Maria
Goodin

The End is Where We Begin

Legend Press Ltd, 51 Gower Street, London, WC1E 6HJ
info@legend-paperbooks.co.uk | www.legendpress.co.uk

Print ISBN 978-1-78955-9-453
Ebook ISBN 978-1-78955-9-446
Set in Times. Printing Managed by Jellyfish Solutions Ltd
Cover design by Kari Brownlie | www.karibrownlie.co.uk

Maria Goodin studied English Literature and French at university before going to train as an English teacher, massage therapist and counsellor. Her writing is influenced by her experience working in the field of mental health, and by an interest in how people process traumatic events.

Her debut novel *Nutmeg* was published by Legend Press in 2012 and *The End is Where We Begin* is her second novel.

Maria lives in Hertfordshire with her husband and sons.

Follow Maria on Instagram
@mariagoodin_author

For my boys.

*"Whether it's them, me, whoever… just make sure
you don't hold everything in."*

Chapter I

Memories

"Happy birthday to you, happy birthday to you, happy birthday dear J-o-sh..."

In the semi-darkness, the room around me seems to fade away as I watch the candles, mesmerised. Fifteen individual orange flames seem to blur into one, melding into the memory of a burning bonfire licking the night sky, bright sparks ascending. The sickly scent of icing gives way to the smell of smouldering wood, and the kids' singing is drowned out by distant voices in my mind; the voices of other kids from long ago...

... What was that noise...?

... Are you scared...?

... Shit! He's bleeding...

I close my eyes, feeling my chest tightening, my throat constricting. Not again, please. Not after all this time.

Run!

We need to get help...

Slow down there, son...

"Dad!" snaps Josh.

My eyes flit open.

"The knife?"

I stare at him. *The knife?* I glance down at the silvery scar that runs across my right palm.

"For the cake?" he elaborates, eyeing me quizzically.

"Oh, right." I quickly fumble in the drawer behind me. One of the kids pulls the blind back up, allowing early-evening light to flood the kitchen once more.

I hand the knife to Josh and head out of the room.

"Don't you want any?" he calls, but I'm already in the lounge next door, pacing, trying to catch my breath, trying to recall the tricks that used to help.

"… so weird…" I hear Josh mumble.

One of the girls says something back that I only half catch. "… not weird… he's totally…"

"Ugh, shut up, that's my dad!" I hear Josh retort, and the girls burst into giggles.

I try to take a deep lungful of air, but it won't come. My throat emits a faint rasping sound. I want them all out of here, urgently.

All of them apart from my son, that is. I want him to stay and never leave the confines of this flat. Here I can keep watch over him. Here he'll be safe.

I hear them talking with their mouths full, laughing at Alex's ability to polish off an entire slice of cake in three mouthfuls. At first they all sound disgusted, but then the boys seem to take it as a challenge to see who can manage it in two. The girls call them gross while egging them on. One of the girls – the skinny one probably, Jasinda, is it? – claims she's on a diet and everyone groans. The girls then start lamenting their ugliest body parts while the boys turn their talk to trainers.

I want to go to my room and shut my door, but I know I can't. It will look too strange and Josh will be concerned. I just pray they eat quickly and go.

Over the din of them talking and laughing, I hear Josh's ringtone.

"Hi," he answers. "Yeah… yeah… yep. Thank you very

much for the money. Yeah. No, that's great, I really appreciate it. I don't know yet, I might just put it in my account. I wanna get a new guitar so... yeah. We're heading out soon. Just bowling, then some food. Uhh, yeah, he's here somewhere, hold on."

No, no, no, I inwardly groan. *Not now, please.*

I quickly turn my back to the doorway, knowing Josh is about to appear, and busy myself with examining the remote control. I know I don't look right. I feel clammy and my chest is starting to heave. Josh has never seen me have an attack, doesn't even know I have them. It certainly isn't something he needs to find out about, especially not tonight. I always need to seem strong for him, even when I'm not, because when you only have one parent, they need to be your rock.

"Dad, she wants a quick word," Josh says, swinging round the doorway. I try to take his phone without looking at him, but he grabs my forearm and gestures for me to hurry up because he wants to go out. I take the phone quickly and turn away, trying to conceal my increasingly laboured breathing. Fortunately, teenage boys can be remarkably unobservant when it comes to other people's suffering, and Josh swings back out the door without another word.

"Is that your mum?" I hear one of the girls ask.

"My mum? Fuck no," Josh mumbles, clearly assuming I'm already in another conversation, "like she'd even remember my birthday."

A jolt of pain and surprise pierces through me. It's not like him, that kind of bitterness. Or is it, deep down? From the outside, my boy seems perfectly well adjusted, but sometimes I feel like I'm just waiting for the emergence of all the ways in which we screwed him up. Every time he's angry, sad, anxious, disengaged, I'm always searching for a deeper meaning behind it. Is that our fault? Did we damage him? Surely, it's got to come out at some point.

I close my eyes and try to drag some more air into my lungs, but it's like my ribs are contracting, squeezing the breath out of me. Luckily, I know that my sister only requires minimal input from me at the best of times.

"Hi," I say into the phone.

"Hi, listen I saw Dad today and he was in a pretty bad way, I just thought you should know. He kept going on about how he hasn't seen you in years, and he was getting quite upset and angry about it. And he was saying all this weird stuff about how he should never have lied to you—"

"What am I meant to do about it, Laura?" My tone is blunter than intended, but I can't be dealing with this right now. I need space. I need air. And I need to get the kids out the door before this damn thing overwhelms me and I end up ruining Josh's evening.

"I don't expect you to *do* anything about it, Jay, I'm just letting you know. It was pretty difficult to deal with, okay? So I'm just telling you because I thought that was the idea, that we keep each other up to date with what's happening, or is that not what we're meant to be doing, because—"

"Okay, okay, sorry," I lie. I just need her gone. On another evening I might be tempted to ask her why the hell she feels the need to tell me all the stuff my dad says. It just makes me feel miserable and it's not like anything's ever going to change. But then that's always been the difference between me and Laura; I keep my pain to myself, she tends to expel it onto other people.

"Anyway, that's not even really what I wanted to talk to you about. My car's still doing that thing, so can I bring it over on Monday after work for you to have a look..."

I move towards the doorway, Laura a grating noise in my ear, and discreetly watch the kids, who have finished their cake and moved into the hallway. They're next to the front door, pulling on shoes. Seven pairs of legs all in skinny jeans. Jasinda and Amelia put their arms around Josh and all three of them hold their phones in the air and snap a selfie as they pull funny faces.

My son's a nice-looking boy, perhaps a little too slender,

but broadening slightly at the shoulders now, a side-parting that makes me worry about the way he holds his neck at an angle in an attempt to keep his hair out of one eye. I don't think it can be good for posture. His skin is fairer than mine, his hair a lighter shade of brown; his mother's genes fighting for their half of him. At least she staked her claim to him on some level.

I hear the toilet flush and Chloe comes out of the bathroom. Josh picks her pink hoodie off the peg by the door, shoves it clumsily at her. They exchange a few words, laugh. They've known each other since they were small, and although Josh denies there's anything between them, I'm certain he's either lying or in denial. I see it in their body language, the way they interact. It might have been some time ago, but I remember teenage love all too well.

Chloe takes a strand of her blonde hair, sniffs it, then holds it out for Josh. He sniffs it, too. He tugs at his own fringe before figuring out that it's just too short to reach his nose, so instead Chloe sniffs it for him. I have no idea what they're doing, but Chloe looks impressed and wraps her arms around his neck. Without missing a beat, he puts his arms around her waist and they stand there hugging, while their friends laugh and jostle around them. I remember the feeling so clearly it scares me; the newness of it all, despite having known each other for years, the uncertainty, the first tentative kisses, the early thrill of skin on skin. And later, those all-important words – *I love you*. The promises – *we'll always be together*. My breath catches in my throat, ever tighter, and I close my eyes, wishing away the memories that have been plaguing me recently.

"We're just friends," he tells me time and time again. He even gets quite irate about it. And so I let it drop, and I stop the teasing and the jibes because I can see I'm pushing my luck. But that's how it started for me, too. We were just friends. And then one day, we weren't.

I watch them sometimes, snuggled close on our sofa,

whispering and teasing each other, or having conversations that look deeper and more meaningful than anything Josh and I ever seem to manage, and I wonder if he's ever going to be brave enough to make a move. I keep my mouth shut, but what I really want to say to him is, "I had that once. That total comfort and ease, the way you look at each other, how happy you are when you're together, the way she makes you laugh. It's rarer than you would imagine. Tell her how you feel, and when you've done that, learn from my mistakes – don't be stupid enough to let her go. Because even at fifteen you can have the greatest love of your life." My mind floods with all the things Josh would say to me if I gave him that speech. All of them are pretty offensive.

"…I don't even know why I took the car there in the first place," Laura is saying, "they're con merchants and the guy who runs the place is such a total dick…"

Chloe releases Josh just as abruptly as she embraced him, distracted by the urgent need to check her phone. At least when I was their age I didn't have to compete for a girl's attention with five hundred other friends.

Alex, for no apparent reason, suddenly pulls Josh into a headlock and rubs at his hair, making Josh whine. The threat of having his hair messed up infuses Josh with enough strength to push the heftier boy off, and after running his fingers through his fringe a couple of times, Josh raises his fists, pretending to square up to his aggressor. In a flash, Alex's fists are up as well, and they start to circle each other as best they can in the narrow hallway, Sam and Joel now cheering on their chosen contestant. Josh and Alex pretend to throw punches at each other, until Alex pulls his fist back too fast and knocks his elbow hard on the wall behind him, drawing a silently mouthed expletive and hoots of laughter from the other three boys.

The camaraderie, the rough-and-tumble closeness of these boys, is in some ways even more painful to watch than the slow-burning relationship between Josh and Chloe. Because despite the passage of time, whenever I see Josh and his three mates, it's like I'm seeing us all over again – me, Max, Tom and Michael. The shoving and piss-taking, the mocking and name-calling, it's the stuff of male bonding that endures throughout the ages. And whereas the rituals between teenagers of the opposite sex seem to mutate from one generation to the next, the glue that bonds boys together is always made of the same ingredients: solidarity, team spirit, a sense of brotherhood, loyalty and even love, all carefully concealed beneath a veneer of ridicule, mockery and tomfoolery.

But then maybe I'm not giving these boys enough credit, maybe things have shifted with time. Josh and his mates are capable of serious conversations in a way we never were – exams, potential careers, terrorism, politics… Perhaps kids have more to worry about now, constantly being exposed to social media and all its accompanying misery. So much has changed in such a short space of time. Or perhaps it says more about the four of us that at fifteen we never discussed anything much more serious than football and breasts. If we'd been capable of discussing even ten per cent of our true feelings then surely it would have helped us cope with what happened back then. As it was, we kept it all inside and tried to act like everything was fine, even though it was anything but.

"Are you even listening to me?" asks Laura.

I try to speak, but no sound comes out. How can you talk without breath?

"Jay? Are you okay, because you've been acting really weird lately. You just seem really distracted. I mean, not that you ever *don't* seem distracted, but even for you… Michael said the other day that you seem like you're not with it. He asked if I thought you were okay, but I said he was way more likely to know the answer to that than me, because God knows you never tell me anything."

The thing about memories is they come whether you want them to or not. When they were little, I used to watch Josh and Alex kicking a football around the park and suddenly

I'd be seeing Tom and myself, whooping and yelling and punching the air when we scored a goal. Years later, I'd see them lounging on Josh's bed playing video games and suddenly I'd be transported back in time to those lazy Sunday afternoons we spent at Max's house. And as Josh has grown older the memories have just kept on coming, more vividly, more painfully. In the last couple of years, his male friendship group has settled into a nice little crowd of four – him, Alex, Joel and, most recently, Sam, and the similarity is at times almost too much to bare. I hope he'll be friends with these boys for ever, that nothing ever drives them apart. For me, there were things that even the closest of friendships couldn't withstand.

"I've gotta go, Laur," I say, my voice barely more than a whisper.

"Okay, so I'll see you Monday, yeah? Are you sure you're okay?"

"Monday," I manage, and hang up.

Josh is the youngest of his friends, born at thirteen minutes to midnight on a sticky July night. So he's not fifteen yet, I remind myself, as if it really makes any difference. I even glance at the time on his phone. Almost five hours still to go. I want the seconds to stop ticking by, I want him to stay fourteen. Because at fourteen everything was good. I was fifteen when it all went to shit, and even though I tell myself that was me, not him, I can't seem to shift the dread of him turning a year older.

"Dad. Phone," Josh orders, suddenly spying me in the doorway. He holds his hands up to catch his mobile, too pressed for time to take the five steps towards me. I throw it to him and he catches it, stuffs it in the back pocket of his jeans.

"Let's go!" he calls, and Joel opens the front door.

I want to step towards him, envelop him in my arms, ask him for the tenth time exactly where he's going tonight and at what times, and to please text me when he gets there and when he's leaving, and who will he be walking home with, and does he have enough money. But I can't even move. I can't even speak anymore. The oxygen won't come.

"See you later, Dad!" Josh calls, followed by a cacophony of goodbyes and thank-yous from his friends.

I step towards the front door, my body making the automatic movement to go after him, to hold him back, but instead, as I feel the tightness in my chest, I find that I'm practically shoving the last of them out the doorway.

"Text you later!" Josh calls, already at the bottom of the stairs, swinging round the bannister into the communal hallway.

And it takes everything I can muster and one great drag of air to call, "Be careful!"

I shut the front door, a wave of relief washing over me, and slump down on the mat, burying my head in my hands. Even after all these years, the feeling is terrifyingly familiar.

"Breathe," I whisper to myself, trying to drag in air, "breathe."

And when I can't even make the word sound out anymore, I continue to mouth it silently.

"Breathe."

"Breathe."

Chapter 2

Breathe

I remember it was my fault we were running late. Mine and that damn polar bear.

"Are you sure this is the right way?" asked Michael, stumbling over some brambles. He was trying to sound casual, but I knew him well enough to catch the anxiety in his voice. We all should have been home by now, and while fifteen minutes wasn't going to mean the end of the world for the rest of us, Michael's dad approached life with military precision. The consequence for him being back late would be well beyond the raised eyebrow and disapproving glance at the clock that the rest of us would get. I was the only one who knew what his dad could be like, but I hadn't been thinking about Michael when I held everyone up that evening. All I'd been thinking about was that stupid polar bear.

"Yeah, this is the right way," I assured him, although I was having doubts.

Tom and I had come this way once before, and I'd suggested it as a shortcut home. But although I remembered skirting the overgrown, abandoned allotments, I didn't remember trudging through them. We stumbled over dried clods of soil, hard and lumpy beneath the soles of our trainers.

"This is the right way, isn't it?" I muttered to Tom, catching my ankle in a tangle of plants. The light was fading quickly and it was becoming a struggle to see where I was walking.

"Yep," he replied, with certainty, "the canal's that way, we just need to drop down there and follow it along."

I could see he was waving his arm, presumably pointing to the things he had just mentioned, but the precise nature of his gesture was swallowed by the descending darkness. I trusted him though. We all did. He was always so sure of himself, it was hard not to. Tom and I lived our lives in competition with one another, and in most matters we were on a par, but he had natural leadership skills I lacked. Faced with options, I often faltered and looked to others for reassurance, whereas Tom quickly made a choice and stuck to it.

"Ah, crap," shouted Max, "not again!" The rest of us laughed mercilessly, the sound of poor Max fighting a losing battle with the stinging nettles overriding any concerns about being late – or lost. "How come none of you are getting stung?"

"I've already been stung!" called Tom over his shoulder. "By a giant hornet!"

"Oh, man up!" I called back. "It was a tiny wasp."

"Our legs aren't getting stung 'cause we're wearing jeans and not gay shorts," Michael told Max, Max's rather tight sky-blue shorts having been the butt of our jokes all evening.

"Yeah, well, that's 'cause none of you have got sexy legs like me," quipped Max. "The ladies were all lovin' my muscular calves this evening."

"Yeah," joked Tom, "if by sexy you mean fat. And by muscular you mean—"

"Fat," Michael and I chimed in at once, leading to more guffaws.

"And if by loving you mean they were all totally ignoring you," Tom added.

"Or looking at you like you were a total div," said Michael.

"They were weighing up the talent, gentlemen," insisted Max, sounding slightly out of breath.

"They'd have trouble weighing anything about you up," I said, evoking yet more laughter.

To be fair to Max, he wasn't really fat, or at least he hadn't been since primary school. In the last couple of years, his height had started to even out his weight, and his developing talent as a goalie meant he was putting his bulk to good use and toning up at the same time. But to us he would always be the lovable "Fat Max".

"I don't know how you can say I look gay, anyway," said Max, "I'm not the one carrying a flippin' stuffed polar bear."

"Yeah, well, that's 'cause you'd have no one to give it to," I retorted, hoping to play the jealousy card, for want of anything wittier to say. Actually, there was no indication that any of them was jealous I had a girlfriend. Far from it, in fact. All I seemed to get were digs about being tied down, and jibes about how it must be *luurrve* and how I'd gone soft. Perhaps they were right. I was feeling a bit of an idiot walking around with a giant polar bear, and as I hugged the soft fur against my chest I was glad of the falling darkness.

"You gonna give it to her tonight then, Jamie?" asked Michael. He was by far the most sensitive one of the group, and the only one to show any genuine interest in my relationship.

"Nah, it's too late. I'll give it to her tomorrow." I hoped she'd be pleased. I'd spent seven quid in my efforts to shoot a cardboard alien with an air rifle, which was clearly more than the bear was worth. But it seemed important, like a nice boyfriendy kind of thing to do. I wondered now if the guy would have taken seven quid for the air rifle. She would have probably preferred that.

"Yeah, you should definitely give it to her tomorrow, Jay," Tom agreed, uncharacteristically helpful.

"You gonna give it to her at her place or yours?" asked Max.

"You should take her down the park and give it to her there, Jay," said Tom.

"You should give it to her wherever it feels right to you, Jamie," said Michael. "You could give it to her at the canal..."

"On the bench down the park."

"In the woods."

"In the back alley."

"Ah, shut up!" I snapped, as they burst into laughter. I'd been an idiot to think they might have been seriously trying to help. "You're so immature."

"Either way, it's definitely about time you gave it to her," sniggered Max, drawing hoots of laughter from the other two.

"Ha ha," I grumbled.

It was then I thought I heard a scream. The boys were still laughing, throwing out ideas about where I could "give it" to Libby, each suggestion more ridiculous than the last.

"The Natural History Museum. Combine it with education."

"TGI Fridays."

"PC World."

I tried to listen beyond their voices.

"Shut up," I told them impatiently.

"Ah, we're just messing with you, Jay Boy," laughed Max.

"No, seriously, shut up!" I snapped, stopping. "What was that noise?"

"What noise?"

The others came to a halt and we stood there, silhouettes against the night sky, the only sound the distant thud and rumble of the fairground music.

And then we all heard it.

"What the heck was that?" asked Max.

"That was a fox shagging," stated Tom matter-of-factly. "It's what they sound like. Like they're being murdered. It's well warped. Haven't you ever heard—"

"That wasn't a fox," I interrupted, "that sounded like someone in pain."

"Sounded like a person puking," said Max.

"It's nothing, let's just get home," said Michael, sounding nervous, and we all resumed walking.

But a moment later there it was again.

"Shhh!" I hissed, listening hard. "Sounds like someone groaning."

"It's over there," said Tom, heading away from us. There were dark shapes looming around us that, so far, had turned out to be inoffensive run-down sheds, shacks and bushes. But now, with the mysterious groaning in the darkness, every shape appeared threatening. I wondered if I could see something moving.

"Where are you going?" I asked.

"To see what it is," said Tom casually. "We've got to go this way anyway. Tenner says it's a fox."

"Are you sure that's the way home?" I asked.

"Yes!" called back Tom, sounding irritated to be questioned again.

The rest of us stood there, unsure what to do. After a few paces, Tom realised that no one was following him and turned around.

"What, are you lot scared or something?"

Challenged, I walked in silence across the uneven earth, Michael and Max following behind. I think I was the first to see amber sparks dancing in the darkness.

"Tom!" I called, keeping my voice low, trying to alert him to what must be a fire burning behind… what? A hedge? A shed? It was too dark to tell what the obstruction was. Either way, Tom was too far in front, or I was too quiet. He just carried on walking, the back of his white Metallica T-shirt the only thing keeping him visible.

"Tom!"

I should have run ahead and grabbed him. Because someone burning a fire in the corner of some shabby, abandoned allotments late at night should have struck me as strange. Because I should have trusted myself that the sound I'd heard was someone groaning in pain. And because every instinct was now screaming at me to go home another way.

The obstruction turned out to be a dilapidated metal

shed, and by the time I was close enough to figure that out, I could smell the burning. When I got there, Tom was already peering round the side. I could hear voices, deep and mumbling. It could have been a couple of old men collapsed in their deckchairs – the last defenders of the allotments – enjoying the summer evening, relieved to be away from their nagging wives for an hour or so. But I knew it wasn't. I felt it. Still, I pushed down my instincts. There was nothing to worry about. At least not until Tom turned to me, panic in his voice.

"Shit," he whispered, "there's some guy on the ground. I think he's bleeding."

Again, again, I have no idea why. Why would I have not just taken his word for it? Why did I have to look? I have no idea now. Disbelief. Morbid curiosity. The same reason I sat through the horror movies Tom put on, watching every rip and cut and scream, even though I felt sick and wanted to close my eyes. Because I had to see for myself.

I inched round the side of the shed. There, not far from us, a man was lying on the ground. He was trying to push himself up. It was hard to tell with his nose pressed against the soil, but I thought he was probably about my sister's age – around nineteen, twenty. On the opposite side of the fire, three older men were talking, glancing occasionally at the guy on the ground, and swigging from a bottle they passed between them. More bottles lay scattered on the ground around the fire.

"What's going on?" I heard Michael ask anxiously.

I felt hands on my back and my shoulders as the others tried to peer round me. Max's heavy breathing was in my ear.

The man on the ground managed to lift himself up slightly, but as soon as he did, one of the other three men stepped round the fire and booted him hard in the ribs. I felt Tom jolt with shock beside me, and I grabbed at his arm and held on tight.

"Jesus!" hissed Michael.

The victim cried out in pain and fell back on the ground. My stomach twisted with fear and disgust. But his assailant was still not satisfied. Straight away, he delivered another powerful boot to the man's side. This time, the victim let out a short grunt, as if he was giving up on even crying out, and rolled up in a ball on the ground.

"Leave him now," one of the other men said. He had some kind of accent.

"Let's get out of here," Tom whispered, pulling at my arm.

"Yeah, let's go," mumbled Max. He sounded loud, right next to my ear. Perhaps he was loud, I don't know. But just then the third man – the one who had been standing smoking a cigarette as if nothing unusual was happening – turned in our direction.

"Shit!" I heard Tom whisper, and he suddenly jerked backwards, pulling me with him.

But in that split second, just before I was wrenched away, the guy lying on the ground lifted his head feebly, gazing straight towards me.

And I saw who he was.

There was a scramble behind the shed, each of us grabbing at each other's arms, pulling at each other's T-shirts with no particular aim in mind. We were like a flock of panic-stricken sheep, fussing frantically but going nowhere. It seemed like Michael made a move to get away, flee in the direction we had just come from, but the rest of us were driven by the instinct to stay as still and as quiet as possible and we grabbed at him, pulling him into a huddle. If we'd have let him go, if we'd have all run then, would that have made all the difference?

We froze, none of us daring to move a muscle, clutching at each other, our faces close.

My heart was pounding, and my legs felt weak. I had never seen anything like that in my life – not that wasn't on TV. The thud of the boot, the cry of pain. Maybe we should have run, but it seemed too late now. Now we just had to stay quiet and hope we hadn't been seen.

I tried to tune into the distant thump of the fairground music, searching for any indication that civilisation was still nearby. But all I could hear was our breathing.

Michael's breath was coming in short, shaky bursts in my right ear. And in my left ear, Tom was breathing quietly, almost silently, as if he was fighting the urge to breathe at all. But Max, opposite me in the huddle, was breathing heavily, and I wanted to reach out and smother his mouth with my hand. In the silence, his breathing seemed too loud, just like everything about Max – too big, too heavy, too noisy. I wanted to tell him to shut up, but I didn't dare speak. Squashed into the middle of the huddle was the polar bear, and I dipped my head, breathing into the soft fur to muffle the sound, feeling the warmth of my own candyfloss breath.

For what seemed like forever, all I could hear was the sound of our breathing, the four of us, clinging together.

We waited.

I think now that we should have run.

I remember her saying: "This one's for two strawberry laces and a flying saucer, okay?"

We were lying on our fronts in the long grass. Libby placed her lollipop into her mouth, picked up her binoculars and handed them to me.

"What's that swimming in front of *Carpe Diem*?"

"Carp what?" I asked through a mouthful of gummy bears.

She removed her lollipop. "*Carpe Diem*. The blue boat two down from ours."

"Is that French or something?"

"No, silly, it's Latin. It means seize the day."

"Stupid name for a boat," I muttered.

I put the binoculars to my eyes, chewing lazily. Magnified grass stems, bulrushes, sun-dappled canal water, a heron

– they all swam in front of my vision as I tried to find a familiar point of focus. I scanned the marina until Libby's narrowboat – *Isabelle Blue* – suddenly came into view.

I held the binoculars steady. I could see my mum and Libby's mum sitting in the bow of the boat, slumped in their deckchairs. Libby's mum was smoking a cigarette; mine was sipping a glass of wine. I swung the binoculars to the right, past *Lady Grey* whose roof was covered in blossoming flowers pots, and onto *Carpe Diem*, a run-down boat with two bicycles and several bags of coal on its roof. There in the water a little black bird bobbed around in circles.

"A moorhen," I said confidently. Placing the binoculars down on the grass, I held out my hand for my prize.

"Nope," said Libby, smugly, "it's a coot."

"Oh, I knew that," I moaned.

"Red for moorhen, white for coot, don't forget it," she grinned. "I get to pick three."

I threw my paper bag at her. It annoyed me that she knew so much stuff. I was meant to be smart, but she knew tonnes of stuff I didn't. And she didn't even have to go to school.

"Cola bottle, shrimp and… oooh, twisty marshmallow thing, I love those."

She dropped my sweets into her own paper bag, which by now was looking significantly weightier than mine, and sat up cross-legged in the grass.

"I don't want to play this anymore," I said, worried that I'd soon have no more sweets left.

"Do you want to go down to the bird hide?" she asked.

"Nah," I said, pulling up a piece of grass.

"Do you want to go build a den?"

I shook my head. It was hot and I was feeling lazy and tired. I wondered if my mum was ready to go home yet, but once she got talking to Libby's mum, there was no stopping her.

"Do you want to kiss me?"

I squinted at Libby. She took her lollipop out of her mouth

and examined its decreasing size, a string of long brown hair falling down over her face.

"What for?" I asked.

She tucked the lollipop back into the side of her cheek and shrugged. "I dunno. To see what it's like."

I pulled up another blade of grass and twiddled it between my thumb and forefinger.

"Mmm... I dunno. I don't mind. If you want to, I guess."

"Sit up then," she ordered.

I slowly lifted myself up. My arms seemed to have gone to sleep.

"You have to close your eyes," she said, tucking her hair behind her ear.

"Why?"

"'Cause that's how you do it, silly."

I closed my eyes and waited, the light filtering through my eyelids.

"Where are you going to kiss me?" I asked, suddenly opening my eyes again. Libby, crawling towards me on her hands and knees, stopped and looked at me like I was stupid.

"On your lips, of course."

"Oh," I said, not sure what I thought of all this. "Okay then."

I closed my eyes again. I couldn't remember what it was like to be kissed on the lips. I seemed to remember being kissed on my lips before – by my mum, I guessed – but I was too big for that now. I had an idea that it might be quite wet.

"Don't do it for too long, okay?" I said, opening my eyes again. Libby's face was so close to mine that the first thing I saw were the freckles on her nose.

She sat back and looked thoughtful. "Three seconds?"

I nodded. "Yeah, okay."

I closed my eyes again, my legs crossed, the grass tickling the bare space between my socks and the hem of my jeans. I heard shuffling in front of me, and then the light was blocked out. There was a warmth in front of my face, and the sweet scent of cherry lollipop. She placed her lips on mine. They were drier and warmer than I had anticipated. Neither of us moved a muscle. I wasn't sure how I could breathe with her face pressed so close to mine, so I didn't. I held my breath and counted the seconds. One Mississippi, two Mississippi, three Mississippi, four Mississippi, five Mississippi...

I was starting to feel the squeeze on my lungs. But if I tried to breathe in now how would I do it? Her nose was pressing into mine on one side, and my free nostril would probably make that weird noise, like the tiniest bit of air coming out of a balloon. Or did I need to breathe out, release the air caught inside my chest? But then I'd be breathing right onto her face. Was that okay? Was she breathing? I couldn't hear her. Was this how you were meant to do it? Because on TV they sometimes kissed for a really long time, and I wasn't sure I could go much longer.

Libby sat back on her heels, returned her lollipop to her mouth and looked at me quizzically. Then she started to giggle.

"You *can* breathe, you know."

I took in a gasp of air with a sense of relief.

"That wasn't three seconds," I grumbled, feeling stupid.

"Yes it was. I did one Mrs Hippity, two Mrs Hippity—"

"It's not Mrs Hippity, stupid, it's Mississippi, like the river."

"No, it's not."

"Yes it is!" I laughed loudly, partly because it was actually funny, and partly to cover my own sense of awkwardness.

"It *is* Mrs Hippity!" insisted Libby.

"Who's Mrs Hippity?"

"I don't know!"

"Mrs Hippity!" I howled, falling back onto the grass.

"You're silly, I'm going home," said Libby, sulkily. She stood up and stomped off through the grass.

I lay on my back, laughing up at the bright sunshine. Once I'd recovered myself, I glanced over at Libby's bag of sweets and thought about how her lips had tasted of cherry. It hadn't been too bad, being kissed by a girl, although I couldn't see myself doing it again any time soon. Maybe if I breathed next time, I decided, it might be better.

I reached over and helped myself to all the sweets she had won from me.

I remember standing there in shock; my knees shaking, my T-shirt sticking to my back, my stomach clenched. I'd read the books, known what to expect, and still it had been terrifying.

The baby was out. He was finally here. I was meant to be important, but I felt like a spare part, standing around awkwardly, being given little jobs to try to involve me. I felt patronised and overwhelmed.

So this was it. Now we had to listen out. Because the first cry meant he was breathing. That he was alive. And it seemed to be taking an eternity.

The nurses were fussing, doing something with him at the side of the room.

Him. My son. It didn't feel real.

I watched the clock on the wall. The seconds ticked by. Eleven, twelve, thirteen… Nobody said anything, but surely we were all thinking the same thing. Why wasn't he crying? I opened my mouth to ask the question, but I couldn't. Maybe I'd got it wrong. Maybe it wasn't meant to happen that quickly. I didn't want to look a complete idiot, but I was sure the cry should have come by now. That's what I'd read.

The first cry is synonymous with breathing…

If he wasn't crying that meant he wasn't breathing, and for a split second I experienced a violent twist in my gut – not fear or desperation, but guilt. Because if he wasn't breathing that meant it was all over.

It meant I was free.

Fourteen, fifteen, sixteen…

This wasn't right. I knew it wasn't. They were meant to cry. I wanted him to cry. Didn't I? *Didn't I?* What was wrong with me? Surely I had to at least want that.

But I couldn't make myself wish for it, couldn't will it to happen.

When the baby cries, his airways are ready to take in that first, big gulp of air, allowing him to breathe on his own...

Seventeen, eighteen, nineteen...

However hard I'd tried to get my head in the right space for this, however hard I'd tried to accept what was to come, I knew that I'd never accepted it at all. It was never meant to be like this, not yet, not now, and I realised in a sudden rush of anguish and self-disgust that I didn't want the cry to come.

I just wanted this to all disappear.

Twenty, twenty-one...

And the silence was shattered.

A painful wail, a chug, a splutter and another wail.

He had taken his first breath.

"There we go," said the midwife, cheerfully, carrying the bundle towards the bed.

I glanced at the other faces in the room, all smiling. None of them surprised or afraid, as if none of them had endured the agonising wait that I had just experienced.

I felt crushed by the weight of some unidentifiable emotion. Disappointment? Self-disgust? Relief?

The nurse in the corner, gathering up towels, glanced at me with an expression of concern. She knew what I had been thinking, I was sure of it. I turned away, red-faced. Could everyone see right to the core of me?

I had wanted him dead. Hadn't I? I had wanted it to be over. No, no, I hadn't wanted him dead. Of course not. Not really. I just...

"You have a beautiful, healthy son," said the midwife, smiling encouragingly at me.

I couldn't see inside the bundle of towels without stepping nearer, but my legs were like jelly. I couldn't move an inch.

I glanced at the clock again.

It would soon be Monday morning. Less than nine hours to go until class started. Maths. There had been days when

I thought a Monday morning couldn't get much tougher than that.

Yet here I was.

I remember my mum asking: "Do you understand what asthma is, Jamie?"

She sat next to me at the kitchen table, her head cocked quizzically to one side, her face a picture of maternal solicitude. I had been given a glass of chocolate Nesquik as a treat, which was strange because I wasn't even ill.

I sucked on my straw and nodded, wide-eyed and sad-looking, playing up to the increased care and attention. I wasn't exactly sure what asthma was, but any explanation was bound to be boring, and stuff happened all the time that I didn't understand without it ever seeming to matter. Besides, my sister was in the corner of the kitchen angrily spreading Marmite onto a piece of toast and I wasn't about to expose my ignorance to her. It sometimes felt like her very reason for living was to mock and belittle me as much as possible.

My mum gave a little smile. "So what's your understanding of it?" she asked gently. "Tell me what you know."

I sighed quietly and felt myself physically deflate in the chair. I should have known she would call my bluff, she always did. It was the teacher in her, always double-checking other people's understanding. Is this what she did with her students, even though they were all grown-ups? They must have found her really annoying.

"You can't breathe," I mumbled, unwilling to attempt any further elaboration.

"Wow, everyone's right, he really is a genius," mumbled Laura, through a mouthful of toast.

"Laura," said my mum sternly, glancing in her direction, "I wasn't speaking to you. And use a plate please."

"I can't even see what all the fuss is about," said Laura,

ignoring my mum's request, "loads of people have asthma. It's not like it's even a big deal."

"I didn't say it was a big deal."

"Well, why are you even talking about it then?"

"This doesn't concern you, Laura."

"Why is everything such a big deal when it involves Jamie? God, I could try to hang myself from my window and no one would sit down and have a heart-to-heart with me about it."

"Don't you have something you need to go and do?" asked my mum, tersely.

"Yeah, Laura, me and Mum are trying to talk," I risked. I would never normally goad Laura, but Mum and I felt like a team right now. Or at least I thought so, until she shot me one of her warning looks.

"Shut up, you little dweeb," my sister muttered scornfully.

"Laura!" snapped my mum. "Go do something. Homework, for example, if you can remember what that is. And, for God's sake, stop rolling your school skirt up like that, I can practically see your knickers."

"No, you can't," Laura sighed theatrically. With a roll of her eyes, she made for the door, cramming toast into her mouth and poking me hard on the back of the neck as she stomped past, the scent of body spray and Marmite wafting after her.

"Ow!" I shrieked, grabbing my neck as if I had been stabbed and looking to Mum for justice.

My mum just sighed and rubbed her forehead.

"So, anyway," she began again, attempting to re-establish her air of concern, "it must have been a bit scary, what happened at school today."

I stared at her, unsure which way to go. I was quite enjoying the sympathy and could easily milk that, but at the same time I was nine now and didn't want to look like a sissy. I took the middle ground and shrugged, which was the most accurate reflection of how I was really feeling. I hadn't actually given the whole "incident" (this is how it was described to my mum when she arrived at the school) much thought. In fact, I'd quickly been distracted by the hunt for a two-headed magpie that Tom swore he'd seen up on the roof of our classroom. Perhaps the "incident" had been scary for the short time it lasted, but I assumed it was a one-off thing, like a nosebleed. Those seemed to appear out of nowhere, for no good reason, and could be scary, all that blood dripping onto your white school shirt. But they passed, just like the asthma had. I figured that, like nosebleeds, asthma was "nothing to get your knickers in a twist about", as my dad would say.

My mum reached out and stroked my hair.

"It must have been quite worrying when you didn't know what was happening. But it's not something you need to be scared of if it happens again. Quite a lot of children have it. It's not uncommon. It just makes it a bit difficult to breathe for a while. The airways get a bit inflamed, a bit unhappy, and that makes them go a bit narrow." She made a tiny space between her thumb and forefinger to demonstrate her point. "There's medicine for it, to make it better, like a little pump, and it's nothing the teachers haven't seen before. Mrs Dray didn't seem too worried, did she?"

This was put out there more as a statement than a question, so I shook my head because I could see my mum was trying her best and I didn't want to contradict her. In fact, Mrs Dray had started to look a bit flushed and her voice had gone all high-pitched, just like the time Annabel Woods's hair got tangled up in the climbing rope during PE and Mr Craven, the caretaker, had to cut her lose.

My mum patted my hand, which seemed to signal the end of our conversation. She made a move to stand, but I didn't want her to go. These moments between us seemed so rare now. She was working on some big project called a PhD, and I was halfway through constructing the Millennium Falcon out of Lego, so we both had our commitments. Plus, I'd noticed that the older you got, the less your parents fussed over you. Not so long ago, whenever I fell over, I would be scooped up into strong arms, kissed and told I was a brave boy. Now I got told to stop being so clumsy and look where I was going, or my dad would ask me if I'd had a nice trip, which was only funny the first five times.

"How do you get asthma?" I asked quickly.

My mum settled back into her seat, reluctantly it seemed to me, and shrugged. "You can be born with it. Or develop it."

"Can you catch it?"

"No."

"Can you give it to someone else?"

"No."

"Can you still do normal stuff if you have asthma, like running and football?"

"You can still do everything, Jamie."

She ruffled my hair and stood up. She was off to do her own thing, whether I liked it or not.

I slurped the last of my Nesquik, images of the "incident" at school today coming back to me. I supposed it had been pretty horrible. I pushed the images away. It was nothing serious or scary, I would try to remember that.

Still, that night I couldn't sleep. Every time I closed my eyes, all I could see was Mrs Dray with her flushed cheeks. "Breathe," she was saying again, "breathe, breathe." And she was taking deep breaths herself, demonstrating how it should be done, as if the problem stemmed from forgetfulness.

"Breathe. Just breathe."

Chapter 3

Action

When Michael's name flashes up on my phone, I'm in two minds whether to answer. The thing is, I've decided on a plan of action, and I'm nearly almost certain it's the right one. So I don't want him talking me out of it. I don't think.

My mood swings easily with the weather, and today, with a bit of sunshine, I might have been feeling more confident about my plan. But although it's a warm day, there are grey clouds in the sky and I'm plagued by a sense of something ominous approaching. Perhaps I should turn back.

In my hand, my phone continues to ring.

The canal water is dark and murky, dotted with the odd drinks can and limp crisp packet. A coot bobs along, searching hopefully for something to eat.

Red for moorhen, white for coot. Don't forget it.

I never did.

I pass a narrowboat tied alongside the towpath, an algae-stained laughing Buddha on the deck. I look away, not wanting to see inside those little windows, not wanting to be reminded.

"Hey," I say, quickly answering my phone before it rings off. All of a sudden I just want to hear a familiar voice. And maybe, just maybe, be talked out of this.

"Hey. You all right?" asks Michael.

"Yep. You?"

"Yeah, good. You on a job?"

"No. I took the day off."

"You what? You never take a day off. What you doing?"

"I'm just... I'm out."

"Out?"

Oh go on, I think, *just tell him*. Not because I want to be talked out of it, because I don't, almost certainly, but maybe a second opinion...

"I'm down by Camden Lock," I tell him.

"Oh, yeah? Stocking up on yet more incense and leather bondage gear?"

"Yep, you know me."

"Too well, clearly. Seriously, what are you doing there?"

"I'm just... there's a... like, an art exhibition thing I want to go to..."

There's a confused pause.

"What?"

"An exhibition. Like where artists show their paintings."

"Yes, I know what an exhibition is, thanks, mate. What are you going to that for?"

Not far ahead, people are standing about on the towpath. Are they looking at paintings? Is this it?

I look over my shoulder, back along the section of path I've just walked. The van's parked just ten minutes away. I could be home in fifty.

"Libby's exhibiting some of her work," I say.

There's a long silence.

"How d'you know that?"

"I found her. I just did an internet search. She's got a website."

Again a long pause.

"So... what? You're there to see her?"

As if he's already talked me out of it, I find myself grinding to a halt. I even take a couple of tentative steps back in the direction I've just come.

"Yeah, that was the plan."

Was? Is! *Is* the plan.

"To talk to her?"

"Yeah."

"And say what?"

"I don't know."

"You don't know?"

"Well, I haven't exactly mapped it all out."

Why did I answer my phone? Now I'm getting doubts in my head. I make a swift turn and head back in the direction I was going in the first place. I know what I'm doing. I do.

"So you were really serious about this?"

"Yes, I told you I wanted to find her—"

"No, you said you'd been thinking about finding her, not that you were going to do it."

"Well, I thought about it a lot. And I decided to do it."

"Are you sure about this?"

"Look, you're the one who told me I had to sort myself out."

"Yeah I know, but I thought it would be more of a mental thing, like working through some stuff in your own mind. Not so much… doing."

"If I could just work through it in my own mind, I would have done that, wouldn't I?"

Michael falls silent.

"*You* told me I had to move on from the past," I remind him. "You said it. And you're right. I do. I need to tie up some loose ends. Make my peace with the past, or whatever, and move forwards. A fresh approach. And I don't know why, but I feel like she's the first person I need to see in order to do that."

"The *first* person?"

I sigh and look up at the clouds. I think it might start raining soon. Is that a sign? Michael clearly thinks this is a bad idea anyway, so I might as well tell him the whole story, everything I've decided on. And I *have* decided.

"After I've seen Libby, I'm going to see Tom. And Max. There's just... there are things I need to say, to just... get out."

Another pause on the line.

I notice I've stopped moving again. I shuffle in circles on the towpath, looking at my feet, risking the odd glance up ahead.

That's it. That's the exhibition. As the people ahead of me shift, I catch sight of the paintings and my stomach flips.

"Okay," Michael says, clearly unconvinced, "well, if that's what you need to do—"

"I don't know," I say, suddenly confused again. "I don't know what I need to do I just... I need to do something."

"Okay," he says, more encouragingly, "okay, then I hope it goes well, I guess. I hope you get whatever you need from this."

I rub my eyes. I shouldn't have answered my phone. I've always been terrible at making decisions, and now this feels like a bad idea, even though last night, lying in bed unable to sleep again, I was sure it was the right one.

I put my phone in my back pocket and stare out at the water, searching for confirmation that I'm doing the right thing. I try to recall my conversation with Michael last week, the moment I realised something had to change.

We'd been driving in my van, the scene for many of our deeper and more meaningful conversations. Or, more accurately, we'd been stuck going nowhere in my van after hitting a traffic jam on the way back from IKEA, the new wardrobe Michael wanted laid out in the back. It's not that we can't hold a meaningful conversation face-to-face, but stuck in a small space without distractions, our eyes diverted by the road ahead, thoughts and feelings flow more freely, and this was one of those times. Plus, it was raining. I always say too much when it's raining.

"What do you think's brought it back on?" Michael asked,

sounding concerned. "I mean, it's been, what, nearly ten years, since you've had those kinds of symptoms?"

I shrugged. "Stress maybe. I don't know. I think it might be linked to Josh, I feel like it started in the build-up to his birthday, months ago, this kind of tightness in my chest. I know that makes no sense, it's just—"

"Josh?"

"Turning fifteen. Just… turning that age."

I saw him nodding slowly out of the corner of my eye and I knew he understood.

"Yeah," he said thoughtfully, "I know. It brings a lot back, doesn't it? Watching him."

I looked down on the blue Corsa beside us also trying to exit from the roundabout. The young couple were arguing about something; her gesticulating wildly at the wheel, him shaking his head despairingly. Relationships. Why bother?

"Do you ever think about it?" I asked quietly.

Michael sighed heavily. "Of course I do."

I watched raindrops gathering on the windscreen like an invading army hastily claiming territory, the wipers intermittently brushing them away before they attacked again.

"I think about it all the time at the moment," I admitted. "More than ever. Me, you, Tom, Max, Libby… everything that happened. Something will happen in the day – a feeling, a word, a sound – and it just triggers all these memories. Memories I didn't even know I had. But they're so vivid. And it's hard, you know. It's really hard."

I traced my finger along the scar under my right thumb. I felt Michael watching me and I knew, without even turning towards him, the expression upon his face: brow knotted in concern, eyes full of a desire to help. This is why I kept things from him, hid them away until I reached bursting point. Because he cared so much. And I wasn't sure he had the resources to care like that.

Michael stretched his legs out, placed his trainers up on the dashboard.

"The past weighs heavily on you, doesn't it?"

I turned away and gazed blindly through the window, rubbed at my jaw, chewed on my thumbnail, my throat constricting with the accuracy of his statement. I had to get a grip on things.

"I mean, it gets to me too at times, of course it does, but you… it's like it overshadows you. It always has done."

I didn't answer. I never realised he understood that about me. How strange to have never known he saw right through me when I felt like I'd been hiding it all. All that effort for nothing.

"We've never talked about it much, have we?"

I shook my head, swallowed hard, suddenly wishing I hadn't brought this up.

"Why is that?" he mused.

Inappropriately, I smiled, even laughed a little. It wasn't funny in the slightest, but it's often what I do when I'm angry, when I'm hurt, when I want to scream something out loud but I know that I can't because I don't want anyone else to be angry, to be hurt. The truth was I'd wanted to talk to him so many times, but how could I?

"None of us talked about it," I said, hearing my own voice tinged with resentment.

He heard it too and turned sharply towards me.

"I *tried* to talk to you about it. At the time. And you shut me down time and again—"

I shook my head. "I don't remember anybody wanting to talk about it."

"Really?" he said, suddenly taking his feet off the dashboard and twisting towards me in his seat, incredulous. "Because I remember very clearly trying to talk about it on several occasions and you literally telling me *I do not want to talk about it*. Believe me, I wanted to. I tried."

"It wasn't exactly an easy thing to talk about, was it?" I said, feeling defensive. "I didn't know how to, I was a kid, I couldn't. But I've wanted to talk to you about it since—"

"Then why haven't you?"

"When? When could I have done that?"

I could feel it now, spilling out, spilling over, leaking through the floodgates that I'd held so tightly shut.

"When would have been a good time to bring it up, Michael? When over the last few years would have been the right time for that? When you were sky-high and unable to take in a single word I was saying, when you were lying comatose on the bathroom floor—"

"Oh, come on—"

"No, you come on. Seriously. When exactly have you been in a place when you could have dealt with that?"

"*I* have dealt with it. *I've* spoken about it."

"With who?"

"With Catherine," he said, as if I'd asked a stupid question.

"Really?"

"Of course. What the hell d'you think? That I wouldn't have discussed it?"

"I don't know. I just... I didn't realise... Yeah, I suppose you would've."

I felt strangely jealous, excluded. It had never occurred to me that the details of that night – a night that felt so secretive, so personal – had been shared with an outsider.

"*You're* the one who's never spoken about it," said Michael. "And you should. Because you need to move out from under the weight of it. I know it was a horrible, horrible thing, and you don't witness something like that and come out the same person, but it's like it shut you down or shut you off or something. I feel like it's always one step forward and two steps back with you. You open up, then you shut down, you invite people in and then you push them away. You're hard, Jay."

"*I'm* hard?"

"Yeah, and I'm bloody hard too, in different ways, I know that, but I've been working on my shit for years. I just think it's about time you started working on yours."

I sighed, inched forwards in the traffic. I gazed ahead at

the line of cars, the grey sky, the concrete industrial buildings lining the grimy North London road. He was right, I couldn't go on like this. Too many regrets, too many thoughts going endlessly around in circles. Too much pushing people away, not wanting them to see to the heart of me, not wanting to risk it all again. Not wanting to have anything worth risking.

"I'm sorry if you've ever wanted to talk to me and haven't felt able to," Michael continued. "I understand why, and I wish things could have been different. But I promise you I'm strong enough to talk about it now. You're right, I couldn't have heard you before. But I can hear you now. So if you want to talk…"

The rain pattered down, and apart from the intermittent creak of the wipers, we sat in silence. Michael rested his head back and I chewed at my thumbnail until I tasted blood. I rubbed my eyes and sighed. He was right, I'd never tried to talk to him about it, not really. Talking about it had only ever been a notion. And maybe I did remember him trying to raise it, trying to explore what had happened and why and how. But when he wanted to talk about it, I wasn't ready, and when I wanted to talk about it, he couldn't. Somehow, we just missed each other.

"I'm sorry too," I muttered.

A horn blasted behind us. I quickly put the van in gear and accelerated into the gap ahead of us, coming to a halt behind the black BMW with darkened windows that we'd been following forever. I suddenly wanted to tell him everything, to get every desperate, lonely thought out of my head in the hope they could be left there, on that wet, depressing stretch of road. But I didn't know where to start.

"I think about Libby a lot," was what came out.

"What, right now or…?"

"Yeah. And just… generally. But a lot right now."

Michael waited for more, gave up, prompted me.

"Think what about her?"

I shook my head. "I really hate the way things were left. I

always have done. And I know it was all a long time ago, but I've always really regretted the ways things went. It was just left a mess, and I wish there'd been a chance to tie it up. There are things I wish I'd said, and I just didn't have the chance. I suppose as you get older you start to think about what you've done with your life, what you'd change. I don't want to always have these regrets."

Michael shrugged. "It was complicated, wasn't it? What could you have said? And then she left—"

"Because of me."

"Maybe."

"Not maybe."

"Well, okay."

"I imagine what it might be like if I could see her now, what I'd say."

"Yeah? So what would you say?"

I didn't even know how to start recounting all the imaginary conversations that had played out in my head over the years.

"I dunno, but I've been thinking about what it would be like to find her," I confessed.

Michael was thoughtful for a long time. "Well, I guess she'd be a very different person now," he said eventually.

I was tempted to make a joke about how long it had taken him to come up with that incredibly obvious statement, but I didn't because I realised that actually I'd never really thought of her as being a different person. I knew she'd be older, that her life would be unrecognisable, but I'd never contemplated the idea that *she* would be fundamentally changed. But of course she would be. No one's the same person at thirty-one as they were at fifteen. Life alters the core of you.

"You know what I heard Josh say the other night just before he headed out for his birthday?" I asked, the memory suddenly jumping into my head. "This friend of his, some girl, asked if his mum had called. And he said, 'Fuck no, she probably doesn't even remember it's my birthday.' How screwed up is that?"

"He's not screwed up. Believe me. I work with teenagers and he's probably one of the most stable, together—"

"I don't mean that's *he's* screwed up necessarily, just the whole situation."

"There are loads of kids out there growing up without one of their parents. Life's no fairy tale, is it?"

"But you know what the tragic thing is? He may be right. It may not even register with her that it's his birthday."

"Of course it does. It has to. She's still a mother, even if she's not capable of being there—"

"Not *capable*?"

"Yeah, not capable, as in not emotionally able to—"

"Give a crap?"

"Connect."

"Connect?" I laugh. "Jesus, that's a generous analysis."

"Yeah, maybe. Well, I've come to see things differently over the last few years. We can't all be who we want to be, can we? However hard we try."

"I think she might have missed the trying bit," I mumbled. We fell silent for a while.

"I guess it was all tied up, wasn't it?" said Michael, eventually. "What happened that night. You and Libby. The way that ended. I can see why one thought leads into another right now."

I nodded. "Sometimes it feels like that one night defined the rest of my life."

Michael sighed, placed his feet back up on the dashboard. "Then you need to stop letting it define you. Find a way to step out from its shadow."

I looked at him, raised an eyebrow, shrugged to show I had no idea how to go about that. He shrugged back. We smiled, a silent agreement that this conversation was over, that we'd hit a dead end.

"I'll tell you something I do know," I said.

"What's that?"

"I'm never driving to fricking IKEA again on a Saturday afternoon."

He laughed heartily. "Well, there you go, my friend," he said, reaching over and slapping my thigh hard, "at least you reached one conclusion on this journey."

And so here I am. Putting my plan into action. My plan to get closure on the past. I thought, for a time, that I'd be with Libby for the rest of my life, a dream built when we were young and life was simple, and when wanting something seemed enough to make it happen. Now the prospect of even walking a few metres in her direction seems too daunting.

But then I remember pacing the floorboards in the middle of the night, lying awake in the early hours, thinking of all the things I wish I'd said and done. I remember the feeling of tightness in my chest, the breath that just won't come.

I don't want to carry these things with me anymore. Libby, Max, Tom... All the relationships, so important to me once upon a time, they all need to be resolved so that new relationships can grow in their place, unfettered by the chains of the past. Jeopardise, that's what Michael says I do. Jeopardise my relationships, my chances at happiness. He's right, and I don't want to be that person anymore.

I put my head down and walk quickly along the towpath, determined to shut out all the questioning voices, all the doubts.

And before I know it, I'm there.

Paintings are propped against the walls and hung on the railings of the bridge, all of them depicting canal scenes: brightly coloured river boats, locks, bridges, water, reeds, wildfowl, kingfishers. Just at a glance I know the first ones aren't Libby's. They're nothing like the paintings on her website, nothing like her. I don't know a thing about art, but these look like classic oil paintings: heavy, intense, dramatic. That was never Libby. Her paintings were always light, airy, slightly removed from reality. She wasn't concerned with showing what was actually there. She said that was what photographs were for. She wanted to interpret, present a different way of seeing things. That was Libby all over. Reality was nothing but a hindrance, nothing that she couldn't think beyond. She never saw the limitations of things, including me. The paintings on her website still carry her same stamp, but, of course, they're better these days, far more skilled but just as quirky.

I wander further along, hearing the voices of bystanders.

I love the colours on that one...

That reminds me of that place we went on holiday... Bathampton, was it?

More paintings. No, this time photographs. Sunlight reflecting off a blue canal, the tiny, shimmering particles captured up close. The intricate detail of a brightly painted narrowboat mirrored in the water. The open gates of a lock, the power of the water captured in full force, tumbling down, shimmering in the winter light. I like these ones. They show canals at their best; places where holidaymakers can make pleasantly slow, relaxing journeys. Places where nothing bad ever happens.

And then the photographs give way to more paintings; subtle tones, blocks of light, undefined edges, angles that don't seem quite right. Libby's work.

My stomach tightens and I can barely turn my head for fear of staring straight at her. But slowly I start to look around me, scanning the faces for one I might recognise.

Maybe I'm missing her. Could she have changed that much? Dyed her hair? Put on weight? If only she'd put a photo of herself on her website.

But then I spot her. She's coming down the steps from the bridge, two polystyrene cups in her hands, concentrating. My heart jumps with the shock of it, adrenaline suddenly pumping through my system. She looks so much older. A grown woman, and yet so familiar. The same brown hair, only shorter, just past her shoulders now instead of halfway down her back. And those dark eyes that I remember. I spent hours of my life gazing into those eyes.

A man in a beanie hat and glasses gets up from a fold-up stool and takes a cup from Libby's hand. They both laugh about something she says, and he briefly places his arm around her, gives her a little squeeze. Is that her husband? I've always imagined she'd be married by now. It was what she guiltily craved, deep down. A bit of security and stability.

I was the only one who really knew that about Libby. It was something she confided in me, like a terrible secret; that underneath all the confused juvenile talk about anti-capitalism, feminism and individuality what she really wanted was to get married and live a regular life. She was a paradox in so many ways. Capable of such original thought, such different ways of seeing the world, and yet all she really wanted was the norm. She felt terrible about it, this aspiration to nothing more than the mundane and traditional, torn between what she wanted to be and what she was raised to be. The one thing she knew for sure was that she wanted to be a mother. The irony of how things turned out wasn't lost on either of us.

I keep looking in her direction, knowing that any minute now she'll look over and meet my eye. But she seems to be looking everywhere but at me. I need to approach her, but my feet are rooted to the ground. Despite all my fantasies about our reconciliation, now that I see her, so changed, I realise we're strangers. We were little more than children when we last saw each other, and now look at us. I'm not great at making conversation at the best of times, let alone with people I don't know, and at the end of the day I don't know her anymore.

My heart is racing and all of a sudden I don't think I can do this. It's fear that's brought me here – fear of the unresolved, of the unsaid, of eternal regrets. And now it's fear that's urging me to turn around, go home, forget I ever saw her.

Fear. My eternal nemesis.

Chapter 4

Fear

I remember saying: "He's going to die."

I'd whispered it without meaning to, without even realising the words were forming on my lips. Perhaps, on some level, I believed it would be helpful, somehow lessen the blow by preparing me for what was inevitably coming my way.

"He's *not* going to die," said Michael quietly but forcefully, putting his arm around my shoulders, "don't say that. It's going to be okay."

"The doctor said—"

"The doctor said they're doing everything they can."

I buried my head in my hands, rocked back and forth on the plastic chair, my thoughts wild and entangled, frantic. I stood up abruptly, strode quickly down the corridor, stopped, strode back. What if one of the doctors returned? I wasn't going to leave this spot. But where the hell *were* the doctors? What were they *doing*? Every second felt like an eternity. I paced quickly, halted, pressed the heels of my palms into my eyes, leaned against the wall, tried to breathe, pushed my hands through my hair, paced some more, gazed up at the strobe lights until they dazzled me, leaving white blotches swimming in my vision. What was I meant to do? Just stand here?

I felt utterly useless. I was meant to protect him. That was my job, to keep him safe. And I'd failed. If only I hadn't left him. All that time I'd spent checking door and window locks whenever I put him to bed, keeping an eye on who was entering the playground behind us, who was getting a bit too close in the supermarket or on the street, making sure the car doors were locked whenever we pulled up at traffic lights, telling him never to talk to strangers, never to go off with anyone we didn't know… none of it had been enough. Because when he really needed me, I hadn't been there to spot the danger.

Instead, where had I been? On a date in a bar, getting cosy with some girl I was only half interested in, all because Michael had persuaded me I needed to get out there, start a relationship, or if not a relationship then just start having a little fun. Do things normal twenty-one-year-old blokes do, he'd said. But look what had happened. I hadn't heard my phone over the music. I'd become distracted by the hand on my knee, the promise of the situation, and had forgotten to even check for messages. And now here we were. And for the second time, I might have been too late to save a life.

On one level it felt unavoidable, like a story I could suddenly see the end of. So, this is how it would happen. This is how my world would fall apart, here in this brightly lit corridor with its nauseating scent of disinfectant. It was almost easier in that moment to give in than to hope, less painful to surrender myself to the horror that was surely to come than grapple with the torment of uncertainly.

I looked at Michael, slumped forward on the otherwise empty row of chairs, his head down, his hands clasped tightly in front of him.

What if he died? What if he actually *died*? What would happen then? I couldn't live with it, I just couldn't. A sense of panic overwhelmed me, making my head spin, my knees weak. I closed my eyes and tipped my head up towards a heaven I wasn't sure I believed in.

I will do anything, I promise, just let him be okay. Please. Please. I'm begging. Let me die. Just let him live.

There was silence, stillness. I felt abandoned to my fate, cast out. Why should He care what I wanted? I was tainted, had been for a long time. I wasn't worthy of His help, and the only voice that answered me was my own.

But you wanted him to die, didn't you?

I shook my head. I didn't. I had never wanted that.

Yes, you did. Don't you remember?

I rubbed at my temples. Shut up. Shut up! It wasn't true. That was never—

Here, in this very hospital, isn't that what you were hoping for? That his first breath would never come? Isn't that the same as wishing him dead?

"No," I groaned quietly, my heart aching. I pressed my fingers into my eyes, tried to stop the hot tears from escaping.

No? Well, then it must be what came before that brought you to this point. The night of the fairground. How long did you think you could get away with that? Cause and effect. Karma. You knew it was coming. You have blood on your hands and now this is justice—

"Jay!"

I spun round to see Laura, her face pale and unfamiliar without make-up, her blonde hair scrunched up in an elastic band, dark roots showing through. I looked her up and down, wondered briefly why she was wearing a Puffa jacket with pyjama bottoms, then realised it must be the early hours of the morning.

"God, I said your name, like, ten times," she said, sounding irritated. Only my sister would vent her annoyance at me at a time like this, and for a second I found comfort in it – a moment of normality in a world that was falling down around me. If my sister could still be angry with me, then surely nothing much had changed. But the comfort was short-lived.

"So," she said, abruptly, "what's happening?"

It might have gone unnoticed by anyone else, but I heard

it – the slight quiver in her voice, the tiny crack. Laura didn't do fear. She shouted and swore and raged at the world, but in that moment, I knew she was scared, and it terrified me all the more.

I shrugged and shook my head, opened my mouth, but nothing came out. My vision blurred through the tears I was holding onto. Laura stepped forward and for a moment I thought she was going to hug me. But if Laura had ever hugged me, then I couldn't remember it, and she wasn't about to start tonight.

"What the hell does that mean?" she said, imitating my shrug but not waiting for an answer. "Well, where the fuck is the doctor?" she said, scanning the corridor. She spied a nurse crossing between rooms. "'Scuse me! Hello?"

I was about to stop her, tell her she wasn't even yelling in the right direction, that all the activity had been down the other end of the corridor, when I heard Michael calling my name.

"The doctor's here," he said, gesturing to a man approaching us.

He had dark hair, glasses. Had I even met this one? There were so many. It was all such a blur. I had shouted at one, told him to get out of my way, to let me into the room with my son for God's sake! Was he the one I'd shouted at?

I tried to move towards him, but my feet wouldn't budge. His face... What was that expression?

It wasn't good. Oh God, it wasn't good.

I clutched at my hair, my breath escaping with a rasping sound through constricted airways. I couldn't hear whatever he was about to say, I couldn't, I couldn't...

"Mr Lewis," said the doctor, his face neither confirming nor alleviating my fears, "come with me please."

I remember rehearsing what I wanted to say.

I like you. A lot. I mean, when I say I like you...

I've been thinking about you non-stop this week. And the week before that. And the week before...

Can I kiss you? Would that be okay? What I mean is, do you want to...

I've been thinking about touching you. Not like that! Well, okay, a bit like that...

Do you like me? I mean, not like a friend, but...

My heart was racing, heat pooling inside my school shirt. I discreetly pressed my palms against my thighs, blotting the sweat against my trousers. The close confines of the narrowboat went from feeling cosy to claustrophobic, and the warmth emanating from the little coal stove suddenly seemed madly disproportionate to its size.

Just say it!

But I didn't know what to say. Words that had sounded right when spoken to my bedroom mirror every evening that week now sounded ridiculous inside my head.

I could just reach out and pull her towards me, cup her chin in my hand and turn her face to mine. That's how it happened in the films. But the idea of just making a pass at her filled me with panic. What if she pushed me off? What if I missed? What if she didn't even like me like that?

I watched her face as she flicked through the textbook on the little table in front of us. I wasn't even sure what she was trying to teach me, had barely taken in a word she'd said that afternoon.

Just say it, you idiot!

I opened my mouth, resolved that I was just going to go for it. But what came out was a tiny squeak at the back of my throat as nerves overwhelmed me. I quickly disguised the squeak with a single cough, which sounded so fake that I then thought I'd better cough again.

"Are you okay?" asked Libby, glancing up at me.

The last shards of afternoon sunshine sliced through the little window behind us, and the long strands of hair that had fallen loose from her ponytail shone golden-brown in the light. My fingers itched to reach out and tuck the strands behind her ear, just like she always did. I ran my eyes over her perfectly smooth skin, the little freckles on her nose, the curve of her lips…

"Uh, yeah, I'm fine," I muttered, tearing my eyes away and pulling at my school tie, which was hanging in a loose knot against my thumping heart, "just a dry throat."

"I'll get you some more water," she said, spying my empty glass.

She shuffled along the seat and squeezed herself out from behind the table, taking the three steps into her kitchen area.

I loved being on this boat, always had done. As a young child, I'd eagerly explored every nook and cranny, like an excitable puppy. Just look where this girl got to live! A floating hobbit house! Even now I was fascinated by the compactness of everything. It was like living inside a tunnel, one tiny room leading into another. Nothing much had changed in the five years since I'd last been on-board – the same spangled curtains hung at the little windows, their tiny mirrors and sequins reflecting the light. The same Indian rug lay on the floor, tattered books still filled every shelf. Stepping onto the boat had immediately brought back memories of that summer we'd been thrown together by our mothers' intense new friendship; the time we'd spent exploring the woodlands, building dens, playing snap, bickering and teasing each other… The time she kissed me in the long grass. Did she even remember that?

"Do you want anything to eat?" asked Libby, ducking down behind the counter that formed a divide between the kitchen and lounge area. "We have, uhh, well not much actually. Some hummus, celery, couscous… Oh, we have rye bread—"

"No, it's fine, I'd better not," I said distractedly, "my dad's cooking tonight so…well, I say cooking, he'll probably get in KFC, that's kind of his idea of cooking."

Don't mention KFC, you idiot, she's a vegan!

"Or pizza. He sometimes just orders pizza."

"Mmm, KFC always smells really yummy when I pass the shop. I'd love to try that one day."

While she was out of sight, I quickly lifted my arms and sniffed, hoping my deodorant was holding up under the stress. For six weeks now I'd been coming down to Libby's boat straight from school on a Thursday afternoon, and even though I'd showered following athletics at lunchtime, and sprayed about half a can Lynx under my arms, I was starting to feel paranoid.

"Apple cake?" she asked, popping up with a plate in her hand.

I quickly pushed out my arms and flexed my fingers to make it look like I'd been stretching.

"No, I'm good," I said, adding a yawn for good measure.

"Please excuse my munching," she mumbled with her mouth full, waving a piece of cake in the air as she placed my water in front of me. "I'm starving. In fact, this is probably dinner for me tonight. I meant to get some shopping, but the cash jar was empty so... actually, I'm not sure I can be bothered to cook just for myself anyway."

"Your mum won't cook when she gets back?" I asked, immediately regretting my incredulous tone. I sounded like a child, like I couldn't make a meal without my mother's help. Which, to be honest, I couldn't.

Libby broke off a piece of cake and popped it in her mouth. She shook her head, making her ponytail swing. "No, I cook normally," she said as she chewed, "Harmonie doesn't really cook. A bit like your dad, so..." She shrugged, leaving this last sentence hanging in the air.

So what exactly? So she was stuck cooking every night? I couldn't even boil an egg. Honestly didn't know how. My mum was out tonight too, at Libby's mum's – sorry, Harmonie's – yoga class, the same place she'd been going every Thursday night for the last five years, but the moment she came in, she'd be checking what Laura and I had eaten, tutting about what my dad had fed us, and asking if we wanted her to whip up anything else.

I wasn't sure if I felt sorry for Libby or in awe of her.

Involuntarily, my hand crept across the seat towards her, wanting to touch her more than ever, but I suddenly didn't feel worthy. Instead I picked at an invisible piece of lint on the seat cushion.

Libby stuffed the last of her cake into her mouth, as if she didn't want to keep me waiting, as if there was anywhere I would rather be right now than sitting next to her. She took a swig from her mug of cold camomile tea (I wasn't even sure what a camomile was), spilling a little onto her cardigan. She rubbed at the deep purple wool, then pulled the sleeves down over her hands, just leaving the tips of her fingers protruding. All the sleeves of her jumpers were stretched at the ends, a fact we'd laughed about a couple of weeks ago when she wore a stripy jumper with sleeves that stretched down to her knees. It was okay, she'd said, she'd knit another one, as if that's what all fourteen-year-old girls did with their spare time.

"So, where were we?" she said in her teacherly fashion, examining the textbook in front of her. "Okay, so I've done a lot of rambling on about conjugating verbs and stuff, which, unless you're a bit of a nerd like me, you've probably found quite boring. So, shall I ask you the questions about hobbies and pastimes and you answer them now?"

I must have looked pained because she laughed. I hated having to speak to her in French. It was humiliating and humbling that thousands of pounds a year was now being spent on my education, but my inability to grasp a foreign language meant I was being tutored by someone who was home-schooled – or, more accurately, self-taught, seeing as her flaky mother seemed to just dump a pile of second-hand books in front of her and leave her to it . To make things worse, we both knew that Harmonie was scathing of the private-school system, so much so that she had shunned my mother for two months after I transferred to Saint John's. And what Harmonie didn't approve of, Libby didn't approve of either.

I wasn't entirely sure how the tutoring arrangement had come about, but it seemed that Libby, principles aside, had suggested the idea after hearing I was struggling in my new school, and Harmonie, who by then had re-established her inner peace and allowed my mother back into her yoga class, had grudgingly agreed.

I found Libby's kindness inspiring and also slightly shaming. On the rare occasions we'd been thrown into each other's presence during the last five years, I'd barely given her the time of day. She didn't have a telly, didn't follow football, didn't go to school, didn't play computer games. What was there to talk about? She, on the other hand, had always tried to be chatty and sociable, unhindered by the teenage awkwardness that had slowly taken hold of me. It was only out of sheer desperation that I'd sat down with her six weeks ago, wondering how I was meant to make small talk with this girl I no longer knew, and who wasn't like any other teenager. Now, here I was, trying to find a way to tell her how much I liked her, desperate to know if there was any chance she liked me too. But how was I meant to do that? How did anybody ever find the courage?

"Do you want to stop?" asked Libby, staring inquisitively at me. I suddenly realised she must have been talking to me.

"Uh, no, it's fine," I laughed, embarrassed. Could she tell what I was thinking? Was it obvious? "Sorry, town and countryside, yeah, let's do it."

"No, we're looking at sports and hobbies," she smiled.

"Oh, right, yeah. Cool. Okay."

She laughed. "Have you got something else on your mind?"

For the first time that afternoon we really faced each other, holding each other's gaze.

Go, go, go! Say it! Now!

"Actually, I... uhh..."

Just spit it out!

My heart was suddenly racing, thumping so loudly I thought she must be able to hear it. My back felt like it was on fire, and I could feel perspiration gathering under my arms.

"I wanted to ask you... err..."

Will you go out with me? Do you want to go to the cinema? Do you like me? Anything! Just say something!

"I've been wondering if… err… I really like you."

I really like you! That's it! I've done it! Oh my God…

"You've been wondering if you really like me?" she frowned, looking wounded.

"No!" I practically shouted, realising what I'd just said. "I mean, I *do*. I do really like you."

You idiot!

"Oh. Ok-ay," she said warily, "but what?"

"But nothing," I said, shaking my head. This wasn't going well.

"Oh, okay. So, you just—"

"I just like you."

"You just like me. Oh, good," she laughed, looking relieved. "I like you too. It's been nice getting together again after all these years. It's been such a long time and, actually, I was always convinced you didn't really like me because you never seemed to say much when we met, so I wasn't sure if you—" She stopped talking and stared at me, realisation slowly dawning on her face. "Oh! Do you mean you… *like…* me?"

I felt heat spreading across my cheeks, so hot my eyes started to sting. I wanted to take a sip of water, but I didn't dare reach for my glass in case my hands were shaking.

"Oh, okay," she smiled, tucking a strand of hair behind her ear. For the first time ever she looked embarrassed and shifted awkwardly on the seat. The silence seemed to stretch forever.

You moron, what have you done?

"Sorry," I mumbled, "I didn't—"

"I like you, too," she said, staring me straight in the eye, smiling.

"You do? I mean… so what, you like me, or you *like…*"

"I *like* you," she said with a giggle.

Shyly, she slid her hand towards me on the table. I stared at the tips of her fingers protruding from the wool of her sleeve. Then I tentatively reached out and placed my hand over hers.

Relief flooded through my body, and suddenly, for the second time in our lives, she leaned in and kissed me.

I remember the order.

"Run and get help!"

I had one job.

Just one job.

I knew that canal like the back of my hand. How many times had I cycled the towpath with Tom and Max? We'd been doing it since we were what, eight, nine? And then there was that summer I'd spent playing with Libby when we were children. We'd explored the woodlands, the meadows, the bridges… How many times had I passed the lock?

And I'd run that towpath. I'd run it so many times that past year. Sure, I might have been failing French, but so what? At Saint John's, what made me stand out – what made me accepted – was my place on the athletics team and that was something I was working damn hard to keep.

So when we realised we needed help – and fast – who else would have gone?

I remember the thud of my trainers along the path, the pain in my chest as I pushed myself, dragging in the warm summer night's air, the sound of my own rasping breath. I remember the fear that help would arrive too late, that something terrible would have happened by the time I got back to my friends. But that fear drove me on, surely made me run faster than I ever had in my life. Fuelled by adrenaline and desperation, I felt like I was flying, air rushing past me, my thighs and calves burning. My pockets were light; they'd taken everything we had on us.

Then I remember skidding to a halt.

I couldn't think which was closer, the Kingfisher pub or the lockhouse. Across the footbridge and down towards the road, or straight on? I set off one way, but then I changed my mind, stopped, searched the darkness trying to get my bearings, started back the way I had just come, but then abruptly changed my mind again and was off once more.

Later, when I ran that same stretch of towpath again and timed myself, I worked out that I wasted approximately fifteen seconds on indecision, and that the Kingfisher was forty-five seconds further away than the lockhouse. So that was a neat sixty seconds of wasted time.

It was the last time I ever ran.

Sixty seconds. That's all.

But it was sixty seconds too long.

I remember sitting on my bed, my back against the wall, my knees pulled up to my chest. My mind was racing. This couldn't be happening to me, it just couldn't. My brain whirred, seeking a way out of this situation. It had to be a bad dream.

I chewed mercilessly at my thumbnail. What was I meant to do now? Was I meant to tell people? Keep it a secret? I wanted to sob. Twenty-four hours ago, I'd thought struggling with my English assignment and fretting over what to buy Libby for Christmas constituted problems. I hadn't even known the meaning of the word.

"What's the matter with you?"

I looked up, alarmed to see Laura standing in my doorway. I hadn't heard her come home. Mum and Dad were out choosing new kitchen flooring, and Laura had been gone for at least a week. These days, we never knew quite where she was or when she'd be back, but it seemed she'd chosen this late Saturday afternoon to make an unexpected reappearance.

"Nothing's the matter," I mumbled miserably, "just close the door."

But Laura, of course, could only ever do the opposite of what I asked her and instead took a step inside my room. She'd recently died her hair jet black and taken to wearing too much eye make-up. I wasn't sure if her pallor was part of the gothic look or just down to late nights and malnutrition.

"Doesn't look like nothing's the matter," she said, eyeing me with what I took for a modicum of concern.

I shook my head forlornly. I wasn't up for Laura's insults. I felt sick to my core and strangely shivery, like I was coming down with something. All I could see was my life spinning out of control and I couldn't grasp it, couldn't pull it back.

"Just go away," I groaned.

Laura tutted. "All right, suit yourself."

But watching Laura leave, I felt more scared than ever. I couldn't do this, let alone do it without the support of my family.

"She's pregnant," I blurted out.

My sister turned and looked at me stupidly.

I tried to think of something to add, but what else was there to say? That was it. That was all there was to it. There were no grey areas with pregnancy – you either were or your weren't. And she was.

God, she really was.

My stomach twisted, and my heart began to race all over again.

And then I added the most important point of all. Because pregnancy didn't have to change everything, not these days. It didn't have to turn your life upside down, unless...

"And she's keeping it. She's already decided. She's two months already."

I could hear the words coming out of my mouth, but it was like I was reading a script written for someone else.

I stared at my feet, noting how the toes of my socks had become threadbare to the point of transparency. It occurred to me that I'd need to let Mum know so she could buy me some more. But soon I was going to be a... a what? A dad? A father? Those words bore no relation to me. Nor did they relate to someone whose mum still bought his socks.

I wanted my sister to say something, do something, to make it better.

"Fuck," said Laura, a hint of amusement in her voice, and when I looked up at her, she was grinning. "So the golden boy has screwed up. BIG time! Wow. So you're not so smart you can figure out how to use contraception, then?"

And then she laughed. She *actually* laughed.

"Mum and Dad are gonna kill you!"

I shook my head in disbelief.

"Just get out."

She held her hands up as if she was about to apologise, but she was still grinning as if all her dreams had come true.

"Just get out!" I yelled, jumping up from the bed. She bolted out of the door and I slammed it hard behind her.

I remember the guy who answered the door to the flat had red-rimmed eyes and dishevelled hair. For a moment I wondered if I had the right place.

"Get your mate out of my flat," he said as way of greeting, without bothering to step aside.

I pushed my way past him. It was two in the morning and I was tired and angry from being dragged from my bed. Although not half as angry as my sister had been when I'd begged her to drive over and babysit my sleeping son for half an hour.

"For God's sake, just let them kick him out on the street then if that's what they want to do," she'd snapped. "It will teach him a lesson!"

But I didn't want that, and from the fact she drove over, I assumed she didn't really want that either.

Inside, the flat was smoky and smelled of fried food. Sections of wallpaper were missing, and the carpet was dirty. Cardboard boxes littered the hallway, spilling out identical pairs of designer trainers.

I stuck my head inside the first two rooms – a small, messy kitchen and a chaotic-looking bedroom. A girl was sitting on the double bed, her head in her hands, illuminated only by the glow of a bedside lamp. She looked up at me, ashen and sad.

I vaguely recognised her from around town. She stuck her leg out and kicked the door shut in my face.

"Lounge!" shouted the red-eyed doorman, as if I knew where that was.

"Jay," a voice said behind me. I turned and with some relief saw Tizzo coming out of the bathroom, zipping up his flies. "Thanks for coming, mate," he said, guiding me into the lounge. "I can't shift him and my brother wants him out his flat pronto. I didn't want to just chuck him out like this, but I wasn't going to have much choice."

In the dim lounge, Michael was sprawled on the sofa. The table in front of him was littered with beer cans, bottles and ashtrays. A black bin liner sat on the floor nearby, showing that some kind of tidy-up operation had taken place before my arrival. I wondered what they had been so keen to throw away or get out of sight. It clearly wasn't the mess itself they were bothered about.

"Michael, get up," I demanded, giving his leg a kick with slightly more force than I'd intended.

"Mate, if that worked I wouldn't have called you," said Tizzo, scratching his shaved head.

I gave Michael a shake and raised my voice. "Michael!"

His head lolled on his shoulders, his face a deathly pale.

"How much has he drunk or… whatever?" I asked.

"Mate, he was already pretty out of it when he got here. You know what he's like, I keep trying to talk sense into him, but—"

"Yeah, right," I mumbled, "sure you do."

"Just shift him!" a voice barked from out in the hallway.

I cursed and tried to lift Michael up from the sofa, but he was a dead weight. He didn't mutter or groan or make any sound at all. I dropped him back onto the stained, sagging cushions and put my ear to his mouth. I couldn't hear anything.

"Turn the light on," I told Tizzo.

"What light, mate?"

"The light!" I snapped. "The main light!"

Tizzo flicked a switch on the wall. In the harsh light of the unshaded bulb, Michael looked more grey than white. My heart started racing.

"What's he taken?"

Tizzo shrugged. "I dunno."

"Bollocks you don't know!"

"Look, mate, he's been crazy lately, you know that."

"Michael," I called, tapping his cheek. "Michael, wake up."

I felt a wave of panic wash over me. I put my palm on his forehead, then his cheek. He felt cold and kind of clammy. Cold enough to be dead? I touched his neck, feeling for a pulse. That was it, right? There it was, I was sure of it. But then it was gone again. My fingers prodded, but I couldn't find anything. Was I even doing it right, searching in the right place?

"I think we should call an ambulance," I said.

"We don't need an ambulance, mate, he just needs to sleep it off."

I studied Michael's face, hesitating. I'd lost all faith in my judgement long ago. But my heart was pounding and my stomach had tied itself into a knot. Nothing about this felt right.

"We need an ambulance."

"Oh, come on, mate, calm dow—"

I pulled my phone out of my jacket and dialled nine nine nine.

"Hey, wait a minute, I wouldn't have called you if I thought you were gonna freak out."

I ignored him and tried to take a deep breath, knowing I needed to stay calm.

"Mate, honestly," said Tizzo, reaching out and gripping my shoulder, "you don't need to call—"

"I'm not your fucking mate!" I yelled, shrugging his hand away.

I looked at Michael and wondered why I had even hesitated.

"I need an ambulance immediately," I told the operator, barely concealing the panic in my voice.

Chapter 5

Reunion

I'm stood staring, frozen like a statue, when she glances over at me, then has to look again. It's a classic double-take, almost comical in other circumstances. My automatic reaction is to look away, hope she hasn't seen me, and then I have to remind myself that *I'm* the one who came looking for *her*. The reality dawns that this is it, I can't hide from her now. I've made my choice and here we are.

We stare at each other for what feels like an eternity but must only be a matter of seconds; her confused, disbelieving, trying to work out if I'm really the boy she once knew; me like a rabbit caught in the headlights. I force my feet to take a couple of tentative steps towards her. She steps forwards too, more decisively, ignoring the potential customer who's asking a question about her painting. Even standing right in front of me, she looks unsure, searching my face for confirmation.

"Jamie?"

The first time I try to speak, nothing comes out and I have to quickly clear my throat. "Hi."

"I wasn't sure if that was you," she says, her fingers going to her throat, grabbing hold of the pendant on her necklace as if for safety.

"Yeah, sorry, I've probably changed quite a lot," I say, hooking my hands into my back pockets, wondering what kind of idiot apologises for changing over the years.

"Yeah," Libby nods, briefly scanning me up and down, "just a bit."

I laugh nervously. "You too." I aim to scan her up and down in a similarly nonchalant way, but I suddenly panic about where my eyes are landing: on her chest, her hips, her legs… It all feels equally inappropriate. I quickly look back to her face, trying not to let my eyes linger on the two-inch scar that runs from the side of her left eye to the top her cheekbone. It's faded with time, but it's still visible, light pink and slightly shiny. I feel a stab of guilt, knowing that I caused her pain, in more ways than one. I quickly open my mouth to make a comment about how well she looks, enquire after her health, say something friendly to break the ice.

"What are you doing here?" she asks without a smile. She sounds almost confrontational and I'm completely thrown. Stupidly, I hadn't prepared for that question, and now I wonder what I *am* doing here.

"I… err… I was wondering if I could talk to you." I suddenly feel exposed, self-conscious, as if the people around us are listening, just waiting for me to cock up.

"Talk to me? What… you came here to see me?"

"I…well… I saw your website and—"

"You saw my website? What, were you googling me or something?"

I definitely don't remember Libby being this blunt. And this is definitely not the way our conversations ever went in my head.

"No. Not googling…I mean, yes, but just to try and find out where you were living or—"

"Where I'm *living*?" She looks mildly horrified, like I've been stalking her.

"Actually," I say, trying to get a grip on things, "do you want to… Are you free to go get a coffee or something?"

She holds up her cup. I notice her hand is shaking slightly.

"Or not get a coffee then. Just, maybe talk—"

"I'm sort of busy," she says, glancing at the paintings.

"Yeah, of course."

"What is it you want? Why are you here?" she asks. Her cheeks, her neck, the base of her throat are getting flushed, just like they used to when she was upset. She pushes her hair behind her ear a little too aggressively so that it misses the hook, falls straight down around her face again, and with that one gesture, so familiar, so unchanged, the years seems to fall away. I stare at her face, the way her brow is furrowed, the set of her pursed lips. She's wearing her angry face.

"I'm sorry, I shouldn't have come, I just… I've been doing some reflecting on my life lately and I'm just trying to tie some things up. I feel like things weren't left well between us and—"

"What, are you dying or something?"

"No," I laugh nervously, scanning her face for any sign that she would even care if I were dying.

"So, what? You're going through an early midlife crisis?"

"No. Well, yeah, maybe. I just know that I didn't handle things back then the way I should have and I suppose I wish things had gone differently, and I thought that perhaps, I mean I know it's been a long time, but I wanted to just see you to… I don't know…"

I'm well aware that I am screwing this up and that I should have prepared *a lot* better, but I didn't expect our conversation to go anything like this. I'm thrown. This was *such* a bad idea.

The guy in the beanie hat gets up from his stool, takes the few steps towards us, touches Libby lightly on the arm.

"Everything okay?" he asks.

"Yeah, yeah," she says dismissively, "he's just an old… just someone I used to know."

I know I have no right to feel the jolt of pain this causes in me.

The guy slinks back to his seat, but not before throwing

me a warning glance. Wondering again if he's the husband, I check Libby's hand for a wedding band, but I'm surprised to find there's nothing there. I'd always imagined her with a husband and a couple of kids by now. I hoped, for her sake, she'd have that.

"Look, I shouldn't have come," I say apologetically.

"I have no idea why you did," she practically snaps, but then immediately looks remorseful. She stares at her coffee cup as if she'd forgotten it was there, quickly shifts it to the other hand and glances at her palm, which is bright pink from the heat.

I take a step back. "Look, I think I've upset you coming here and that's the last thing I wanted—"

"I have no idea what you wanted. I don't know why you've come. Because, what, you wanted to smooth things over or something?"

"Yes, I guess so," I nod, as if she's understanding me now. Smoothing things over sounds the right kind of idea, making things neat, doing away with the horrible jagged edges that result from something being broken.

"Okay," she says, swiftly hooking her hair round her ear again, "well, consider things smoothed then. I mean, it was all a long, long time ago, so… I mean, really, I honestly can't believe you came all this way to find me." She's talking fast, looking agitated. I think I've shocked her by showing up like this. Well, of course I've shocked her. What was I thinking? "You know I have an email address on my website, you could have just used that."

"Yeah, I know, I didn't like the idea of just suddenly contacting you—"

"So you thought it would be better to just turn up in person?"

"Yeah, it seemed the better option, but clearly—"

"Libby!" calls the man in the beanie, gesturing to the sky.

"Look, I'm not sure what all this is about, but I've got to go," she says, moving towards her paintings.

I hadn't even noticed it starting to rain. The other artists are hastily taking down their pictures or covering them over with plastic sheets. Libby goes to unhook one of her paintings from a railing, fumbling with her coffee cup.

"Let me help you," I say, going after her.

"No, it's fine—"

"No seriously, I kept you talking and now—"

"I was about to pack up anyway. I don't know why I bother doing these things."

"Well at least let me help you get them out of the rain," I say, searching for the painting's fastening.

"Seriously, it's fine!" she snaps, hot coffee suddenly erupting from underneath the lid, spilling down her forearm as she searches for somewhere to put the cup in among the sudden chaos of tarpaulins and frames.

I quickly take the drink from her.

"Damn!" She wipes her arm across her T-shirt. "Just have it," she says, waving the coffee – and me – away. She begins packing up with an angry, frantic energy.

"Yeah, sure, I'm sorry, I'll just go," I say, taking a couple of steps backwards. "I shouldn't have bothered you. I just thought… I don't know what I thought actually, but anyway, I'm sorry—"

I turn to leave, coffee dribbling down the side of the cup onto my wrist.

What have I done? Never in a million years did I imagine it would go that badly. What the hell was I thinking when I decided…

"How's Josh?"

I turn around again. She's stopped what she's doing and is looking intently at me, one of her paintings clutched in front of her like a shield. I feel like she's throwing me a lifeline, a reprieve from the mess I've managed to cause.

"He's good," I say, gratefully.

She nods thoughtfully. "Good."

"He's doing really well at school. Going into his GCSEs.

He's got a girlfriend." This last bit's not exactly the truth but I think it virtually is, or would be if he could summon the courage to ask Chloe out. Plus, on some level, I feel it might connect us, me and Libby, remind us of what we once were, where we came from. And for a moment something does seem to shift. We hold each other's gaze, searching for something, a connection. Dots of rain cling to her hair. I'm just about to ask how she is, open things up, take us over this bumpy start, but she cuts me off.

"Okay, well, take care then," she says flatly, attempting a forced smile.

And then she turns away.

I walk for a few seconds along the towpath and then I stop and turn around. Sadly, I watch her back, bending and stretching as she works, and wonder how on earth I could have got it so wrong. And then I realise that I didn't even get around to saying the most important thing of all, the thing I've always wanted to tell her, that I really want her to hear.

I never even managed to say I'm sorry.

Chapter 6

Sorry

I remember turning the corner and Addison saying in his smug, plummy voice: "Well, hello there, Hutton." My heart sank. Did we really need to give this kid such grief every time we saw him? "And what are you doing loitering out here? Not skiving lessons again I hope."

Hutton didn't say anything, just sighed as if he was resigned to what was coming his way. His face – delicate and pale with dark, wary eyes – always wore the same tired expression. His narrow shoulders slumped and he put his head down, hoping to carry on past us through the alleyway that led from the old stone school buildings to the perfectly maintained sports pitches. He already knew he wasn't going anywhere though.

"Er, Hutton?" said Addison, putting out a hand to stop him. "You were just asked a question." He looked to us. "It's not very polite of him not to answer, is it, boys?"

Watts and Smith shook their heads and sniggered. I shrugged non-committally and gave a half-hearted smile. What else was I meant to do? I felt bad for the boy, but over the last few weeks I'd managed to convince myself that he just needed to stick up for himself. This was all part of the private-school culture, wasn't it? The way boys imposed hierarchy. Besides, whatever had been going on between them had started well before I joined the school.

"Are you going to give us a song, Hutton?" smirked Smith.

"*Aaaveee Mariii-aa*," sang Watts, shrilly.

"Ah yes, our little choir boy," sneered Addison. "You better watch out, Hutton, I think the Reverend Peterson has got his eye on more than that sweet, angelic voice of yours. A pretty boy like you…"

The others snorted with laughter.

"Come on, Madame Nedelec's going to skin us," I said, hitching my bag up on my shoulder, hoping we could just get going. But I knew that wasn't likely. Hutton was just going to have to dig deep and find some balls.

It hadn't been easy for me either, being accepted at this school. I'd been an outcast when I arrived at St John's two months ago. No one had talked to me for weeks. For the first time ever I was alone and friendless, floundering in agonising isolation without Tom and Max by my side. They'd always been there, ever since I was five years old, my little gang. I'd felt lost without them, and I'd never been more miserable in my life.

I knew my parents wanted the best for me, but in the early weeks I'd felt angry at them for transferring me to St John's. I wished I'd never started messing about at Allenbrook, wished I hadn't drawn everyone's attention to the fact that even in the top set I was bored out of my mind. I'd bought into my parents' vision of a better future for myself, but now I felt conned. I didn't fit in here. I was nothing like the other boys. I wasn't rich. I didn't even live in one of the nicer parts of Timpton, let alone one of the expensive surrounding villages a lot of the other kids came from. I couldn't guess how my parents were finding the money for me to come here. I hadn't come up through the prep school and didn't have a clue about house colours and speech days. I was an outsider, and it showed.

It was only when I got out on the running track that anyone looked up and took notice of me. Sporting ability was currency at St John's and thank God I had something to offer. I threw myself gratefully into the first group of boys who extended the hand of friendship. Smith, Addison and Watts were all sporty, clever and sharp. I didn't feel totally comfortable with them yet, but what could I expect? I wasn't going to find another Tom and Max. The kids were just different here, and as my mum kept pointing out to me, I had to make an effort to fit in with them, not expect it to work the other way around.

So what if my new friends could be a little patronising and arrogant? As my dad was always saying, we're all just products of our upbringing. I could turn a blind eye to anything so long as I wasn't an outsider anymore. Even this thing with Hutton. Maybe all the taunting and the teasing didn't sit comfortably with me, but I reasoned that was the private-school way, wasn't it? Isn't that what toughened them up, made them leaders? I'd had to fight to fit in, why shouldn't he? Besides, these rich kids had so many privileges, with their big houses, fancy holidays, prefect-looking families… A little hardship wasn't going to dent Hutton's golden-plated life.

These are the things I told myself when we hid Hutton's PE kit and earned him a detention for not having the right equipment; when we stole his blazer after cross-country, leaving him shivering all afternoon in his thin school shirt; when we pulled his bag from his shoulder on the walk home and threw it between the four of us before chucking it over a garden wall. And when I say "we", I don't mean I ever instigated it, or that I ever really wanted to do it, but I was there and part of it, the silent accomplice. I didn't join in when they called Hutton a fag or a retard. In fact, to date I'd never even spoken to him. But I was still there. I tried to think of it as ribbing, making fun, taunting. I couldn't bring myself to see it as the relentless bullying it was.

"I need to go," mumbled Hutton, trying to pass Addison.

"You're bunking off again, aren't you, Hutton?" said Addison. "And you know we're going to have to report that, don't you?"

"Screw you," Hutton mumbled.

All four of us looked at each other in surprise. He had never spoken back like that.

Go on! I secretly thought, willing him to stand up for himself, not considering what might happen if he did.

"Er... sorry, Hutton, I think I misheard you," said Addison, coming right up in his face. Smith and Watts crowded in beside him.

It seemed ironic that my new friends thought life in a comprehensive was all fighting, drugs and sex. They asked me a million questions about life at Allenbrook, hanging on my every word like I was giving them insider knowledge about life in Borstal. I embellished a bit, giving them what they wanted to hear, but the truth was that until I came to St John's I'd never been touched by bullying in my life, just as I'd never been offered drugs or had a girl pin me against the wall and shove her tongue in my mouth until I went to a party at Watts's house.

"I said screw you," mumbled Hutton again. He made a move to pass us, but it was like watching a fly trying to extricate itself from a spider's web. We all knew he wasn't going anywhere.

With a thud, Addison dropped his bag to the ground.

I was never really sure what happened next. I didn't see who lashed out first – I assume it was Addison – but the next minute all three of them seemed to be on Hutton, pulling at his blazer, dragging his bag from his back, shoving him between them. And then someone spat and I saw it hit the side of Hutton's neck, a globule of saliva just above his perfectly pressed shirt collar. Hutton always looked immaculate, his blonde hair neatly cut, his shoes shined, his tie perfectly straight. But now Addison was pulling on Hutton's tie like he was trying to drag a struggling dog on a leash, and his blazer was half pulled from his shoulders.

"Hey, come on, you lot, just leave him," I heard myself say.

"You're such a loser, Hutton," snarled Smith.

"Repeat what you just said to me, Hutton!" demanded Addison, jabbing at his shoulder.

"Come on, just leave him," I said, a bit louder this time. This was going too far.

"Go on, say it again!" barked Addison, shoving Hutton in the chest, sending him stumbling backwards.

"Just get off him!" I snapped, and before I knew what I was doing, I'd grabbed Addison's shoulder and was dragging him off.

"What do you think you're doing?" Addison growled, knocking my hand away. He glared at me. He wasn't used to anyone standing up to him, let alone manhandling him.

"What are *you* doing?!" I shouted, suddenly incensed by this behaviour. "Just leave him alone. You're out of order!"

"*I'm* out of order?"

"All of you! What's he even done to you?"

Addison squared up to me. He was broader than me and a good few of inches taller, so that I had to arch my neck to look him in the eye.

"Don't go all wimpy on me, Lewis," he said menacingly. "I thought you were meant to be tough."

"Oh yeah? Well, I don't know where you got that from," I retorted, before realising the idiocy of what I'd just said.

Addison smirked. "Perhaps from the fact you're a comp boy from the wrong side of Timpton?" he suggested, smugly.

"I'd rather be a comp boy from the wrong side of Timpton than a stuck-up, arrogant, bullying dickhead like you," I said defiantly.

Addison's face flushed red. "Go back to the sinkhole you somehow managed to crawl out of, Lewis," he spat, grabbing his bag from the ground and striding off.

Smith and Watts exchanged glances, unsure what to do, before grabbing their own bags and heading after Addison.

"You've gone and made life hard for yourself, Lewis," called Watts, glancing back at me. I wasn't sure if it was meant as a final piece of friendly advice or a threat.

I sighed heavily and hitched my bag up on my shoulder, contemplating life ahead of me at St John's now.

Just then, I heard the sound of someone clapping slowly.

I turned to see Hellie Larsen and her two sidekicks approaching. It was only at sixth form that St John's admitted girls, and the small number meant I probably should have known all their names, but seeing as I was relatively new and still some way off the sixth form myself, the only name I knew was Hellie Larsen. Everybody knew Hellie Larsen's name.

"Hurrah for the hero!" cheered Hellie, smiling at me. She was dressed in a smart, pastel-pink suit, her platinum hair tied up in a high ponytail.

I flushed, unsure how to respond. I wasn't even sure if she was being sarcastic or complimentary.

"So, it's Lewis, is it?" she asked, her accent an intriguing mixture of Scandinavian, American and cut-glass English.

I nodded.

"Well, Lewis," she said, smiling at me over her shoulder as she continued on her way, "you're my kind of friend."

I stared after her, hearing her friends giggling and whispering.

"You didn't have to do that," Hutton mumbled.

For a moment I'd forgotten he was there. I turned and I glared at him. If it wasn't for him I wouldn't have got into this situation.

"They'll probably be out to make your life hell too now," he added.

It is that what they'd done? What *we'd* done? Had I really been part of making someone's life hell?

I looked at my shoes, feeling ashamed. I hadn't told anyone what had been going on with Hutton. Not my parents, not even Max or Tom. I'd convinced myself that it was irrelevant, but the truth was I'd known how wrong it was. My dad would have been so disappointed in me; my friends wouldn't have believed I could be part of such a thing. They would have all told me to stop hanging out with Addison, Smith and Watts. But where would that have left me? Alone, again. Was I really that weak? I couldn't believe I'd been such a sheep. Is this who I was without Tom and Max by my side? I felt disgusted at myself.

"I'm sorry," I said, "for… you know for… all the stuff…"

The apology wasn't well expressed, but I sincerely meant it. I felt horrible.

Hutton shrugged.

"'S'okay," he said quietly.

I shook my head. "No, it isn't, it's shit. And I'm sorry."

We stood in silence for a moment. The wind picked up around us, brown leaves blowing down the alley, over our smart shoes.

"What's your name anyway?" I asked. "I mean, your real name."

"Michael," he said, with a shiver.

"I'm Jay."

"I know."

"Oh right," I said, feeling stupid. "I hate this dumb system of calling everyone by their surname."

"I hate everything about this place."

I nodded. I could see why he would hate it. I suddenly realised that I did, too.

"I've got to get to French," I sighed, ambling away.

After a few steps, I stopped and turned around.

"You coming or what?"

Michael eyed me warily for a moment, and then slowly moved to catch up with me.

"I'm really sorry," I mumbled again as we walked along, as if saying it enough times would wash away my involvement.

"Okay," said Michael, looking straight ahead of him, "you can stop apologising now."

I remember staring out at the still water.

"I'm so sorry," I whispered.

My breath clouded against the grey November sky. I

imagined jumping into the canal, the shock of the freezing water whisking this horrible moment away. Out of the corner of my eye, I saw Libby wrap her arms around herself and shiver against the cold.

"I honestly thought we were done," I told her again.

It was a quiet, early Sunday morning. From our place on the bridge, we watched smoke rising from the chimneys of the narrowboats lined up neatly along the water's edge, the scent of burning wood carrying through the air. A few of the boats betrayed evidence of last night's festivities: a burned-out barbecue in a bow, two empty wine glasses on a roof. Scraps of fireworks littered the towpath, along with the odd blackened sparkler. The morning felt dead and bleak, a hangover from the celebrations. The odd dog walker trudged along the towpath, bundled up against the cold, but other than that there was no one else out.

"It didn't take you long," said Libby, bitterly.

I shook my head sadly. "I didn't mean for it to happen. Like I said, I just... I was in a bad place. I'd had a bit to drink, so had she... I thought you and I were over, otherwise I never would have—"

"Was it because we hadn't... you know. Because I kept saying we should wait—"

"No!" My voice sounded louder than I had expected, amplified in the stillness of the air. I pushed my cold fingers through my hair. "I honestly thought... you said we were done."

"I said I was done with the way you were behaving."

"You said you couldn't handle our relationship anymore."

"*You*. I said I couldn't handle *you* anymore! And the way you were acting. I just... I needed a break."

"But I didn't know it was a break! Of course I didn't know that, otherwise I never would have gone with her! I thought you were finished with me. I mean, why *wouldn't* you want to finish with me? Look what I did to you!"

I gestured to her face and then quickly looked away, unable to bear what I had done.

"It was nothing to do with that," said Libby adamantly, touching the scar. "I told you I forgave you for that. It was all the other stuff I couldn't handle. The drinking and getting suspended and behaving so closed off. It was so totally unlike you. Every time I thought it was getting better, it seemed to get worse again. I didn't know what you were going to be like from one moment to the next."

"I know I was being a pain in the arse, but I just didn't know how to deal with what happened that night after the fairground. I could see I was going to drive you away but I couldn't stop, and then when you said you'd had enough... What was I meant to think?"

"You were meant to think I'd had enough and that I was taking time out!"

"But all you told me was you'd had enough! It would have been handy to have added the bit about taking time out!"

"I thought... like I said, I just assumed..." Her voice trailed off and she tucked her chin inside her thick knitted scarf.

That was the worst thing of all: that she'd just assumed. That she'd had that much faith in us that it never occurred to her we were over. Whereas me, the moment I thought we were finished, I'd been overwhelmed by hurt and regret and anger and gone and put the final nail in the coffin. How could we have been on such different pages? Perhaps when you had a dad who came and went with the seasons it seemed normal to separate and then come back together. Her parents had been doing that for years, over and over. But that wasn't how I was raised. In my world, you were either together or you weren't. And I had honestly believed we weren't.

Then, last night, Libby had come round to see me, said she'd had time to clear her head and wanted to move forwards, that she hoped the time out had done us both good but she didn't want to be apart any longer.

And all I could think was *what have I done?* There she

was, sitting on my bed talking to me, just like she had done several times a week in the year we'd been together, and it was as if nothing had changed, as if it could all be fixed and we could find our way back to where we were before.

Only I knew that everything was different.

I already regretted going to Manchester. Now I would have done anything, absolutely anything, to take it back.

I should have told her straight away, but it was hard. Libby talked a lot when she had a point to make, and when she was on edge, both of which were applicable at that point. And so I'd just let her carry on pouring her heart out, talking as if our weeks apart had been nothing but a bump in our road, while I stood there in stupefied silence, unable to believe she was there. That she had – it seemed – never stopped being there. I felt like I'd stepped off a high bridge, only to realise that there was something to live for after all. And so when she put her arms around me and tentatively kissed me on the lips, I let her, thinking that maybe I could keep what happened in Manchester a secret, make a pact with Hellie to keep it buried forever; beg her, bribe her, blackmail her, whatever it took so that it never got out. Libby was the best thing that had ever happened to me and we had to go back to how we were, whatever it took.

Guilt hammered at the door of my mind until the early hours of the next morning when, sleep-deprived and drowning in regret, I finally gave into the realisation that I could never keep this from Libby. I knew telling her would ruin everything, that my second chance with her would be gone, but I couldn't live with the deception. It wasn't right. Plus, what would happen when we came to take that next step in our relationship? It was meant to be the first time – for both of us. We'd talked about it, edged towards it, but agreed to wait a little longer. What was I meant to do when the moment came? Make out it was my first time too? I couldn't do it.

I knew Libby wouldn't scream or cry or storm off when

I told her. Her mother had raised her to believe that women should be strong and independent, and never emotionally enslaved to a man. She did Harmonie proud: pursing her lips, retaining her dignity, maintaining an agonising silence as we stood on the bridge that Sunday morning and I told her everything. But I knew how much it was hurting her and I hated myself for it, hated myself for ruining any chance we had of getting back together.

"We could pretend it didn't happen," said Libby, suddenly, gazing out at the dark, still water.

I turned to her, shocked and confused, but she just stared straight ahead. I studied her profile; her freckled nose just rising above the folds of her knitted scarf, her eyes steely and resolute, her cheeks tinged pink with cold, the scar she would always bear because of me. Hope shot up in me like a fountain, but then dropped again. I shook my head slowly.

"But it did happen," I said, regretfully, "we can't just pretend it didn't."

Libby turned to me. "But we can move on from it. We can still make this work. It was just a…"

"A mistake," I finished, unable to believe what was happening.

She nodded. "I don't want to lose you," she said, tears glazing her eyes, "I can't imagine not being with you and I don't care about what happened with that girl. I just want us to go back to how we were."

I stared at her, speechless.

"I promise I would never have done it—" I gushed.

"I know," she interrupted.

"And I'll change, I promise. I'll go back to the old me. I'm gonna put what happened that night of the fairground behind me. I think I just need to try and forget about it. Things will be like they were before, I promise."

"Okay," she nodded resolutely, tucking a flyaway strand of hair behind her ear, swallowing down her tears, "okay."

My heart felt like it was about to burst out of my chest. I

could have cried with the relief of having her back. I wrapped my arms around her, buried my face in the thick wool of her scarf, breathed in the familiar scent of her hair, felt the soft, chill skin of her cheek against my lips once again.

"I'm sorry," I mumbled in her ear, not because I believed I had betrayed her, but because I should have had more faith in us.

I remember my mum sighing.

"I'm sorry, Jamie, I really am."

I shook my head and smiled bitterly. "Sure you are," I mumbled.

"I didn't want things to turn out like this. Nobody wants their marriage to come to an end."

Try not sleeping with another man maybe. That might help.

"I've been trying to make this work for so long," she muttered, her elbows slumped on the kitchen table, her fingers wrapped in her hair. "I wanted to make it work, wanted us to stay a family... but I can't carry on like this. I know you must be upset with me."

Upset? Upset! I was more than upset. I was hurt. And angry. And disbelieving. But most of all I was terrified.

"You said you'd be here to help. When the baby comes. You said—"

"I will be here. I'm not going to be leaving Timpton. I'll be available as much as you need me."

I'll need you all the time! I wanted to scream at her. *How am I meant to do this without you?*

"But you won't be *here*," I said.

"I won't be in this house, but I'll be around. Nothing's changed. Me and your dad meant every word we said, we're going to help you as much as we can. And there's no animosity between us, we'll still work as a team to help you. But we don't even know how much time the baby will be spending here, Jamie. We have no idea how all this is going to work yet."

"I know that!" I snapped. "We don't know *anything*, that's the whole point. The whole situation is just…" *A nightmare*, I wanted to say, but how could I say that about my own baby?

Several months after the initial blow, it seemed like everyone was expecting me to man up to the situation, come to terms with the position I'd put myself in. *You made your bed!* my mum had snapped at me during of one of many stress-fuelled arguments. She'd even started buying "bits and pieces" for when the baby arrived. But I couldn't come to terms with any of it.

I still awoke each morning believing I was back in my old life. As I opened my eyes, I spied books scattered around my bedroom, my bag, a calculator, pens… But then, as my brain stretched and yawned, it started to dawn on me that everything looked different. Instead of seeing one of the smart suits my parents had bought me for sixth form hanging on the back of the door, hooded tops and jeans were scattered around the room. In place of my leather satchel emblazoned with the crest of St John's, a rucksack slumped beside my desk. And then every morning the realisation hit me, making my stomach lurch. St John's had suggested, not too politely, that I might be better off continuing my A levels elsewhere, given my current situation. If, indeed, continuing my A levels would even be possible.

"And after we lifted your suspension and allowed you back to school," the headmaster had tutted with a despairing shake of his head, "what a waste of a second chance."

Fast-forward a few weeks and at least the local community college didn't care for smart suits, crests and stuck-up attitudes. They didn't even care if I turned up or not.

"Jamie, I know everything's hard right now," said my mum, reaching out to touch my hand.

I pulled it away.

"I just can't believe you're doing this. To Dad. To…" I was about to say "to Laura", but would she even be bothered? She'd moved in with Steve, her dopey new boyfriend, and only ever called in for food, washing or money. I wanted to say "to me", but I wasn't sure if I was allowed to need her anymore. If you're about to become a dad yourself, is it okay to still need your mum? I had a feeling that I was expected to be all grown-up now. And yet my parents still paid for everything, my mum cooked my meals, my dad drove me into the college where he worked…

My dad. My heart ached when I thought about what he must be going through. How could my mum be leaving him? Hadn't he always been there for her? Hadn't he supported every decision she'd ever made? All the hours she'd spent buried in her thesis, the conferences, the meetings, and then, later, her long working hours at the university. Or had she been with *him* all that time? It made my stomach turn to think about it. And the way my dad had been ever since the pregnancy announcement – unflappable, stoical, quietly supportive. My mum always said he must have the patience of a saint in order to spend so many years teaching maths to young people who had failed their GCSE first time round and were highly likely to do so again. She'd always urged him to move on, to get into management or higher education like her, but he was committed to his job, as challenging as it could be.

Still, as much as I appreciated my dad's patience and understanding, those qualities weren't going to help me handle a baby. My mum was the one who knew what she was doing when it came to these things. She was the one I needed.

"Your dad understands that I haven't been happy in a long time," she said. "He understands that I need to go. I'm grateful to him for all the years we've been together—"

"*Grateful?*"

"Yes, grateful," she repeated, tersely, "for being a good father, a good husband. But I'm not just a wife and mother, Jamie, I'm a person, a human being. I have my own needs and desires and ambitions, and I've been supressing those for a long time."

I stared at the tabletop, following the familiar patterns in the wood grain with my finger. I didn't want to hear about my mum's desires. Why was she suddenly talking to me about such things? Because now it was evident that we had both had sex she thought we could be open about such things? I'd done it once, just once, and it felt like the biggest mistake of my life. Because, unlike her, I didn't get to walk away. And mixed with the anger and the hurt came a surge of jealousy.

"You said I needed to own up to my responsibility," I said, bitterly, "but you… you're just walking away from yours."

"I've done my time!" she snapped, colour rising in her cheeks.

"God, you make it sound like a prison sentence!" I retorted. "I'm sorry we've been such a burden!"

"You haven't! I didn't mean it like that. I just mean that I've been here for as long as I can be. You and Laura are both grown up now."

"So now I'm a grown-up?" I asked angrily. "Because four months ago when I told you about the pregnancy, I was a child. That's what you said, wasn't it? That I was just a child and how could I possibly have a baby? But now that it suits you, I'm suddenly a grown-up, and so it's okay for you to just leave?"

"If you really want to know, I'd been planning to leave when you turned sixteen all along! It was only the fact that you stupidly got yourself into this situation that meant I stayed as long as I did! I thought I had to be here, I thought I at least had to stay until everything got settled, but I just can't do it! Because if I stay then that's it, isn't it? I'll never fucking leave!"

I stared at my mum in shock. I don't think I had ever heard her swear before. And to hear that she'd been wanting to leave us… My *mum*? It couldn't be true.

"What do you mean you'd been planning to leave all along?" I asked, quietly, unsure I wanted to hear the response. "How long have you and Jack been…?"

My mum sighed heavily and rubbed her eyes. "I didn't mean… I just meant I'd had it in my head for a while—"

"No, you said *all along*. What does that mean? How long

have you been—" I searched for a word that didn't make me feel too disgusted, "—*with* him?"

My mum rubbed at her eyes. "Our history," she said quietly, "goes way back."

I already knew that Jack had been my mum's boyfriend in her college days. They'd kept in touch and, over the years, he'd call in for a visit now and then. I didn't know what he did for a living and didn't much care, but I knew he travelled a lot. He wore battered leather jackets and smelled of cigarettes, and he tried to make conversation with me in a way that showed he had no kids of his own. I'd extricate myself from these situations at the earliest opportunity and go hang out with my dad in his workshop. My dad, for his part, always greeted Jack with polite detachment and then left my mum to entertain him. I would sometimes hear the two of them talking about their college days, the places they'd travelled, the memories they shared. My mum seemed giddy around him, laughing loudly and talking too much, but I also had memories of harsh whispers, hushed disagreements and sudden, unexpected exits. Had he been trying to lure her away from our family all along?

"My feelings for him never really went away," my mum continued, quietly. "I resisted them for a long, long time, but…" She looked up at me imploringly and I glared angrily at her, willing her to get to the point. "We've only been together these past six months or so," she conceded, "but I think it's always been heading—"

"Six months! You've been having an affair for *six* months?!"

"I was going through a tough time, Jamie! I needed someone to talk to, he was here and—"

"Dad was here!"

"But your dad's part of it, Jamie! He's *in* it! He's been under just as much stress as me. I just needed to talk to someone outside of it all and then…" she trailed off with a long sigh.

Six months ago. So around the time I "lost my way", as my dad referred to it. My mum referred to it as me becoming a "complete bloody nightmare". It started after that night at the fairground, gradually at first and then building momentum, until I didn't know what to do with all my stress and anger other than stay out all night drinking until I forgot about everything, shouted at the people around me, turned every disagreement into a fight, and finally got myself suspended from the school my mum had so desperately wanted me to go to. Then, just as I was coming through it, the final blow; there was a girl, something had happened, she was pregnant, it was mine. My mum had cried and ranted and raged for most of a month – I'd ruined my life, wasted my opportunities. I was only a term into my A levels – how on earth was I planning on finishing those? In the moments when my dad had managed to calm her down, she had been the mum I wanted – putting her arms around me, telling me it would be okay. But her stress and disappointment would soon get the better of her again. I was the one she'd pinned her hopes on.

And so it was me, was it? I'd been the one to finally push her into the arms of another man. Not Laura, who had been a constant, steady source of concern and frustration for years, but me, the good boy only recently – but quite spectacularly – fallen from grace. I was the reason our family had disintegrated.

"You don't get to pin this on me," I said defensively, standing up so abruptly that my chair fell backwards and clattered against the kitchen floor.

My mum frowned and looked exasperated. "I wasn't… Where are you going?"

"What else is there to say?!" I snapped.

My mum, her face pale and exhausted, opened her mouth, searching for the words to make things better, but nothing came out.

"Just go then," I said, storming out of the kitchen.

"Jamie, come back!" I heard her shout, as I ran up the stairs. "I'm sorry!"

Chapter 7

Struggles

I'm concerned and bemused by the amount of time my son spends glued to his phone. Concerned because surely it can't be healthy, and bemused because I can't understand why anyone would want to be connected to other human beings twenty-four hours a day. I can count the number of people I care about on one hand, easily, and I know what they're up to because they talk to me about it all the time, whether I want them to or not. I love them, but they exhaust me, all of them. One day, once Josh has left home and my dad's no longer around, I plan on moving to the Peak District, renovating my great-great-grandad's crumbling two-bed cottage and living in splendid isolation, working by myself, hiking and biking by myself. I could be happy like that. I really think I could.

But Josh isn't like me. He's sociable and outgoing, the centre of his friendship group. I suppose I was more like that once, but even at his age I always needed my time alone, my space apart from the world. He can't seem to go an hour without being on social media, commenting on someone else's life, sharing details of his own. Maybe he's just typical of his generation. But I think it's also in his genes.

His mother was very outgoing, very extrovert. Her threshold

for boredom was non-existent, as evidenced by the fact that her infatuation with her newborn infant burned out within a matter of weeks. She loved being the object of gossip and revelled in the scandal of her pregnancy. Josh brought her all the attention she desired, and in those early weeks I felt my son belonged more to her gaggle of friends than he did to me. But as everyone else's interest in the baby died down so did hers. And then she was off chasing the next thing that would make her centre stage. When I first met her, I thought she was fearless and uninhibited, and I was fascinated and perhaps a little in awe. Later, I realised she was needy and desperate, and her vulnerability made her more human to me. It took a little longer to realise she was completely and inexcusably self-centred, but by then it was too late.

So, no, maybe my son's not so much like his mother after all. Maybe he has her better parts – her sense of adventure, her air of confidence, her zest for life. But he has none of her selfishness, none of her clawing need for approval. He enjoys attention, but he doesn't rely on it. He likes to be heard, but not to the exclusion of others. Perhaps my introverted genes have balanced out her more dramatic ones. Perhaps, somehow, out of the mess that was us, we created something that was just right.

Anyway, when I walk in from work and find Josh lying on the sofa texting, Snapchatting, WhatsApping or whatever else, I'm hardly surprised.

"All right?" I ask from the doorway.

He makes some kind of non-committal noise without bothering to look up.

The TV's on, even though he's not looking at it, as are the lights, despite it being a bright summer's evening. Aren't today's teenagers meant to be concerned about the environment? I flick the light switch off and bite my tongue, determined not to start the evening by making a fuss about his waste of electricity. Or the mess he's created by leaving plates, glasses, crisp packets and biscuit wrappers around the lounge. Or the fact that the washing I asked him to put away is still sitting in a pile on the coffee table. What helps me restrain myself in these situations is the guilt I feel at leaving him to his own devices almost every day of the summer holidays while I work.

"I'm gonna jump in the shower," I tell him, already stripping off my T-shirt, "can you get some water boiling for dinner?"

He smiles, but it's not at me. It's at his damn phone. But it isn't the smile that usually spreads over his face when he's texting – that of a sniggering schoolboy, the one that tells me he's exchanging rude or snide remarks with one of his mates. It's a soft, contented smile. I have a feeling it's Chloe.

"Josh?"

"What?"

"Water—"

"Yeah, yeah."

I'm about to walk away when my curiosity gets the better of me.

"Who are you chatting with?"

"What?" he asks, glancing up for the first time. "No one. I mean, just, you know, friends."

He's lying, I know. He looks shifty.

"Put that washing away please," I say, heading for the bathroom, knowing I'll get no more out of him.

According to Josh's friends, I'm meant to be the laid-back, lenient, easy-going dad, since I'm about fifteen years younger than most of their parents. I'm meant to be the cool dad, the one that lets Josh get away with things they're not allowed to, the one who's more like a friend than a parent. Evidently, I'm not that dad, which they find highly amusing. They rib Josh about it all the time – the way I lay down rules, monitor his homework, correct his grammar. In front of his friends he takes it in good humour, shaking his head despairingly and muttering about how lame I am. But when we're alone it's another matter. Nothing causes more arguments between us than me "doing my anal parenting thing".

"Why can't we just eat in front of the TV for once like normal people?" Josh complains, slumping into a kitchen chair.

"The amazing thing about on demand, Josh, is that you can watch what you want when you want," I tell him, sliding two bowls of pasta onto the table, "which means you're not missing anything."

"Seriously, we are, like, the only family I know who never eat dinner in front of the TV."

"We are *like* them? You mean we resemble them?"

I know this is going to antagonise him, but I'm easily irritated tonight. I've been going in circles in my head all week, dissecting last week's encounter with Libby, feeling increasingly angry at myself for the rubbish way I handled it and sad about the outcome.

Josh tuts. "I mean we *are* the only family I know."

"Really? The only family you know? Somehow I can't imagine the Stapleton-Porters sprawling on the sofas at mealtimes."

"Actually, they do. Well, not her parents maybe, but last time I had dinner at Chloe's, we ate in the games room in front of the telly."

"That's because you were about nine the last time you ate dinner at Chloe's."

"No, I wasn't. It was, like, a year ago."

"What's the games room anyway? Where they keep the billiard table?"

Josh rolls his eyes. "Yeah, Dad, it's where they keep the billiard table. It's right above the servants' quarters."

I like to tease Josh about Chloe's family being rich, mainly because it seems to annoy him, but also because it's a way of venting my envy. It's not so much their wealth I'm jealous of; in reality, they're not really what you would call rich, and I've never been particularly materialistic anyway, which is handy under the circumstances. But it's the comfortable middle-class security of the Stapleton-Porters' lifestyle I begrudge. I know I have no right, but they have one of those perfect-looking lifestyles that brings to mind the families I knew at St John's and aggravates the chip on my shoulder. They've been able to give their child everything I would have liked to have given mine – great birthday parties, nice holidays, music lessons, a lovely home. And, most importantly, two parents.

"So you've never sat down with Chloe's parents to eat?" I ask.

Seeing as she's been brought into the conversation, I'm reluctant to let talk of Chloe drop. I want him to open up about his feelings for her. Josh can be a typical cagey teenager, but with a little probing he tells me most things. I think.

"No, we've never sat down to eat dinner with her parents. In the same way we've never sat down to eat dinner with you."

"Because?"

"Because it would be cringeworthy. Plus, you've never asked her to stay for dinner."

"Well, maybe I should."

"Maybe you shouldn't."

"I could get to know her better."

"You've known her for, like, seven years."

"Yeah, but I never get to have a proper conversation with her. It might be nice to find out what's going on with her these days, what she's up to…"

Josh frowns at me as if I've lost my mind.

"What for?"

I shrug. "I don't know."

I'm not even sure why I'm suggesting this now. The idea of sitting down and making polite conversation with Chloe over dinner would probably be just as painful for me as it would for her.

Josh shakes his head, bemused. "You're hardly Mr Sociable, Dad."

"All right, forget I mentioned it."

"I'll do that."

Josh shovels pasta into his mouth, his head bent over his bowl. I pick at a couple of pieces of fusilli. I'm not hungry despite the fact I haven't eaten anything since a bacon roll at ten o'clock this morning. My appetite's been non-existent ever since my ill-fated trip to Camden.

"Can I go out after dinner?" Josh asks.

"Where?"

"Just into town."

"With?"

"The usual."

"Specifically?"

"Specifically, the same people I always hang out with."

"To do what?"

"Don't know. Whatever."

I chew slowly and stare at him, waiting.

"Probably go to the park for a bit," he offers.

"You'll come home before dark," I order, wagging my fork at him.

"I'll come home before dark," he sighs, as if he's heard it all a million times, "and I won't talk to any strangers and I won't take the shortcut home and I won't walk too close to bushes people could jump out from and I'll watch out for any cars or vans pulling up alongside me."

I hate his smart-arse attitude, but I'm also glad he's able to reel off all these safety precautions. He thinks I'm over the top, but he has no idea of the dangers out there.

"Have you done any work on your assignment today?" I ask.

"Yeah."

"Can I see?"

Josh probes his pasta.

"Well, I mean I didn't get that much actually done. But I thought about what I'm going to do next."

"Well, thinking about doing something isn't the same as doing it, is it?"

Josh sighs, reaches for his glass and very slowly gulps down an entire pint of orange squash. Then he picks up his fork again.

"Josh?"

"What?"

"It's not the same thing, is it?"

"I've got the whole summer."

I shake my head despairingly. I am so sick of having to bang on about schoolwork.

"Josh, come on—"

"Dad, just drop it okay? I'm doing it."

"Yeah, except you're not, are you?"

"Oh my God, will you just get off my back about this project?!"

"I'd love to not *have* to be on your back all the time."

"Really? 'Cause, seriously, it's, like, non-stop."

A tense silence falls between us while we pick unenthusiastically at our food.

"You know what would be way more useful to me than doing this dumb music assignment?" he finally mutters. "If you'd actually let me get some experience—"

"Don't even start this again."

"Why?!"

"Because you're too young!"

I could kill Michael for having put this idea in my son's head. I know he thinks Josh is talented, and that he wants to nurture that talent, but suggesting my child jumps in on one of his gigs was way out of line. He should have asked me first, but when he gets excited by an idea, he just never stops to think.

"It would just be a couple of songs—"

"No. You're not doing a gig in a pub—"

"The Canal House!"

"Which is a pub! It still gets rowdy down there when there's a band."

"What exactly do you think would happen to me?"

"That's not the point. You've just turned fifteen—"

"Exactly! I'm not a child anymore!"

"That's exactly what you are! And it's my job to keep you safe."

"I *am* safe! I couldn't be any bloody safer!"

He stands up and angrily scrapes the reminder of his pasta into the bin.

"Where are you going?"

"Out," he mumbles, leaving the kitchen, "unless you think leaving the flat is too dangerous."

I open my mouth to call him back, but suddenly I feel exhausted and can't face the drama. It's been a horrible week of regret and rumination following my meet-up with Libby, and I need to shift this mindset. I glance out the window at the clear blue evening sky.

There's somewhere I want to go. I've been thinking about it a lot this week, and there's plenty of time before it gets dark.

A few seconds later, I hear the door slam.

Exactly one year on from the night of the fairground I walked all the way to the cemetery. It took me well over an hour, and by the time I got there, my new trainers had rubbed both heels to the point of bleeding. It seemed fitting, like a penance. I vowed I'd do that walk on the same date every year.

I never went again.

Until now.

I park the van on the main road, and by the time I walk apprehensively through the wrought-iron gates, the sun is going down. The evening air is cool against my bare forearms, and the scent of freshly mowed grass and this afternoon's rain lingers. The cemetery is huge, but I know exactly where I'm heading. Our lives rush forward like high-speed trains, but he'll forever be in one place.

The grave is beautifully kept, as unaltered by time as the grief of those who tend it.

I crouch down, my eyes scanning the chiselled lettering on the headstone.

Barclay James Macintyre
Beloved son of Carole and Peter
Forever in our thoughts

I shake my head slowly. "If I'd done things differently that night…" I whisper.

I close my eyes and there we are again, for the millionth time, trapped in an eternal loop, stumbling over clods of mud in the darkness, laughing. The sweet taste of candyfloss in my mouth. The distant thud of music. The soft fur of a polar bear beneath my fingertips.

… wearing gay shorts…

… gonna give it to her tonight…?

… so immature…

… what was that noise…?

… just a fox…

… are you scared…

… Tom…!

… Shit! He's bleeding…

… let's go…!

He looks straight at me, firelight reflected in his swollen eyes. Blood running down his bruised face, a strand of hair plastered to his forehead.

I know him.

I know who he is.

With a sharp intake of breath, my eyelids spring open. I put the tip of my thumb between my teeth, bite down hard, gaze at the headstone there in front of me.

Beloved son

Forever in our thoughts

I close my eyes again.

We need to get help!

I am racing, my trainers pounding the towpath, my breath jagged and painful.

Then turning in circles, the inky star-studded sky spinning above me.

Which way? Which way?

The lockhouse or the Kingfisher?

The Kingfisher or the lockhouse?

Turning, turning…

And then I'm flying, the blackness of the canal rushing by at my side.

I burst through the door of the pub, music spilling out into the night, faces turning towards me.

Slow down there, son.

Hey, isn't that Richard's boy?

My knees hit the floor and I'm on all fours, a nauseating swirl of faded blue carpet filling my vision, the stench of stale beer, flecks of crisp trodden into the pile. And blood. My own blood.

Steady on, young man.

Nine nine nine, I gasp, *you've gotta call nine nine nine.*

And then I vomit sweet, sickly pink liquid onto the swirling pattern beneath me.

I open my eyes again and drop onto my knees, feeling the dampness of the grass seeping through the denim of my jeans. I count in a whisper.

"One. Two. Three. Four. Five. Six. Seven…"

How much can be accomplished in sixty seconds?

You can ignite the fire that will burn down a forest. You can give the final push that will bring life into the world. You can give the order to start a war. You can press the button that will send a rocket to the moon.

But you can't save a life once you've made a wrong decision.

Regret weighs heavily on my chest, squeezing the breath out of me. I can feel it starting. The band around my ribcage, the tightening in my throat. I try to count, breathing slowly, deeply. I open my mouth, my lips and tongue uncomfortably dry, as I try to drag in some air.

Zzzzzzzzz.

The vibration in my back pocket startles me.

I stand up quickly, digging frantically for my phone, blood rushing to my head. The world tips sideways slightly before righting itself.

I know it's going to be about Josh, I just know it. A rival group of lads from another school, an addict with a knife, a drunk driver…

But by the time I have my phone in my hand the buzzing has already stopped. It was just a text message coming through. No emergency then.

Hi. Hope you don't mind me texting like this. Found your number on internet. You took me by surprise Monday. I would like to talk. Can we meet? Libby.

The breath that's been trapped inside me rushes out with a sigh. I reread the message six times. Relief floods through me that I didn't do the wrong thing in finding her, that I haven't just made things worse.

My thumb fumbles across the keys.

Yes, that would be great.

I pause, unsure what else to write. Thanks? When? Where? Why?

And then I just press send, because what else is there to say? It would be great, that's all.

I push my phone back into my pocket and stare at the headstone, my sense of despair subsided.

For the first time in ages I feel like I might be able to start my journey towards some kind of peace, some kind of resolution to everything that started that night.

For the first time in ages I feel hope again.

Chapter 8

Hope

I remember that when I left Hellie in drizzly Manchester – trudging out of her halls of residence with a holdall, a hangover and a sense of regret – she'd promised to call me over the Christmas holidays. She'd be coming home for three weeks and we'd have to get together, she'd said, kissing me goodbye on the cheek. Yeah, sure, I'd smiled, feeling nauseous and disorientated.

So when it reached January and she hadn't called, I welcomed in the new year with a sense of relief. My life was once again on track. I was overwhelmingly happy to be back with Libby, grateful my school suspension was over, and I was moving on from the trauma of last year. I was no longer anxious or angry all the time. I was no longer having nightmares. I just wanted to leave what had happened in the past – all of it, including Hellie. I imagined that's what she wanted, too.

So when she phoned me one Saturday afternoon at the end of January, I was disappointed.

"The thing is," I told her quietly, not wanting to be overheard by my parents, "me and Libby are back together. We have been for a few weeks now."

"So?"

"So I'm really sorry, Hellie, I just don't think I should see you. Not after, you know…" my voice dropped to a whisper, "what happened between us."

"Chill out, Jay, you're safe. I'm not looking to screw you again."

Hellie was always straight to the point, her capacity for bluntness hidden beneath her blue-eyed, blonde-haired angelic veneer and the gently undulating rise and fall of her accent.

I sighed inwardly, knowing that if I saw Hellie I was going to have to be honest with Libby about it. But could I refuse to see Hellie? Was that a terrible thing to do after what had happened between us? After all, she hadn't done anything wrong. Well, technically, I was still adamant that *neither* of us had done anything wrong, seeing as Libby and I – in my books at least – had no longer been a couple. But still, if I met with Hellie then Libby was bound to be upset. I couldn't put my relationship back on the line.

"I just… I'm really sorry, I just don't think I should. It's just that me and Libby… it was kind of a misunderstanding and now—"

"I'm pregnant."

I don't think there has ever been another moment in my life when my brain has refused to compute in such a way. The processor whirred round and round but struggled to produce one single piece of output.

"Did you hear what I said?"

A stream of thoughts suddenly rushed through my mind, all of them desperately trying to lead me to the safety of denial.

She's wrong. She's lying. She's joking. It's someone else's, she just wants me to know. Why would she just want me to know? For support, of course! You're meant to be her friend. Maybe she's got a boyfriend. Maybe they planned it. Would she have planned it? Probably not, given that she's eighteen and at university…

"It's yours," she said matter-of-factly, "just to clarify."

I looked around me, stupidly, as if the answer might lie somewhere nearby.

"But I thought…" I muttered, confused, "…you said…"

"Nothing's a hundred per cent safe, is it? I was taking it every day, just like you're meant to. But these things happen."

These things happen?!

My heart started to pound, the information infiltrating its way into my brain. My legs suddenly felt numb.

This is a disaster! God, this can't be happening! What does this mean? What am I meant to do? Jesus Christ, I only did it once!

"Take some time to freak out. I freaked out at first as well. But now I've got my head around it and, well, it'll be okay. It's not ace, but, hey, it's manageable."

"Not ace"? Talk about the understatement of the century!

But then it dawned on me what she was saying. It was *manageable*. Of course. For a moment the shock had overwhelmed me, but of course it was manageable. There was a way out of this. It would be all right. This could be fixed.

"O–okay," I stammered, "erm… so what happens now? Do you… shall I come with you to sort it out? I mean, I'll come with you, we… we can go together—"

"I've already been to the doctors, just to get it totally confirmed."

"Oh right. Okay. And… so, what happens now?"

"Well, you know, you've got school, so you should probably just focus on that. And I'm going back to uni tomorrow evening. My parents want me to stay at home, but screw that."

"You've told your parents?!" I asked, unable to contain the horror in my voice. Why had she gone and done that? There was no frigging way I was telling mine!

"Well, yeah, I figured I might as well do it now. They're not thrilled, as you can imagine."

I tried to visualise telling my parents about this, but all I could see was the excruciating moment when my dad cornered me in his workshop last year and initiated "the talk". I'd been so desperate to escape that I'd mumbled *I know, I know* in response to every sentence he uttered, before practically shoving him out of my way and rushing back to the safety of the house.

No, there was no need to tell my parents about this. What would be the point? This was a mistake that was going to the grave with me.

But Libby.

What about Libby?

I couldn't keep this from her any more than I could have kept the fact I slept with Hellie from her. I simply couldn't live with the deceit.

But maybe it wouldn't make a difference. She knew what had happened between me and Hellie anyway. Surely that was the worst of it. This… this was just a crappy, unfortunate by-product of something she had already forgiven me for. But it would be dealt with. It would soon be a thing of the past. God, surely after everything me and Libby had worked through this wouldn't derail us now.

"Okay, so look," I said, sudden determination in my voice, "this is my responsibility too, so just tell me when you have an appointment and I'll come with you. You don't have to do any of it on your own."

For a moment I felt almost like a grown-up. I was owning up to this, taking responsibility, being supportive.

"Okay," said Hellie, her voice softer, appreciative, "that's good. I mean, like I said, I wasn't expecting anything from you, but actually that's kind of nice to hear. God, most boys your age would probably run a mile. Most boys *my* age would probably run a mile. But then I've always thought you're really mature. And in the long term you can be as involved as you want. There's no pressure. You know my parents are loaded, so financially it's no problem."

I nodded silently, my brain struggling to catch up.

In the long term?

"And, look, don't feel like you need to tell your parents right now. We can keep it quiet awhile. My dad's pissed, but he's not going to go hammering on your door or anything. And as for your girlfriend... I don't know. Hopefully you can still make it work. It's not like we're going to ever be a couple, right? Just 'cause we're having a baby, it doesn't mean anything really needs to change. Especially for you."

Having a what?!

"What...? But I thought..."

On the end of the line, voices suddenly erupted loudly and then gradually faded. It sounded like Hellie had switched the TV on.

"You thought what?"

"I thought... So you're not getting rid of it?"

"The baby? No, that's what... Is that what you thought I was saying? God no, I'm morally opposed to abortion. Oh God, is that what you thought I was saying? No, sorry if I confused you. I'm keeping it. Definitely."

It felt like the room was sliding, the walls coming in towards me, all the hope of a couple of minutes ago suddenly wrenched away. I closed my eyes and bit down on my lower lip until it hurt.

There was absolutely no frigging way this could be happening.

I remember that I couldn't look her in the eye. Couldn't allow myself to feel anything at all. We were at the end and it was going to hurt.

We stood in silence in exactly the same spot on the bridge where just a few weeks ago we'd made up, put our arms around each other and clung onto the glimmer of hope that was our future. This time, it was a bright, frosty Saturday afternoon. There were dog walkers again, meandering along the towpath, wrapped up against the cold air, stepping aside for the cyclists who weaved around them. Families were out enjoying the sunshine. But apart from all the activity, the landscape was unchanged. The same narrowboats were still moored in the same order, smoke puffing from their chimneys. I even noticed a piece of rubbish – a stream of transparent plastic wrapping – that had been stuck in the bare branches of a nearby tree the last time we had stood here. Not much had altered really, and yet in my world everything was totally different.

I knew it was wrong and utterly selfish, but part of me was still hoping – desperately, irrationally – that Libby would want to stay together despite the baby. She was liberal, used to unusual family set-ups. I figured she wouldn't have to be involved with the baby, and it's not like Hellie and I would ever be together.

I'd made all these points to my parents in a foolish, gushing tirade of emotion at eleven o'clock last night, following an exhausting day of thrashing out the finer details of what any of this would mean for our family.

My dad had sighed and looked at his feet a lot. My mum had wrung her hands through her hair and paced furiously up and down the lounge.

"Have you got any idea what's happening here?!" she'd shouted. "Are you in any way able to comprehend the magnitude of this? It's a baby, Jamie! A human life! Have you any idea how much responsibility that is? Libby isn't the issue! She's not even on the radar! Fretting over the state of your teenage romance is not the bloody priority here!"

"I know that! I know it's not the priority, but it's still *something*. Something I have to sort out!"

"What on earth makes you think that a sensible girl like Liberty would want to be involved in this mess?! Or even that she *deserves* to be involved in this mess?"

"Libby," I mumbled, "she hates being called Liberty."

"After everything you've already put that girl through, I can't believe you'd even consider trying to drag her into this! *She* is focusing on her education! *She* is focusing on getting into a good university one day! All the things that *you* should have been focusing on while you were out drinking and getting into trouble and getting girls pregnant! And, yes, I do understand this has been a tough year for you, but, no, I don't think you can keep using that as an excuse! And how the hell am I going to explain this to Harmonie? I've already had to plead your case on several occasions, not least because you managed to scar her daughter's face for life! And there was I telling her you were a good lad really, you'd just been through a rough time but you were sorting yourself out now… Ha! And now you've gone and proved her completely right and made me look a bloody fool!"

"I can't believe you're worrying about what Harmonie is going to think of you! So it's *not* okay for me be thinking about how Libby fits into all this, but it *is* okay for you to be worrying about her flake of a mother?! Well, I'm sorry if you get kicked out of your stupid yoga class again!"

"Libby *doesn't* fit into all this, Jamie! You've made your bed and now you have to lie in it – alone, if you can manage that! The fact that you are even *thinking* about getting Libby involved in this just shows that, a, you really do have no comprehension of what is coming your way, b, you are just as selfish as most boys your age, and c, you are completely deluded! Because as much as that girl might think she's in love with you, I imagine that even she must have her limits! Just like we all do!"

"Jamie," my dad had interrupted, calmly but forcefully, "I know right now you're struggling to take all this in, and it's going to take some time to get your head around it. It's going to take us *all* time to get our heads around it," he added, glancing at my mum, "but I think what your mum's saying is that you're going to have a *lot* to deal with over the coming months, and it's going to mean change. Big change. In every part of your life."

Deep down, I knew they were right. I could burn myself out trying to cling on to the way things were, but it was all in vain.

My life was turning upside down and there was nothing I could do to stop it.

But still, in spite of myself, in that moment on the bridge, after I told Libby about the pregnancy, I allowed myself to entertain the tiniest glimmer of hope that she might still want to be with me, in whatever form that might take.

"So are you and Hellie going to be… together?" Libby asked, quietly, her hands pushed deep in her coat pockets, staring down at the sparkling surface of the water.

I shook my head, sadly. "No. I mean, I don't know how it's all going to work at the moment, but it's not like that between us. It never will be."

She nodded, thoughtfully.

We watched silently as a red narrowboat chugged out from underneath the bridge and made its way slowly, peacefully along the canal, causing a couple of ducks to bob gently in its wake.

Libby suddenly turned and looked up at me, squinting against the light. Her skin looked unusually pale, but the tip of her nose was pink. She was wearing the same knitted scarf that she'd worn all winter, the one I'd buried my face in the last time we'd stood here, overcome by relief that she was willing to take me back. Now I ran my eyes over her cheeks, her chin, her hair… all so familiar. And I knew that I'd never touch her again.

"We could stay together," she said, her eyes imploring, full of hope. "I know it sounds messy, but people's lives are messy, and it's not like you meant to get yourself into this situation, and it's not like normal relationships have ever really been a feature in my life. I mean, you and Hellie won't be a couple, and who's to say she won't get a new boyfriend, so there's no reason you and I… I mean, look at my parents…"

As she talked fast, anxiously, coming up with all the logical reasons that I'd already been through in my mind about how and why we could still make this work, all the reasons I'd prayed she would come up with on her own, I felt hope swell in my chest once again, just like it had the last time we'd stood on this bridge.

But as I watched her – pretty, clever, full of ambition, her whole life ahead of her – I knew with sudden conviction that my parents were right. I couldn't do this to her. I was sixteen. She was fifteen. We were just kids. And although my own selfish longing wanted to wrap her in my arms and believe in what she was saying, all of a sudden I didn't. I didn't believe any of it anymore. This baby was going to change everything. And it was going to be the biggest challenge of my life. I didn't know if I had the resources to get myself through this, let alone contend with the complications of Libby being involved. And she deserved so much more than this mess I was in. As hard as it felt now, she'd move on, find another boyfriend, build a life for herself, and one day, maybe, look back and remember me as her first love, but nothing more. I had to face the truth. We'd finally come up against something bigger than both of us.

As she talked, I shook my head, slowly, watching her eyes fill with tears. Her voice trailed off and she reached out to touch me, but I pushed her hand away.

"You know it wouldn't work," I told her.

And she did. I could see it in her face. I watched as the hope she was trying to cling on to vanished as quickly as it had materialised. She composed herself, taking a breath, holding her head a little higher, blinking back tears and nodding resolutely. She wasn't raised to have some boy break her heart.

"I should go," I whispered, unable to stand this any longer.

Libby clenched her jaw, nodded, forced the tiniest of smiles.

Swallowing the lump in my throat, I strode past her, over the bridge, down the steps and along the towpath without looking back, telling myself not to think, not to feel. It was the only way I was going to get through this.

I remember bursting through the door of my dad's workshop,

a timber building at the end of our garden where he did everything from fixing car parts to carving pieces of furniture.

"Dad, can you come help?" I shouted desperately over the drumming of the rain. Even the short walk from the house had soaked me and I could feel water running off my hair, dribbling down the back of my neck.

My dad was sitting at his worktable, hunched over something that looked like the inside of a radio, his glasses perched on the end of his nose.

"Hmm?"

He didn't look up.

"The baby won't stop crying. I've tried everything. Nappy, bottle, burping, hushing, singing… Can you just come and make him shut up? It's doing my head in."

My dad repositioned the head of the lamp, examined the array of tools on the tabletop, picked up a small screwdriver and went back to work.

"Well, I'm a little busy right now, son," he muttered.

I pushed my hands through my hair, smelling rancid milk on my forearm from where I'd already tested the temperature of a bottle four times today, starting at two o'clock this morning.

"Dad, I'm serious," I told him, already halfway out the door, expecting him to get up and follow as usual.

"So am I."

I frowned at him.

"You have to be joking. You're not busy. What are you even doing?"

"I'm tinkering."

"Tinkering isn't being busy," I said, impatiently, shooting a glance back towards the house. I'd left the baby on the lounge floor where he couldn't fall off anything, and it wasn't like he could do much other than lie in one place, but my anxiety was mounting with every second I was away. And I could still hear his bloody screaming. "Come on, Dad, you're the only one who can calm him when he gets like this, you know that."

"And where's Hellie?" he asked, laying his screwdriver down and picking up a small piece of wire.

"How the heck should I know?" I shrugged, bitterly.

Despite the communal living arrangement being Hellie's idea, I hadn't seen her since yesterday morning. She'd suggested living like this would be easier for now, and given that my mum had moved out and Laura's bedroom was empty, it seemed to make sense. But it was starting to become clear that moving out of her own home and into ours had more to do with irritating her parents than any ideology about sharing the early months of parenting. Two weeks after the baby came home, she'd started going out for long stretches of time, and six weeks in, she was staying out overnight without bothering to inform anyone of her whereabouts. I felt angry, trapped, exhausted, overwhelmed and desperate, and I couldn't handle it anymore. The baby didn't seem to like me or Hellie or my mum or Laura or anyone who touched him apart from my dad, who was the only one of us with the peace of mind to settle him.

"You know, son," said my dad, removing his glasses and leaning back in his tatty office chair, "you need to do this yourself."

"I can't do it myself!" I snapped. "I've spent the last frigging hour trying to do it myself! He hates me! I've tried everything and all he does is scream louder!"

"He's trying to tell you something."

"He's not trying to tell me anything, he just likes screaming for the hell of it!"

"Try and listen to what he's telling you."

"Oh, come on, Dad! I can't do this."

My dad nodded. "Yes, you can." Then he put his glasses back on and returned to his tinkering.

"You have to be kidding me!" I shouted, slamming the door behind me so hard that the whole workshop shook. I stormed back towards the house, the dark clouds and pouring rain making it easy to forget that this was summer.

I scooped the baby off the floor, holding him away from the wet fabric of my T-shirt, jiggling him a little too frantically. The noise of his screaming drowned out any ability to think.

"Shh, shh, shh, SHH, SHH!" I told him with increasing frustration.

"WAHH! WAHH! WAHH!" he screamed, his little red face scrunched up and angry.

"Oh my God, will you just shut up," I whispered. "Please, please, please, just shut the hell up."

I walked him around the house, into my room which looked more than ever like a bomb had hit it, into Hellie's room which was now a strange mixture of the punk-rock posters that Laura had left behind and Hellie's expensive perfumes, floaty scarves and pieces of silver jewellery, into my parents' room, where my mum's bedside table now sat bare. I had a sudden image of opening my parents' window and throwing the baby down onto the drive, knowing that the blessed relief of silence would follow. I could feel my body yearning to make the necessary movements, my left arm itching to take the baby's weight, while my right arm reached out for the window latch…

I fearfully shook the images from my mind and turned away, only to be faced with the sight of myself in my parents' full-length mirror. My hair was dishevelled, I had a stain down my T-shirt, my face was strangely grey, my eyes were puffy and bloodshot… I'd looked like this last year, when I "lost my way" and started drinking until I was sick. But this time there was no fixing it. I was helpless and there was no way out.

I felt a sudden surge of rage at my mum for not being here anywhere near as much as I'd expected. And then an even bigger surge of rage at my dad for being here and refusing to help. And then at Hellie for being useless. And at Laura and all my friends for being free…

"WAHH! WAHH! WAHHH!"

My chest started to feel tight, like I couldn't get air into my lungs, like there was a belt around my ribcage being systematically tightened. I felt my heart rate accelerate as I started to panic. I tried to inhale deeply, to drag in some air, but I couldn't quite catch my breath. I thought about my dad down the bottom of the garden, how far away that was.

I walked back into my room, craving the familiarity of my stuff, my environment. I jigged the baby up down up down, trying to prevent my fingers clenching around his tiny limbs, trying to ignore the need in my arms to hurl him away from me.

I slumped down on my bedroom floor, surrounded by bits of my clothing, the baby's clothing, a maths textbook, a packet of baby wipes, a calculator...

The baby screamed on my knees.

I clenched my eyes shut and tried not to cry. No one could help me right now. I needed to calm myself down.

I needed to focus on my breathing, but the constant screaming wouldn't let me, so I needed to make the baby quiet, but I didn't know how the hell to do that!

He'd had milk, he'd been changed, he'd been winded. He had a Babygro and a cardigan on, so he had to be warm enough. I'd been shocked by the stifling temperatures on the maternity ward, the fact that even in that kind of heat the babies had all been forced into cardigans and little beanie hats. But, apparently, keeping small babies warm was essential, especially ones that had been born a bit prematurely like ours. We'd been subjected to a scolding by the health visitor when she came for her first home visit last month.

"Baby should have more clothes," she'd said sternly, handling him like he was no more than an aubergine in a greengrocer's. He was wearing nothing but a nappy, a doll-sized T-shirt and a pair of blue socks.

"I put a cardigan on him this morning," Hellie had said, playing the angelic mother and glaring at me. "I don't know why you took it off."

I'd shrugged. "It's July. It's warm outside."

"Yes, but we're not outside, are we?" the health visitor had said abruptly. "Stick to Babygros." She scribbled something damning in her report book.

But as I looked at the baby screaming on my knees, I noticed that his ears, cheeks and fingers were tinged bright pink. Sod what they said. He was too hot, I was sure of it.

I tore the poppers of his Babygro open, prised out his tiny limbs. His skin was warm and blotchy, his little chest rising and falling rapidly as he wailed. I unpeeled the fastenings at either side of his nappy, loosening it just enough to let some air circulate. I held his naked tummy against my damp T-shirt.

For a moment I just stayed there, listening to his crying, feeling his tiny body squirming awkwardly against mine. But then the crying started to subside, turning to more of a moaning, then a mewing, then finally, finally, there was silence.

For a second I contemplated the idea that I might have actually gone deaf.

But when I looked down at him, his eyes were flitting back and forth, contentedly examining the blue of my T-shirt, his little fists clenching and unclenching, grasping the material.

I turned him over onto his back so that we were facing each other. His eyes peered into mine, fascinated, like he was seeing me for the first time. The pinkness that had mottled his skin had subsided. I noticed that his chest was rising and falling almost imperceptibly now, his heartbeat having returned to normal. And with some surprise I noticed that mine had, too.

I couldn't help it. I smiled. I even gave a little laugh. I'd done it. I'd figured out what the problem was and I'd calmed him down all on my own.

I held my little finger out to him and he clenched it tightly in his first.

And for the first time since his birth I felt hope that I might be able to do this after all.

I remember telling him: "This has to stop."

"I know."

"You keep saying you know."

"I *know*."

Michael sat on the edge of the bed with his head in his hands, while I paced slowly around the increasingly small amount of space that was available for pacing. My sister's old room was becoming a dumping ground for every wandering soul who came and went. Even though she'd been gone for almost four years, traces of Laura still remained: a wonky ceramic bowl she made at school, an old teddy bear perched high on a shelf, and those faded punk-rock posters that no one could be bothered to take down. Then there were Hellie's contributions: some expensive jeans and tops in the wardrobe, a vanity mirror and some items of make-up. I didn't know when she'd next be back, or even if she would, so I left it all there, month after month, like an open-ended question. And then finally there was Michael's stuff. A couple of guitars, some scattered clothes, cigarette packets and bottles.

Far too many empty bottles.

Sometimes I wondered who Michael would have become if he'd never met me. What if Tom had never introduced him to metal music and Max had never shared that first cigarette? What if I'd never given him his first sip of alcohol? I knew he'd made his own choices, but still, I couldn't help but wonder… Was part of this my fault?

"I'll stop. I will," he muttered.

"When?"

"Today."

I turned my face to the ceiling and sighed heavily. It was like listening to all our previous conversations on replay.

"Yeah, but you won't, will you?

"I will," he muttered, rubbing at his eyes. Last year, he'd had a large, weeping angel tattooed on his forearm, its dark wings wrapping around his pale skin. Now a demon was emerging just above it, his twisted, angry face adorned by sketchy horns that couldn't be completed until Michael had the funds to pay for it.

"I can't have you around Josh if you're going to be doing this," I said, sounding almost apologetic.

Michael looked up at me. His face was white and his dark eyes were bloodshot.

"Josh doesn't know what's going on," he protested, "he's three."

"Exactly. He's three. He's not a baby anymore. He sees things, he hears things. He understands things."

Michael shook his head, dismissively. But I'd been thinking about it, and I knew I was right.

"I'm serious, mate. You need to sort yourself out. Or I can't have you here."

Even at that point, I wasn't sure if I meant it. Where else would he go? After his GCSEs, Michael had spent eighteen months driving himself into a state of misery, trying to get to grips with his father's business, but he'd struggled, just like he'd struggled at school. He was hopeless at his new role, out of his depth and full of anxiety. He'd quit more times than I could count but had always gone back as part of his endless, self-defeating mission to win his father's approval. He'd started drinking and doing God knows what else just to get through, had fallen in with a few shady types he'd met on the local music scene, and finally got himself thrown out of both the business and his father's home. Apart from a bit of gigging and busking, he hadn't worked in almost two years, and if he wasn't sleeping here, he'd be crashed out on the sofa at one of his new "mates'" places. I didn't want that. I wanted him to be safe. I wanted him to get his life sorted out. But looking at him now – unwashed hair, nicotine-stained fingernails, empty bottles at his feet – he looked so far removed from that neat, innocent blond-haired boy I once knew that it was hard to believe he was the same person.

"Josh looks up to you, Michael, you know that. He worships you, for God's sake."

"But I wouldn't ever do anything—"

"It's not that I don't trust you with him, I do. But you know what he said to me the other day? He said, *Why won't Michael wake up? It's daytime.*"

"I was asleep!"

"You were passed out!"

"He doesn't know the difference!"

"He knows something's not right! Look, I just can't have this around him! First Hellie, and now you. He needs people around him who are going to be stable, who don't change from one minute to the next because they're hung-over or stoned or drunk or—"

"Okay!" Michael snapped. He glared angrily at me, but his expression quickly changed to remorse. "You're right, I don't want Josh to see me like this," he said, shaking his head sadly.

I could see I'd touched a nerve. Maybe this was my way in. God knows I'd tried everything else over the past few months. Shouting, swearing, begging, pleading, even shoving him hard into a wall out of sheer frustration. And fear. Fear that he was going down a path he might not come back from. But nothing worked. He apologised and promised to change and then went out and did it all over again.

But for Josh's sake, maybe, just maybe, he might turn himself around. When my dad had been out at work, Michael had been the one who'd watched over Josh for hours on end while I'd poured over my A level textbooks and occasionally even managed to make it in to college for the odd tutorial. He'd walked him around and around the house, naming every object they'd come across, sung him songs, played him tunes on the guitar, made up lyrics with his name in. He'd been the fun one while I'd been desperately trying to knuckle down to study. I was pleased at that point that Michael didn't have anywhere else to be, and I felt like I owed him big time. But what had started out as the occasional wild weekend had spiralled out of control, and I felt like I had no choice but to give him an ultimatum, even if it was just to shock him back to his senses.

"Josh is growing up, Michael," I said, sitting down on the bed beside him, "and I want you to be a massive part of his life. Because he thinks you're the best. He adores you. God,

I think he'd like *you* to be his dad. But this..." I gestured to the mess around us.

"Yeah, I know," he sighed, pinching the bridge of his nose. "It's fucked up, isn't it?"

"Look, you stop drinking and I'll stop, too."

"You can't do that."

"Yes, I can. It's not like I've always made the best choices when I've been drinking," I said, thinking of the night I slept with Hellie, and the night I scarred Libby's face forever. "We'll stop together, okay? Plus, you clean yourself up and I'll get Josh one of those guitars you were talking about. And you can start to teach him, just like you said you wanted to."

Michael shook his head. "Nah, you were right, he's too little."

"No, like you said, he's smart and he's got good concentration. He can just have a play around to start with, see what sounds he can make. But I want you to be the one to do it with him."

Michael fingered a small rip in his jeans and nodded thoughtfully.

"Wouldn't that be cool?" I asked, probing for some confirmation that I was hitting the spot.

"Yeah, that would be pretty cool."

"And then he'd always have the memory that his Uncle Michael was the one who gave him his first guitar, the one who taught him his first strings or chords or whatever."

Michael laughed at my musical ignorance. "Well, we'd better not leave it up to you."

"Exactly," I smiled, "he needs you."

"Well, I do have a pretty mean version of 'Froggy Went A-Courtin'' I could teach him."

"Yeah, not that version."

"Really? Not that version?"

"No, not till he's eighteen. Just the normal version, if that's okay."

Michael turned to me and smiled, his pink eyes regaining

a little bit of life. "I'll do it, okay? I promise. I'll sort myself out. You get him that guitar and I'll start teaching him. And I'll be as clean as a whistle."

I nodded and smiled, full of hope that I'd finally given him a reason to step off the path of self-destruction. Full of hope that this time he would change.

I remember Brenda saying: "He seems much more like his old self, doesn't he?"

I nodded, squinting against the bright sunshine.

"Yeah, he does."

"I think it was all the stress, you know. Ever since the takeover, the college has just gone bureaucracy-mad. I was up until eleven o'clock last night doing paperwork. I can't wait to follow in your father's footsteps and retire. One year to go and counting."

I watched my dad dribbling a football slowly around the garden, Josh chasing him in fits of giggles, tripping over his own poorly coordinated feet every so often.

"Oh, he's having a little lie-down again!" my dad would joke, making Josh giggle so hard he could barely get back up again.

"I guess he must have been more stressed than he seemed," I said.

"Oh, he's definitely been stressed," confirmed Brenda, removing her sunglasses and examining them for smudges. "I know he always seems as cool as a cucumber, but how could he not be stressed? Thirty years teaching in the same place and then someone comes in and tells you to do it all differently? And then everything at home. Your mum and...well... you know... everything else."

Brenda was a friend of my dad's. In fact, it turned out they'd been friends for years. Apparently, they used to do the crossword together every lunchtime and share packets of Jaffa Cakes. I didn't even know my dad liked crosswords.

Or Jaffa Cakes. She was a small, neat woman with a gentle, motherly way about her, despite having never married or had children of her own. Whenever she came round, she brought comfort food – cakes, casseroles, lasagnes – and fussed over us "boys", which is how she referred to myself, Josh and Michael collectively. She knew a surprising amount about each of us, and with a sense of disbelief, I realised that my dad – so quiet, self-contained, and reserved – must have spent years spilling out the details of his home life to someone none of us even knew existed.

"Stress can do such funny things to your brain," said Brenda. "I'm not surprised he was losing the plot a bit. I won't be surprised if I end up going a bit doolally myself soon."

Over the past year, I'd become increasingly concerned about my dad's mental state. He'd become forgetful and absent-minded, and he'd get frustrated and agitated about the smallest of things. None of it would have been particularly alarming or even that unusual for a man in his mid-sixties, but it just wasn't my dad, who'd always been extraordinarily calm, organised and sharp-minded. Laura and I had engaged in several hushed conversations about the best way of conning him into seeing a doctor, but it seemed those conversations had been unnecessary.

Now, a month into retirement, he seemed bright, full of energy, and his "senior moments", as we'd started to refer to them, appeared to have subsided. It was a weight off my shoulders. With him back to his old self I was even starting to think that maybe I could apply for university. Like he kept saying, now he was retired, he had all the time in the world to watch Josh, and as long as I stayed local, why couldn't I make it work? After all, getting through my A levels had seemed impossible two years ago, but I'd made it. Just.

"That was some wonderful football playing!" grinned Brenda, as my dad walked across the grass towards us, holding his giggling grandson upside down.

"You're going to be the next star striker for England, aren't you, Jamie?" my dad joked, turning Josh the right way up and plonking him down. My son stumbled towards me, arms outstretched, laughing.

"Am I?" I asked, scooping Josh up in my arms. "It's clearly been a while since you've seen me play, Dad."

"You mean Josh," Brenda corrected him.

"Sorry?" my dad asked, scratching his head.

"Josh," she repeated. "You said Jamie."

My dad smiled vacantly. "Oh, yes!" he laughed, realisation catching up with him. "Too many Js!"

They laughed heartily. I quite envied that way the smallest things seemed to evoke a disproportionate degree of hilarity in older people.

I absent-mindedly stroked Josh's sweaty head and watched my dad enjoying himself with his old friend. It was just a mistake, that's all. Too many J's. So easily done. He was fine. Fit, strong, healthy and as sharp as ever. I'd do it. I'd put in my application for uni and look at starting next year.

With the sun warming my back and my happy, tired son resting his head against my shoulder, I really felt like the future was opening up. I couldn't believe how far I'd come. Everything seemed infinitely more manageable than it had just a few months ago, and for the first time since Josh's birth I felt genuinely hopeful about our future.

Chapter 9

Reconciliation

"You all right, Jay?" calls Stewart from behind the bar. "You look a bit on edge."

He finishes arranging bottles on the shelf behind him and runs a hand over his smooth head. It's like he has to check every so often whether the hair that deserted him in his twenties has come back yet.

"Uh… yeah, I'm fine," I tell him, picking my coffee up and moving tables for the second time, "I'm just… I'm meeting someone, that's all."

Where would Libby want to sit? In the corner? Does that seem too intimate? In the middle of the room? Does that seem too exposed?

"Oh yeah?" Stewart laughs mischievously. "I think I know who that might be."

"Really?"

Jesus, can't Michael just keep his mouth shut about my business?

"Yeah, she was in here Friday night asking after you. I won't repeat some of the language she used. Women get pretty miffed when blokes don't return their calls, you know?"

Oh God. Rachel. Tall, blonde, Australian Rachel who seems

to think – perhaps understandably – that there's something going on between us. Rachel whose hands were all over me at Michael's gig the other night, right here in the centre of this room. Squashed in among the crowd of hot, sweaty bodies, the music pulsating through me, I'd been swept along with it. Arms around each other, some suggestive comments (mainly from her), lips against each other's ears (the only way to make ourselves heard), her hand snaking under my T-shirt as we watched the band play. I hadn't meant anything by it and had no intention of taking it further. I was trying to get my head sorted right now, not add further complications. But it seemed like I'd inadvertently gone and done that anyway. I'd meant to reply to her texts, but while I was figuring out a way to politely nip things in the bud, I'd forgotten to reply at all.

"Oh yeah, no, it's not her," I mutter, glancing at the doorway for the hundredth time.

"Really? 'Cause she seems to really like you. And, mate, that girl, she's seriously..." he quickly checks around, presumably to make sure his girlfriend, Irena, is nowhere to be seen, "*hot*," he mouths.

I nod, distractedly. Perhaps I shouldn't have asked Libby to meet me here. I'd said I would go to her, but when she insisted on coming to Timpton, this was the first place that popped into my head. Perhaps the familiarity of it seemed appealing at the time, but now I wonder if we should have met on more neutral ground. Stu and Irena are a great couple and I've known them a long time, but my meeting with an unknown woman is bound to set their gossip radars to high alert. Fortunately, the place has almost emptied following the lunchtime rush, but the chances of getting through the next hour without someone I know walking in are practically zero.

The Canal House is made up of two parts: an old, brick structure at the front, containing oak tables and an open fireplace, and an airy, high-ceilinged extension at the back, housing the bar, an assortment of leather sofas and a pool table. It's the acoustics in this part of the building that make it a great venue for live music, as well as the fact that the glass doors fold open all along the back, allowing the crowds to flow outdoors onto the large terrace that overlooks the canal. Michael plays here a lot with his band, Halo, and that's how I know so many of the regulars, which is both a blessing and a curse. On the one hand, I feel at home here; Stu and Irena are always welcoming, and there's usually someone to pass the time of day with if I feel in the mood. But while Timpton's a fairly large old market town, it can be hard to walk through the centre without one of the Canal House locals stopping me for a chat, which can be a pain in the backside. I like talking to people in small doses, on my terms and when I choose.

"So, if it's not Rachel," Stu pipes up again, sounding intrigued, "then it's…?"

"None of your business?"

"Oohh, what a slap in the face!" jokes Stu. "Well, whoever you're meeting, it looks like she's got well under your skin, for one reason or another."

"What makes you think it's even a woman?" I ask slightly irritably, taking a sip of my coffee and somehow managing to spill it in the process. "Shit," I mutter, wiping the back of my hand across my chin and checking my T-shirt.

Stu laughs. "'Cause no bloke makes a guy look that jumpy. Not unless it's your bank manager you're meeting."

I glance through the glass doors at the empty terrace. It's a warm day, but there are grey clouds looming ominously overhead. Then I look back at Stu, smug smile on his face, eyebrow raised questioningly. I think I'll take my drink outside and risk the rain.

But just as I'm standing up, in she walks, looking flustered and rosy-cheeked. My heart starts to race. I'm the first to admit that I can be pretty socially awkward at the best of times, but sit me down face-to-face with an ex-girlfriend whose heart I unintentionally broke and who I haven't seen in over fifteen years and suddenly this seems like a nightmare scenario. This would actually be a good time for my feet to move towards her, but instead they decide to stay rooted to the wooden floor, letting her stand there alone, scanning the room, wide-eyed and lost.

She spies me but doesn't move. Or smile. It's like she's in two minds about whether to turn around and bolt. But while every part of my body remains frozen, she visibly takes a deep breath, stands a little taller and heads towards me.

"Hi," she says, already slipping her bag from her shoulder and starting to remove her jacket, meeting my eye for only the briefest moment. She's wearing a blue V-neck T-shirt, and I notice her chest and throat are flushed. She fumbles to place her jacket over the back of a chair, while I spend way too long searching for something to say. But then we both speak at the same time.

"Did you find it—"

"It's hot in—"

"Oh, we can go outside—"

"Yeah, I found it fine—"

I give an awkward laugh, while her lips struggle into a forced smile.

"Outside sounds like a good idea," she says, gathering her jacket and bag back up.

"Can I get you a coffee?" I ask.

"I'll just have a cold drink."

I glance over at the menu above the bar, searching for a list of cold drinks. "I think they have—"

"It's fine, I'll get something and meet you outside."

"Well, let me pay," I say, quickly pulling my wallet from my back pocket.

"No, it's fine, I'll get it," she says abruptly, walking away.

I stand there, wondering whether to go after her, but then I remember that Libby was always fiercely independent about money. She would never take cash from me, even when she had none – which was all the time. She'd been brought up to distain materialism, and I learned early on in our relationship that she didn't accept gifts easily or comfortably.

As Libby orders her drink from Stu, he gives me a quick wink over the top of her head. I quickly grab my coffee and open the back door, gratefully stepping into the fresh air. I've just sat down at a table when Libby emerges with a glass and a bottle of Appletiser. I rush to stand up again, pull a chair out for her, offer to take something out of her hands; her jacket, her bag, her glass, her bottle…

"It's fine," she insists, struggling to set everything down.

When we're settled opposite each other, the silence, which must be all of ten seconds long, seems to stretch forever.

"I was surprised to get your text," I say, apprehensively.

"Um, yes, well," she fumbles, quickly tucking her hair behind her ear and grabbing for her bottle of drink, "I decided I was maybe a bit rude when you came to see me, and I apologise because that wasn't really necessary—"

"No, it was my fault. I shouldn't have—"

"—so I thought maybe I should just come and say sorry or something," she ploughs on, "because, you know, I didn't need to be so blunt, but you just caught me totally off guard, I mean, you were absolutely the last person I expected to see that day, and God, it's been such a long time, and at first I hardly recognised you, but when I realised it *was* you, I was just so taken aback—"

She talks fast, waggling her bottle in such a way that I'm amazed she doesn't spill any.

"—so I'm sorry I was so off that day. It hadn't been a good day actually, and then, what with you and the rain and… anyway, I hope you didn't mind me just texting you like that. I was hoping I had the right person, actually. I googled your name and it showed up under a trades directory with a Timpton number next to your mobile number, so I thought that must be you and… anyway. Here we are."

She quickly splashes Appletiser on top of the ice in her glass, sending some of it slopping over the side and onto the tabletop. She stares at the settling fizz, her hands clasped together in her lap. I don't dare reach for my coffee, fearful that I'll spill it again.

"I still don't understand why you came to see me," she says suddenly, her eyes still on her glass, "after all this time."

I stare at the table, trying to recall my rehearsed response. I've spent the last three days preparing for this question, in the hope of sounding slightly more coherent and slightly less like a stalker than I did last time. But the words have gone completely out of my head. There was something about trying to get closure, wanting to move on, feeling tied to the past... but all that just sounds so self-centred now. This isn't just about me. I feel like I owe her something. An explanation, an apology.

"I always hated the way things were left," I say, honestly, "and I suppose I've always wanted to say sorry."

"There's nothing to apologise for," she says, hastily.

"I feel like there is."

"What?" she asks, looking me straight in the eye for the first time. "What is it you did that was so wrong?" There's an edge to her voice that makes the question sound like a challenge.

"I just... I know I put you through a lot and there were times when I behaved like an idiot—"

"Of course there were times when you behaved like an idiot. You were a fifteen-year-old boy who went through a pretty harrowing ordeal. I mean, I probably should have been more supportive."

"God, no. You *were* supportive—"

"Well, I seem to remember I spilt up with you, so not that supportive really," she scoffs.

"No, you were right to—"

"Actually, I don't think I meant to split up with you," she says, peering at the clouds as if she's trying hard to recall. "I seem to remember just wanting a break from you, but I don't think I really understood how relationships worked, which, you know, is probably normal at that age, especially given that my parents weren't exactly the best examples. But anyway," she waves her hand, dismissively, "it was all a long time ago."

"I've just always felt that it ended in such a mess," I tell her, "the way we got back together, and then having to tell you about the pregnancy, and then having to break it off and—"

"Oh, and I didn't make that any easier!" she suddenly laughs, shaking her head as if she's just remembered something embarrassing. "Didn't I ask you if we could still make it work somehow? God, I was just so young and naïve! Well, I mean we were, weren't we?"

"I've just always hated the fact that you got hurt and—"

"We were just kids, Jamie!" she frowns, as if this conversation is totally ludicrous. "Kids get hurt. First relationships and all that. I mean, yes, it was messy, but love is, isn't it?"

For a moment we meet each other's eye and I feel a tiny stab in my chest, the sense of loss all over again. Because that's what it was: love. And, yes, we were kids, and, yes, it was a long time ago, but it mattered. Because it's the only time I've ever been in love, and I know that now for sure. I've tried to find it again, tried to replicate what I once felt, but it's always been like grasping at thin air. At times, I've told myself I've had it, only to acknowledge I'm kidding myself. At other times, I've told myself that the feeling never existed in the first place, that what I remember is nothing but a distorted memory intensified by the passing of time. But looking at Libby now – even though she's so different and in many ways a stranger to me – I recognise enough of the girl I used to know to enable me to recall that feeling. And I know it was real. And I know I don't want to go the rest of my life never finding it again. Which is why I needed to see her. So that I can make my peace with her and move on, leave her in the past where she belongs. Because I don't want to be trapped by my best memories any more than my worst ones.

"You were a really important part of my life," I tell her

truthfully, "and the last thing I ever wanted was for you to get hurt."

She shakes her head and looks as though she's about to laugh again.

"And I know it was a long time ago," I cut in quickly, "and I'm sorry that I came barging into your life again after all this time, but I just wanted you to know that I'm sorry about how things turned out. And I realise you moved on long ago, and maybe you don't ever give it a second thought, but I do. Because I was the one who hurt you. And I regret that. I regret a lot of things. And I don't want to go through the rest of my life with these regrets. Not if I can find a way to... I don't know, to apologise, to—"

"And you're honestly not sick or anything?" she interrupts.

This time, I'm the one to shake my head and laugh, realising how ridiculous this clearly all sounds to her.

"No, I'm not sick."

She looks at me seriously. I feel horribly exposed.

"Okay," she nods, "I don't think you need to say sorry, but if it makes you feel better, if it helps you deal with whatever stuff you've got going on at the moment, then fine."

She gives me the tiniest smile, and I want to feel something. Some kind of release. But I don't feel anything, other than a sense that I've somehow missed the mark.

"You went through quite a trauma that year, Jamie," she says, her tone softer now. "Then you got yourself in a difficult situation and you handled it the best way you knew how. You stepped up and there are a lot of boys who wouldn't have."

I look into her wide, brown eyes and for the first time I see something of the old Libby; the kind, compassionate girl who tried so hard to help me through those difficult months when I couldn't sleep for fear, when I couldn't take criticism without lashing out, when I couldn't find a way to deal with life having so closely witnessed death. The girl who was always so much wiser than her years.

"Whatever happened, I've always known you didn't mean

for anyone to get hurt. I've never held it against you. So don't feel bad. There's really no need."

And there it is; a shift, almost imperceptible, but I feel it in my core. That's what I needed to hear, then. That she never held what happened against me.

"And you and me, we would have probably ended anyway, one way or another. I mean, all that talk about forever," she pulls a doubting expression and shakes her head, "we were just children really."

I nod and smile sadly. I know what she's saying is right; we were just children, it was all so long ago, it's all forgotten, in the past, of no consequence now. But that talk about forever; it *had* been real. At least for a while. But perhaps she doesn't remember that now.

We sit in silence for a moment, and finally I feel calm enough to pick up my cold coffee and take a sip. I've said what I wanted – I think – and she's heard me. This thing I wanted to do is done. Maybe it wasn't the life-changing release I was hoping for, but I think perhaps it will make a difference. Maybe I can leave something here today that I should have left behind a long time ago.

Libby finally reaches out for her drink and takes several, long, slow gulps. She takes so long in fact that I wonder if she's stalling. I don't know what's meant to happen now and presumably neither does she.

I watch her as discreetly as possible, composed enough now to really see her, to take in all of her altered features. She has tiny lines round the edges of her eyes, unnoticeable to me until now. The freckles on her nose are still there, but sparser and faded. Her face looks slightly rounder than I remember. In fact, everything about her is slightly softer. It suits her. When we were together, she was always on the skinny side, a little gangly. Perhaps it was her vegan diet, or the fact that there was never much food in the fridge, but she never seemed to quite catch up with the other girls her age with their new curves. I can still remember Libby's flat stomach and jutting hips under my hands. Now here she is, no longer a girl but a grown woman with flesh on her bones, strong and healthy-looking, all the changes that were just starting to take place when I knew her now fully complete.

She sets her drink down and gives me a little smile while she taps her fingers against the side of her glass, her ring making a *ching* sound with every tap. Then she brings her hand up to her face, touches her lips, fiddles with her earring. And suddenly I notice the diamond ring sparkling in the light.

"You're engaged?" I ask, nodding to her hand.

"Oh, yeah!" she smiles, flashing her hand at me proudly.

"Congratulations," I smile, feeling both wistful and relieved. It's another reminder that things have moved forward, that nothing I did to her mattered in the end. She's found happiness. She'll soon be married and having the family she always craved, albeit with someone else. And that's fine, it's how it should be. We're in a different time and place.

"Yeah, I'm getting married later this year, so… yeah, I'm very excited. Um…Will, he works in London and… well, we've been together six years—"

"Wow."

"Yeah, I know! So… yes. Getting married, looking for a house… so much to organise!"

"Big wedding?"

"Yes, that's the plan," she says, still fiddling with her ring, "the whole traditional thing."

I'm not surprised. It could have gone either way with Libby. She could have been planning a barefoot wedding beneath the harvest moon just as much as a stiff white dress and hotel buffet. She was always so contrary and conflicted about her beliefs and desires. But I always knew that the future she guiltily whispered about when it was just the two of us, sharing our hopes and dreams, was the one she really wanted. Predictable. Stable. Ordinary.

"It's possibly even going to be in a church. Harmonie's not amused, as you can imagine."

She looks at me and we both laugh a little.

"But then she's living in an actual house now, so—"

"You're kidding."

"No, she's finally on dry land. In Essex. All those years I wanted to live like other people and *now* she decides it's a good idea. Can you believe it?"

"No, actually," I smile.

"Yeah, and sometimes my dad even lives there with her, which is even weirder."

"Really?"

"Yeah, I mean, he still has his boat and he's always on the move, but sometimes he stops for a couple of months with my mum and… I don't know." She shrugs and shakes her head. "You know what they were like."

The intimacy of this statement throws me for a moment. Yes, I do know what her parents were like, just as I know that her favourite colour was yellow and that her favourite food was raspberry jam and that she always wanted a sister… but I'm sure all these things have changed.

I open my mouth to ask about her fiancé, just because it seems like an obvious next question, but then I think better of it. It's too personal and none of my business.

Libby fiddles with the label on her empty Appletiser bottle. "Actually, my dad's seen you a few times over the years," she says, "you know, when he's stopped around here." She waves her hand towards the canal, as if his boat might be moored just on the other side of the wall that separates us from the waterway. "So I knew you were still in Timpton."

"Yeah, I see him around town now and then," I admit.

Seeing Libby's dad always left me unsettled for a few days afterwards. It was like a piece of her returning out of the blue. I'd never approached him. I hadn't even been sure he'd recognise me, although clearly I'd been wrong about that. Even when I was with Libby, I'd only met him a handful of times, and although he'd been friendly enough, he'd also seemed edgy and distracted, like he was already itching to be off somewhere else. Libby always said he was a free spirit, not designed to be in one place for too long. My mum used to say he was more like a freeloader, turning to Harmonie every time he was broke and down on his luck. "Funny kind of feminist," she used to mutter.

"I even saw your dad in here once," I add, nodding towards the bar. I don't mention that it was eight o'clock on a Sunday evening and that he could barely stand, or that I'd left as soon as I saw him.

"I think he still likes to drink down at the Kingfisher mainly," says Libby.

"Right," I nod, placing my empty mug down on the table. "I never go there."

By this I mean I go out of my way not to even walk past the place. I don't like to remember the last time I was there, the night I burst through the doors breathless and panicked, pleading for someone to call nine nine nine.

Libby meets my eye for a second before we both look away, and I know she understands.

"So, um, are you a full-time artist now?" I ask quickly.

I lost track of the things Libby wanted to be. A geologist. A historian. A doctor. A radiologist. An artist. An architect. She was so smart and studious she could have been anything she wanted.

"Oh, no. The painting's just a sideline. I was actually working for this big advertising company in London, on the creative side of things."

"Wow, really?"

"Yeah, lots of very prestigious clients, well-known brands... It was, you know, a lot of... um..."

"Pressure?"

"I suppose you could say that. So I'm just taking a little break right now. Sort of re-evaluating. Figuring out my next career move. I mean, I've has some offers, but..."

"Sounds like you can take your pick."

"And you're an electrician," she says, swiftly switching

the focus to me. "I was surprised when I googled your name and it came up under the trades directory. That's what made me unsure if it was actually you. Because it just had your initial. You know, J. Lewis, and I thought Lewis is a fairly common name and I never saw you going into that kind of work."

"Uh, no, well, things didn't go quite the way I thought—"

"No, of course not," she says almost apologetically.

"I scraped through my A levels in the end, and my dad offered to support me through university and take care of Josh, but… well, that wasn't really an option in the end. Plus, I think my mum wanted me to go down the academic route way more than I ever did. I suppose I just didn't know what else I was going to do. Or maybe I just wanted to keep her happy."

"Oh well, we can both be disappointments to our mothers then!"

We both laugh politely.

"Are they well anyway, your parents?" she asks.

"Um, yeah," I lie, not wanting to drag the tone of the conversation down.

"And Josh? You said he's doing well?"

"Yeah, great. I mean, he's a challenge occasionally, but you know, he's fifteen, so…"

"Fifteen," she mutters, shaking her head disbelievingly. "I can't believe it's been that long."

"It's crazy, isn't it?"

"Do you have any photos?"

"Oh, yeah. Do you want to see?" I ask hesitantly, unsure if showing her photos of the child that ended our relationship isn't somehow a bit weird.

"I wouldn't have asked if I didn't," she smiles.

I quickly scan through my photos and then hand her the phone.

"Oh my God," she says, her smile fading as she contemplates the picture. She looks at it for a long time. "He looks so much like you at that age," she says quietly.

"Really? You think?"

"It's like going back in time and looking at the fifteen-year-old you."

When the screen suddenly times out and goes blank, she looks up like she's coming out of a dream. She hands me back the phone.

"That's so weird," she mutters, looking unsettled, and I wonder whether that wasn't such a good idea. Slowly she stands up and takes the few steps over to the wall, peering down at the canal. She gazes to her left, in the direction of the marina where her boat was moored for all those years.

"Have you ever been back?" I ask her.

She shakes her head and folds her arms around herself. The clouds still threaten rain and now the warmth has gone. Summer's never quite settled in this year, and it doesn't look like it's going to.

"I came to see you, you know," I say, although I'm not sure why I'm telling her this now. "A couple of months after we broke up. I knew I shouldn't have done, but I just wanted to make sure you were okay. And to say… well, pretty much what I've said today, really. That I was sorry for how things had ended. But you were gone."

Libby nods slowly. "We went north. Harmonie got offered a business opportunity," she says vaguely. She turns towards me and shrugs. "But anyway, long time ago."

I feel relieved by her explanation. I'd always assumed she'd left because of me, but clearly – and a bit embarrassingly – I've overestimated my own importance.

She comes back to the table and picks her jacket off the chair. "I should get going," she says.

There's so much I want to ask her, so much I want to know. But, of course, that was never the point of today. It was never going to be a question of reviving a friendship. I'm looking to let go, sever, move on, not rebuild something new out of the ashes of the past. It's been strange, brief, and somehow both more and less than I had hoped for. But it's done.

I stand up quickly, grabbing my phone and wallet from the table. "I need to get back, too."

Libby pulls her bag onto her shoulder.

"So, uh…" she splays her hands out in front of her, the universal sign for *how do we end this?*

"Yeah. Um… thanks for coming. It really meant a lot, being able to just see you again and say, you know, what I said."

She shrugs. "It's fine."

We look at each other for a moment, and suddenly I have an overwhelming urge to reach out and put my arms around her, just like I would have done so many times in the past without a second thought.

"Are you…?" she asks, gesturing towards the bar.

"Yes, right, let's go," I say, and lead her back inside.

"All right, Jay?" I hear someone call as soon as I'm through the door.

Leo, Michael's drummer, is playing pool in the corner with Stu. Leo's massive frame is hunched over the table, carefully lining up a shot, his eyes on the ball. His long hair hangs limply around his face.

"You enjoy the gig at the weekend?" he asks without looking up.

"Yeah, great," I say, head down, focusing on getting out of here.

"You looked like you were having fun with, er… what's her name? Rachel?" He lets out a long whistle between his teeth, takes his shot, misses and curses quietly. The moment he straightens up and spies Libby walking behind me, he flashes me a guilty look, as if he's put his foot in it.

"You guys want to play?" asks Stu, stepping forward.

"No, we're just leaving," I say, quickly, shooting him a warning look, which he chooses to ignore. Instead, he holds the pool cue out to Libby.

"No, it's fine, thanks," she smiles, but those few words are enough encouragement for Stu to start a conversation.

"You from around here?" he asks, smiling broadly.

"Oh, well, not really," says Libby. "I mean, I used to be. I grew up on the canal, but I'm living in North London now."

Stu wags his finger between myself and Libby. "And you two know each other…?"

I narrow my eyes and shake my head at him so slightly that only he would notice.

"We used to be… umm…" Libby looks at me uncertainly.

"Friends."

"Friends," she affirms, "when we were young. And then we just met up again at… well, at an art exhibition."

"An art exhibition?" asks Stu, raising an eyebrow at me.

"Well, my exhibition," Libby clarifies with a dismissive wave of her hand. "I do some painting and Jamie came long…"

"Jamie came along?" repeats Stu gleefully, putting an emphasis on my name. No one round here ever calls me Jamie.

"What kind of painting do you do?" asks Leo, pulling up alongside Stu. He's a gentle giant of a guy with a soft, rounded belly.

"Oh, nothing much. I just like splashing colours around really," Libby laughs, self-consciously. But while the last thing I want to do is drag out this conversation, something in me won't stand by and hear her diminish her talents in that way.

"Libby paints canal scenes," I clarify. "They're fantastic."

A blush rises in her cheeks, and she throws me a smile halfway between thankful and mortified.

"Oh, hey!" exclaims Leo, jabbing Stu in the arm with his pool cue. "You want a canal scene painted on the outside wall, don't you?"

"I do!" grins Stu, pointing to the wall surrounding the terrace. "I want a canal scene painted right around that wall there. Cheer the outside area up, make it in keeping with the scenery."

"Or people can just look at the *actual* scenery," I say, drily.

"But you can't see the canal when you're sitting down, smart-arse," Stu corrects me , "all you can see is wall."

"That's a great idea," nods Libby, considering the wall like she can already see the painting taking shape. "You could have canal boats, and people walking dogs, and kingfishers, people on bikes... Oh, actually, you could have the seasons changing as the painting goes around. Spring, going into summer, then autumn—"

"Yeah, I like it," nods Leo, thoughtfully.

Stu claps his hands together loudly. "Yes! Great! When can you start?"

Libby laughs, but her smile falters when Stu doesn't laugh with her.

"I'm serious!" grins Stu.

"Oh, no, I don't... I mean... I don't do murals."

"But could you?"

Libby looks to me, slightly flustered and confused.

"Libby doesn't even live around here," I tell Stu.

"Well, North London's hardly far! Seriously, how much would you charge for something like that?"

"Stu," I say, more firmly, "Libby didn't come here looking for a job. And we were just—"

"Well, actually, I *am* sort of available for work at the moment..." Libby says, thoughtfully. "I mean, I've never done a mural before, but maybe..."

"Fantastic! Well, look, let me give you my number."

Libby seems unsure, but after a short hesitation she takes her phone out of her bag and taps in the numbers Stu gives her, while I try to get my head around what's going on. I invited Libby here to get something off my chest – and now she's being offered a job? So she's going to be back?! What does that mean? How will that work? This wasn't what I envisaged at all. I was prepared for seeing her once. Just once.

Oh God, Stu! I could literally kill you right now!

Libby's brought her website up on her phone and Stu and Leo are both looming over her, gazing at the screen, enthusing about the quality of her paintings – and rightfully so. She's a good artist and a nice person and I wish her all the opportunities she could ever want. But just not here. I don't want her here. Because watching her familiar face, her careful smile, the way she tucks her hair behind her ear, the way she uses her hands to express what she's saying – too much, too fast – the way she laughs – halfway between gay abandon and self-conscious restraint – I realise with a sinking heart that today isn't going to help me move on. Not in the way I wanted. Yes, I feel forgiven. Yes, I feel freed from the guilt of the hurt I caused. But I don't feel freed from my lingering feelings for her. If anything, I'm reminded more clearly than ever of exactly what I lost.

"Call me!" Stu orders Libby, heading to the bar to serve a couple who have just walked in.

Leo pats Libby so hard on the shoulder that she has to steady herself, and then he heads back to the pool table. "Jay, tell your friend we're not taking no for an answer!" he booms.

My friend?

Yes, maybe that's what she could be after all. My friend. We're adults, and whatever I feel can be handled in an adult fashion. So she might be around for a while. So I might end up seeing a bit more of her. Okay, that's fine. It might even be nice. Perhaps getting to know her again properly will help whatever I feel to subside.

"Well, maybe I'll be seeing you again after all," shrugs Libby, turning to me with a smile that suggests she's both excited and a little overwhelmed by what's just happened.

"Maybe," I shrug back, as if it wouldn't faze me either way.

Friends. I could do that. What could be so hard about being friends?

Chapter 10

Friends

I remember Max staring at the screen and shouting: "Boom, and you're dead! Again."

He pushed his glasses up his nose and studied the score. "Two hundred and eighty-five points to... er... twelve."

Tom, who was lying on his bed flicking through a football magazine, gave a snort of laughter.

Michael put the controls down next to him on the rug with a defeated sigh.

"May I please use your bathroom?" he asked Tom, politely.

"*May* you?" repeated Tom, without looking up. "Yes, you *may*, sir. Go hither to the end of the landing and turneth right into the room with a bog in it."

Michael stood up and carefully picked his way through Tom's mess of a bedroom.

"You don't have to take the piss," I told Tom as soon as Michael had left the room.

"I wasn't."

"*May I* take the piss?" asked Max, and Tom laughed.

"What's wrong with *may I*?" I asked.

"Why doesn't he just say *can* I, like everyone else?" frowned Tom.

"Because *can I* means *am I able to*," I retorted, "and I'm pretty sure Michael is *able* to use your toilet. He was asking permission—"

"Oh, shut up," groaned Tom. "What else is that posh school teaching you? How to hold a teacup with your pinkie finger in the air?"

"How to curtsy?" asked Max, already loading up the next game.

"How to hold a spiffing garden party?"

"How to eat a cucumber sandwich?"

"No one needs to be taught how to eat a cucumber sandwich, you moron," I tutted.

"Max doesn't need to be taught how to eat anything," quipped Tom, puffing his cheeks out.

Max, taking the joke in good humour as always, snorted like a pig.

"So, what do you think of him anyway?" I asked, tentatively.

"Well, he's crap at video games," said Max.

"And his hair's a bit prissy," said Tom.

"He's a bit quiet."

"And his clothes are a bit stiff."

"And he looks like he needs some sunlight."

"And some fun."

"And he says *may* I."

"But apart from that," said Max, "he's fine."

Tom shrugged. "'S'all right."

"He's just a bit shy around new people," I said. "Be nice. He's cool. Really. He's funny."

Max and Tom exchanged doubting looks.

"Really," I insisted, "you'll like him once you get to know him."

I knew they weren't convinced, but I really wanted them to all get on. Michael and I had become good friends over the past few months, spending nearly all our time together at school, and I didn't want to keep my two worlds separate anymore.

Michael sheepishly entered the room again and we all fell silent for what felt like an awkwardly long time. Sitting on the bed next to Tom, I pinched his toes hard through his socks and he shot me an angry look. I glared at him and nodded towards Michael, urging him to make conversation. He responded by delivering a discreet kick to my thigh.

"So, Michael, what football team do you support?" chirped up Max.

Thankfully, you could always count on Max to be friendly. He had an ability to put anyone at ease. The fact that he was pudgy and wore glasses could have made him something of a social pariah, but in fact his warm personality and self-deprecating wit made him hugely popular with boys and girls alike.

"I don't really follow football," said Michael, sitting down on the rug again next to Max.

Max and Tom looked at each other, and then at me, in silent confusion. Whatever our ability, whichever team we supported, we spent a *lot* of time talking about football.

"We don't do football at St John's," I reminded them.

Tom raised his eyebrows and shook his head despairingly. He thought St John's sounded stupid and took every opportunity to make this clear to me. In many ways, I agreed with him. I still couldn't get used to all the petty rules and regulations, the ceremonies, the pointless traditions – but it *was* starting to feel like my school, and there were times when I looked around me at the history, the facilities, the buildings and couldn't believe how lucky I was. Tom's derision was starting to grate a bit.

"So, what do you like? Rugby?" Max persisted, as if this was the only sport played in private schools.

"Yeah," nodded Michael, earnestly, "I'm the prop forward."

Max looked him up and down wordlessly, taking in his

narrow shoulders and delicate frame. Then Michael smiled, and Max, realising he was joking, laughed.

"You had me there for a moment!"

I was relieved to see Michael employing his usual deadpan humour, but Tom only raised his eyebrows, unimpressed.

"Michael really likes music," I interjected.

"R 'n' B? Hip hop?" asked Max hopefully. Tom and I told him all the time that his music was garbage.

"I'm not sure," Michael said. "Anything, I suppose."

"Like what?" Tom pressed. "Which bands?"

"Um... I don't really know the names of that many bands. But I sometimes hear stuff I like. Like when I'm in shops or...I don't know, just out places."

Max and Tom flashed each other a discreet frown, although not so discreet that Michael didn't spy it.

"My dad doesn't really like me having music on in the house," he explained, uncomfortably. "Well, not unless it's his kind of music."

"Which is what?" asked Tom.

"Classical stuff mainly. Mozart, Beethoven, Bach."

"So is that what you like?" asked Tom, a smile playing at the edge of his lips.

Michael shrugged. "It's okay, I suppose."

Max nodded encouragingly. "Cool, everyone likes different things." But after that even he wasn't sure what to say and the conversation ground to a halt.

I squirmed. This wasn't going to work. I had school in common with Michael if nothing else. We could joke about teachers and other students and all the stupid things we were made to do. But none of that was transferrable, and the gulf between my old friends and my new one suddenly seemed too big.

We remained quiet, Tom returning to his magazine, Max tutting that the game he wanted to play wasn't uploading, and me picking at a bit of cotton hanging off my sock. Only the music playing on Tom's stereo saved us from awkward silence. Michael, sitting crossed-legged on the rug, looked painfully aware that this social experiment was failing. He hummed along quietly and didn't look up for some time.

"I like this," he offered finally. "Who is it?"

"Who *is* it?!" spat Tom, incredulous.

"Guns N' Roses," Max quickly stepped in. "You could say Tom's a fan of old metal."

"*Classic* metal," Tom corrected him, "it's timeless."

Michael nodded thoughtfully and Tom raised an eyebrow at me, as if to say an unfamiliarity with Guns N' Roses had pushed things beyond the limit of his tolerance. I glared at him in a way that suggested he was pushing me to the limit of mine. He rolled his eyes and sighed quietly.

"Do you know Metallica?" he asked, grudgingly.

Michael's eyes narrowed thoughtfully and then lit up. "'Nothing Else Matters'?"

"Yeah," nodded Tom, surprised. "So you *do* know some decent music."

"I love that song. I don't know how I've heard it…"

"You've heard it," said Tom standing up, "because it's one of the greatest fucking songs ever written." He swiftly scrolled through his iPod and the song in question started to play through the speakers. Then he picked up his guitar and sat on the edge of the bed.

Max and I exchanged withering looks. Heavy metal was a passion that neither of us really shared, and while Tom was a decent guitar player and singer, he wasn't quite as good as he thought. Michael, on the other hand, looked enraptured, and hummed along with increasing confidence as Tom played. In contrast to Tom, his pitch was spot on.

"You sing?" asked Tom, when they reached the instrumental.

Michael nodded, and I was so desperate for him not to set himself back by explaining he was a chorister that I quickly interjected.

"Michael plays keyboard, too. He's really good."

Michael looked at me, confused, and I shot him a warning

glance. It was actually classical piano he played, but I didn't think Max and Tom needed to know that right now.

"I'd really love to learn the guitar," said Michael.

"So why don't you?" asked Tom, still strumming along.

Michael shook his head, dismissively. "My dad thinks it's a waste of time. He gave me the choice of violin or piano. Plus, they don't teach guitar at our school."

Tom shrugged. "I'll teach you, if you want."

Michael smiled sadly. "Thanks, but there's no way my dad would buy me a guitar."

"I've got a spare one," said Tom.

"My dad still wouldn't give me the money for lessons."

Tom frowned at him like he was out of his mind. "I'm not gonna charge you, you idiot."

Michael grinned. "That would be incredible. I'd just need to make sure my dad doesn't—"

"Screw your dad," said Tom, suddenly turning up the volume and jumping up onto the bed as the next track came crashing through the speakers. He started headbanging and pretending to rock out on his guitar. "Your dad needs to get with the music!" he shouted.

Michael smiled up at Tom like he was some kind of god.

Max jumped onto the bed next to Tom and started playing air guitar. I felt a wave of relief wash over me, hopeful that some kind of bond was being forged, and hopped up there with them, rocking my head in time to the music and playing the imaginary drums.

"Come on, Blondie!" Max shouted at Michael.

For a moment Michael looked shy, but then he too climbed onto the bed and started miming into an imaginary microphone. All four of us were jumping, banging our heads and rocking out on our imaginary instruments, and I could just about hear Tom's mum yelling at us from downstairs.

Suddenly there was a loud crack, and we tumbled on top of each other as the centre of Tom's bed folded in. We looked at each other in stunned silence.

"Shit," said Tom, examining the way his bed now dipped in the middle. "That's not good."

Michael looked to each of us, eyes wide with horror.

"That's rock 'n' roll, baby!" shouted Max.

He threw his head back, letting out his characteristic, contagious, big belly laugh. Tom sniggered, I hooted with glee, and then suddenly all three of us were in peals of raucous laughter. Michael studied us for a moment, clearly shocked that this was how the rest of us spent our Saturday afternoons, before breaking into a grin and starting to laugh along. When Tom's startled mother appeared in the doorway, there we were, arms and legs flung over each other in a heap on the collapsed bed, laughing uproariously at the ceiling.

I remember that for a while there was nothing but the sound of our breathing. Then I could hear them talking again: deep, hushed voices, mumbling behind the shed. There was a sudden thud and a cry of pain; another boot in the side for their victim. I winced and closed my eyes tight, clutching at the polar bear that was wedged between the four of us, squeezing its cheap, under-stuffed body. Someone shouted in a foreign language, a strict order to stop. He had already told them once and was losing his patience.

When I dared open my eyes again, Tom was staring straight at me, his eyes steely and shining. It was almost dark now, but I could see what he was trying to communicate to me: *Let's go, quietly, slowly.* I nodded and looked to Max and Michael, both wide-eyed and frozen. A silent agreement was reached and we carefully extricated ourselves from the huddle. Ever so slowly, we started to feel our way across the hardened earth, heads bent, straining to see the ground beneath our feet, at pains not to tread on anything that might crackle or snap. I flinched at each tiny crunch of the earth beneath our trainers.

And then I felt the hand on my shoulder. Hot and heavy, applying just enough pressure to stop me.

I turned quickly and found myself staring up into a pair of pale, narrow eyes. They reminded me of the eyes of a snake. I opened my mouth, ready to tell the others to run, but they had already ground to halt in front of me, stopped in their tracks by a tall, lanky figure.

We were hemmed in.

"What are you boys doing?" asked the lanky figure in a slow, thick accent.

No one answered. My heart was drumming fiercely and my head was racing, trying to think of a way out of this situation.

"He asked you a question," said Snake Eyes behind me, squeezing my shoulder a little tighter.

I opened my mouth but nothing came out.

"We got lost," said Tom, "we were trying to get to the canal."

"Oh, lost," the lanky man nodded, "you boys don't want to be lost out here in the dark on your own."

"No, there are some strange people around," said Snake Eyes, gripping my shoulder, his accent slightly subtler than his mate's, "you wouldn't want to run into any of them. Come. We have a nice fire going. Come join us."

I saw the whites of my friends' eyes darting about in the darkness as we looked to each other.

"Thanks, but we need to get going," said Tom. He took a few steps forwards, and Max and Michael made a move to follow. The hand on my shoulder gripped me tighter and held me still.

"We insist," the voice behind me said. I watched as the lanky man shifted in front of the others, blocking their path.

With a sudden surge of panic, I realised that we weren't going anywhere.

"We really need to get home," said Tom, anxiety creeping into his voice.

"Are you the only one of your friends to talk?" asked the lanky man. "Can they not speak?"

We all stood silently, not knowing how to respond.

"'Course they can speak," said Tom on our behalf.

"But you are the leader, yes? Like me. All groups need a leader, yes?" His voice was slurring and he laughed as if his comment really amused him. "I like leaders. I am leader of my friends, too. Come. You bring your friends to meet my friends."

He reached out and put his arm around Tom's shoulder.

"We need to go," I said suddenly, fear making me weak in the knees.

"Yeah, we do," agreed Max.

"Yeah, sorry," Michael mumbled, ever polite.

"I don't think so," said Snake Eyes behind me. "You see, I think we might have a problem. I think you might have seen us being – how shall I say – a little heavy-handed with one of our friends?"

"We didn't see anything," said Max.

"No, nothing," agreed Michael.

Both men laughed.

"Well, that's good," said the lanky man – the Leader – "because, you see, to outsiders it may have looked a little unkind. But that is only because you do not know the context. You see, this friend of ours, he has been a very bad friend. He has betrayed our trust. And when this happens a leader must take action, do you not think?" he asked, addressing Tom. "They must show that they are not to be messed with."

Tom was silent, as still as a statue, the arm of the Leader still draped around him. A surge of fear rushed through me and I wrenched myself free from the grip on my shoulders. I had no plan, I didn't know what I was doing, I just knew we had to get out of here.

"Come on, let's go," I said, pushing Michael and Max forwards. As I stumbled past Tom, I grabbed his arm, "Come on, Tom," I urged, yanking at him.

But Tom pulled his arm free and stayed where he was. I turned towards him, confused. What the hell were we meant to do? Go with these people? What other choice did we have but to try and walk away?

But then I spotted the glint of the blade.

The Leader had a knife in his hand, dangling casually from the hand resting on Tom's shoulder.

My stomach felt like it was going to drop right out of me.

The familiar hot, weighty grip settled back on my shoulder once more.

"Come," said the voice behind me, "let us all be friends together."

I remember flashing the torch one, two, three times.

"I don't think he saw," said Tom beside me, his face white in the glow of the street lamp. "Do it again."

"No, look he's coming," said Max.

A window at the side of Michel's house opened and we watched as one leg emerged and then the other. He lowered himself carefully onto the pitched roof below, shuffled down the sloped tiles on his bottom, turned over onto his belly and then disappeared from our view, hidden by the garden wall. In a few seconds he would emerge through the side gate.

"I'm gonna live in a house like these when I'm older," mused Tom, looking around him at the large, detached houses lining the wide, leafy avenue.

"Yeah, right," Max scoffed. "Good luck with that."

"What? I can get this if I want to."

"By doing what?"

"I dunno. Whatever these people do."

"These people didn't go to Allenbrook. They'll have come from some posh school like St John's. If anyone's gonna get a house like this it'll be Jay."

"Why should he be the only one?"

"'Cause he'll be the one to get the best qualifications. That's what his parents are paying for. Plus he's got the brains."

"I'm easily as smart as Jay."

"Yeah, but you go to a shit school, so tough luck for you."

"So what? I work hard. I'll go to a shit school and still beat Jay in my exams."

"No, you won't," I muttered, stuffing my hands into the pockets of my jeans. It was too cold to be out tonight and this wasn't really where I wanted to be.

"I bet you I can do better than you," insisted Tom.

"Bet me what? You don't have anything."

"God, why do you two always have to turn everything into a competition?" groaned Max.

"I'll bet you fifty quid," said Tom, sticking out his hand.

"It'll take you forever to earn that when you're working in McDonald's," I told him.

"Ha ha. Go on. Fifty quid says I do better than you."

"Whatever." I shook his hand unenthusiastically. "You better start saving."

"Hey," said Michael, jogging up to us, "where are we going?"

"The park," said Tom.

"I don't wanna go to the park again," groaned Max, "it's boring."

"Not if we liven things up a bit," said Michael, reaching inside his jacket and pulling out a bottle.

Tom unzipped his own jacket and also pulled out a bottle. "Great minds think alike," he grinned.

We lay on the tennis court looking up at the night sky, our heads swimming pleasantly, our bodies warmed by the alcohol. We'd talked about football, music and video games. Michael still had a lot of gaps in his knowledge, but he was catching up fast and he'd slotted into our friendship group so perfectly that it was hard to remember a time when four had been three. It was like there had always been a space there for him, just waiting to be filled.

"How much d'you reckon your house is worth, Blondie?" asked Tom, rolling over to light Michael's cigarette.

Michael took a long drag. "I dunno," he shrugged, "not that much. A million maybe."

The rest of us laughed.

"Not that much!" we spat.

"It's not that much compared to some of the other houses round our way. Or some of the other kids at school. Some of their families have serious money."

"Tom wants to be as rich as your dad one day," explained Max. "He bet Jay fifty quid he'd beat him in his exams."

"Which he won't," I added. Apart from on the running track, I'd never been a competitive person – except for when it came to Tom. He drew it out of me, and so far it had always been to our mutual benefit, forcing us both to push ourselves just that bit harder.

"Well, you'll probably all do better than me," Michael sighed, "I'm thick as pig shit."

I tutted despairingly, hating the way he always put himself down. He wasn't thick – far from it – he just lacked confidence, getting so flustered and overwhelmed by schoolwork that he seemed to stop functioning properly.

"Aren't you gonna go work for your dad anyway?" asked Max. "In which case what does it matter how you do in your exams?"

"Yeah, you're set for life anyway," said Tom, a little bitterly. "You'll get a job *and* an inheritance."

"I don't give a crap about the money," said Michael. "I'd give it all up to not have to work with him."

"So why don't you?" said Tom. "He can't force you."

Michael didn't answer. His relationship with his dad seemed complicated, and none of us could quite get our heads around it. We all had the impression that his home life was a source of unhappiness, so it seemed best not to talk about it. We were his friends – there to cheer him up, take his mind off whatever problems he might be having. It was the same when

Max's dog got run over, or when Tom's dad was hospitalised, or when my grandfather died... A good laugh with your mates was always the fix.

"Did your mum work, Blondie?" asked Max.

"She was a model," Michael replied.

"No way!" chimed Max and Tom simultaneously.

"Yeah. Not, like, a famous one, but—"

"Was she hot then?" asked Tom.

"Oh my God, Tom, I can't believe you just asked Michael if his mother was hot!" exclaimed Max.

"His *dead* mother," I pointed out, and all of us – including Michael – laughed at the tastelessness of it, while Tom insisted it was a reasonable question.

"Actually, your mum *was* pretty stunning," I said, once the laughter had died down, "from the photos I've seen."

"Well, that was well before she got sick," said Michael. "She didn't look much like that at the end."

We all fell silent for a moment. I reached out and pinched Michael's cigarette from his fingers. I knew I shouldn't smoke, but occasionally, when the temptation was there...

Max belched loudly, breaking the silence.

"Sorry."

"God, you're disgusting," I groaned.

"What?" he protested, innocently. "Better out than in, that's what I always say."

"I can't imagine working with my dad," said Tom, sitting up and taking a swig from one of the bottles. "What a nightmare."

"Your dad's all right," I said.

"Yeah, but his job... God, man, I would die sitting in those fucking council offices all day, pushing papers around a desk. And then coming home to us lot. It's no wonder he's friggin' nuts."

"Well, your dad's gotta pay for all you kids somehow," said Max. "'Specially with another one on the way."

"Or my parents could just stop having sex. Which they

should have done a long time ago. I mean, they're both forty, for God's sake. It's disgusting."

"You might finally get another boy to add to the Wilson clan," suggested Max.

"Screw that, then I'll have to share my room. I'd share a room with Jay's sibling, but not mine."

"Dream on," I muttered.

"I do, my friend, every night."

"My sister would eat you for breakfast."

"That's what I dream about."

"Plus she has a boyfriend now."

"Oh, no way!" cried Tom, disappointed. "Who?"

"This bloke that's living opposite us. He's moved in with his uncle across the street for a while. Got into some kind of trouble back home so his parents sent him away for a bit. His name's Rocket."

"Rocket? What kind of crap name is that?" asked Michael.

"I dunno. A nickname, I guess. He's all right actually."

And by "all right" I meant he was the coolest bloke I had ever met. He'd started taking Laura out to the big clubs in London, where he somehow knew all the DJs. He high-fived me whenever he came round and said *Hey, dude!* with a chilled-out grin. He gave me cigarettes without anyone knowing, including Laura. He normally wore a beat-up biker's jacket and red chequered shirt, and he had black hair that hung just past his collar. He was that cool that I didn't even mind the thought of him shagging my sister.

"No one's parents should have sex," chirped up Max. "Once they become parents that should be it. It should be the law."

"Yeah, although Jay's safe," said Tom, "there's no way his dad will be able to get it up anymore."

"Or if he can he won't be able to keep it up for long," added Michael, "not at his age. One benefit of having an older dad – you don't have to worry about him having sex."

"Out of the things I worry about, that's honestly not one of them," I told him.

"He could be using Viagra," suggested Max, helpfully.

"That's true. He could be keeping it up for ages with Viagra," said Michael.

"Could we please stop discussing my father's erections?"

"I sometimes hear my parents having sex," piped up Max. "My dad makes these weird hooting noises, like an owl."

"What the hell?!" I cried, and we all laughed loudly. "That's so disturbing."

"You mean he doesn't call out to Jesus?" asked Tom, referring to the family's involvement in the church. "JESUS! JESUS! JESUS! OHHH, JESUS!" he yelled, his voice echoing across the night sky, making us laugh all the more.

Gradually we fell silent, and after a while a conversation about music started between Michael and Tom.

"You okay, Jay Boy?" asked Max. "You've been kind of quiet tonight."

I'd tried to enjoy the evening so as not to drag anyone else down, but I wasn't really feeling it.

"I'm okay. I just… I had a bit of an argument with Libby yesterday, that's all," I admitted reluctantly.

"Oh yeah? A lovers' tiff?"

"Yeah," I sighed, "and it was so stupid. I mean, it was about nothing, really. But somehow it all got blown out of proportion. I don't even know how. I'm sure it'll just blow over, but I don't know. It feels a bit shit."

Part of me was yearning to tell Max all about it. Just like a part of me was yearning to tell him that Libby had said she loved me, and that I'd said it back, and that we'd spent a cold evening in the bow of her boat huddled under a blanket whispering about our imagined future together, and that I'd been both freaked out by the seriousness of it and genuinely excited, and that I really wanted to take things further with her but I was too nervous to try, and that sometimes I felt overwhelmed by the fear of losing her… But I knew that if I shared any of these things I'd be laying myself wide open to my friend's mockery.

Maybe, just maybe, Max might say something sensitive and supportive – after all, he was a genuinely kind person, a Christian, a scout, and a lifelong friend – but it was just as likely he'd shout over to the others and within seconds I'd be the butt of their jokes. Because our friendships, as tight as they were, were forged on a mixture of fun, laughter, derision and humiliation. The ways we expressed our loyalty and affection for one another – an arm around the shoulder, a bear hug, some humorous words of wisdom – all fell safely within the age-old guidelines of male bonding. But venturing beyond those sacred boundaries? Sharing our fears, anxieties and emotions? Putting something genuinely personal out there and not knowing what you would get back? It was all too much of a risk.

It feels a bit shit.

That was about as emotional as any of us liked to get.

"Girls can be a bit mental, can't they?" said Max, confirming that a deep and meaningful discussion about the nature of relationships had probably never been on the cards. "They get angry at the stupidest things, turn even the littlest thing into an argument."

"Well, it wasn't all her fault," I conceded.

"It's periods and stuff, isn't it?" continued Max. "Makes them go bonkers. Every month my mum loses the plot. Last week, she hit my dad over the head with her copy of *Caravanning Monthly* just because he didn't offer her a cup of tea. I mean, talk about overreaction."

I smiled, comforted by the fact that there were households like Max's out there where being hit on the head with a camping magazine constituted drama. I loved spending time at his neat little house. It was so calm and quiet, and his parents so kind and mild-mannered, that it felt like a retreat from the chaos of the world. His mum brought us trays of orange squash and biscuits. It was like being enveloped in a warm, fluffy hug.

"Who's overreacting?" asked Michael, latching on to the end of our conversation.

"Libby," Max told him. "She's got PMT and is being argumentative."

I opened my mouth to protest, wondering why I ever bothered sharing anything when people didn't listen properly, but Tom interrupted.

"Okay, so we're back on Libby again, are we?"

"What's that meant to mean?" I asked defensively.

"Nothing. Just that even when you're actually with us and not her for once, you're still *talking* about her."

I felt anger swell in my chest. I'd been stressing myself out lately over dividing my time between Libby and my friends and my schoolwork. My mum was constantly pushing me to study harder, my friends were always nagging at me to go out. Was it any wonder the only person I wanted to be with right now was Libby? It sometimes felt like she was the only person who cared what *I* wanted.

"What's that meant to mean, when I'm *actually with you*?" I spat, sitting up and glaring at Tom. His eyes looked sleepy and unfocused in the light of the moon.

"It means when you see fit to grace us with your presence."

"I still hang out with you all the time!" I protested.

"Yeah, okay, whatever."

"You have to be kidding me! I saw you Wednesday. I'm here tonight, aren't I?"

"Well, only because you've fallen out with Libby, obviously. Which explains the last-minute message saying you were coming out after all."

"I just didn't think I was going to be able to get my prep done in time!"

"Prep," scoffed Tom, "or homework as us commoners call it."

"You know, screw you!" I shouted, suddenly jumping to

my feet. The tennis court spun and liquor rose in my stomach with a burn. "I'm getting so sick of your snide little remarks about my school. *And* my girlfriend! You're becoming a right pain in the arse!"

"Whoa," said Max, slowly hauling himself to his feet, "come on, guys."

"Why don't you just go hang out with her then?" spat Tom, sitting up. "If we're such a pain in the arse!"

"You! *You're* the pain in the arse!"

Michael stayed lying down but put his hands over his face and groaned.

"Then go be with her, like I said!" snapped Tom.

"What the… Where's that even come from?!" I asked, spreading my hands out wide in confusion. "I wasn't even talking to *you* about her!"

"For once."

"Time to go home, boys," chirped Michael, quickly scrambling to his feet.

"Yep," said Max, putting an arm on my shoulder and steering me away. But I wasn't having any of it. Months of repressed frustration at Tom were finally being given a voice thanks to his goading and Michael's vodka.

"None of this is even about Libby and you know it!" I snapped, pointing a finger at Tom, who was now on his feet, swaying slightly. "It's about the great fat chip on your shoulder. You've been weird with me ever since I went to St John's, just because you can't stand the fact I'm going to a private school when your parents can't even afford the subs for football anymore!"

Tom, drunk and defensive, suddenly lunged at me, shoving me hard and sending me stumbling into Max whose sturdy frame prevented me from falling to the ground.

"You think you're so special now, don't you?!" he yelled.

I wordlessly shoved him back.

"Stop!" barked Max. He grabbed me by the upper arms,

his large goalkeeper hands holding me still, while Michael tentatively blocked Tom's way.

Tom and I glared at each other, our eyes wide and angry, before I broke free of Max's grasp and with a quietly muttered *Screw you* strode off towards home.

Anger.

The one emotion that's always permissible among boys.

I was lying on my bed in the dark, still fully clothed and fuming, when my dad knocked on my bedroom door.

"Tom's here," he said quietly, poking his head around, "he wants a quick word."

I sighed heavily and dragged myself upright. I was starting to develop a headache.

"Don't wake your mum," he whispered as I pushed past him onto the dark landing. "And have you been smoking?"

"Nope," I lied, trudging down the stairs.

"I'm going to bed," he mumbled, "and you do the same please."

Tom stood on the doorstep, his hands deep in his pockets, looking sheepish.

"What do you want?" I asked coldly.

"I'm sorry," he said, kicking gently at the doorstep, "I was a dick."

"I just don't get what your problem is lately," I complained.

He sighed and looked everywhere apart from straight at me.

"I dunno," he muttered, "it's just… it's weird not having you at Allenbrook anymore, that's all. And then you started going out with Libby, and I don't mean to be a div about it, but what with your new school and your new girlfriend, it's just I don't see you as much and… I dunno. I don't know why I'm being such a prick."

In the glow of our porch light, his eyelids looked heavy. I stared at him and finally understood what his attitude had been about these past few months. Part of me wanted him to just say it. But I knew he wouldn't. Out of all of us, Tom was probably the person least likely to wear his heart on his sleeve. Plus, he didn't need to say it. Not really. I knew what he was getting at.

I thought about telling him I missed him too, but I was only going to say that if he said it first.

"I know I'm being a bit crap at meeting up lately—"

"No, it's fine," said Tom, shaking his head. "I get it. I just..." He trailed off with a shrug.

"I'm sorry about what I said," I muttered, "about the football subs. I didn't mean—"

"Yeah, I know."

We stood there for a minute in silence, Tom kicking gently at the door frame with the toe of his trainer, and me staring at my socks.

"Is your dad... I mean, is everything okay?" I asked tentatively, wondering if there was anything else on his mind.

Tom shrugged. "Not really," he mumbled.

I didn't know what to say, or how much I could ask. I didn't really understand what was wrong with Tom's dad, none of us did. Depression was a word you heard sometimes, but it didn't mean a lot to any of us. It seemed best to either make a joke about it, like Tom often did, or not talk about it at all. I chose the latter option, not wanting to show my ignorance or say the wrong thing.

"Go home, you div," I said.

"We cool?" Tom asked, sticking out his fist.

"Yeah, we're cool," I told him, bumping my first against his.

He turned and sauntered down the garden path.

"Later, dickhead," he called quietly.

"Later, shitface," I called back.

And just like that we were friends again.

Chapter 11

Celebrations

Hello Tom
Apologies for contacting you out of the blue. The
hospital gave me your email address

DELETE

Hi Tom
It's been a long time. I heard you were at a hospital
in Surry now so I spoke to

DELETE

Dear Tom
I hope you are well. It's been a long time.
I was wondering if I might be able to visit you? I
have some things I'd like to talk to you about. I have
been doing some thinking about the past and

DELETE

Hey Shitface

DELETE

Tom,
Been a long time. Hope you are well. Any chance
we can talk?
Jay

SEND

Apparently, Stu slid off the sofa and positioned himself on one knee in the middle of a particularly violent episode of *Game of Thrones*. I suppose it's half-heartedly romantic, and it seems to sum up his relationship with Irena; deep-seated affection tinged with a hint of hostility. They constantly bicker behind the bar and she snaps at him, calling him an oaf and an idiot or other things in Polish that he may or may not understand, so that anyone who isn't a regular at the Canal House might feel slightly uncomfortable and question their professionalism. But most of us know it's just their way. They've been a solid couple for years, and news of their engagement is a cause for celebration, hence tonight's barbecue. I just don't feel like celebrating, that's all.

I've not been sleeping well again. My meeting with Libby last weekend – far from bringing me the peace of mind I'd been craving – has led to a new kind of turmoil. On the one hand, I feel genuine relief in knowing she's never held a grudge against me, and I'm grateful to have had the chance to say sorry, whether she thought I needed to or not. Some of the guilt has been lifted from my shoulders by seeing that she's happy, successful, unharmed by the mess I made. I don't know why I ever imagined otherwise. But a new kind of unrest has taken hold of my mind. Lying awake at night, unable to shut my thoughts off, I find the past playing out even more vividly than before. I'm in the long grass, nine years old, the warm sun on my face…

Do you want to kiss me?

And later, on her narrowboat, when we had to get to know each other all over again, when we were changed, teenagers, fumbling to find the words.

… I really like you…

And then when we were a couple. Hours spent just talking, laughing, lying on her narrow bunk innocently holding each other, or taking our first, tentative, clumsy steps in kissing, touching… I remember the newness of it all, the excitement, the longing… but most of all I remember that feeling of connection. We fit. It felt easy. It felt right.

But after the night of the fairground nothing felt right anymore. And nothing really ever felt easy again.

It's pointless, wondering what if. What if I'd handled my emotions better? What if I'd fought harder to stay together? Could we have ever made it work, despite the baby, despite everything? Probably not. She was right. We were just kids.

But still. What if?

I don't know why I keep wasting my time on these thoughts. I'm an idiot.

She sent me a text the day after our meeting, which I fretted over for forty-eight hours before replying.

Hi. Good to see you yesterday. Just to let you know I agreed to do Stu's mural. I'm planning on working on it weekends, pending weather. Take care. Libby.

I should have been happy for her. She'd looked genuinely enthusiastic to have a new project. Perhaps after her stressful career with the big advertising company she just wanted to get back to her roots, indulge her love of painting for a while, feel the sun (what there is of it) against her face. But the truth is my heart sank when her text came through. I was responsible for her coming here, but now I just want her gone. It had never been part of the plan to see her again. I'd just wanted to say my piece and move on. That was the idea of closure; box things up, seal shut with industrial-strength tape and send to archive, never to be thought of again.

But now she was sticking around, and she was texting me, and what did that even mean anyway? *Good to see you.* Was that an invitation to friendship? Was I meant to go and see her at the Canal House, call in one weekend, admire her mural and make chit-chat about her progress? Because, having given it some thought, I'm just not sure we could ever be friends. There's far too much water under the bridge.

Or was her text saying exactly the opposite? *Take care.* Was that a final goodbye, her signing off, an over-and-out? Was she warning me where she would be and when so that I could stay away, saving us both the embarrassment of more awkward conversation?

In the end, I replied with a brief message which was carefully worded to convey neutrality, but which probably just made me sound like a disinterested and cold-hearted dick.

Thanks for meeting with me. Hope the painting goes well.

I still don't know what to do. Today's Saturday and as it's been dry, I'm guessing she might have already started work on the mural, but luckily I've been busy finishing off a job that overran, visiting my dad and ferrying Josh between friends' houses, so going to see her hasn't been an option. Tomorrow, though, I need to make a decision. Should I call in and see her? Would it be rude not to? Would it be weird to do so?

I'm still agonising over it when I arrive in front of the Canal House. I only intend to stay an hour at the barbecue. Josh is a good excuse for getting away early. If I'm honest, he's always been my excuse for lots of things – for not dating, for not committing. His growing older and more independent is highly inconvenient. What will I have to face when I don't have him to hide behind? Anyway, just for tonight I can say he's home alone, which was true at the point of leaving the flat, but probably isn't any more, seeing as his friend Sam was on his way over to play video games. In reality, Josh won't be bothered in the slightest that I'm not there.

The sun is starting to dip, and barbecue smoke carries on the air over the roof of the Canal House and right out to the high street, along with the sound of talking and laughter. Knowing the bar is likely to be even more busy than usual, I open the gate and make my way down the side alley and straight through to the terrace at the back. The tables – adorned with tea lights for this special occasion – are all taken, and groups of people are mingling in the spaces in between, laughing, drinking, eating hotdogs and burgers. It's not a private party – far too much revenue to be lost on a Saturday night to warrant closing the place – but all the regulars have turned up.

"Jay!" I spy Leo across the terrace, a good few inches taller than anyone else. "All right, mate?"

I give him a nod.

"Where's Michael?"

I briefly scan the crowd and shrug.

Ah, crap. Don't say he's not here. He's like my buffer in these situations, allowing me to take a back seat. He's always up for a get-together. Unless... I check my phone with a sinking feeling.

Not going to make tonight sorry, not feeling so good.

Normally he would have been one of the first to arrive, but the text was only sent ten minutes ago. That means he intended to come, he tried, he spent some time working up to it, not wanting to let Stu and Irena down, not wanting to let me down, but in the end, he couldn't bring himself to do it.

I hold my phone up towards Leo and shake my head sadly. He nods, understanding. There's not that many people that know the other side of Michael, but Leo's one of them. Michael's had to cancel too many rehearsals and even the odd gig for any members of his band to be left in the dark.

You okay? I type back. We both know that I don't really mean *are you okay* because clearly he's not. What I mean is *Is there anything I can do? Do you need me?*

I sigh, my heart suddenly feeling heavy.

"Heeeyyy!" Irena dives towards me and kisses me on both cheeks. She's in high spirits, her usual brusqueness evaporated. "I was asking people where were you. You don't have a drink, no? Come, have something to eat—"

"I'm good, I'll get myself a drink in a minute," I tell her, "but, listen, congratulations—"

"'Bout bloody time, isn't it?" she scowls, her accent still thick after all these years. "That son-of-a-bitch slowcoach, it took him seven years, you know?"

"Well, all good things are worth waiting for. Plus," I add, nodding at her slight swell of a belly, "he's doing the honourable thing."

"That's right," she smiles, stroking her little bump. "And now I think it's your turn, isn't it?" She pokes me hard in the chest. Even when she's being playful she looks aggressive, her raven black hair and thin, pencilled-in eyebrows doing nothing to soften her demeanour. "Who are we going to find for you, eh?"

I smile and shake my head. "No one. I'm good thanks."

"No one is good on their own. Especially not you. You are wasted. You and Rachel, I think I can see—"

"You cannot see *anything*."

"She would be good for you, I think. Let you have a little fun. She's a beautiful girl, isn't it?"

"Stop trying to set me up with people."

She places her hand on my upper arm, bright red nail varnish adorning fingers that by the feel of her grip must be made of steel. Matchmaking is Irena's passion, and she doesn't like to be held back.

"You are infuriating," she says sternly. "I don't know what I can do with you."

"Don't do anything. Just enjoy your evening."

"But where is Michael, anyway?" she says, scanning the crowded terrace.

"Sick. A bug."

"Oh, you kid me! I thought he is coming. Poor him. But still," she says excitedly, peering around, "your friend is here! Yes, over there."

Seated at a table with a group of people I vaguely know is Libby, wearing the same jeans and blue T-shirt as last weekend, cradling a glass and looking around uncomfortably. My stomach flips.

"Why is she still here?" I ask, sounding far more accusatory than intended.

"What is point in her going home?" says Irena, taking a step back and looking a little alarmed by my tone. "She is going to stay here and then carry on tomorrow with the painting. No point coming and going."

"But... doesn't she want to get back? To her fiancé, or... I don't know... I mean, it's not that far for her to get home."

Irena shrugs and frowns at me. "Well, is nearly an hour, and what for? Just to come back in the morning? No, we agreed. She can stay here. No problem for us. We have the little attic flat. Is sitting empty. And she seems nice. Nice for me to have a girl friend to chat to. Why do I want to hear about football and this boys' rubbish all of the time?"

"So, you mean she's going to stay *every* weekend?" I ask, realising I sound slightly horrified.

Irena frowns and shrugs. "I don't know. We will see."

For a moment I contemplate making a discreet exit. I could make my way back through the bar, say a quick congratulations to Stu, who will be stuck serving drinks all night anyway, and then quietly slip away. I've shown my face, that's all I really needed to do.

Irena follows my line of vision, gazing over towards Libby. "Ahh, but perhaps I am climbing up the wrong tree with Rachel," she says sagely, "perhaps it is this Libby who is someone you like."

"No! God no. She's just a friend. I mean, she *was* a friend. A long time ago."

"Well, go say hello to your old friend," Irena orders,

suddenly reverting to her usual brusque self and slapping me on the arm. "She knows nobody. Go talk to her!"

As Irena marches off, I stand motionless and watch Libby. She smiles politely at something the guy next to her says – a bloke called Nick, who's all right when he's sober but turns into a bit of a letch when he's had a few. And by the way he's leaning into Libby, he might have had a few already. I watch her laugh unconvincingly at his joke and then turn casually to the two women on the other side of her, smiling, trying to get in on their conversation instead of being stranded in a one-on-one with leery Nick.

Libby was always confident when it came to chatting to people. She was socially developed beyond her years, comfortable in her own skin. She spent most of her childhood around adults and learned to communicate in an adult fashion at an age when most of us were shifting awkwardly from one foot to another and trying not to look like our very existence was a cause for embarrassment. But she never had any friends. How could she? She didn't go to school, didn't mix with people her own age – except me, obviously – and very occasionally Michael, Tom and Max. We'd all hang out now and again, but in truth it never worked that well.

She got on well with Max – everyone did. He was used to making nice chit-chat due to all the church events he had to attend, and the two of them could hold something of a proper conversation. But Michael – having been in single-sex education from the age of seven and still painfully shy around anyone but us – didn't know what to say to her. And Tom was too crass, full of sarcasm and bad language. A couple of times she pulled him up on his use of expletives – those that referred to parts of the female anatomy in a particularly derogatory way. She was never fearful of expressing her point of view, and I loved that about her, admired her sense of conviction, but being told off like a naughty schoolboy didn't go down well with Tom, who doubled his use of offensive language. To make matters harder, although Libby was well-rehearsed in the art of conversation, she didn't know anything about normal teenage life: TV programmes, video games, celebrities... it meant nothing to her. Thinking back, I can't imagine what the two of us spent so many hours talking about, or what we could have possibly had in common. I think maybe she was more the talker and I was more the listener. I don't know. All I know is somehow it worked. Easily. Comfortably.

Right now, though, Libby doesn't look all that comfortable. The two women (I don't know their names, but I think Michael might have had a very brief thing with one, or possibly both, of them) are too engaged in what appears to be a hilarious anecdote to notice Libby. Nick keeps edging in close, talking in her ear, and she smiles and replies politely, but she's leaning away slightly, trying to avoid what I imagine might be beer breath.

I can't just leave her. I at least have to check if she's okay.

I weave my way through the groups of people towards her, checking my phone again as I go, wishing Michael would text me back and let me know how he is.

Libby spots me as I approach her table and stands up swiftly. She looks strangely happy to see me, like she's been awaiting my arrival. She steps forwards, a little unsteady, and with a hint of disappointment I realise her enthusiastic greeting is probably directly related to her alcohol consumption.

"Hi," she smiles, pink-cheeked, tucking her hair behind her ear.

"Hi," I respond, stuffing my hands into the back pockets of my jeans.

We stare at each other, waiting for the other one to speak, then we open our mouths at the same time and pause there, like two overly polite strangers standing by an open door. *After you; no, after you.*

"Having fun?" I ask, braving the first move.

"Um... well..." she glances around her, "I... well... I suppose..."

I laugh a little at her poor attempt at diplomacy, and so does she.

"Well, I wasn't expecting this tonight and I don't know anyone, so…"

"Bit weird?"

"Bit weird," she nods.

I glance at Nick, slumped in his seat, eyeing Libby up and down, his eyes swimming lazily.

"All right, Nick?" I call abruptly.

"All right, Jay," he drawls, raising his depleted pint to me, before shamelessly going back to ogling Libby.

God, I'm glad I don't drink if that's what blokes become after a few pints. He's not a bad guy really, always friendly and harmless enough, but still, I suddenly have an urge to grab him by the throat and chuck him over the wall into the canal.

"Do you want to…?" I find myself suddenly saying, gesturing somewhere else, anywhere else.

Libby looks longingly in the direction of the canal.

"Actually, do you want to take a walk?" she asks, tentatively, gesturing to the steps in the corner of the terrace that lead down to the towpath.

"Yeah, sure," I say, so desperate to be out of here and away from all these people that I'm not even worrying about what Libby and I will say to each other or how awkward it's bound to be.

"Thanks," she smiles, gratefully, and I realise that she probably was genuinely pleased to see me arrive. We might be out of touch, but at least I'm not a complete stranger. She grabs her half-empty wine glass from the table and then stands expectantly in front of me, waiting for me to lead the way.

"You can't take that off the premises," I tell her, realising I sound like a complete killjoy. "Stu's the one who gets in trouble…"

"Oh, of course!" she says. She takes a gulp of the wine, examines the glass, clearly decides it's not worth leaving the rest, and downs that, too. She places the glass back on the table, squeezes her eyes tightly shut and grimaces.

"Oooh... bad idea. I'm not really used to drinking."

"You okay?"

She nods, and I lead the way through the gathering towards the steps, quickly checking my phone on the way. Still nothing. I drop Michael another quick message.

Text me U R OK

"Michael was going to come tonight, but he's not well," I say over my shoulder. "He would have liked to have seen you."

"Oh, that's a shame, I would have liked to see him, too," she says, sounding genuinely disappointed. "I was looking at all the photos of him and his band on the pub wall. God, he looks so different! And I hear he's really good."

"He's amazing."

"Oh, what do you think so far?" asks Libby, just as we reach the top of the steps.

I turn to her blankly, and she gestures the length of the terrace wall. With all the bodies blocking my view, I hadn't even noticed the bricks have been painted white. Well, half have been painted white.

"Er... well... not much to go on so far..." I say, trying to be polite.

"No, I thought I'd at least have the base done today," she says with a thoughtful frown, "but it's taking somewhat longer than I thought it would."

"Yeah. Well, it's a long wall," I say, following it with my eyes around the perimeter of the terrace.

"It is indeed," she nods with a grimace. "I'm not sure if I've bitten off more than I can chew. So, you know, if you enjoy painting and have a spare hour or so, feel free..."

I'm pretty sure she's joking, but I have a frustrating need to jump to people's assistance – my sister, Josh, Michael, my dad, my clients – I end up running myself ragged half the time trying to help them all out.

"Yeah, sure," I shrug, "I can come down tomorrow. I'll get Josh along as well, it'll keep him out of trouble."

What?! What am I saying? Now we're going to be painting a wall together? This is just too weird. Isn't it?

"Oh," says Libby, clearly taken aback. "I was just kidding, you don't have to do that."

She looks a little embarrassed and now I feel awkward. Of course she was only kidding.

"Oh, okay, sorry, I wasn't sure if you were being serious or—"

"Although, actually, I mean, if you guys *are* free…"

"Yeah. So long as it's just a case of slapping a bit of white paint on."

"Well, great, if you're sure?"

No. No I'm not sure. I have absolutely no idea what's happening here. One minute we're taking a walk, now we're going to be painting a wall together. What the hell have I started?

"Shall we…?" I say, gesturing to the steps.

"After you."

I hesitate, letting a group of women come up from the canal path. They're made up for a night out; skintight jeans, strappy tops, hair knotted up… Ah, crap. Rachel.

"Hello, stranger," she smiles, greeting me at the top of the steps with a hand on the shoulder and a kiss on the cheek. In heels, she's almost as tall as me. "I assume you lost my number, or…?"

I'm embarrassed that I forgot to text her back. "Rachel, I'm *so* sorry, things have been manic and—"

"Don't worry," she smiles, playfully punching me on the arm, clearly having regained her chilled-out Aussie demeanour. I wonder now if Stu was winding me up, telling me she was angry at me. She's always seemed so laid-back. "Although I have been hoping to bump into you."

She cocks her head to one side, her shiny lips curling at

one corner in a sexy smile, her smoky eyes running over my face. God, Stu was right, she really is incredibly hot.

"I had a good time the other night," she says, "I was hoping we might be able to do it again sometime."

I shift awkwardly, wondering how that must sound to Libby who's hovering behind me.

"Umm… yeah," I say, scratching at my neck, "why not?"

"Great. So, do you want to buy me a drink?"

"I… actually I was just going to get a bit of space for a minute," I tell her, glancing down at the towpath.

She comes in close and places her fingers gently on my forearm. "Do you want some company?" she asks, smiling coyly.

"Actually," I say glancing back at Libby, who is waiting patiently, "we were just—"

"Oh God, I'm sorry," Rachel says, more to Libby than to me. She quickly removes her hand from my arm as if she's been touching something that doesn't belong to her.

"No, it's fine, we're just… This is Libby. She's an old… er… an old friend of mine."

Libby smiles and gives a little wave.

"Oh, right," smiles Rachel, looking relieved. "Well, listen. I'm going to be here a while, so maybe we can catch up later, okay?"

As she passes by, she places the flat of her palm against my stomach, letting it linger there a moment. I swallow hard and try not to let my eyes follow after her.

"Sorry 'bout that," I mumble over my shoulder to Libby.

"No problem," she says, and I catch a little smirk on her face before we descend the steps.

We wander slowly along the towpath in silence. I rack my brain for something to say, but where do I start? Should I bring up the past, the only shared territory we have in common? Stick to the present? Enquire about her fiancé, wedding plans, living situation...? But is any of that really my business? We've spent hours on this towpath. Two little kids cycling their bikes, exploring the woodlands, finding bugs, sharing their sweets... And years later, holding hands, talking, laughing, kissing, sometimes arguing. And now here we are again, third time round. Silent.

I open my mouth to say something, anything, but just then my phone buzzes. I dig it out of my back pocket with a sense of relief. But it's not Michael. It's a message from Josh.

Wot time r u back?

I reply quickly, mumbling an apology to Libby.

Hour tops. Why?

He responds straight away.

Wot dissolves superglue?

"What the hell?" I sigh.

"Everything okay?" asks Libby.

"Yeah, sorry, just Josh," I tell her vaguely, typing back.

What's it on?

"God, it's just one thing after another," I say, shaking my head.

"Teenagers, eh?" Libby quips.

"You don't know the half of it," I sigh.

Skin, Josh replies. *I'm glued to Sam.*

"Oh, for God's sake," I mutter. "I'm really sorry, do you mind if I make a quick call?"

"Of course not."

We stop walking and she diplomatically turns to study the narrowboats moored at the edge of the water, while I wait for Josh to pick up. I'm half expecting him to answer in a state of panic, but instead I'm immediately met by the sound of the two boys laughing as if this is the funniest thing ever.

"We've glued our arms together!" Josh shouts breathlessly.

"How the hell...?"

"I don't know. We were just seeing what would happen."

"You were just seeing what would happen if you put superglue on your arms and stuck them together?"

"It was an experiment. We didn't think it would dry that fast. Or stick so hard."

"What are you doing with superglue?"

"Making a model airplane. Sam's mum bought it for him. We think she was probably drunk and forgot he's not, like, seven anymore."

I hear Sam burst into laughter, which seems inappropriate, but having never had an alcoholic mother, who am I to judge how he handles it?

"And this model airplane kit for seven-year-olds came with superglue?" I ask, sceptically.

"Well, no, but the glue it came with was taking too long to dry and it wasn't very strong, so…"

"So you thought you'd try superglue. Because it's very strong and dries very fast. It sounds like you already had the answer to your experiment right there, Josh."

"I'm not saying there was a whole lot of logic in this, Dad," he says, making Sam laugh even louder.

"Well, how much of you is stuck together?"

"Like, a quarter of our forearms."

"What?!"

"No, not a quarter, I dunno, like, a bit."

"Oh, for Christ's sake, Josh."

"What do we do? It said use nail varnish remover on YouTube, but we don't have any."

"Funnily enough, no. Have you soaked it?"

"In what?"

"Water. And soap."

"No, 'cause it just said use nail varnish—"

"Look, put your arms in some hot, soapy water for ten minutes or so and if it still doesn't come off, then walk down to Tesco and get some nail varnish remover."

"We can't go to Tesco, we're stuck together!"

"Well tough! You shouldn't have been such morons!"

"Oh my God," he groans dramatically, as if this was somehow my fault.

"Look," I sigh, "I'll be back in an hour, then I'll go out to Tesco if I need to, okay?"

"Okay."

"Thank you!" I hear Sam shout just as I end the call.

"Everything okay?" asks Libby, turning to me.

"My idiot son and his idiot best friend have somehow superglued their arms together," I explain, returning my phone to my pocket.

Libby clamps her hand over her mouth, looking both horrified and amused.

I shake my head despairingly, but smile. I'm slightly worried my evening will end with a lengthy wait in A&E, but I can also see the funny side.

"Kids," I sigh, as we resume walking side by side.

"The teenage years must be extremely challenging," she says.

"*Every* year's extremely challenging."

She laughs as if I'm joking.

"I think it's a lot easier now, actually, than it used to be."

"Really?"

"Yeah. I mean, the early years were…" I search for the word, but nothing really sums it up adequately, "hard."

"I can't even imagine."

We fall silent for a while, the last sixteen years like a gaping chasm between us. Where to even begin?

Libby fiddles with her necklace.

"So, is Hellie…?"

"Haven't heard from her in years. She moved to the States when Josh was three."

"And she's never kept in contact with him?"

"Nope. Nothing."

"Wow."

"Wow indeed." I make no attempt to keep the bitterness out of my voice.

"I mean, I heard on the grapevine that she left, but I had no idea it was quite so… er…"

"Final?"

"Right."

"She wasn't really on board from the start, to be honest. Not long after Josh was born, this guy she knew offered her a bit of modelling work in the US, and then it seemed to turn into promotion work or acting or something and... I don't know. She came and went. And then she just... went."

"And so, what, you brought him up on your own?"

"God, no, I couldn't have done it on my own. My dad was there to help for a few years, but, well, then he couldn't anymore. But my sister did a lot, and so did Michael. I don't know what I would have done without them."

"But I mean you didn't, you know, you didn't meet anyone?"

"What, a woman?"

"Well, last thing I knew that was your gender of preference."

I laugh and so does she.

"Yeah, well, it still is. But, no, I'm not with anyone, if that's what you're asking. I haven't had much time for all that and... I don't know. That's probably a lousy excuse. I mean, there have been people, here and there, you know..."

"Yes, so I gathered," she says with a smirk, raising an eyebrow at me.

"Uh, no, Rachel, she's just a friend."

Libby smiles sceptically.

"A friend I might have given the wrong impression to," I add with a guilty smile, and Libby laughs.

I'd forgotten how much she laughed, how much she smiled, and how that always made me want to smile, too. I was thrown by our first couple of meetings; her cold reserve and sharpness. But I can see now that her warmth is still there. She's not so different, after all. Plus, I suspect the drink has loosened her up a bit. If I wasn't worrying about my conjoined son and my mentally unstable best friend, I might even start to relax around her.

"So, what about you?" I dare to ask. "How did you meet…?"

"Will. Erm… we met at work – not the job I just left, another one. An insurance company. He's the head of finance, so…"

She stops there as if this is everything I need to know about Will. I have an image of a corporate guy in a smart suit ordering people around. He'd be pretty rich, wouldn't he, if he's head of finance? I never imagined Libby ending up with someone like that. Wasn't that everything she stood against? But then I guess that was a long time ago. And even back then she was confused and contradictory about her values.

I want to ask more about Will, but at the same time I don't want to know. I'm happy for her. She deserves love, stability, security. But it's strangely hard, thinking of her with someone else, even after all this time.

"So, you said you were working for an advertising agency?" I ask, slightly confused by what she does exactly. "On the creative side?"

"Umm… well, yes," she says, sheepishly, "but not being particularly creative, unless you call arranging biscuits into nice patterns on a plate creative. I was just doing secretarial stuff. It was just a temporary job. As was the job at the insurance company. Except there I got to stand behind reception all day and wear a weird uniform that made me look creepily like an overgrown school girl."

"Hopefully that's not what attracted Will."

She laughs. "Hopefully not. But I… umm… I'm still, actually, working out what I want to do."

I nod, thinking this makes sense in so many ways. Behind the confident, determined exterior, she was always conflicted, muddled, lost. And it sounds like in some ways she still is.

"Well, it can be hard, finding your path in life. I'm sure you'll figure it out," I say, cringing at my own words. I meant to sound reassuring, but instead I think I just sound patronising.

"I kind of thought by this age I'd have already figured it

out. I did have a plan, once. I started an archaeology degree, but, I don't know, I struggled a bit at uni. I found it hard, trying to integrate. When you haven't been to school, haven't been used to groups of people your own age… I don't know. Maybe I'll go back one day."

"Well, you've still got your whole life ahead of you, really. There's lots of time to make changes and choices. I don't see myself hanging round here forever, doing what I'm doing. I'd like to move to the Peak District before too long, renovate my great-great-grandad's cottage, work less, enjoy the outdoor life a bit more."

"So, don't you want… I don't know, don't you want to meet someone maybe, settle down, have more kids…?"

"Christ no," I laugh. "I mean, meet someone, maybe, but kids? No. No way."

"Has it been *that* bad?" Libby laughs.

"No. No, it's just been…"

I look out at the water, the evening sun bouncing off the surface in shimmering, golden sparkles. In my mind's eye, I see that hospital, the strobe lights, the plastic seats. *I need to prepare you, Mr Lewis. We're doing everything we can, but he's in a critical condition…*

"…it's been challenging, like I said."

"So, you're done," Libby states.

"Yeah, I'm done. Definitely. I mean, this one has literally glued himself to his mate, so…"

Libby laughs. "Yes, I see your point."

"Don't let me put you off, though. They're not all as crazy as mine."

"Oh, you won't put me off. I can't wait to have kids."

"You want to start a family soon?" It feels way too personal a question for this stage in our… whatever this is. But she was the one who put it out there.

"Absolutely. Wedding vows out the way and then…"

"And then down to business, eh?"

"You could put it that way," she laughs.

"You still want to have four of the little buggers?"

She shakes her head at the memory, cringing. "Er... no, maybe not four. A couple will do fine. God, I must have terrified you, with all my talk about marriage and kids the minute we were old enough!"

"Well, a little maybe," I concede, and we both laugh.

"I've always thought it was kind of ironic," she says, "that I was so keen to have kids, but you were the one who ended up having one."

"Yeah," I nod, "I've thought that too. But it wasn't really a choice."

"No, but clearly you've made a good job of it."

"Again, he's glued himself to his mate."

"Understood. But who was the first person he called? You. And I could tell from the way you spoke to him that you two have a good relationship."

"Did you get that from the fact I called him a moron and then hung up on him?"

"Absolutely."

We come to a halt, both of us staring towards the bridge where we once made up, and then only weeks later went our separate ways. I can't believe we've wandered this far. I glance discreetly at Libby's profile. She looks confused, like me, to suddenly find herself here.

"So many memories..." she mutters.

I don't respond. I don't know how to. Sometimes you stop, look at your life, and wonder who the hell you are and how the hell you got here. It's mind-blowing beyond words.

"It took me a really long time to get over you," she says, quietly.

The intimacy of her statement shocks me. I feel a stab in my chest. *Do you want to know how long it took to get over you?* I want to ask her. But I still don't think I know the answer to that question.

I can smell smoke. There's another barbecue going

on somewhere nearby. Music emanates from one of the narrowboats, and the tinkle of conversation carries on the air.

"Maybe I shouldn't have come here," says Libby, wrapping her arms around herself.

"Here?" I ask, thinking she means this exact spot.

"Back to Timpton. When I left, I never thought I'd come back. And now I don't really know what I'm doing here." She shakes her head, sadly. "I don't know what I'm doing anywhere, really. I mean, God, look at you, you've done so much. You have a teenage son, your own business, your own place…"

"Me? I'm just muddling through, working all hours, trying to meet the bills. You're getting married," I remind her, "I'm guessing you're gonna buy a nice house in the suburbs, have two point four kids… I mean, six years together, that's something."

She nods, but she doesn't look convinced.

"I guess."

"You guess?"

She looks up at the sky.

"Things are just never quite as you imagine they're going to be, are they?"

I study her face, suddenly so sad, so different from just a few moments ago.

"But you are… I mean, you're happy, aren't you?" I ask, confused, willing the answer to be yes.

But just then my phone buzzes.

I watch her, waiting for an answer.

"Don't you have to check that?" she asks.

Irritated by the interruption, I pull my phone from my back pocket. It's Michael. I can't believe his timing.

Am ok. Run out of meds. Mix up at Dr. Need to sleep. Text U tomorrow.

I stuff my phone back in my jeans and look to Libby again, but somehow, in that split second she's manage to plaster a smile back on her face.

"I had way too much to drink this evening," she laughs. "I'm not used to it. Do you mind if we head back?"

"Yeah, sure," I say, and I smile despite the fact I suddenly feel unsettled.

We start to retrace our steps, and I'm just about to steer the conversation back to where we were, when my phone rings. I never turn my phone off or refuse to answer it. Not after that night Josh got sick and I missed the calls. But sometimes I just wish I could be uncontactable.

"God, I'm so sorry," I tut, looking at the screen, "it's my sister, I have to take it."

I answer the call, weary now of all the disturbances.

"What?" I ask abruptly.

"It's Dad," she says, "he's in a bad way. Can you get over here?"

"Where's Brenda?"

"She's not back yet. Her niece's wedding, remember?"

"Can't you handle it, whatever it is?"

"Would I be fucking calling you if I could?"

I sigh and run my hand over my head.

"Twenty minutes," I agree, thinking Josh is just going to have to wait.

I hang up.

"Wow, you're really in demand," quips Libby.

I rub my eyes.

"Like you wouldn't believe."

One evening. One friggin' evening to myself, is that too much to ask? Not even an evening – an hour! I mean, it's not like I really wanted to come, but still, the idea that I could go out for an hour and be left in peace… Heaven forbid!

As Libby and I walk back to the pub at an accelerated pace, I try to remind myself that this is just life. Everyone has responsibilities. Everyone has pressures. Idiotic kids, unstable friends, sick parents, demanding sisters… I don't want to feel annoyed with them. And I don't want to feel resentful. So I clench my fists at my sides and try to take a deep breath.

And I tell myself not to feel angry. Because anger has never served me well.

Chapter 12

Anger

I remember shouting at her: "You weren't there, you have no idea what it was like!"

"I know I wasn't there! I can't know what it was like. But maybe if you talked to someone—"

"I'm talking to you!"

"This isn't talking, Jamie, this is shouting!"

I paced restlessly in circles. I kicked at one of the metal lamp posts that dotted the canal path near the marina, gently at first and then harder, giving it a boot that sent a sharp pain shooting through my toes and up my calf.

Libby stood by, wringing her hands, watching me anxiously. I hated the fact that she looked so anguished. I didn't want to raise my voice. I didn't want to be like this. But for weeks now this feeling inside – this churning fear, and anger, and hyperactivity – had taken over me. I couldn't sleep. I couldn't stop. And there was only one thing that ever seemed to take the edge off.

"You're drinking too much," said Libby, "it's not right. You need to stop."

"I'm not drinking too much."

"Yes, you are. And it's not helping. I'm going to speak to your parents, Jamie—"

"You aren't going to say a word to my parents!" I snapped, glaring at her. I heard my own voice, loud and angry, echoing against the water's surface and the surrounding woodland. Was that really me, shouting at Libby like that?

Her eyes were wide and startled for a moment, before regaining their steeliness.

"It's not like they don't know, Jamie!"

"Well, then you don't need to talk to them!"

She sighed and rubbed her forehead, strands of long hair falling around her face.

"I'm worried about you," she said more gently, holding her hands out imploringly. "This is so unlike you. And I don't know what to do. You're scaring me."

I looked up at the purple-tinged sky. It was a warm evening and the light was just starting to fade. I gazed at the narrowboats up ahead, their glorious colours blurring slightly after the drinks I'd had with Michael earlier.

I hadn't hung out with my friends much since that night at the fairground. In fact, seeing as we were now all on study leave for our GCSEs, I hadn't even been at school to see Michael. But on those few occasions we had got together, we'd got drunk in miserable, awkward silence until an argument had erupted, angry words, accusations and recriminations flying back and forth between us until we all sulked off in our own directions. Everything had changed for each of us, the bond we once shared now strained out of recognition.

"My mum knows this person—" said Libby, tentatively.

"I don't need to talk to some psycho shrink person. I need to talk to you!"

"But then talk to me!"

"I *do*! I *am*!"

"You don't! You don't tell me anything! You flip at the tiniest thing, you shut me out, you drink, you got yourself suspended! Your GCSEs are happening and you're barely doing any revision! This isn't you, Jamie!"

"I know that!"

In anger and frustration, I grabbed a stone from the path and flung it up at the light. Glass smashed, flying in jagged, sparkling pieces towards the ground. In that split second, I felt a kind of satisfaction with my aim, a sense of release at the sound of my own petty act of destruction. But then I heard Libby cry out.

She was clutching at her face.

The realisation of what had happened hit me and I rushed towards her.

It took us less than five minutes to get back to where her boat was moored, but in that time, against my advice, Libby had tugged the shard of glass free from where it had embedded. I'd taken my T-shirt off and she was holding it against her cheek, blood seeping through the fabric. She was pale and silent in the face of my endless apologies.

After a hasty and fumbled explanation of events, Harmonie quickly bundled Libby inside the boat, but when I tried to follow, my entrance was barred.

"I think she needs the hospital," I blurted out, anxious that Harmonie might be planning on using some new-age approach to try and heal the wound.

"Of course she needs the bloody hospital!" she snapped. "You could have blinded her!"

"I know," I said, wringing my hands, "I'm sorry, I—"

She jabbed her finger at me aggressively, rows of bangles jangling on her arm. "I don't want to hear it! You've caused her nothing but stress and unhappiness lately. I know you've had a hard time, but don't push that onto her. You're all the bloody same. Nothing but trouble in the end. Now get off my boat and let me deal with this."

"But can't I—?"

"No, Jamie! You've done enough."

And with that she ducked inside, shutting the door on

me, while I stood silent and shocked, wondering what I'd turned into.

I remember asking Laura if she was okay and knowing perfectly well the response I'd get.

"What the fuck do you care?"

I almost walked away right then, but as mean as she could be, she was still my sister.

"You just look kind of… washed out lately."

"Wow, thanks. No wonder you've managed to bag yourself a girlfriend with that kind of charm."

I sighed and stood up from the kitchen table, ready to take my sandwich elsewhere.

"Seriously though," muttered Laura, popping two pieces of bread in the toaster, "why do you give a crap?"

It was one o'clock on a Saturday afternoon and I'd just come back from athletics practice at school. I was still in my jogging bottoms and T-shirt adorned with the school emblem. Laura, on the other hand, had just crawled out of bed and was wearing her pyjamas. I watched her spoon coffee and a huge amount of sugar into a mug.

"I know you like to think we all hate you, Laura, but it's not totally true."

She mumbled a comment that sounded like *yeah, right.*

Lately, Laura hadn't been home much. She'd been spending a lot of time with Rocket, going to the clubs in London. When she *was* home, she was even more moody and distant than usual, and any modicum of motivation she'd had seemed to have evaporated. She'd lost her job for oversleeping too many times, but she didn't seem to care.

It was clear from the start my parents had never liked Rocket, but I'd assumed that was because they were old and boring and wouldn't know cool if it smacked them in the face. Now I was starting to wonder if they had a point. Even though I was slightly in awe of his bad-boy image, he didn't seem to be a great influence on my sister. I knew he'd got her dabbling in drugs, and although I assumed it was nothing serious, I was starting to think Laura was easier and nicer before she met him, which was really saying something.

"Your family actually cares about you, Laura," I added, really pushing the boat out now with my display of emotion, "not that that seems to bother you."

I turned to walk out the door, taking a bite of my sandwich as I left.

"All you care about, Jamie, is being number-one son," she retorted, bitterly. "Being Mum's little superstar."

I stopped and turned around. "What the hell are you talking about?" I mumbled through my mouthful.

"It's always the same. It always has been. You're such a little wonder boy, aren't you? The hard-working student with his fancy new school and his sports trophies and now a cutesy little girlfriend to top it all off. So sickeningly perfect!"

"I was just asking if you were okay, for God's sake. This has got nothing to do with me—"

"It's got everything to do with you!" she snapped, throwing her teaspoon into the sink with a clatter and glaring at me. "Because everything is always about you! How well you're doing at school, how well you're doing on the running track, whether you're being stretched enough, whether you're working hard enough…"

"Jesus, I'm sorry for even asking!"

"God, I had to literally be thrown off my A levels before anyone even noticed I was struggling! Whereas you, you somehow deserve constant attention, constant monitoring—"

"Do you think I like having Mum on my back all the time?! Do you think I like feeling as if I have to measure up to her expectations?!"

"Yes! I think you fucking love it! Because it makes you her golden boy, the one who gets all the attention! Just like you always have done!"

"That's crap, Laura."

"Really? Then how come you're the only one asking if I'm okay? I mean, I can literally do anything, can't I? I can lose my job, stay out night after night, hang out with anyone and nobody really gives a crap, do they? Where as *you*, *you're* a different matter. Everything *Jamie* does has to be considered in the minutest detail to make sure he's achieving his potential—"

"And do you think that's *fun* for me?! Don't you think that's stressful, having to worry all the time about whether I'm worthy of all this money they're spending on me, whether I'm going to do well enough—"

"I think that's love!"

We glared at each other, eyes blazing.

"You know, I have memories of me and Mum when I was little," said Laura, sadly, "spending time together, doing stuff, being happy. And Dad. I remember potting plants with him, building that little wall at the end of the garden, making that old rope swing. But now, he's always out there in his workshop, and if he spends time with anyone, then it's always you—"

"But it takes two, Laura. I've seen Dad try to make conversation with you and you give nothing back. And the only reason I'm the one hanging out with him is because I actually like learning some of the stuff he can teach me. If you want to learn how to, I don't know, build a circuit board or whatever, then you can just as easily go hang out—"

"But why should I have to?! Why can't people come to *me*, ask what *I'm* up to, what *I* want to talk about?!"

"Because we've all given up trying! You give nothing! You're never here for a start, and when you are, you barely do more than grunt at people! It has to work both ways! You're always just so… so mean! And angry! And no one ever knows what the hell about!"

"I'm angry at you! *You're* the one I'm angry with! Because before you came along, *I* mattered! But I stopped mattering because clearly I was never going to fulfil Mum's ambitions for her, so what the hell was the point in me?!"

I slammed my plate down on the kitchen table, refusing to be the scapegoat for all her problems.

"Well, I'm sorry for being born!" I yelled.

"Good! Because I wish you never had been!"

She strode straight past me and slammed the kitchen door behind her, leaving me with the echo of her hate-filled words.

I remember how Josh stood in the corner of the lounge, his face pressed against the wall, while Hellie crouched down nearby and tried to coax him out of his hiding spot.

"Come on, Joshie, come and give Mummy a hug."

I hovered in the background, barely able to watch, but unsure whether to intervene.

Defeated, Hellie sighed, stood up and turned to me.

"What's going on with him?" she frowned.

I stared at her, stunned by her question. Her fair hair had been bleached almost white by the Californian sun, and her skin has acquired a bronzed glow. The American in her accent had strengthened to the point that it now overpowered the blend of Scandinavian and cut-glass English. Everything about her testified to the length of time she'd been away, and yet her ice-blue eyes searched my face, waiting for an answer as to why her son was rejecting her.

"What do you mean, what's going on with him?" I asked, incredulous. "He's confused. You've been gone three months. He needs time—"

"Time for what? I'm his mum."

I held my palms out, dumbfounded by her stupidity.

"Are you turning him against me?" Hellie asked, eyeing me suspiciously.

"What the…? You're kidding me, right? You've been gone more than you've been here for the last year, and you're blaming *me* for the fact he's acting like this!"

"I don't know what you tell him about me when I'm not here," she stated, calmly.

"I don't tell him anything! What the hell would I tell him? I don't know what you're up to any more than he does!"

"I just don't think this behaviour's normal," she said, gesturing to the tiny figure in the corner.

"Of course it's not normal! But it's not normal that his mother's never here!"

"I was raised by nannies all over the world. I went to boarding schools from the age of seven. I was sent to board in the UK when I was twelve. But do I treat my parents like this?"

"Yes! Your parents email *me* to find out what's happening with you because they haven't heard from you in months!"

"Look," said Hellie, holding her palms up to me in a futile gesture that was somehow intended to calm the situation, "I do appreciate what you're doing here—"

"You *appreciate* it?!"

"I do. I know at the moment my career is taking me away a lot—"

"Your *career*?" I laughed, bitterly. "Is that what you call it?"

"—but maybe if he had a bit more structure, a bit less chaos," she said, gesturing around her. "Children need order."

I followed her eyes around the lounge, taking in the mess. My sister – on a break from the most recent boyfriend – had temporarily moved back into her room, and Michael – when he wasn't spending the night with God knows who doing God knows what – was sleeping on the couch. My dad – increasingly confused and erratic in his behaviour – was spending most his time tinkering in his workshop, and I was back at college, now on a vocational training course while trying to juggle parenthood. If it wasn't for Brenda doing most of the washing and cleaning and cooking, I think we'd have descended into total chaos. As it was, toys and games littered the lounge floor, along with guitars, bags, blankets, books… But despite the disarray, every single one of us cared for Josh, played with him, read to him, tickled him, held him. Did Hellie seriously think the *mess* was the problem?

"You know, if you need money for a nanny or childminder or whatever they're called," said Hellie, scanning the mess, "then my parents—"

"I don't want your parents' money!" I yelled in disbelief. "He's *our* son, *we* need to support him! I don't want a penny from your parents, I just want to stop living in limbo, waiting to see what you're going to do next!"

Three years of suppressed rage rose up in me like molten lava pushing up through a volcano. Three years of sleepless nights, exhaustion, confusion, not knowing whether she was staying or going, trying to be patient for the sake of our son. Three years of shelving every one of my own needs, hopes and ambitions while she swanned around the world on her trust fund, doing whatever the fuck she wanted. Three years of responsibilities I'd never imagined having at the age of twenty, all on my shoulders. I clenched my jaw so hard I thought I might crack my back teeth.

"You," I said quietly, my voice trembling with barely contained anger, "are the issue here, Hellie. Not me. *I'm* here. *I'm* the one up in the night because he's upset over you leaving again. *I'm* the one dealing with the fits of anger after you've gone. *I'm* the one dealing with the endless questions about where you are, the acting out, the scribbling on the walls, the bed wetting, the refusal to speak for hours on end. And the reason he's doing those things is because of *you*, not *me*!"

Hellie crossed her arms and shook her head at the ceiling dismissively.

"You need to decide if you're in or out, Hellie," I told her, "because you can't keep doing this to him. You need to make a choice. Not just about whether to be physically here or not, but about whether to be a mother. Because, let's face it, even when you're here you're not. You talk to him and play with him for a couple of hours and then you're off out again, bored by him."

"That's not true—"

"Of course it's true!" I shouted, wringing my hands through my hair, unable to believe that she could deny it.

"And so you're the perfect dad now, are you?" she said, colour raising in her cheeks.

"I'm *here*!" I yelled in exasperation. "I'm not perfect, but I'm *here*! Which is where you should be, but you're not because you're too selfish!"

"I'm not selfish!" she snapped. "But the opportunities to do the things I want aren't here on this crappy little island!"

"You should have thought about that before having a baby! And maybe before lying to me about being on the pill!"

"I didn't lie," she spat.

"Whatever," I retorted.

We'd been here before. More than once she'd told me she wasn't on the pill when we slept together, that she'd lied in order to get me to sleep with her. It was because she'd wanted a baby, wanted to piss her parents off, wanted to trap me… the reason changed each time. And then she'd change her mind, say she'd just been messing with me, that of course she'd been on the pill, why the hell would she have intended to get pregnant? One thing I'd found out too late about Hellie was that she liked to screw with your head. I didn't know what the truth was. What did it even matter?

"You need to make up your mind, Hellie," I said, my hands balled into fists at my side, "because we can't go on like this. I mean, what even *is* this?" I asked, gesturing between her and myself. "You live here, sort of, when you can be bothered, but why? We're not a couple, we never will be. This whole situation is just so fucked up! I can't go on like this. I need to know what's happening, and you need to decide if you're in or out!"

"You can't give me an ultimatum!" she snapped.

"I'm not giving you an ultimatum, I'm asking you to make a fricking choice!"

"You can't demand that I make a choice!"

"And I can't let you keep on doing this to him! He doesn't

understand what's going on! It would be different if you actually acted like you gave a shit when you were here, but you don't!"

"Don't tell me what I can and cannot do," she said sternly, "I'm his mother. I can take him with me right now if that's what I choose to do."

I froze, chills running up my spine. Could she do that? Would she? It had never occurred to me she could take him, simply because she'd never shown anything but a fleeting interest in him. But suddenly it seemed like exactly the kind of erratic, impulsive thing she might try to do just to spite me.

Overtaken by a sense of panic and fury, I suddenly found myself up close in her face. "If you ever try to take him from me…" I spat at her through clenched teeth, but I didn't know how to finish the sentence. Then what? What would I do?

Hellie glared at me. Then she shook her head slowly and turned away with a sigh, as if she'd had enough, as if this just wasn't worth the fight. She gathered up her jacket and the two holdalls that only an hour earlier she'd dumped on the armchair and walked out of the lounge. A few seconds later I heard the front door click shut.

As if emerging from a nightmare, I took stock of my surroundings, my hands trembling with rage. It was only then that I spied Josh in the corner, his face still buried silently against the wall. I couldn't believe we'd just left him there, a forgotten witness to our bitterness and threats. His two parents at war with one another. Me, who'd sworn and shouted and let my fury pour out. And Hellie, who'd left without even glancing back at him.

I remember sitting on an upturned crate, Max next to me, watching the remains of the polar bear burning on the fire, his black eyes gazing up at me pathetically.

The Leader – his long, skinny arm draped over Tom's shoulder, the knife dangling from his hand – was talking drunkenly in faltering English about leadership, respect, his country, his people. His victim was still lying face-down by the fire, unmoving, defeated.

The four of us kept looking at each other, wide eyes darting in the flickering light, asking the same silent question: how the hell do we get out of here?

Suddenly an argument erupted between the Leader and his two henchmen, Snake Eyes and Muscles, as I'd come to think of him, due to the bulk of his biceps. Muscles, until this point, had been fairly quiet, but now angry words flew back and forth between the three of them in a language we didn't understand. The Leader removed his arm from Tom's shoulder and drunkenly squared up to Snake Eyes. He snatched the bottle out of his hand, threw it to the ground, where it smashed, and shouted furiously, waving the knife in Snake Eyes' face.

The four of us eyed each other desperately, unsure what to do. Were things about to get really nasty? Was this a chance to make an escape?

As the arguing continued, their victim on the ground rolled over slowly. He raised his head off the dry earth, looked around him as if seeking someone out, and then settled his gaze upon me. One of his eyes had swollen shut. His lip was cut and bleeding, his nose bruised. But he was still recognisable to me. It was the black hair that gave him away. And the chequered shirt.

Hey, dude...

The fire cast flickering light and shadow across Rocket's face. He mouthed something at me as best he could with his damaged mouth, but I couldn't make it out.

And then I got it.

Run, he was saying. *Run*.

I glanced anxiously at Tom, who caught my eye.

It was now or possibly never.

I looked at Rocket lying on the ground. I'd get help, I'd

get the police. But I couldn't do anything for him unless I got out of here.

And so I jumped up from the crate, grabbing Max and pulling him after me. Immediately, Tom burst into action, running into Michael and pushing him forward. But Muscles spied us and shouted. Moving swiftly, the Leader stepped in front of me, holding out the knife. With a burst of adrenaline, I knocked his arm out of my way and pushed on through, all four of us making a desperate bid for freedom.

Out of the corner of my eye, I saw the two henchmen make a sudden move to come after us.

And then there was a cry of pain.

I stopped and turned, saw Rocket crawling on the ground, the broken bottle glistening in in his outstretched hand. And the Leader cursing, clutching at his calf.

The two henchmen wavered, unsure whether to pursue us or return to their leader's side.

"Jay, come on!" I heard Tom yell.

I glanced at my hand. Blood was dripping from my palm where I'd knocked the knife out of the way, but I felt no pain.

I couldn't go back. The only thing I could possibly do now was get help.

I took one last glance at Rocket and ran.

Chapter 13

Complicated

Josh and I step out onto the terrace at the Canal House, mugs of tea in our hands, courtesy of a blurry-eyed Stu, who's busy tidying up inside following last night's engagement celebrations. Irena's still cocooned in bed, suffering from morning sickness. It's half nine on Sunday morning, and apart from the chinking of bottles being tidied away, the place is quiet, the air bright and still.

"Thank you *so* much for coming," beams Libby, squinting against the morning sunshine, a paintbrush dangling from her hand. She's wearing loose cotton trousers and a khaki shirt that are both splattered with white paint. She looks tired. Without make-up and with her hair tied back, her scar stands out, pale pink and shiny. Guilt forces me to avert my eyes.

"I'm really grateful for the help," Libby smiles. "I think once this base coat's done, I'll be fine, I just had no idea it would take so long. I thought one coat would be enough, but it's not and..."

"It's fine," I reassure her, and then gesture behind me. "Libby, this is Josh. Josh, Libby."

"Hi," smiles Libby, giving him a little wave.

"All right?" he nods, awkwardly.

Libby continues to stare at him, searching his features.

Josh shuffles self-consciously and stares at his pristine trainers.

"I really do appreciate your help," she tells him, shaking away whatever thoughts she'd been having. "This might not be much fun for you—"

"It's not meant to be fun," I interrupt, "it's punishment."

I grab his arm and hold it up for Libby to see. A red-raw strip of skin runs down the inside of his forearm. Hard, white specks of superglue are still stuck here and there.

"Ouch!" she recoils, as Josh snatches his arm back and glares at me.

"Punishment for being an idiot," I clarify.

"Oh, well," sighs Libby, "we all do silly things when we're teenagers, don't we?" She raises an eyebrow pointedly at me and smiles.

Josh smirks. She's already won him over.

"Yeah, Dad," he mumbles. "I mean, I got a bit of glue on my arm, you got thrown out of school and had a baby... We all do dumb stuff, don't we?"

I shoot him a warning glance and he rolls his eyes defiantly before wandering over to inspect the paint pots and brushes that have been laid out on old sheets.

I shake my head despairingly at Libby and we both snigger a little as if to say *Kids!* Again, I wonder how we got to this point, to this age where we're the grown-ups.

"So..." I open, taking a sip of hot tea and trying to hide the fact I've just scalded my lip.

Libby smiles at me, waiting. I nod towards the half-painted wall, unable to swallow.

"Oh! Right!" she exclaims, remembering why I'm here. "So, just grab a brush and get stuck in basically!"

I place my tea down on one of the tables. Breadcrumbs, bits of gherkin and smears of tomato sauce still litter the terrace from last night, the barbecue now cold in the corner.

"How much needs doing?" Josh asks, his eyes following the line of the wall as if this is a Herculean task.

"All of it," I tell him, in a tone that implies this should be obvious.

He stretches his arms up high, revealing a pale, lean midriff that doesn't match the rest of the tan he's picked up over the summer. "Seriously?" he mutters through a yawn.

"He hasn't seen half nine on a Sunday morning for a while," I tell Libby in a low voice.

"Yeah, I think I could have done with more sleep myself," she says, rubbing her temple. "And much less wine. I hope I didn't say anything… I mean, you know, if I said anything weird, then just forget—"

"No," I tell her, reassuringly, "you didn't say anything—"

"Oh good, 'cause I have a tendency to talk rubbish after one glass of wine, let alone three. Well, I have a tendency to talk rubbish all the time, but… Oh! How was your dad?"

We crouch down next to each other and start painting, while Josh takes a paint pot and brush to the other end of the wall, as far away from us as possible.

"He was… umm…" *Violent? Aggressive? Offensive?* "… He was okay. It was just a bad evening."

"Is he…?"

"He has Alzheimer's." I spit it out quickly, the words still carrying their sting even after all these years.

"Oh my God, I'm so sorry," she says, stopping what she's doing and looking at me.

I paint silently, staring straight ahead, my grip tightening on the brush, pushing down my own anger and sadness, willing her to stop looking at me. After a while, she resumes her own painting.

"He was diagnosed when Josh was four," I tell her, wondering why I always measure my life by my son's age, as if my own existence is merely a shadow of his. Do all parents do that? "It had been clear for a while things weren't right, though. I think I was just in denial. But we're sort of at the stage now… well, it's getting harder."

"Does he live by himself?"

"No. He's still in the house. I mean, you know, our family house. But he has a partner. Brenda. They got together not long after my mum left. She moved in after he got his diagnosis. Josh and I had to move out at that point, so she kind of stepped in."

"You moved out because he was ill?"

For a moment it sounds like an accusation, but when I glance at Libby's face, I see nothing but concern and a desire to understand. No one's accusing me of abandoning my dad but me.

"I couldn't have Josh around him," I rush to explain. "Having a young child around... All the noise and chaos, it wasn't doing my dad any good. He'd get angry and flustered. Plus, he'd get confused. He'd think Josh was me when I was little, and then he'd get confused about who *I* was, and who everyone else was... In the end, he started doing dangerous things: leaving the gas on, leaving the front door open... He started a fire in the kitchen one day, that was pretty much the final straw..."

I trail off, guilty for revealing these details about my dad who'd always been such a calm, private, capable person. In his rare moments of lucidity, he'd always been mortified by his own behaviour, and so I kept his secrets for him, told no one who didn't need to know. Or at least that was normally the case.

"I'm so sorry," says Libby again, her voice full of sympathy, "it must so hard for you all. Your dad was always so competent, wasn't he? I mean, with all the things he used to build, and his teaching... he was so clever. And so patient. I remember how he taught me all about a car engine, took it all apart, showed me how it all worked."

"Yeah, we were meant to be going to the cinema to see *X-Men* and we missed the start," I say, smiling at the memory.

"And you were annoyed."

"I thought you were just trying to get out of seeing it."

"No, I was genuinely fascinated by what he was teaching me!"

"I realised that later."

"And we ended up running to the cinema with me covered in grease and oil!"

"And you spent the whole film asking what was happening because we'd missed the beginning."

"I did that with every film—"

"Yes, you did! Every film we ever watched, you spent the whole time asking who everyone was and what was going on and I always wondered how someone so clever—"

"It used to really irritate you!"

"Because I couldn't concentrate and then *I* didn't know what was going on!"

We laugh at the memory of it.

"I'm still just as bad with films, you know. It drives Will crazy. I don't know what it is. He says I just have appalling concentration."

We fall silent for a moment, the mention of Will bringing us back to the present time.

"Nah, you were just bored by most of the mainstream crap that was out there," I tell her. "You used to like all that arty stuff, independent films, things with subtitles."

"I still do. Although Will won't watch them with me, so I just don't bother normally. It's no fun watching films on your own, is it?"

I disagree with her, but I don't say so. I've spent hours sitting in the dark watching films in blissful solitude, so long I can't imagine it being any other way.

"Well," I say, searching for something that will take us back to where we were a minute ago, pre-Will, pre-the-stress-of-adulthood, "I never did get to find out what happened at the start of *X-Men,* so if you ever find out—"

"You'll be the first to know," she laughs.

We paint quietly for a while. Josh has his headphones in, and he's painting slowly, sloppily, with the same minimum effort he affords most tasks.

"So," starts up Libby again, "when you moved out of your house, what did you do? Where did you and Josh go?"

"Well, at that point Brenda moved in. And she had a little flat on the outskirts of Woodside – right down the road from where Michael grew up actually – and the mortgage was paid off and everything, so she let me and Josh move in there. The primary school was one of the best in the county."

"Yeah, that's a nice part of town."

"Really nice. The flat was tiny. Just one bedroom, so I spent the next four years sleeping in the lounge, but I don't really know what we would have done otherwise. I mean, even once I started working, I wasn't earning anything near enough to rent somewhere."

"But how did you manage? I mean, with work and childcare…"

"Actually my sister was…" *Argumentative? Erratic? A bitch?* "…amazing, if you can believe that."

Libby eyes me like I've lost my mind.

"Yeah, I know! But, seriously, she adjusted her working hours to do school drop-offs, she covered sports days if I couldn't be there. I honestly don't know what I would have done without her. Or Michael. I mean, without the two of them…"

I don't mention the ups and downs, the fact that Michael was sometimes like a second dad to Josh – chipping in with school pick-ups, taking him to the park on the weekends when I had to work – and at other times incapable of getting out of bed or lifting his head off the floor. I know other people might question my judgement, but he was one of the few people I always trusted with my son. The only person Michael had ever been a risk to was himself.

"And your mum?"

I shake my head and no doubt make a poor job of hiding my bitterness.

"Nope. She made promises before Josh was born about how she'd help with everything, but once she'd moved out… I mean, she helped a bit at first, but then, after about a year, she followed Jack to Ireland, got a lecturing job. We barely spoke for years."

"My God, it's so weird how things turn out, isn't it? How people surprise you – in good ways or bad."

"Sure is," I mutter, trying not to dwell on thoughts of my mum. Over the years, my anger's dissipated, and I've started to see her side of things. She was right, I guess; I made my bed, it was my job to lie in it. But still, when I look at Josh now, not far off the age I was when Hellie got pregnant, I still wonder how she could have abandoned me to it.

"I mean, look at you," piped up Libby, "who would have thought you'd cope with a child? You were just a boy who didn't know how to boil an egg… I mean, literally!"

I nod and smile. "And you thought that was outrageous."

"It was outrageous! Fifteen years old and no egg-boiling ability! You couldn't work your washing machine, didn't know how the iron worked, couldn't read bus timetables because Mummy and Daddy used to drive you everywhere—"

"Yeah, okay, okay."

"Couldn't even work the oven! Do you remember when you tried to cook me a special meal for my birthday and it was still raw?"

"Yeah, all right," I smile, "just because you were little Miss Independent. I was your average teenage boy—"

"But look at what you did!" She looks over at Josh, staring again like she's never seen a human boy before. "You raised a son. On your own."

"Oh no, not on my own," I protest.

"Well, as a single parent, I mean. And he seems like a good boy. I mean, he's here first thing on a Sunday morning—"

"Not through choice, I promise you."

"Nevertheless. It's impressive. I'm really proud of you."

I turn to her, surprised, and she blushes, before quickly going back to her painting.

"I mean, *you* should be proud of *yourself*," she says with an awkward laugh.

I watch Josh, lazily painting away, nodding his head to whichever black-eyed androgynous vocalist is attempting to burst his eardrums today. It's never occurred to me that I should be proud of myself. Proud of him, yes, but not of myself. I've always seen myself as someone who screwed up, had a child too young with a girl I barely knew, wasted my education, wasted my opportunities. I dwell on the things I haven't provided for my son – a nice home, a proper family unit, a range of horrendously expensive extracurricular activities that a lot of his friends seem to have access to. A mother. He should have had so much more.

"So, anyway," I say, not used to talking so much about myself, "what about you?"

"What about me?"

"Well, what did you do after..." *After I broke your heart? After I screwed up that great thing we had?* "...you know, after you left here?"

"Well, like I said, I went to uni, flunked out of that, did various jobs, rented various rooms, moved about a bit. Then I met Will." She shrugs, as if the rest should be self-explanatory.

"So, what about all the stuff you wanted to do?"

"Trek the Andes, traverse the desert plains on camel back, do an archaeological dig in Egypt...?"

"For starters."

She laughs. "Well, it turns out you need this little thing called *money*."

"Ah yes, I know it well. Or not so well, in fact."

"Likewise. And... I don't know... I suppose if I'd really wanted those things that much I would have worked harder, made them happen. But perhaps I changed, too. Or perhaps I was never really that person in the first place. Perhaps that was just the hippy-chick I thought my mum wanted me to be."

"Sounds like where you are now couldn't be more different. About to marry a City boy, settle down in a nice part of town, have a couple of kids, start shopping at Waitrose..."

I'm just toying with her, but she playfully takes the bait.

"That's right," she quips, "I'll be off in my Audi to stock up on quinoa…"

"… And organic baby food…"

"… Choosing a kitchen island…"

"… For your massive house in Woodside."

She laughs. "Will's not *that* rich. We can't *all* have the privilege of living in such a posh area, sending our kids to the county's best school."

"Yeah, well, I admit I got lucky there for a while. Although I felt like a right fraud. The parents at that school used to look at me like I was scum."

"Seriously?"

"God, yeah. I was just some scruffy young bloke always turning up late to everything, always rushing, never seemed to have the right bag or book or paperwork…"

"Well, I promise that when I'm dropping off little Tarquin and Geraldine, I won't look down on any teenage, single parents that cross my path."

"You'll just mow them down in your Audi."

"Damn right I will."

"Tarquin and *Geraldine*?"

"Well, I don't know. What do posh people call their kids these days?"

"I have no idea. Josh used to have a Sebastian in his class at primary school. And a Portia."

"Oh, Portia. Good one. Portia and Sebastian it is then."

"I'm holding you to that."

Libby chuckles.

"God, listen to me," she sighs, "you must think I'm a right sell-out, abandoning all those ambitions for a quiet life in the suburbs. It's certainly what my mother thinks, anyway. The idea that I'm actually marrying a man – *enslaving* myself to him – is bad enough, but the fact that we're planning a *nice* wedding and planning on *buying* a house… all materialistic, capitalist blah blah blah."

"But I thought you said *she* was in a house now?"

"Ah, well, that's an interesting point, the irony of which is not lost on me, but apparently is on her. But it's different, you see, because she rents her house with two artists and a lesbian reiki master, and apparently it was their destiny to come together, and it's a communal living arrangement, and they grow their own organic chard…"

"Ah, well, for a minute I thought she was being hypocritical, but if she grows her own chard…"

"Yeah, that makes all the difference, doesn't it?"

I notice she's slapping her paint on a bit more vigorously, and it's clear that she's outgrown the unquestioning adoration she once had for Harmonie. I can relate to the disappointment and anger at finding out your parents were never perfect like you thought, that they were just human all along. It's a universal rite of passage. Josh used to tell me I was the best daddy in the world. Now he rolls his eyes at me every day in distain, each of my flaws and weaknesses magnified by his critical teenage eye.

"Well, I don't think there's anything wrong with wanting a bit of security in life," I tell Libby, wanting to reassure her. "I know it was hard for you growing up. You never had much—"

"That's not actually why I'm *marrying* Will," she says, eyeing me like I've just accused her of being a gold-digger.

"No, God, I didn't think… I mean, I know that. I just meant you shouldn't let your mum make you feel guilty—"

"I don't."

"Oh, okay, it just sounded—"

"Well, I mean I *do*, obviously, because it all goes against my upbringing and she *tries* to make me feel guilty. But, unfortunately, I didn't fall in love with some lentil-eating cloth-weaver – although Lord knows she tried to introduce me to enough of them – I fell in love with Will."

I feel a stab of jealousy, followed by a flash of anger with myself. What the hell is the matter with me?! She's not mine anymore. She's not *mine*!

"Well, that's good," I say firmly, concentrating hard on the strokes of my brush, the white gradually covering over the brickwork, "that's good that you're... that you found someone who makes you happy. That's all that really matters."

I'm struck by how much I mean it, how much I want her happiness. She deserves it. She deserves the love, the family, the security that she always craved, and if that happens to come with a few nice things, then all the better. And no one should ever make her feel bad about it.

"If Will makes you happy, then it sounds like you've found what's right for you," I tell her.

She dips her brush in the paint pot and stirs it around again and again. I watch her out the corner of my eye. She looks lost in thought.

"Well, exactly," she mutters, stirring slowly, "I mean, that's what really matters."

She keeps stirring for so long that I wonder what to say. Does she look sad?

I'm about to ask if she's okay when she looks up, a smile plastered back on her face.

"Your tea's getting cold," she says.

We talk more about our families, our jobs, the changes in Timpton. It feels strange, having an adult conversation with her. We used to talk excitedly about our hopes, dreams and ambitions. Now she's trying to explain Will's plan to get an off-set mortgage and we're lamenting the arrival of a Wetherspoon's in the town. As we fill each other in on the details of our lives, it all seems so far from what we had once envisaged when we were young and the world was full of possibilities.

She asks about Michael, but I'm careful what I say, protective of his privacy. We also touch briefly on Tom and Max, but there's not much to say there. I'm not going to tell her about my plan. I don't want her knowing she was just the first step in my strategy to move on from the past, the first person on my list of people to go and see.

In the moments of silence, memories of our shared past flood my mind. Some of them are innocent and some are intimate. Either way, it doesn't feel right to bring them up between us like some kind of shared secret, not when she's engaged to someone else. Besides, she might not remember. Relationship-wise, she moved on years ago to something far more serious, far more grown-up than anything we ever had. It's just me that got stuck.

But it's okay. Because the more we talk about where we are now, the more I'm assured that this is not the same Libby I used to know. This isn't the girl I held in my arms, the one who was so full of life and dreams and a thirst of knowledge. This is a grown woman, with stresses and responsibilities just like me. We're totally different people to who we were back then, and it's good to realise this. It's helping me let go. Whatever fantasy I've been entertaining all these years, I'm reminded that it's just that: a fantasy.

Finally, we meet Josh towards the end of the wall. He hasn't covered much ground, but at least it's something.

"Oh my God, my back's killing me," he groans, stretching out.

"You're the young one! You shouldn't be complaining," teases Libby.

"Yeah, stop whinging," I tell him, flicking my paintbrush out and slapping a bit of white paint on his arm.

"Hey!" he cries. He hastily swipes back at me with his own paintbrush, but I dodge him. Somehow he ends up painting his own elbow.

"Ah, man!" he cries, and I laugh.

"Boys, boys," chides Libby.

Josh goes for me again, a bit more aggressively this time, and daubs paint on my wrist.

"Whoa, it's a draw," I tell him, holding my hands up in surrender.

"Thank you so much for your help," Libby interrupts, "I really do appreciate you both giving up your Sunday morning."

"No problem," I tell her, "we weren't doing anything. In fact, our Sunday mornings have just become free, so any more help you need…"

I stare purposefully at Josh, who rolls his eyes slightly. He recently decided to quit kickboxing, something we've been doing together every Sunday morning for the past two years, and I'm not happy about it. It's a big, bad world out there and I've had him doing everything from karate to judo to taekwondo since he was eight years old. But he gets bored, impatient, restless. I worry that he's inherited his mother's inability to stick with anything.

"Well, I need to start painting the sky next, which is really easy," Libby says with a cheeky smile, "so if you ever fancy trying your hand with a bit of blue…"

The playful tone to her voice suggests she's joking, but I can tell there's also a little bit of desperation in there. She's not seriously expecting us to give up more of our time, but clearly she feels a little overwhelmed by this project. The problem is that I was only joking, too. I wasn't really expecting to come back. I was just trying to get Josh to reconsider his Sunday-morning options, using a little reverse psychology. In fact, the idea of coming back suddenly fills me with turmoil. Because the truth is that I've enjoyed working alongside Libby today. Far too much. And whatever I might tell myself about how getting to know the older, changed version of her is helping me move on, it's not. It's really, really not.

"Umm… yeah," I shrug, feeling cornered, "I'm sure we can help again. Oh, but, unless…" I look to Josh hopefully, "was there something else we needed to do next Sunday?"

Surely, he's got to think kickboxing is better than this, I think. *Surely.* But, of course, he's not going to let me win. He'd rather drag himself out of bed at nine o'clock every weekend than let me back him into a corner.

"No," he says, pointedly, "we're totally free next Sunday."

"Are you sure there's not something—"

"Nope. Totally free."

The charged glare we exchange would be imperceptible to anyone else.

I look to Libby and manage to muster a smile. "Count us in."

"Oh, that would be great!" she grins. "I promise it's nothing harder than today. I'll do all the detailing afterwards, I just need you to slap on a few different hues of blue."

I take in her brown eyes sparkling with relief, her warm smile, the streak of white paint in her hair... Oh God, what have I got myself into?

At eleven o'clock that evening, I'm sprawled on the sofa, illuminated only by the light of the television. I was looking forward to catching up with the latest episode of *The Walking Dead*, but I don't think I've heard a word of it. Hollow-eyed zombies parade in front of my vision as I stare blankly at the screen.

I can't decide whether this morning was a step in the right direction or a disaster. I mean, this is what I wanted, wasn't it? To build bridges with Libby, to know she's okay, to feel forgiven. I never dreamed that we'd be able to laugh together again, that we'd build something of a friendship. But I also wanted to let go of her, of the pull I had towards the past. Instead, my memories have been reawakened. They race through my mind more vibrantly, more clearly and with more feeling than ever before.

Really, when I think about it, though, this was bound to happen. Seeing her again was always going to stir up feelings. Perhaps I'm just confused as to what those feelings are. Perhaps I think they're something they're not. Yeah, I think I just underestimated the effect seeing her again would have. I think I'm just muddling up my feelings now with my feelings from the past. I think it'll be fine. I think it'll all settle down. I think the more I see her, the easier it will get. Or perhaps I should see less of her. Maybe I shouldn't see her at all. In fact, I think what I really need to do is get back in the game, get out there, start dating again...

"What are you doing?"

I look up with a start to find Josh standing in the doorway, wearing tracksuit bottoms and his bed T-shirt.

"Just watching TV," I tell him, but when I glance at the screen, I find the programme's finished, and all that's showing is the TV menu.

"Why are you lying in the dark with your arms wrapped over your face?"

"Was I?"

Josh wanders over to the sofa, muttering something about me being a weirdo, before grabbing my ankles and pulling them off the sofa. He slumps down next to me.

"Aren't you meant to be in bed?" I ask him.

"Can't sleep."

"Everything okay?"

He gazes blankly at the screen.

"Anything you want to talk about?"

He sighs quietly.

"Did you ever…" he begins and then falters, "…did you ever fall for someone that it would have been better not to have fallen for? Like, you wish you didn't like them because it's way too complicated, but you just can't help it?"

I unwittingly let out a stifled laugh, struck by the irony of his question. A couple of weeks ago, the answer would have been a resounding no. I've strictly avoided complications where matters of the heart have been concerned. Any relationships I've had have been simple, straightforward, brief. I haven't "fallen" for anyone.

But now here I am, going around in circles, trying to convince myself that I don't feel whatever it is I feel for my soon-to-be-married ex-girlfriend. "Complicated" doesn't even begin to sum it up.

"Yeah, it's a bit crap when that happens, isn't it?" I sigh.

"It's not exactly convenient," he confirms.

"No, well, love isn't very convenient," I tell him, wearily. I almost add *and that's why I tend to avoid it*, but I don't want to inflict my cynicism onto him. I'm well aware that what I do isn't healthy. Hence why I set out to "fix" myself, starting with finding Libby and putting her in the past. Talk about digging yourself deeper.

I study Josh's profile in the blue glare of the television. He looks like he's got the weight of the world on his teenage shoulders. I wonder why he doesn't just come out and say it: that he likes Chloe but he doesn't know how to handle it. However, despite his need to share every single inane, superficial aspect of his life on social media, Josh can still be fiercely private when it comes to his genuine thoughts and feelings.

"So what's so complicated with... with this person, anyway?" I ask.

He shrugs. "I dunno. Everything. We're already friends and I don't want to put my feelings out there and risk ruining our friendship, but at the same time I really like them, and I think they feel the same but... I dunno, maybe it would be better to leave things as they are."

I remember the feeling of being fifteen, knowing I liked Libby but being too scared to tell her, wondering if I'd lose our friendship if I declared my feelings. I was glad I went for it though. So glad. Thinking this is a useful parallel, I share it with Josh, grasping the rare opportunity to impart some parental wisdom. He knows my relationship with his mother was just a one-off thing, that there's nothing useful I can offer him there in terms of relationship advice. But maybe there's something he can learn from my past experience with Libby.

"So how long were you two together for then?" he asks.

"Just over a year. "

"So were you, like, you know...?"

"No," I say adamantly, "we weren't. Because we were too young and not ready—"

"I was going to say were you in love with her," Josh hastily interrupts.

"Oh. Right. Well... yeah."

"How did you know?"

I shrug. "I dunno. I just knew. Why? D'you think you're in love?"

I hope I'm not pushing my luck here. I don't want him to clam up or, even worse, flee for his room. I can see this is tough for him, but, selfishly, part of me wants to string this out. This closeness, this sharing of confidences – it's precious, and becoming rarer year on year.

He sticks his lower lip out and shrugs slowly, studying his bare feet, wiggling his toes. "Maybe. I don't know. I mean, I think about them, like, non-stop. I mean, literally, they are, like, all I seem to be able to think about... Does that count as being in love?"

"God, I hope not," I mutter.

"Huh?"

"I mean, not necessarily," I correct myself hastily. "You can find yourself constantly thinking about someone for all kinds of reasons, can't you? Like, maybe they intrigue you, or... I don't know... you have a weird obsession of some kind—"

"What? I don't have some weird obsession!" he protests, eyeing me like I've lost my mind.

"I'm not saying you do. I just don't believe that thinking about someone all the time in itself means you're in love with them," I tell him. And myself.

"Yeah, I guess," he says thoughtfully. "But still. I think I am."

"Well, why would that be such a bad thing?"

He lets his head slump back against the sofa cushion. "Well, it's just not a simple situation, Dad."

"No. It rarely is."

We sit in silence for a moment, both of us lost in thought.

"So, you think I should just go for it?" he pipes up. "Just admit how I feel?"

"What's the worst that can happen?"

"Total and utter humiliation?"

"Or, they feel the same way and... bam."

"Bam?"

"Yeah. Bam."

"What's bam?"

"You know. Cupid's arrow. The big L. Destinies colliding…"

He rolls his eyes at me. I'm relieved to see a smile back on his face.

"Seriously, if you never take a risk you'll never know, will you?"

I say it as if it's a no-brainer, the simplest thing in the world, but I know full well I'm being a complete hypocrite. When it comes to matters of the heart, I stopped taking risks a long time ago. But if my son realises I'm a lying fraud, he doesn't show it.

Josh nods thoughtfully, stands up and stretches. "I'm going to bed."

I watch him go, knowing it's late and he must sleep but regretting that our moment of closeness has ended.

He stops in the doorway and turns around. "You don't, like, still have a thing for Libby or anything, do you?" he asks, tentatively.

"God, no!" I hear myself say a bit too quickly. "Why would you say that?"

"I just wondered. Like, 'cause of the way you were talking and laughing and stuff. I've just never really seen you like that with a woman before."

"Well, to be fair, you don't see me around that many women," I say.

He scratches at his messed-up hair. "I guess."

He heads out of the room.

"The big L," he chuckles quietly. "Oh my God, no wonder you're single."

When he's gone, I put my arms back over my face.

No, I don't have a "thing" for her, I think, annoyed by his insinuation. What I have is a bit of confusion. A bit of a mix-up in the wiring between my thoughts and my feelings. A bit of a tendency to retreat into the safety of the past. A bit of a hangover from earlier times.

What I absolutely, categorically, definitely do not have for Libby is a "thing".

Chapter 14

Denial

I remember a guy I didn't know sitting down next to me at the bar, slapping his hand on my shoulder and yelling something in my ear.

"What?!" I shouted over the chanting.

"I said your mate's a blast!"

I looked back to Michael, who was standing on a table in the centre of the room, a shot glass in each hand, commandeering the attention of a large group of people. Some of them were friends, some loyal fans, some were just people who saw the posters for Breaking Days and turned up to give the band a go. Michael had already entertained them with his music, but that wasn't enough for them. Or, it seemed, for him.

"Down it, down it!" they chanted.

Michael knocked the shots back to a resounding cheer. Part of me wanted to go over and tell him to stop, that he'd had enough and it was time to go, but I quashed the urge. I couldn't do that, not when he was having so much fun.

Some girl with one side of her head shaved grabbed the empty glasses from him and thrust his guitar into his hands.

"Play, play!" the chanting started up again.

"I can't hear you!" Michael yelled, putting his hand to his ear.

They chanted louder.

"You lot are insane!" he cried, throwing his head back and laughing. "Drinks all round!" he yelled to the bar staff. "On me!"

A loud cheer went up.

I glanced over at Tyler and Theo – Michael's bandmates – who were leaning further down the bar, swigging bottles of beer, observing his antics somewhat coldly. Through the dark hair that fell in sweaty strands over his face, Tyler met my eye. We all knew that Michael was struggling for money, and that anything he had managed to scrape together he owed to them. Studio time was expensive, as was publicity. There was some serious interest in the band, and it looked like they might be on the verge of a big break, but Michael was ruining their chances. He was unreliable, one minute bursting with the kind of energy, creativity and enthusiasm that would see him writing new material for two or three days straight, and the next flat and despondent, refusing to engage. Tyler and Theo looked like they were just about ready to walk, but everyone knew that without Michael they were nothing.

Michael wobbled on the table, stumbling towards the edge. Strangers' hands reached out and grabbed him, pushing him back onto his stage, demanding another song. He started to play. As the evening had gone on, his voice had acquired a raw, rasping edge to it that just made it all the better. He was forgetting words, missing the beat, but no one seemed to care.

A petite girl with short auburn hair and a lip piercing jumped up on the table beside him, lifted her arms high in the air and started to gyrate her hips in time with the music, displaying a dragon tattoo on her waist where her black vest top rose up. The crowd whooped and, spurred on by their attention, she tucked herself in tightly behind Michael, snaking one hand underneath his sweaty T-shirt. He grinned over his shoulder at her while he continued to play off-tune, and the crowd whistled and hollered.

"Jesus!" exclaimed the guy who had sat down next to me. "Your mate's having the time of his life, isn't he? Good on him!"

I watched Michael. His guitar was now gone – perhaps stolen by one of the crowd – while he entwined himself in an increasingly provocative embrace with the auburn-haired girl, his damp T-shirt being pushed higher over the white skin of his ribs while he clutched at her backside and the crowd hollered.

Yeah, he was having the time of his life. And like the guy said, good for him, right? I knew he wasn't always like this; that the self-doubt that had plagued his earlier years was still there, that he'd sometimes get so down that he didn't even want to get out of bed. So, when he was happy like this, exuding confidence, why would anyone want to stand in his way? This behaviour, it was good, wasn't it? Not the drinking maybe. But seeing him so excited, so full of life... Surely that was a sign he was doing better. It was a little extreme perhaps. A little excessive. He needed to curb the spending of money he didn't have, the endless stream of girls, the creative binges that lasted for days and left him exhausted... But still, anything was better than seeing him so low.

Yeah, this was good. He was showing signs of being a happier, more confident person than he ever had been. And so long as that was the case, then all the other behaviours would iron themselves out.

He'd be fine, I told myself. It was all fine.

I remember Mr Robson saying: "I want you to tell me the real reason you don't want to run anymore."

"I've told you the reason!"

I glared at him defiantly. He held my gaze with hard,

piercing eyes, the muscles in his jaw working. I looked down at my school shoes.

"I've told you the reason, sir," I repeated more respectfully.

"And I don't believe you, Lewis," he said sternly.

I shrugged, exhausted. Mr Robson might not have seen me running lately, but in my fitful dreams I never stopped. Night after night, my feet pounded the canal path, never taking me forward.

"Look, Lewis, the school are aware that you have been though a… distressing experience lately. But in the face of adversity we need to pick ourselves up, dust ourselves off and get back in the saddle. That's everything that this school stands for. We're all about raising resilient young men, and I wouldn't be doing my job if I were to make concessions and excuses for you and allow you to wallow in self-pity."

"I'm not wallowing—"

"Then what is it? Because I don't buy this excuse that you're too busy focusing on your exams, especially when all your teachers *and* your own mother informs me that's certainly not the case. And even if you have got a lot else on, is it acceptable to let your teammates down? Is it all right to just waste all the hard work and training you've put in? I don't think so."

He waited for me to respond, but I just stared at the school logo on the breast of his polo shirt, feeling anger rise in me. Whatever he thought he knew, it was all bullshit. He knew nothing.

"I think you're scared, Lewis."

"I'm not scared," I scoffed. "What would I even be scared about?"

"Failure," he said without missing a beat.

I rolled my eyes dismissively and shook my head.

He sighed, the severity in his features softening slightly, and shifted his weight. I could see his fingers wiggling inside the pockets of his regulation navy-blue tracksuit trousers.

"Your mother told me you were the one who ran to get help—"

"I just don't want to run anymore!" I snapped. "Why is it such a big deal? I'm bored of it. I'm just sick of running, that's all there is to it!"

"And I said, I don't believe you."

"I don't know what you want me to tell you! I hate running! I don't ever want to run again, okay? Ever!"

"Master Lewis—"

"Just fuck off!"

My voice echoed down the empty school corridor, bouncing off stone walls that had stood for hundreds of years, no doubt without witnessing such an offensive outburst. I could feel my face burning with anger. Mr Robson didn't look mad. He just looked disappointed.

But just then, Dr Turner, the Headmaster, appeared at the end of the corridor, fresh from the morning chapel service. He strode towards us, his black gown flowing behind him. He studied me coldly as he approached.

"Master Lewis!" he barked. "My office. Now."

I remember her asking me: "Did you see his face? Once he was dead?"

I nodded slowly, gazing at the shadows on her bedroom wall. My head felt woozy from the alcohol.

"What was it like?"

No one had ever asked me that question. No one, apart from Hellie, would have dared.

"Empty," I told her, "like he'd left. Like he'd upped and gone away in the time I'd been gone, and what was left was just an empty container."

We were sitting on her bed, her body warm next to mine. She hugged her legs and rested her head on her knees, waiting for me to tell her more.

"And so pale," I continued, "like all the blood had drained out of him."

"Did he look peaceful?"

I shook my head. "No. Not peaceful. Kind of… shocked."

"I remember watching my baby brother asleep in his cot," she said. "His eyes were just a tiny bit open. He looked so still and peaceful. I didn't know he was dead."

Out of the corner of my eye, I studied her pale, angular features. Her hair, white in the glow of her bedside lamp, fell around her face in gentle waves.

"I didn't want to tell anyone he was gone, so I just stood there looking at him."

"Why didn't you want to tell anyone?" I asked, a shudder running down my spine.

"Because then they would have moved him. And it would have all been over."

I leaned my head back against the wall, feeling the faint thud of music coming from the bedroom next door. Out in the corridor, two girls, drunk, laughed loudly on the way to their rooms. Tonight had been fun – kind of. We'd drunk cheap beer in the student union bar. She'd even got me to dance. And for a while I'd forgotten about everything. After all, hadn't that been the whole idea of coming here? I might have told my parents it was an opportunity to see Manchester Uni, get a taste of student life. Maybe I'd want to apply here next year, I told them. After doing far worse in my GCSEs than predicted, and having made a shaky start to my A levels, I think they were pleased I was taking any interest in my future. But in reality I just needed to flee, get away from everything that had happened back home – the night of the fairground, my own rage and fear, my suspension from school, Libby dumping me. And for a while it had worked. For a while I'd put it all out of my mind. But now here we were, Hellie and I, coming down from our high, talking about death and heartbreak, and suddenly I felt miserable again.

"I thought it must be nice," she muttered, "to be as peaceful as my baby brother. To just have everything go away."

She reached out and fiddled lazily with the strap of my watch.

"I tried to throw myself from a speeding car once," she added matter-of-factly.

I already knew this. The whole school did. Rumour had it that she'd been under some kind of psychiatric care for a while. Nothing Hellie Larsen ever did stayed quiet, and that's just as she wanted it. But what nobody ever knew was why she did it. For attention? To kill herself?

"Sometimes I just want to get out of myself," she said when I asked her, "get out of the moment I'm in. I guess it was just one of those times."

Her hand slid over mine.

"Don't you ever feel like that?"

The warmth of her touch felt good. I'd missed someone holding my hand, tucking their body next to mine.

I thought of Libby and my heart felt like it might break with the sense of loss.

And then anger rose in me. Anger at myself for having lost her, anger at her for having given up on me.

Yes, I knew what it was like to want to get out of yourself.

I knew, as soon as she kissed me, that I wasn't going to take this all the way. It would be too much too soon. I knew it was over with Libby, that I'd driven her away, but I'd always believed my first time would be with her, and it was too early to think differently.

But, just for that moment, kissing Hellie made everything feel better. It made me forget. And what did it matter anyway? What did anything matter anymore? It was only a kiss. Nothing more.

And then we found ourselves lying down, pressed together on her narrow mattress. So what? We could touch each other, even remove a couple of items of clothing. It meant nothing.

We could stop – *would* stop – soon. I wasn't going to take this all the way.

She was on the pill, she said. That's fine, I told her, but that's not where this is heading. However good it feels. However much it helps to take all the other thoughts and feelings away. This isn't what I came here for.

So we should stop.

Or we could take it a tiny bit further. Why not? Who gave a crap anyway? We were here now.

Just a little longer. Just a little bit more. Just because it felt so good.

But then I'd stop.

Because this really, really wasn't going all the way.

Chapter 15

Stars

After the night of the fairground, my friendship with Tom quickly withered. We were hostile towards each other. Angry. Stressed. We drank and fought. We should have spoken about it – all of us should have – but instead we bottled it up inside, not knowing how to express the things we'd felt that night. Fear. Panic. Helplessness. These weren't things we knew how to discuss. Instead, Tom buried himself in his schoolbooks, while I rebelled and barely looked at mine. Fast-forward a few months and Tom was preparing for university while I was up to my eyeballs in nappies.

I knew there was a good chance he wouldn't reply to my email. I had no right to ask for his help. He didn't owe me a thing. So when his reply popped up in my inbox, I opened it with trepidation. Would he tell me to shove it? Politely reply that the past was the past as far as he was concerned?

> *Jay*
> *Sorry for the slow reply. I was surprised to hear from you. It's been a long time.*
> *Yes, I think a meet-up is long overdue.*
> *Best*
> *Tom*

I'm not sure what to make of his tone. It doesn't sound like the Tom I used to know, but then again why would it? He's thirty-two now, a grown man. Still, I'm glad he's replied. There are things I want – things I need – to say to him.

I quickly tap out a reply and send it before I lose my nerve.

Tom
Thanks for agreeing to meet. I can come down to the hospital sometime in the next couple of weeks if that suits?
Jay

It feels cold, perfunctory, and matches the tone of his own email. It's sad that such a long, close friendship full of laughter and mockery and jibes has become a sterile exchange of words. He was my first friend, my closest friend, for so many years. Perhaps we'd be meeting once a week for a pint down the Canal House if the course of our lives hadn't taken such a sudden turn.

I delete the junk from my mailbox, thinking for the hundredth time that I should really get round to unsubscribing from all these things I unknowingly subscribed to in the first place. In fact, I'm deleting so fast, I almost don't notice it. It's only the first three letters of her surname embedded in the email address that make me stop in my tracks.

My stomach tenses. What the hell does she want?

I open the untitled message with a sense of dread.

Dear Jay
I hope you are well.
My parents have no doubt told you that I am currently living in New York. I intend to come over to the UK in the next couple of months and I would like to see Joshua. We haven't had much of a relationship over the past few years and I would like to address that.

Obviously I will work around whenever is convenient
for the both of you.
I look forward to hearing from you soon.
Love Hellie xx

My heart's pounding in my chest.
WHAT THE…??!!!

Luckily, it's Saturday afternoon and Josh is hanging out with Sam again, the two of them having become pretty much inseparable since the start of the summer.

I immediately call Michael, my hands trembling with anger.

"Yo," he answers, lazily. I wonder if I've just woken him. Given that he's a chronic insomniac, he chooses to nap at all kinds of hours. But his sleep patterns are the least of my worries.

"You won't believe this! She's just emailed me saying she wants to come and see Josh! No explanation as to why she suddenly wants to see him, apart from the fact that – quote – *we haven't had much of a relationship over the past few years.* How about NO fucking relationship?! And who's fault is that? She going to – quote – *work around what's convenient for us!* Can you believe this? I mean, what the hell?! She even put two fricking kisses on the end! I mean, why now? He's just going into his GCSE year and she thinks NOW is a good time to totally throw his life into chaos? This is just so bloody typical of her!"

My rant is initially met with silence. As I pace rapidly around the flat, I can hear Michael trying to kick his brain into gear.

"I take it we're talking about Hellie here?" he says, his voice dry and groggy.

"Well, who else would be this bloody inconsiderate?! I mean, so this is it? This is how she gets back in contact? After all these years? NO mention of whether *Josh* might like to see *her*! NO mention of whether I'm happy for her to come waltzing back into our lives! Just an assumption that it will be fine. She even called him Joshua. I mean, she never even called him that when she was here! When the hell have we ever called him that?!"

"Okay, okay, calm down," Michael soothes. "I know you must be shaken—"

"I'm not shaken, I'm fucking livid!"

"Okay, listen, you know she's not quite right. No sane person sends an email like that. She's not all there, clearly."

"Clearly!"

"Yeah, well, we know that, don't we? I take it you haven't told Josh about this."

"No, he's out."

"Okay. Look, I'll come over."

"No, don't come over. I just want to bash something and I don't want it to be you. I mean, seriously, is that what you do after twelve years? Just drop a few lines in an email? Is she out of her mind? What does she even want?!"

"I don't know, mate, she's a law unto herself. Maybe she's just decided she wants a relationship with him. Maybe she's been doing some soul-searching like you and wants to make amends for the past. I mean, we all make mistakes—"

"Oh my God, are you seriously sticking up for her?!"

"No. Calm down. I'm just saying you always knew this was likely to happen. You've always said it probably would. I'm just trying to guess what might be going on in her—"

"She must know this is his GCSE year, right? I mean, she was schooled in the UK, so she does know how important this year is, right?"

"It might not have even crossed her mind. I mean, it's not like she has any involvement in his education or—"

"Or anything. She's had absolutely no fucking involvement in anything! Her son nearly died and I didn't even know how to get hold of her! I just... I can't believe... I mean... AGGHHH!"

"What the hell did you just kick?"

"The sofa. Shit, I think I might have broken my toe."

"Look, take a deep breath and, whatever you do, don't reply. Give it at least forty-eight hours."

I slump down on the sofa and rub my foot, the phone clamped between my ear and shoulder.

"Jay?"

"What?!"

"Forty-eight hours."

"Yes, yes, okay. I heard you."

I sigh deeply.

"Anyway, sorry, how are you?" I ask, remembering he wasn't having the greatest week either.

"I'm okay."

"You feeling better now your meds have been sorted out?"

"Yeah, and I talked things through with Catherine, which helped."

"I woke you, didn't I?"

"It's okay, I needed to get up. Tyler and Theo are doing an acoustic set down at the Canal House later and I'm going to pop down for a bit. You wanna come?"

I almost jump at the chance. Anything to take my mind off this email. But then I realise that Libby will probably be there. I'm not sure I can handle any more emotional turmoil right now. Then again, I've already signed up to helping her paint tomorrow morning, so what difference does it make? Plus, I think it'll be okay. I've managed to put her out of my mind a bit the last couple of days. Perhaps whatever I thought I felt is dissipating with time.

"Yeah, I'll come down for a bit," I agree.

Once I hang up, I read through the email five more times, just to check it really is as outrageously brief and inappropriate as I remember. Josh is already struggling to focus on school. What's this going to do to him? And what's to say she can even be trusted? How many times did she let him down, tell him she'd be there when she wasn't, before she finally abandoned him all together? It's not that I don't want them to have a relationship. She's his mother. They *should* have a relationship. But I also need to protect him.

I know Michael's right and I should wait forty-eight hours before replying, but I'm also impulsive when I'm in a rage and prone to ignoring good advice.

Hellie
Why the hell have you decided now is a good time

DELETE

Hellie
So you have finally decided you might be missing out on

DELETE

Hellie
I'm sure you'll appreciate that with his exams approaching this is already a demanding year for Josh. It's not simply a question of you turning up and seeing him. I never have – and never will – deny you access to your son, but we will need to discuss at length how best to handle this.
Jay

SEND

The Canal House is busy as ever on a Saturday night, but I go through to the back room where the band is playing, knowing Michael will be somewhere nearby. I spy him sitting on one of the leather sofas with Libby. They're deep in conversation, happily catching up on the past.

I quickly evaluate the seating situation. The gap next to Libby is the most obvious place to sit, but the idea of being pressed so close to her fills me with dread. I don't think I want that, and I'm worried she won't either. Instead, I gesture for Michael to scoot up. There's a moment of awkward confusion while he struggles to interpret my sign language, and then the two of them shuffle down, creating a space for me next to Michael.

Tyler and Theo are singing a song about searching for something you just can't find, and although it's just them on their guitars, the acoustics in the high-ceilinged room mean the music's fairly loud.

Libby peers around Michael and gives me a friendly wave. I raise a half-hearted smile in return, even though I kind of wish she wasn't here. I feel stressed out and fed up, and really could have done with talking things through with Michael tonight. Plus, seeing her again immediately tells me that whatever feelings I've been battling haven't dissipated during the week at all. They've just been lying in wait for her return.

"You guys been catching up?" I ask eventually.

"We have!" they both chime, turning to each other and smiling.

"I think we've pretty much crammed sixteen years into the last half hour, haven't we?" says Michael.

"Yeah, it really is amazing how—"

"—Little we've done."

They laugh and then an awkward silence falls. Michael's eyes dart between myself and Libby, as if he's weighing something up.

I busy myself placing my phone and wallet on the oak coffee table in front of us, pouring lemonade into my glass and taking several gulps.

"They sound all right," I comment, nodding towards the singers.

Michael crosses one foot over his knee and takes a sip of his sparkling water.

"I hear they used to be better," he quips, "before they kicked their fantastic lead vocalist out."

Personally, I was relieved when Breaking Days broke up. I'd never liked Tyler or Theo much. They were part of a wider group of people that I considered to be dragging Michael into a downward spiral. Ironically, they were the ones who kicked him out after his behaviour exceeded even their limits of acceptability. Nowadays, Tyler's a driver for Tesco and Theo works in a call centre. Each of us has grown up, moved on. But I still don't like them.

"Ohhh, no way," Michael suddenly calls, shaking his head, "tonight's my night off!"

I look up to see Theo holding a guitar out to him, while Tyler sets up another stool.

"For old times' sake!" calls Theo.

A few shouts of encouragement go up around the bar.

"Get up there!" Stu calls to Michael, gathering glasses from a nearby table. "Keep my clientele happy!"

There are some hoots of laughter and a bit more egging on.

"Oh, Jesus," mutters Michael quietly, as he reluctantly stands up and weaves his way towards the band to a spattering of applause.

As he slings the guitar strap around his neck and exchanges a few words with his former bandmates, the empty space between me and Libby gapes awkwardly. We both sip our drinks and wait silently for him to start.

The three of them play one of their old songs about wanting to rewind time and not being able to. It's a good song with a heart-wrenching melody, too catchy to be depressing yet full of bittersweet regret. It's one of the more uplifting songs they could have chosen, given that most of what Michael wrote back then was dark and full of pain. The lyrics strike a chord with me. How many times have I wished I could rewind time? It's like the soundtrack to my life.

After a while, Libby shuffles a little closer, perching uncertainly on the edge of the sofa next to me as if she might need to flee at any moment.

"He's got a great voice," she says over the music. "I can't believe how much he's changed. He used to be so shy. He'd barely say a word to me."

She gazes at the band, mesmerised by the music, but I'm distracted, acutely aware of her proximity to me. Out of the corner of my eye, I study her hands clasped around her wine glass. I notice she's not wearing her engagement ring, presumably because she's spent the day painting. Her nails still have flecks of white paint on them, even though she's clearly made an effort tonight, wearing a thin, short-sleeved blouse with jeans and a dash of make-up. I find my eyes travelling over her wrists, up her bare arms, examining her sun-kissed skin...

"How did the painting go today?" I ask, trying to refocus.

"Oh, good. I finished before the rain started, so..."

"You finished?"

"I mean, I finished for the day."

"Oh, right."

"Yeah, not *finished* finished, obviously! Don't worry, there's still *loads* for you to do. I mean, if that's still okay. For tomorrow, I mean. Is that...?"

"Yeah, yeah. No worries. We'll be here."

The band finishes to a round of applause and a couple of ear-piercing whistles. They decide to take a break, and to my slight disappointment Michael stays chatting with Tyler and Theo, leaving me alone with Libby.

I take a long sip of my drink and scratch at my neck.

"So are you staying here again tonight?" I ask.

"Yeah. Actually, I'm going to be staying here during the week as well. Just for a little while."

"How come?" I ask, trying not to sound too alarmed.

"Well, they said they need some help in the pub, and I need a job. Poor Irena's really suffering with this morning sickness still, and it kind of just makes sense. Plus, I can work on the painting, because just doing it at weekends… well, it's going to take longer than I thought."

"But have you ever worked in a pub?" I ask, half hoping to put her off. "There's a lot to learn."

"I've done pretty much everything!" she laughs.

I don't know what to say. So now she's got a job here? She's going to be living here?!

"Well that's… great. But what about Will?"

"Oh, he's fine with it. It's just temporary anyway."

She quickly takes a big glug of wine.

"Actually, the little flat here's really nice," she says. "Have you seen it?"

I shake my head.

"Oh, come and have a quick look!"

Above the pub is Stu and Irena's flat, and above that, it turns out, is a small converted attic space accessed via a narrow stairwell. There's a double futon, some drawers, a narrow wardrobe, a tatty armchair, a camping stove and a small fridge all in one room. Next door there's a toilet and sink. The slope of the ceiling means I can only stand up straight in one half of the room.

"I just have to pop downstairs to use the shower," Libby explains. "I have everything else I need though. I can even cook. I mean, I don't because Stu and Irena insist I eat with them, but I could if I wanted to."

I gaze out of the skylight above the bed into the descending darkness. Drizzle speckles the glass.

"It's… compact," I say, looking around me.

"I lived for eighteen years on a boat, remember?" she smiles. "I'm used to compact."

"Well, when you and Will move to your posh house in Woodside it's gonna feel like a mansion after this!"

Libby looks down at the bare floorboards and shakes her head, not taking the bait this time. My attempt at humour hasn't even raised a smile.

"Yeah," she shrugs, "well, to be honest, even the smallest flats I've lived in have felt like mansions to me. All these jokes about living in a big house and whatever... none of that matters to me really. I'm not used to having space. I don't know how to fill it. It's not a house I want, it's a home. There's a big difference."

I study her face, wondering what's going through her mind, until she looks up at me, all smiles again.

"And the best thing about this place," she grins, "is this."

She scoops a disgruntled-looking cat off the armchair and presses her face into his matted grey fur.

"This is apparently your favourite place to hang out, isn't it, Crumble? So you're gonna keep me company, aren't you?"

She waggles the cat's paws as if he's waving at me. He looks utterly fed up to have been disturbed, but he tolerates the abuse.

"I always wanted a cat when I was younger," Libby tells me, as if I don't already know this about her.

"Don't you need a blind or something over that skylight?"

"Well, the sun did wake me up at the crack of dawn last Sunday, which was a pain. But, on the other hand, when I was trying to get to sleep, I just lay there gazing at the stars for a while. It was really nice. It reminded me of being back on the boat. Just sitting in the bow, gazing at the stars... I used to love that."

"Yeah, I know you did," I say distractedly, pondering how you might fit a blind if you needed one, "you taught me all about the constellations."

As soon as it's out of my mouth, I regret it. It's too personal, too intimate.

I remember she'd been shocked to discover I knew nothing about astrology and had taken it upon herself to educate me. We'd made ourselves a bed of blankets in the bow of the boat and snuggled close, our breath forming faint clouds of vapour against the cold evening air. We'd started off talking in hushed voices, her pointing up at the evening sky while I played with her hair, distracted by her closeness. We'd ended up clumsily tugging and pulling at each other's clothes underneath the covers, hands searching, feeling, exploring undiscovered territory…

"Do you want to…?" I'd asked her.

"I'm not sure," she'd said.

"It's up to you."

"Do you have a… you know."

"Yes. But only… you know, just in case. I wasn't thinking…I mean, we don't have to."

"Do you want to?" she asked.

"Umm… yes. But only if you do."

"I don't know if I feel ready…"

"That's fine."

"Can we wait?"

"Sure. Whatever you want."

"We've got all the time in the world, haven't we?"

"Yeah," I told her, "we've got forever."

The way she looks at me now, the way her eyes dart away, the slight colour that rises in her cheeks, tells me that she's been reminded of that evening, too.

She quickly places the cat down on his chair, but he's fed up now and runs past me and out of the door.

"Erm… should we…?"

"Yeah," I say, awkwardly rubbing the back of my neck, "we should…"

"It sounds like the band's started up again."

"Yeah, let's go—"

"Actually, you know what? I'm kind of tired. I might stay here and call it a night if that's—"

"Yeah, I need to go pick Josh up from the cinema anyway so—"

"Are you okay to—"

"Sure, I'll see myself out."

"Oh, I meant tomorrow. Are you okay to get here about

half nine again? Or whenever. I mean, whenever you're ready is fine, don't feel—"

"Half nine's fine."

"Oh, watch the—"

"Ouch!"

"Yeah, the ceiling's really low there. Are you okay?"

"I'm fine. No worries."

I leave hastily, rubbing my head, feeling awkward and clumsy on more than one level.

I lied. I don't have to pick Josh up from the cinema for ages. He doesn't see why I won't just let him and Sam walk home together, seeing as Sam lives just at the end of our road, but I'm not having him wandering through town on a Saturday night at closing time. I've been on the end of hassle too many times myself. And at fifteen you don't see the risks. You don't worry about who's lurking in the dark. You don't think twice about taking a shortcut. You're untouchable. Until the moment you're not.

Kicking myself for my clumsiness with Libby, I head straight through the bar and out onto the street, dropping Michael a quick text to let him know I've left. The light has almost faded and I walk slowly through town, letting the light drizzle dampen my T-shirt. I gaze through the windows of shut-up shops and cafés, my solitary reflection staring back at me. I pass the Indian restaurant, where a couple are holding hands across a white-clothed table, oblivious to everything around them. I wonder what it takes to create and maintain that kind of intimacy. I wonder if I'll ever have it, whether I'm even capable of it. I think I might have been, once, but it feels like a lifetime ago.

I pull out my phone to text Josh and confirm I'll be there at eleven, but I get distracted by the red flag on my email box. I click on it with some trepidation.

Dear Jay

I appreciate your concern for our son and understand that my email has come out of the blue. I know that I have not always done the right thing by him and that makes me regretful but there is no reason for things to always continue the same way and I am in a better place now with more of an ability to have a relationship with him. I think your right that we need to discuss this and I can meet with you first to talk about things if that's best. Let me know what you want.

I understand that this is not an easy situation but I would appreciate your help.

Love Hellie xx

I stop dead in my tracks, staring in disbelief. The illuminated screen of my phone glows back at me in the darkness, gathering tiny specks of rain.

Help? She wants my *help*?!

Her email summons a sense of outrage in me. Why was she not there to help when I was up night after night with a child who missed his mum? Why was she not there to help when I was at the hospital with him? Why was she not there to help *ever*?! And why, after a lifetime of private education, is she incapable of using proper fucking punctuation?!

I put my phone back in my pocket, incredulous.

My help? *Jesus effing Christ.*

Chapter 16

Help

I remember Amber inviting me into their run-down little flat in the worst part of town.

"He's in the lounge," she sighed, picking up her jacket. "I'm going out. And, by the way, we're over."

"You're what?" I asked, shocked.

"We're over," she sighed. "I can't do this anymore, Jay. I love him, but I've had enough. I don't know what to do. I think he needs help of some kind, but I can't force him. And I just..." she sniffed, tears welling in her eyes. "It's exhausting."

I nodded, disappointed but sympathetic. I liked Amber, Timpton's very own girl with the dragon tattoo. When she'd jumped up on that table behind Michael and snaked her hands under his T-shirt, I'd assumed she'd be just another of his one-night stands. But, almost two years later, here they still were, living together in the cheapest place their rent could afford, and through all his extreme ups and downs she'd stood by him. Until now.

Amber leaned down and ruffled Josh's hair. "There's a couple of biscuits in the tin if you want."

"Yay!" cried Josh, running off to open the cupboard.

Amber and I exchanged sorry smiles. Then she left.

"Just stay here for a minute," I said, sitting Josh down at the plastic picnic table in the kitchen.

The lounge was gloomy, the curtains still drawn even though it was the afternoon. Michael was lying on the saggy sofa, staring at the ceiling.

He was still wearing his suit trousers and a dishevelled shirt, even though his dinner with his father had been the night before last.

I perched quietly on the tatty armchair next to him. A wilting pot plant sat on the old coffee table they'd found outside someone's house and carried back to the flat. They'd tried to turn this place into something of a home.

"You can't keep doing this to yourself," I said, quietly.

He didn't respond.

"You have to stop seeing him," I said.

"Would you stop seeing your dad?" he muttered.

"No, but my dad doesn't leave me feeling like shit."

"Yes, he does."

"Because he's sick. Not because he's a total bastard. And he leaves me feeling worried not..." I gestured to Michael's listless body, "...whatever this is."

The place smelled of stale cigarette smoke. I wanted to draw the curtains and fling the window open wide, but at times like this Michael developed a vampiric intolerance to sunlight.

Michael's shirtsleeves were pulled down to his wrists, cufflinks still in place, disguising the numerous tattoos his father wouldn't approve of. His father had moved away from Timpton, but Michael was summoned, every six months like clockwork, to a different fancy restaurant in London to indulge his father's love of fine dining. Michael struggled through each meal, spinning lies about his job, his income, his flat, his girlfriend... He said Amber was a restaurant manager instead of a waitress and showed off old photos of her at family weddings, pre-lip piercing and looking smart. She knew she was being misrepresented but was surprisingly understanding, having also come from a stuffy, hard-to-please family. She'd been understanding about everything – his drinking, drugs, mood swings, inability to hold down a job… but it seemed she had a limit.

I had no limit though. I owed him. I could never shake off the guilt of how I first treated him at school and what that bullying might have done to him. I could never repay him for getting my son to the hospital on time, for looking after Josh when I was studying or working, for being there for me at every twist and turn. I wasn't ever giving up on him.

"Michael, I think you need help," I said.

"I'm okay," he mumbled, putting his hands over his face. "I've stopped drinking, haven't I?"

"This isn't about the drinking though, is it? It's not even about your dad. This has been going on—"

"I'm fine," he groaned. "Last week, I was in a great place, I couldn't have been happier—"

"But that's not normal."

"Everyone has ups and downs."

"Not like this, mate."

He was silent for a moment.

"Amber's leaving," he muttered.

"I know."

"She's given up on me. And you should, too."

"That's not gonna happen. I'm not going anywhere and we're going to get you some help, okay?" I said determinedly.

He removed his hands from his face and looked over at me with eyes so dead and pained that I wondered why it had taken so long to reach this point.

"We're going to get you some help," I repeated.

I remember there were dozens of them in the playground, lots of tiny little bodies running about in brightly coloured T-shirts and sun hats, shouting and screeching. It was almost impossible to keep track of your child the whole time.

It was a hot day, and I sat with Brenda and Dad on a park

bench feeling drowsy. All of our minds were elsewhere, mulling over the doctor's diagnosis. Alzheimer's. What did that mean? Where would it lead? Usually I was hyper-vigilant, watching Josh like a hawk. But not at that moment.

"Help! Daddy, help!"

I was up on my feet before I was even sure it was Josh, my eyes searching frantically for him, my heart pounding. I couldn't believe I'd taken my eyes off him!

"Help!"

I ran through the playground, ducking and weaving, searching under slides and inside tunnels.

"Josh?!"

God, where was he?! Who had him?!

I turned in circles, and in a frantic blur I spied the bushes where someone must have been lurking, the car that was speeding out of the car park, the gang of teenage boys who suddenly looked shifty, the dishevelled man who was pulling something metal out of his pocket, something that glinted in the sun...

"Daddy, help!"

"Josh?!" I yelled in a panic, causing everyone to turn and stare.

This was it! I knew it! I'd taken my eye off him for one second and someone had hurt him – was *hurting* him – and I couldn't get to him because I couldn't find him because I'd stopped watching—

And then there he was, being led across the playground towards me by a man in sunglasses.

I rushed towards him, snatching him up and away from the stranger, who went from smiling to shocked in the blink of an eye.

"He... he couldn't find you," stammered the man, "I was just..."

I glared at him, my breath coming in short, sharp bursts.

"Thank you," said Brenda to the man, suddenly appearing by my side, "that was very kind of you."

The man gave Brenda a smile but shot me a look which suggested he thought I was out of my mind.

"What happened?" I demanded, holding Josh tightly in my arms and checking him over for damage. "Did someone hurt you?"

"No," Josh frowned, "my shoelace came undone."

I stared at him in disbelief.

"You were screaming like that because your shoelace came undone?"

"Yes. Because I wanted to climb the slide. And you said once before that if I climb the slide with my shoelaces undone I could fall and break my neck."

I plonked him down on the ground, my hands shaking.

"I can't believe you were screaming like that because your shoelace came undone!" I snapped.

"I don't know how to do them up," wailed Josh, tears springing to his eyes.

"Come on, Sunshine," I heard my dad say, scooping my son up and carrying him away, "let's fix your shoelace and then you can show Grandad how fast you can whizz down that slide."

Brenda gave my arm a little rub before shooting me a sympathetic smile and following after my dad.

I looked around me, catching the puzzled stares of parents before they discreetly turned away. The car that looked like it had been speeding out of the car park was only just crawling through the exit barrier. The gang of teenage boys – just three of them I saw now – had been joined by their parents, who had just walked out of the café. And the dishevelled-looking man was nothing of the sort – he just had that weary, unshaved look of a father with a toddler. He was sipping on a can of energy drink, which glinted in the sun.

I remember Josh asking: "Daddy, what's wrong?"

"Nothing," I told him, struggling to catch my breath. "School jump... school jumper on, okay?"

Josh pulled his tiny red jumper over his head, arms flailing, searching for the sleeves.

I sat on the edge of the floral sofa, my head in my hands, and focused on trying to drag some air into my lungs. My forehead felt clammy against my palms. I glanced at the carriage clock on the shelf and concentrated on the second hand ticking round.

Come on, come on, come on.

Josh, his jumper stuck over his head, flapped one of his sleeves up and down like a trunk and made a loud elephant noise.

"BBBBRRRR!" he trumpeted. "BBBRRRRR!"

I tried to breathe slowly and deeply, but I could feel my chest tightening, my lungs begging for more air.

"BBBRRR! Daddy, what aminal am I? BBBRRRRR!"

"Josh, shh," I muttered quietly.

"Guess, Daddy! BBBRRR!"

"Shush!" I snapped.

Josh pushed his head through the hole and peered at me, wide-eyed.

I felt a stab of guilt. He was just trying to inject some fun into the morning, but the noise really wasn't helping.

I waited for the knock on the door, willing it to come quickly. I felt my head growing light and as I glanced round the room, the objects seemed to shift and blur; Brenda's collection of ceramic pig ornaments, her pot plants that were slowly dying under my care, her bookcase full of crime novels, my pillow and duvet discarded on the floor, Josh's plastic cars and Spiderman toys, our breakfast plates still covered in crumbs... There was once neat orderliness in Brenda's little flat. Now, since she'd entrusted the place to me and Josh, there was chaos.

"Auntie Laura!" Josh cried, jumping up.

I hadn't even heard the knock.

I stayed where I was and let him open the door.

"Hey, munchkin!" I heard her squeal.

She followed Josh inside and stopped abruptly when she saw me.

"You look like crap," she stated.

"I'm fine."

I stood up quickly, grabbed Josh's school bag and thrust it into her arms. I tried to keep my voice steady.

"Thanks. I've called. I've... I've told them he'll be late."

"Again."

I ignored her and opened the front door, desperate for them to be gone.

"You gonna see a doctor today?"

"I'm fine, it'll pass," I told her quickly.

"Jay, for God's sake—"

"I don't have time!" I managed to spit out, wondering when the hell I was meant to get to a doctor. What was I meant to do? Take time off the job I was already barely hanging onto by the skin on my teeth?

"Make time!"

"I'm late for work."

"Yeah, me too!" she shouted, gesturing to the smart suit she wore behind the hotel reception. I couldn't imagine how she had conned any interviewer into thinking she had good customer service skills.

"I'm sorry," I sighed, running my hands over my head. The bristles still surprised me.

"And what the hell happened to your hair?"

"I rubbed glue in Daddy's hair and he had to shave it all off!" beamed Josh with delight.

"You need to get some help with this," Laura told me, sternly.

"I don't need help—"

"What's the matter with you?! Why is it such a struggle for you to ever ask for help?!"

"I did! I asked *you* for help!"

"Not me! Not just someone who can take Josh to school! I mean medical help! From a fucking doctor! Whoops, sorry—"

"Auntie Laura said *fucking*."

"And I shouldn't have done that, Josh, so just ignore me. It's just your daddy drives me effing mad sometimes and I don't know why he has to be so effing stubborn all the time and why he can't just get the effing help he needs!"

"I'm fine," I growled.

"You know what you are?" Laura hissed. "A *martyr*. You would rather suffer than seek help because you get some kind of perverse pleasure from your own suffering."

"Yeah, I love it," I wheezed, bundling them out into the hallway.

"Bye, Daddy!" Josh called over his shoulder. Laura held his hand down the stairs, shaking her head angrily.

I closed the front door and slumped down on the sofa. For a moment I monitored my breathing, unsure whether this thing was going to take hold or not. It could go either way. Was it leaving, freeing me from the threat of its clutch?

If I left for work now I wouldn't be too late. I needed to get paid in full this month. No deductions for poor timekeeping or missed hours.

I'd be fine. It would pass. It always did.

I grabbed my jacket, trying to ignore the band that was tightening around my chest.

I didn't need help. I didn't *want* help. I just wanted to get to work.

Chapter 17

Truth

Given the enormity of the situation with Hellie, I shouldn't even be thinking about Libby, but as I head through the crowded streets of Covent Garden that's exactly what I'm doing.

The morning after we watched Tyler and Theo play at the Canal House – when she showed me her attic room and I fled like an awkward schoolboy – Josh and I turned up to help her paint the wall again. Following a brief demonstration in how to slap on and roughly blend two tones of blue paint, Josh once again plugged his headphones in and took himself off to the far end of the terrace, leaving me and Libby together. But it was clear something had shifted between us. It felt like I'd overstepped a boundary the night before, mentioning the constellations, reminding us both of that private time on the boat. If I ever wondered whether she remembered that evening, there was no room for doubt now. It sat between us like an unspoken intimacy that we were both shuffling around, trying to avoid disturbing any further. Instead, she talked about Will a lot, supplying tedious details about his career, his family, his plans for the future. I told her (probably equally tedious) details about Josh's schooling, his GCSEs, his lack of plans for the future. It was all excruciatingly polite and, most importantly, neutral. The situation's been playing on my mind ever since, keeping me awake at night, making me feel agitated and confused.

I could entirely do without today, but there's no turning back now.

* * *

I'm struck how much she's changed since I last saw her. She looks thinner, her hair's a bit longer and darker, and she's wearing glasses. I watch her for a moment through the café window. She's peering thoughtfully into her coffee, chewing her bottom lip, checking her watch anxiously.

I weave my way through the customers queuing for their drinks and in between the busy tables. Chatter mingles with the bang and hiss of the coffee machine and the clatter of cups and saucers. I feel hot and claustrophobic before I even reach her table.

She looks up and I see her eyes travelling the length of me, sizing me up. She stands and takes a couple of steps forwards. Hesitantly, she reaches out and places her hands on my upper arms. When I don't stoop towards her, she stands on tiptoe to plant a brief kiss on my cheek.

"It's lovely to see you," she smiles awkwardly.

I stand rigid, angry at her for tearing me away from more pressing matters at home, angry at her for so many things.

But then, as always, I soften.

"Good to see you too, Mum."

We meet once, maybe twice, a year. The conversation is always slightly stilted and awkward, and it pains me to remember the closeness we once shared. I think it pains her, too. But at least we talk. Laura – more stubborn and less forgiving – hasn't spoken to her in years.

With time, I've learned more about her relationship with

Jack, and it's helped me view her leaving with a maturity I wasn't capable of at the time. I understand that Jack was the love of her life, and that they were together, on and off, throughout most of their twenties. He was spontaneous, creative and carefree. He made her feel alive. But he had no interest in ever settling down and having children, and that's what finally tore them apart. In the end, her desire for a family outweighed her desire for him, and before it was too late she turned to my father – fifteen years older, steady, reliable and adoring. She thought she could turn off her feelings for Jack, but instead they haunted her throughout her marriage. And maybe that's why I understand her now more than ever. Because if there was a switch to turn off your feelings for someone and leave them in the past, I'd have used it by now. But there's not. I get it. I honestly do now believe that she tried her best.

As for Jack, I don't feel anything for him. I no longer see him as the devil who swept in and stole my mum away from us, but I also don't have much respect for him. For all those years, he kept her hanging on, trying to convince her that they'd be enough for each other. But if he really loved her that much, why would he expect her to give up her dream of a family? I know that my feelings for Libby, whatever they really are, are one-sided and that she's committed to someone else, but even if I thought I stood a chance with her, I would never, ever pursue it. She wants children. I absolutely don't. The fact that I could never give her what she wants is reason alone to keep my feelings to myself. I would never want her to compromise on something she so desperately longs for. She deserves more than I could ever give her.

"There's something I want to talk to you about, Jamie," says my mum, anxiously.

We're sitting on a bench in a small, unkempt public garden near Russell Square after a slow, uncomfortable walk through the streets of London. I have the feeling that today we're both preoccupied by other things and would rather be somewhere else.

"Jack's sick," she tells me. "He has cancer. It's terminal."

And there's why she seems so distracted.

"I'm sorry," I say, and I genuinely am. Not for him – I barely know him – but for her. "How long does he have?"

"We don't know. Maybe six months, maybe more. But the thing is…" she sighs quietly and shakes her head. "I don't know how to do this… The things is, there's something you need to know."

I wait patiently. A pigeon jumps onto the arm of the bench and I carefully brush it away, sending it hopping onto the concrete.

My mum clasps her hands together and brings them to her lips like she's praying. She takes a deep breath.

"Jamie," she says, turning towards me and clearly trying, but failing, to meet my eye. "Jack's your biological father."

I turn to her, but she's staring at the ground, her hands clenched tightly in front of her mouth, the tips of her fingers turning white.

"What?"

A tear slips from her eye.

"Perhaps we should have told you, I don't know. But we all agreed…"

"I don't… he's what?"

"Your dad knows. I mean, Richard. He knows. He's always known. And we all decided – the three of us – that it would better if we just carried on—"

A strangled sound escapes from her throat. She removes her glasses and wipes at her eyes.

"God, I know this must be a shock—"

"I don't… I… what? I mean… *What*?!"

All of a sudden the ground feels like it's spinning beneath my feet. I lean forwards and put my head in my hands, nausea washing over me. The pigeon pecks at my shoes and I kick it away fiercely, sending it flying, wings flapping in alarm.

"What the fuck?" I whisper.

"I know it's a lot to take in." She places her hand on my shoulder and I shrug her off.

"How…? I don't understand. How can he be…?"

"We had a very brief affair," she says hastily, as if getting it out quickly will somehow lessen the torment. "When I found out I was pregnant, I knew it was Jack's baby and I told your dad. I even told him I'd leave if that's what he wanted, but he didn't want me to. He didn't want to lose Laura. He didn't want to lose me. Jack didn't want children – I told you that before – and Richard was willing to raise you like his own child—"

"So hang on," I say, hunched over and digging my fingers into my scalp, "all three of you agreed on this?"

"It just made sense all round. Jack didn't want a baby. And he certainly didn't want the responsibility of Laura. That was never what we had in mind. It wasn't what anyone wanted. I wasn't looking to break our family up—"

"Oh my God," I groan. "Does Laura know?"

"Of course not."

I shake my head in disbelief. I can't get my thoughts straight. My dad. My life. All of it a lie.

"We never expected to have to tell you—"

"So why are you telling me now?"

"Because he wants to see you. He's dying and he wants to talk to you—"

"About what?"

"To make his peace with you, I suppose."

"His what?" I laugh.

"He might not have been there, but he's always kept a close interest in you."

"A close interest in me? He hasn't seen me in years!"

I try to understand what's going on, but I feel oddly detached from the situation. I try to feel something, anything, just so I know I'm really here and this is actually happening, but I can't. There's nothing there. I'm hollow.

I laugh quietly, bitterly, pieces of the jigsaw suddenly falling into place.

I remember asking why I was the only one in the family with blue eyes and being told it was a generational throwback to my grandmother. I remember everyone saying I'd grow to be six foot three like my dad, and later being vaguely surprised when I ground to a halt three inches beneath him. I remember wondering how my parents could have possibly found the money to pay private-school fees. But they didn't, did they? It was him.

I stand up and start to walk away.

"Where are you going?" my mum asks.

"Home," I say, numbly.

But then I stop, turn around.

There's something that Laura's always suspected, and I've denied, but now, finally, I want to ask her. Because what is there to lose now? Why don't we just say it all?

"Did you know that dad was getting sick?" I ask. "Is that why you left when you did?"

She shakes her head but doesn't look shocked. "No. I didn't know. And that's not why I left when I did. I just couldn't do it anymore. It was just time."

I study her lined face, her watery brown eyes behind her glasses. I desperately want to believe her, but I feel like I don't even know who she is anymore.

Over the years, I've tried to see things from her point of view. I know now that parents are flawed and imperfect. I know now what it's like to fall for someone despite your better judgement. And I know how hard it is feeling trapped by responsibility. I understand that at sixteen I was no longer a baby, that it wasn't her job to deal with the fallout of my mistakes, and that I had to own up to the consequences of my actions.

But I also know that's all bullshit. It's just what I tell myself to reason away the hurt and the anger.

Because if Josh ever found himself in the situation I was

in – scared, overwhelmed, life careering off track – it wouldn't matter if he was sixteen or sixty.

I will always, *always,* be there for my son when he needs me.

"Christ, what's up with you?" asks Laura when she opens her front door, searching my face with a look of mild horror.

She's wearing a little black dress and a lot of make-up, clearly heading out for the evening.

"I need to talk to you," I say, pushing past her.

"Err… firstly, bit rude. And, secondly, I have a date."

"With who?"

"Mark. The guy who owns the garage."

"You said he was a dick."

"Yeah, but he's a hot dick with tickets to this club I want to go to."

"Well, cancel."

"I'm not gonna cancel just 'cause you're obviously in the midst of another crisis," she says indignantly.

But clearly she sees something desperate in my face. Her expression changes from annoyed to wary to concerned.

"Okay, I'll call him," she says, nervously, "just go and sit down."

After the shock comes the understanding.

"You know, for all those years I wondered why you were the favourite one," Laura muses, staring at the whisky in the bottom of her glass. "You, Mum, Dad – you all used to tell me that it was in my head, that I was imagining it. But I wasn't, was I? I was right. She favoured you because you were his."

We're sitting on her lounge floor, slumped against the front of her sofa, the lights down low. Josh is staying at Sam's house. It's gone two in the morning and we just can't stop talking about it.

"I always felt guilty," I tell her, "for the way she treated me. Like I was somewhere to pin all the hopes and aspirations, while you... I dunno, I think you did always get the raw deal."

Laura shrugs. "Yeah, but then I could see she put you under a lot of pressure. It must have been hard for you, having her pushing you all the time. And I didn't exactly make things easier for you."

I lean my head back against the edge of the sofa cushion and close my eyes, growing drowsy.

"Nope. You could be a prize bitch at times."

I can feel myself slipping into sleep, but a change in Laura's breathing besides me makes me open my eyes. She sits forward and hugs her knees. Is she crying? *Laura?*

"What the hell's the matter with you?" I mumble.

"I really was *such* a bitch to you."

"It doesn't matter," I sigh, exhausted.

"Of course it fucking matters! I mean, I told you so many times I wished you weren't my brother and now..."

"Now what?" I ask, suddenly wide awake and sitting up. "Now *what*? I'm not your brother anymore? 'Cause you'll always be my same pain-in-the-arse sister. As far as I'm concerned, this changes nothing."

Laura wipes at her eyes, smudging her mascara across her cheeks. Her sparkly earrings were long ago discarded on the carpet and she's picked so much at a thread in her tights that she now has a ladder running from thigh to ankle.

"I wouldn't even blame you if you didn't want to be my brother after the things I've said to you in the past," she says, shaking her head sadly.

"Shut up," I say, putting my arm around her. "What the hell would I have done without you over the last fifteen years? How would I have managed?"

She rests her head against my shoulder.

"I do love you really," she tells me, her voice cracking.

"Christ, now I know you're pissed. You're gonna regret telling me that in the morning."

She laughs through her tears. "You won't even remember I said it. You've got a memory like a sieve these days."

I butt my foot against hers.

"Least I haven't got weird chimp feet," I say, referencing the fact that her second toes are longer than her big ones.

She slaps me hard on the stomach.

I swear and then give her a squeeze, before resting my head back on the sofa and closing my tired eyes.

"I love you too, you crazy moo," I mutter.

As he slumbers in his armchair, I hold my dad's hand, feeling the grey hairs of his knuckles, the dry, calloused pads of his long fingers. These capable hands that have spent decades fixing and tinkering.

Brenda places a mug of tea beside my chair.

"You can wake him, if you like," she says. "Silly man keeps falling asleep in the afternoons and then doesn't sleep at night."

"No, I don't want to wake him," I say quietly. "Let him rest."

I take in the white stubble of his chin, the lines around his eyes, the slack skin around his neck. I remember riding high on his younger shoulders, racing those long legs across the park, being pulled in for a hug by those strong, wiry arms. It never bothered me that my dad was a little older than everyone else's. I knew he was fitter and sharper than any of them.

Brenda sits down on the sofa with a sigh. She's older than my mum – much closer to my dad's age – and so totally different. She's quiet and unassuming, insistent on good grammar and exemplary manners, but she's also as tough as an ox, a no-nonsense kind of woman who gets things done without complaining. Even this new revelation – that my dad raised another man's child – hasn't fazed her. *He'll have had his reasons for not telling me*, she said.

I don't know how she's managed with my dad for so long – his tempers and wanderings, his demands and emotional outbursts. But recently the cracks are starting to show. She simply can't cope with this anymore, and we're going to have to make choices. For the last few months, we've been trawling through websites and leaflets, speaking to doctors and social services, visiting community centres and respite homes. All of us – me, Laura and Brenda – all know some big decisions need to be made. But none of us wants to make them.

"Are you sure you don't want something to eat, love?" asks Brenda. "I could do a toasted sandwich?"

I shake my head. I can't eat today, just like I haven't been able to eat for the last three days since meeting with my mum. I feel wobbly inside, and my breath feels strained and tight. Every time I try to eat something, I get heartburn. And I'm so, so tired, although I can barely sleep.

"When did you know you loved my dad?" I ask, my eyes fixed on his face.

I hear Brenda swallow a mouthful of tea.

"I don't think there was single moment," she says, "he just sort of grew on me. A shared word search in the staffroom, a shared packet of Jaffa Cakes… I finally looked forward to going to work just for that time together. But I knew he was married. I never imagined we'd be anything other than friends."

"But how did you carry on like that, day after day, when you were secretly in love with him?"

"Well," she sighs, "for me it was that or nothing. I was resigned to the fact that he had a wife and family. And anyway, I never would have imagined he'd be interested in me, romantically speaking. So, friendship was better than nothing."

I think about Libby and I wish I could feel like that, but I just don't. I'm tired of struggling with my feelings for her, trying to keep them in check. I don't want to be her friend anymore. I just want to be free of her.

My dad stirs in his chair. For a second he opens his eyes and looks at me. I smile, but there's no recognition there, and he quickly closes his eyes again, falls back asleep. What breaks my heart most are the times he gets angry and agitated about me never visiting, telling Laura that his son never comes to see him.

I'm always here, Dad. Always.

Suddenly I remember Laura's phone call on the night of Josh's birthday, how she told me Dad had been distressed, saying he never should have lied to me. Was this what he was talking about? The lie about my parentage? Laura thought he was talking nonsense. She would have told him to quieten down, have a nice cup of tea.

I wonder what it took for him to raise another man's child as his own, knowing the biological father of that child was the true keeper of his wife's heart. What did it take for him to allow that man to visit his home, speak to his wife, see his child, year after year? What did it take for him to allow that man to pay for his son's education?

I know what it's like to be offered money to help raise your child. My life – *Josh's* life – could have been so different if I'd accepted the money Hellie's parents were willing to give me. Maybe I was wrong, maybe I was being selfish, but surely every man wants to be able to support his own child. At twenty-one, whether I like it or not, Josh will have access to a trust fund he doesn't know exists. He'll be a wealthy young man. But until then it's my job to support him. It takes a bigger man than me – a man like my dad – to shelve his pride.

"I should go," I say quietly, but I can't let go of my dad's hand. I feel like I've already lost him once.

I hear Brenda take another sip of her tea.

"You stay as long as you need to, sweetheart," she says. "This will always be your home."

Chapter 18

Empty

I remember…

   …

…nothing.

My mind is blank. I feel empty, spaced out, detached from reality.

Everything that went before feels like a lie.

I feel like a lie.

The memories stop. My thoughts stop.

I

Feel

Nothing.

Chapter 19

Secrets

I haven't told Josh the truth yet.

It's already been so hard for him, watching my dad decline. He makes a joke of it when his grandad can't remember his name or can't recognise his face, but I know it breaks his heart. How will he feel to find out his real grandad's a man he's never met? I don't know. I don't even know how *I* feel.

I have a sense of being numb, outside of myself. I can't think straight. I can't focus on anything. All the thoughts and memories that have been streaming into my brain for the past few weeks have vanished, leaving nothing but white noise. I'm functioning on autopilot, going through the motions of the day without anything registering. I just feel hollow.

But I have to tell Josh. Better to get it over and done with.

I get up from the sofa and head towards his bedroom, when suddenly he comes crashing out into the hallway.

"Why didn't you tell me?!" he snaps.

For a moment I wonder how on earth he knows. Who would have told him? Laura? Michael? But why would they?

"Why would you not tell me that my mum wants to see me?!"

Ah. That's the other thing I haven't told him.

"I saw the emails!"

My brain scrambles to catch up, but then I realise with horror that I said he could use my laptop after he somehow managed to drop a can of baked beans on his brand new one and killed it. I was so busy ranting about his carelessness and how much the damn thing had cost me (and so startled that he was actually going to do some work on his music project) that it didn't even occur to me that the increasing number of emails I've been exchanging with Hellie via my phone would be accessible on my laptop.

"Why were you looking at my email account?" I demand, knowing full well this really isn't the point.

"I wasn't! I was just trying to log you out so that I could log into *my* email account!"

I run my hand over my head.

"Look, I was going to talk to you about this—"

"When?"

What am I meant to say to that? *When I felt sure that she wasn't going to lose interest in you again after five minutes? When I felt certain she wasn't going to break your heart with her selfishness?*

"When were you going to tell me she wanted to see me, Dad? When you'd persuaded her not to bother? When you'd put her off the idea completely by telling her how damaging it would be for me?!"

"Hang on, that's not what I was trying to do—"

"Really? Because from what I read, *she* wants to build a relationship with me, and *you* have been trying to convince her not to!"

"You can't be serious! If that's how you've read it, then you need to read it again because—"

"I *have* read it!"

"Then you'll know I was *not* trying to put her off! I would *never* do that! I was trying to look after your best interests—"

"How the hell do you know what my best interests are?!"

"Because I'm your father!"

"And she's my mother!"

I clench my jaw. I want to snap back, *No! No, she's not! She gave you up! She gave up her right to be your mother!*

"She got in contact over two weeks ago and you said nothing! Nothing! You should have told me! It should have been *my* decision what to do next! Instead, *you* decided it might be best if she gets back in contact after I've finished school?!"

I pinch the bridge of my nose and sigh.

"Josh, that's not what I said. I just wanted a bit of time to sort things out with her—"

"Why did you tell her that seeing me would screw up my GCSEs?"

"That's not what I was saying! I was trying to make her see that now might not be the best time. You've got so much going on—"

"That's literally all you care about, isn't it? How I do in my precious GCSEs! You are *always* on my back..."

"Because I want you to fulfil your potential!"

"...pushing and pushing..."

"Because I don't want you to waste your life!"

"Like you did? Because you had me?"

"What?"

"Oh, come on, Dad! We all know that what you really wanted was to go to university. And then I came along and screwed up your plans. So now you're pushing all your hopes onto me—"

"That's not true."

"Yes, it is! You're not scared that *I'm* going to waste my life, you're just pissed that *you* wasted yours!"

I stare at him, dumbfounded.

"Josh, I don't give a crap that I didn't go to university, and whether you believe it or not, I have only ever wanted what's best for you, and I have been trying to protect you—"

"I am sick and tired of you trying to protect me, Dad! I don't need protecting!"

"Of course you do!"

"From what?!"

"From everything!"

"From my own mother?!"

"Yes, from your own mother!"

He stares at me, waiting for an explanation, but what am I meant to tell him? That she only ever used him as a plaything or to get attention, that she dropped him for the first offer that was slightly more interesting, that I suspected she only ever *had* him to piss her parents off? I have never, and will never, tell him the whole truth.

When he was little, I used to say that Hellie loved him but that she didn't have the right skills to be a mummy, in the same way that I didn't have the right skills to be a chef or a teacher. Later, I told him that she simply couldn't cope with motherhood, but that certainly wasn't his fault and wasn't really even hers. It seemed to soften his sense of rejection, but it was only one side of the story. I feared that the other side – his mother's utter selfishness and her blatant disregard for him – would have hurt him too much.

It's been years since Josh asked about Hellie and yet here he is, apparently desperate for a reunion with her. Did I really believe he wasn't bothered about not having a relationship with his own mother? Did I really believe he'd made his peace with the situation and moved on? How stupid have I been?

"Why did she say you gave her an ultimatum?" asks Josh, his cheeks flushed.

I wrack my brain trying to remember the content of our email exchange.

You chose to walk away, Hellie, so I'm sure you will understand that I am cautious to ensure any future contact is made with a sense of commitment...

It's difficult to think of it as a choice Jay when I was given an ultimatum...

"I didn't give her an ultimatum," I tut, realising what he's referring to. "I asked her to make a choice – about whether to stay or go. So that neither of us were just living in limbo any longer, waiting to see—"

"So you told her if she wanted to carry on working abroad, then she couldn't see me anymore."

"No! No. Absolutely not. It wasn't like that."

"That's how she seemed to think it was."

"That's her twisting things, as always."

"But you told her to make a choice."

"No. Well, yes, but that makes it sound—"

"Why would you make her choose?!"

"It wasn't like that! I never made her break off contact! She could have contacted you at any point. She could have *seen* you at any point! I never would have stopped her, I just told her to stop messing us around—"

"And so you forced her to choose – me or her career."

"There *was* no career!"

"But you forced her to choose."

"She should have chosen you! That's what *I* did. *I* chose *you*!"

"You had no choice! You were stuck with me!"

"Yes, because *she* left!"

We glare at each other.

"I didn't mean… I mean, no, I wasn't *stuck* with you, I *wanted* to be with you—"

"You never *wanted* me! No seventeen-year-old boy wants a baby—"

"I *did* want you!" I insist, but even as I say it, I'm tormented by the memory of standing in that hospital, secretly hoping that his first breath would never come. "You weren't planned, but I *did* want you!" I repeat vehemently, as if saying it with enough conviction might erase the shame of what I once felt.

Josh shakes his head as if he doesn't believe me and I feel sick to the core. Is that what he's always felt deep down? That I'm the one who got stuck with him through default because his other parent left?

"Look, I never told her to leave. You don't understand how it was—"

"You had no right to keep those emails from me!" he fumes.

"But the emails weren't *to* you, they were to *me*! We – me and her – we have to sort some things out before we take anything forward—"

"You should have told me!" he yells, fury blazing in his eyes.

"Okay, yes okay, you might be right—"

"It involves me! *Me*! Were you even going to ask me how *I* feel about this?"

"Of course I was! I just wanted to clarify where *she* was coming from first. I was pretty shocked by this, Josh. I might not have handled it correctly, but I wasn't expecting this email from her out of the blue and I was trying to negotiate things—"

"You didn't need to *negotiate* anything, Dad! This isn't Brexit! All you needed to do was talk to me about it!"

"Okay! Okay. I'm sorry. I screwed up. I should have just told you about it and asked what you wanted to do."

"But you didn't. Because you always think you know what's best for me. What GCSEs I should do, when I should study, what I should do with my future, whether I should even be allowed contact with my own mother... I mean, were you this much of a control freak with her? 'Cause I'm not surprised she left!"

I blink at him in disbelief. He really thinks the fact Hellie left was *my* fault?

"Forget it," Josh spits, turning away and heading back to his room, "I'm going out."

I follow him as he grabs his phone and hoodie from his mess of a room.

"You're not going out," I tell him, blocking his doorway, "we're going to talk—"

"I don't wanna talk!" he shouts, shoving me so hard in the chest that I stumble out of his way. I'm taken aback by his strength and his anger. He's never laid hands on me before.

"Wait!" I snap, grabbing him, but he breaks free with a quick twist of his arm.

"Get off me!"

"We need to talk about this! Josh!"

But it's no use. He's already out the door, slamming it behind him.

I'm left alone in the hallway, shocked and dazed.

"Shit!" I spit, banging my fist against the wall. "Shit, shit, shit!"

That evening, I drive around in the dark searching for my son. It's well past closing time on a Friday evening and only a few people walk the streets – the odd couple who've been out for a quiet drink with friends, the odd group of mates who've had a few – or way too many. I drive with the window down, the intermittent noise of their shouting and laughter making me nervous. I don't want Josh out there alone.

I've been reassuring myself that despite my fears he's probably big enough to take care of himself. Six years of karate, judo, kickboxing... I remember the way he twisted his arm free of my grasp earlier today, not randomly but with applied technique. But I'm starting to slip into panic. I've called everyone I can think of and no one's heard from him. I've driven around town twice, walked through the park, explored the grounds of the closed-up leisure centre, the skate park, the underpasses...

I pull into the deserted car park of the Canal House to phone my sister. An hour ago, I promised to call her with an update, and it's more than my life is worth to break a promise to Laura. But I'm distracted by a figure lurking in the darkness.

I get out of the van. "Libby?"

"I thought that was you," she says, stepping forward into my headlights, wrapping her arms around herself.

"What are you doing?"

"I'm looking for Crumble. He's normally back in by now. Stu and Irena told me not to bother, but you just don't know, do you? People can be so mean after a few drinks."

My stomach flips. I don't need a reminder of this.

"What are *you* doing?"

"I'm looking for Josh. We had an argument and he ran off and I can't find him anywhere and I'm going out of my mind because this isn't the kind of thing he does. I just don't know where else to look, no one's heard from him…"

"Oh, God. Okay. Umm…" she searches for a suggestion.

"I'm just gonna carry on driving around for a bit."

"Do you want me to come with you? Two pairs of eyes are better than one."

I check my watch. It's gone midnight.

"I'll come with you," she says decisively, heading for the van.

We drive in silence through the dark streets, peering through our windows for any sign of a boy in black jeans and a grey hoodie. I've called Sam, and Sam's texted their other friends, but there's been no responses, perhaps because they're all asleep, perhaps because their parents confiscate their phones at bedtime like I do with Josh. I don't know what else to do.

Just then my phone rings.

"It's okay, he's here. He's just turned up at our door," Michael says.

My body slumps back against the seat.

"Okay, I'm coming—"

"No," he says, quickly, "we made a deal that if I told you where he was then he could stay here the night."

"A deal? He's not a in a position to be calling any shots, Michael! I've been going out of my friggin' mind!"

"I know, I know. Look, he's really wound up and I think if you turn up here he'll probably just make a run for it again."

I pull into a side street and park up.

"Can you just put him on the phone?"

"He won't talk to you. Look, it's late, just let him stay here tonight. Let everything calm down a bit and I'll drop him back in the morning."

Feeling that I have no choice but to agree, I hang up and lean my head on the steering wheel.

I feel Libby place her hand gently on my shoulder, and the

relief that Josh is safe is suddenly sabotaged by a whole host of other mixed-up feelings which shouldn't even be featuring on my radar right now. I wish she wouldn't touch me.

"Safe and sound?"

I sit back and nod.

"I'm not giving you a very good impression of life as a parent, am I?"

"*Well*," she says, trying to be diplomatic, "I can see why you might not want another one."

I laugh quietly, relief washing through me, although she's way off the mark. Not wanting another one has nothing to do with the millions of daily stresses and strains that come with parenting, and everything to do with the nightmare of being told my five-year-old son might die of meningitis. I am never, *ever* risking an experience like that again.

"Take this as a reflection of my parenting skills more than anything. I'm sure you'll fare much better."

"I'm sure this wasn't your fault."

I tell her about the emails from Hellie. I even read her a few of the more outrageous lines – and by the glow of my phone I see her frown and shake her head, indignant at Hellie's sense of entitlement after all these years.

"What did you ever see in her?"

I shake my head, sadly, and experience a strange sense of the past repeating itself. This is a question Libby asked me so many times when we were trying to work through what had happened, trying to get our relationship back on track.

"It wasn't about what I saw in her. We were just two unhappy, drunk kids—"

"But why were you even friends with her in the first place?"

"Because she had another side to her. And because by the time I'd seen what she could be like—"

"So what was this other side to her?"

The way she says it sounds like a challenge. We look at each other, eyes shining in the darkness, and suddenly I feel like we're teenagers again, back in that place where we were thrashing it out over and over; her pouring out her jealousy and hurt in an endless stream of questions about this girl from my school that she'd never even heard me mention, and me explaining, however many times it took, that it meant nothing, that I thought we were finished, that I was angry and hurt and just got swept along…

"It doesn't matter," Libby says, shaking her head as if she's not sure why she even asked the question, "she just sounds so… I mean, I just wondered how you ever ended up—"

"It's not something I meant to happen, you know that."

"I know."

"It just happened."

"And if it hadn't, you wouldn't have Josh."

"And that's why I can't regret it."

"I never asked you to regret it."

I search the shadows of her face. I have no idea what's happening here. It's like we're going through it all again, sixteen years later: the bitterness, the upset, the need to understand where we went wrong.

She turns away and looks out the window at the row of red-brick houses lurking in the darkness. In the thick silence that lies between us, I feel my heart thumping. I don't see it coming, I don't even know why I do it. Blame it on the endorphins that have rushed in after an evening of stress and panic.

"The only thing I regret is losing you."

She stays turned away from me and I wait. I don't know what for. I bite the side of my tongue, perhaps to stop me saying more, perhaps to punish myself for having said too much.

The silence between us seems to stretch forever.

"It was your decision," she says eventually, her voice barely more than a whisper. "I said we could have still tried to make it work."

I stare at the back of her head, straggles of dark hair caught inside the neck of her T-shirt. "I didn't have a choice," I say, "once I knew about the baby—"

"It was still a choice."

"But what was I meant to do?"

She takes her time to answer.

"You could have given us a chance."

I think of our first meeting at the Canal House, the way she'd scoffed at the idea of us ever having stayed together, the way she dismissed the notion like it was some kind of childish fantasy.

"I *wanted* to," I say with more feeling than I intend, as if I need her to know, after all these years, that letting her go was one of the hardest things I ever did. "But I just… I wanted you to be happy. And free."

"Of you?"

"Of me, of the mess I was in—"

"But that should have been *my* decision."

I think of Josh this evening telling me exactly the same thing.

We sit in silence and I barely dare to breathe.

"We should go," she says.

I look out at the dark street ahead of me, and when she doesn't say anything more, I go to turn the key in the ignition. But then I stop. There's so much I want to tell her: that I haven't been able to stop thinking about her, that I've been flooded with memories of the past, that my dad isn't who I thought he was, that I'm worried I've screwed things up with my son, that I feel like an empty vessel…

"Libby, are you happy?" I ask, because in the midst of everything else that's going on, right now this is what I really want to know.

There's a long pause.

"Why are you asking me that?"

"Because I want to know. And because I'm still allowed to care about you, aren't I? I still want you to be happy."

She opens her mouth to speak, but then turns away again.

"Can we just go?"

We drive through the dark streets in a silence so awkward and confusing that it's almost painful. When we pull into the car park of the Canal House, she fumbles in the dark to open the van door. I reach over her and lift the latch, so close I can feel the warmth of her body, smell the scent of her hair.

"I hope you and Josh manage to sort things out," she says, stepping onto the concrete, about to close the door behind her.

"Libby—"

We stare at each other.

"I need to go," she tells me.

Once more I know something's shifted between us, taken us into a place it feels forbidden to go, where sentences are left hanging and nothing seems to make sense. But I don't understand it and I don't know what to do with it.

I nod. "Okay. Well, thanks for coming with me."

She offers me a weak smile, shuts the door and heads across the dark car park, leaving me wondering what the hell happened tonight.

I wait at home the next morning until Josh comes back from Michael's, pushing past me at the front door and heading into his room without a word.

"I'm tired," he mumbles, when I try to talk to him.

"Have you had breakfast?"

"I'm not hungry," he says, kicking off his shoes and flopping down on the bed. "I just want to sleep. Can you shut the door?"

I stand in the doorway, uncertainly.

"Please," he grumbles.

I close the door sadly.

That evening, I insist Josh stays home. We need to talk. But my explanations are met with stony silence, as are my apologies. I get nothing back but contemptuous glances. He simply isn't ready to engage.

In the end, I wonder if it's best to let the dust settle, talk things through in a couple of days when he might have calmed down. My main concern at the moment is to build a bridge between us, so the next morning I try a different tack.

"Why don't we go to kickboxing?" I suggest, when he slopes into the kitchen. "Burn off some steam?"

He lazily flicks the kettle on, peers inside a box of Shreddies as if they disgust him, and then opens the cupboard.

"We'll stop at McDonald's, get some pancakes on the way."

Josh gazes at the almost-empty shelves as if he's longing for an alternative breakfast option to suddenly materialise in front of him, but when it doesn't, he shrugs.

"Whatever," he mumbles.

Josh eats his pancakes in the van just as he always eat them – drowning in syrup, rolled up and devoured in a couple of gluttonous mouthfuls. This is a good sign, I think, seeing as he refused to eat any dinner last night. But he still won't talk to me, and we make the twenty-minute drive to the gym in silence.

"Ah, welcome back!" beams Rob as we enter his class.

Josh walks straight past him without an acknowledgement.

I open my mouth, about to call him up on his rudeness, but Rob sidles up next to me.

"Don't worry," he says, his Dutch accent creeping through, "let him work it out in here."

"He might need more than the hour then," I mutter.

Rob laughs. "I'll make sure he works hard and burns it all off."

Rob has a calm, reassuring presence about him that I think might be good for Josh today. Nothing ever seems to faze him. I can't imagine what it takes to be that calm, but if it's the punishing fitness regime, vegetarian diet and strict avoidance of caffeine, alcohol and sugar that does it, then I don't think I have what it takes.

"Right," shouts Rob to the class, clapping his hands, "so pair up, gloves and pads on, free pad work starting and ending with twenty straight punches. Go!"

Josh grabs his boxing gloves and gets ready to pair up with one of his usual partners – a guy called Nicco who's about his age, or a regional champion called Steph who matches his size but could probably kick the crap out of anyone in this room.

"Hey, let's partner up for a change," I suggest to Josh.

He raises his eyes despairingly towards the ceiling but doesn't protest.

I hold the pads for him and I can tell he's wound up from the way he attacks them. This is meant to be a warm-up, but the thud of his gloves and the thwack of his feet against the pads ricochet off the walls, and I have to plant my bare soles into the floor to stop myself stumbling backwards. Within a few minutes he's red-faced, sweat glistening on his forehead.

"Twenty straight!" Rob yells.

I hold the pads at shoulder height and Josh punches fast: left, right, left, right...

"You're done," I say, when twenty's up.

The other pairs around us have stopped, but Josh keeps going, lost in the rhythm.

"Stop, you're done," I repeat. I take a step back, go to lower the pads, and THUD! a punch comes straight in against the right side of my face.

I'm bent over, stunned, when I see blood dripping onto the floor.

"Whoa!" Rob shouts, running over. "What happened?"

I straighten up, holding the back of my hand against my bloody nose, to find Josh glaring at me, panting. His anger is evident to everyone.

"What the heck, man?" I hear Nicco mumble to Josh.

But Josh just rips off his gloves and throws them to the side of the gym before striding out the door.

"This is ridiculous," I whisper to Michael as I head out of his neat, modern flat.

"It'll all pass," he says quietly, "just give it a few days."

I look behind him, down the hallway into the lounge where Josh was standing a few seconds ago. But he's already gone, off to the spare room with a single holdall and his guitar.

"I've really screwed this up," I mutter.

"Don't go thinking this is all about you," says Michael, leaning in the doorway. "What he's going through is massive. His mum getting in contact after all these years... He's gonna have all kinds of thoughts and feelings going on. Anger, confusion, fear that it won't work out, fear that it will. He's processing, and he's taking it out on you because he knows it's safe to. You might just have to be his punchbag right now." He nods at the bruise that's come up under my right eye and across the bridge of my nose. "Literally."

"Well, you're the youth worker, so I'll take your word for it, but it's a bit hard to be his punchbag when he's refusing to even live at home."

"Look, just give it a couple of days. I'll try and talk to him."

I nod and force a grateful smile. My eyes are drawn to the shelf in his hallway, displaying signs of cosy coupledom: two sets of car keys in a glass bowl, a photo of the happy couple on holiday in Thailand... I feel a yearning in my soul for a similar shared life, a shared love.

"And how are you doing?" Michael asks, placing a hand on my shoulder. "Apart from all this stuff with Josh? What about all the other crap?"

I shrug.

I'm tempted to tell him that I think I'm losing my mind, because I know he'll understand how that feels. I'm tempted to tell him that I've lost my sense of self, that I don't feel sure of who I am anymore, that I keep having nightmares and I have a sense of things spinning out of control, that my breathing's got bad again... But he's taken on enough by watching over my son.

"I'm okay," I lie.

He smiles and shakes his head, sadly.

"Why do you always pretend?" he asks.

Chapter 20

Gone

From my head being empty, now all I seem to do is think and think and think. My feelings are elusive, escaping me every time I try to catch a glimpse of them. I'm just living in my head, asking one question after another.

Am I still me? Am I different now? Who are my wider biological family, my grandparents, aunts, cousins... Does it even matter? Do I even care? How would my dad feel if he understood that I know the truth?

And then, of course, there's the bigger question: am I going to see Jack before he dies? I know what it's like to have regrets, to want to tie things up and make them neat before it's too late. Would I deny another man the peace that I've been searching for?

My mum phones several times a day and leaves concerned messages, but I can't face answering her calls. What am I meant to say? Where would I even begin? I just want her to leave me alone.

And alone I am.

It's almost two weeks since Josh left. He's been hopping around between Michael's, Laura's and Sam's places, and although we're in contact, things are tense between us. I ache for his presence, his laughter, even his backchat. I can't believe this is happening, that something's come between us to such an extent that's he's actually moved out, that he really has that much anger towards me.

He has to come home soon. The new school year's started and this just can't continue. But for a little bit longer I'm willing to let him have his space. In fact, just for now, it's probably best that he's not here to see me. I'm lost, shattered, but I don't want him to know that. I want him to feel I'm here for him – waiting, solid, strong. I don't want him burdened by my sadness and confusion. And that's why I've chosen not to tell him about my dad, not yet. You might say I haven't learned my lesson about keeping secrets from him, but I simply can't throw another thing at him right now.

I pace the quiet, empty flat in the evening, unsure what to do with myself. I was supposed to be staying with my dad for the night while Brenda's away visiting her sister, but at the last minute, Laura stepped in. Initially I felt grateful, but now I think I could have done with the distraction. My natural reaction in times of stress is to retreat from the world, but tonight I can't stand being with myself for a moment longer. My instinct is to head to the Canal House and surround myself with familiar faces, but I guess Libby will be there and I don't know if I can face her. Despite having a million more pressing things to think about, our conversation in the van the other night keeps going round in my mind.

The only thing I regret is losing you...

What made me say that? It was too much. Too honest. Too exposing.

You could have given us a chance...

Did I give up too easily? Could things have been different?

All these confused thoughts are making me feel increasingly and irrationally angry towards her for the stress she's brought into my life. I didn't want this when I set out to find her, and I sure as hell don't need it right now. I've been going to the Canal House for years. I have friends there. It's where I talk, laugh, offload. And now I feel unable to go there because she's suddenly decided to settle back in town?

Sod it, I think, grabbing my wallet and phone. I'm not staying away just because of her.

When I arrive at the Canal House, I almost turn and walk straight out. Libby's there, as expected, clearing glasses from tables, seemingly settled into her new role, and I don't know what I'm thinking or feeling when I look at her but I wish it would just go away.

I head for a seat at the end of the bar, tucked in the corner out of the way. It's no surprise to find that Stu and Irena are, as always, already clued up on what's been going on in my life.

Before I sit down, Irena draws me in for a brief, firm hug. Her growing stomach feels round and hard and for a second it startles me. I could count on one hand the number of times I reluctantly felt Hellie's stomach when she was pregnant, and we certainly had no reason to hug during that time.

Irena releases me and punches me affectionately – but quite hard – on the arm.

"We were worried about you!" she frowns.

"Crap couple of weeks, huh?" smiles Stu sympathetically from the other side of the bar.

It's midweek and as the place isn't too busy, Irena is happy to serve while I fill Stu in on the finer details of Hellie's emails, Josh's anger, my dad's deterioration, my *other* dad's dying wish to see me...

"Jeez," whistles Stu, "it never rains but it pours, eh?" He leans across the bar conspiratorially. "You know what might cheer you up?" he asks, glancing behind me.

I turn to see Rachel and one of her Aussie friends playing pool on the other side of the room.

"I'm not sure that's gonna solve my problems, mate," I tell him wearily.

"Suit yourself," he shrugs, heading off to serve a customer.

I'm gazing into my glass of lemonade, watching the tiny bubbles fizz, when I feel a presence beside me.

"Hi," says Libby tentatively, edging onto the bar stool next to me.

"Hi," I say without even looking up.

"I've been wondering how you are. I saw Michael and he told me about your dad… You know, not being your dad… And I was going to text you. I did text you, actually. Well, I wrote you about six texts, but I didn't know what to say so I deleted them. They all sounded so inadequate."

She talks fast, and out of the corner of my eye, I see her checking over her shoulder, scanning the room.

"How's the new job going?" I ask, wondering if she's anxious to get back to it.

"Oh, fine. I'm helping out in the kitchen mainly, clearing tables, waitressing, and then the painting, of course. Thank goodness it's been dry the last couple of days and I've actually made some progress! Do you want to…? You should come and have a look…"

"Yeah, I will," I tell her, a bit dismissively, "maybe another—"

"Oh sure! Another time, of course."

We fall silent and I play with a beer mat. I was feeling better after my chat with Stu, but I suddenly feel my stress levels rising again. As if I haven't got enough going on right now without… this. I wish she wouldn't sit so close to me. I wish she hadn't said those things the other night that made me think that if only I'd given us a chance we could have made it work. It's bad enough to spend years thinking about what you lost. But to think you might never have lost it in the first place…

"I can't imagine how you're feeling right now," she says. "You already had so much going on and now this. It must be so confusing."

I tap the beer mat on the bar.

"Nothing's changed really," I shrug. I don't feel this is true, but I want it to be.

"No, of course not! I mean, your dad's still your dad, he still raised you, that's what counts. Look at my dad. The biology's all there, but can I really call him a dad? Being a dad isn't really about DNA, is it? It's about doing all the dad stuff."

I don't respond. This is too hard. I wish she'd leave me alone. For good.

"I'd been thinking actually," she continues, "about asking you if I could visit him. He was always so nice to me. God, he really used to make me laugh! And he was so patient, answering my endless questions about how things worked, letting me try things out in his workshop…"

I'd forgotten how often Libby used to get involved in my dad's "little projects", as my mum called them. How he used to let her tinker with wires and gears and circuits, while I lingered impatiently, wanting her to myself.

"He used to like teaching you things," I say, my anger towards her dissipating a little with the memory. "You had more interest than I did. And more aptitude."

Libby glances anxiously over her shoulder again.

"Well, I don't know about that," she says quickly, "it's probably no coincidence you became an electrician. I'm sure you learned a lot from him. But if you think it would be okay to visit him… I mean, if he'd like that…"

I don't tell her that he probably wouldn't know her. She clearly doesn't realise quite how bad things are and I can't blame her for that. But I'm touched by her offer. Generally, Alzheimer's has an amazing ability to keep people at bay.

"I'll have a think," I tell her.

"Oh, sure, I mean, maybe it would be too much, but just let me know."

I look at her for the first time and she offers me a little smile. She always tried her best to comfort me. Even when I was too angry and stressed and sad to hear her, she kept trying until I finally pushed her away.

I feel a sudden urge to talk to her now, to share my struggles in a way I never could back then, but just as I open my mouth, a man appears behind her, placing his hand casually on her shoulder. She quickly jumps to her feet.

So here's her distraction.

"Will this is Jamie, Jamie this is Will," she says hastily, waving her hand between us.

"Ahhh," says Will, eyeing me as if I'm the missing piece of a puzzle. I'm the ex-boyfriend who tracked his fiancée down after sixteen years for the sake of a garbled apology she apparently didn't need. I know what I'd think in his place: that either I'm still in love with her or I'm slightly unhinged. Well, he'd be wrong about that, because I'm pretty sure I'm both. He smiles and extends his hand. "Nice to meet you," he says, politely, although the vice-like handshake makes it clear he doesn't mean it.

"You too," I say, increasing my grip in return.

He's about my height, maybe slightly taller, slim, fit-looking, clean-shaven, with glasses, neatly cut sandy hair and an aura of self-assurance. He's apparently come straight from work as he's wearing a well-cut suit, although he's loosened his collar and removed his tie.

"Libs, I should probably get going," he says.

Libs?

She offers me an apologetic smile before following him towards the door, where they stand close, chatting. He places his hand on the bare skin of her arm and whispers something into her ear. I look away, anywhere but at the two of them.

"All alone?" I hear a voice ask.

Rachel slides onto the stool Libby's just vacated.

"You look kind of unhappy," she says, making a sad, pouty face.

"Nah, I'm great," I lie, draining the rest of my lemonade.

"Let me get you another drink," she says, beckoning Stu over.

"Actually, I'm just leaving."

"Oh, come on," she whines.

"What will you two be having?" Stu asks, flashing me a look of encouragement.

"I'll have a beer," says Rachel, "and..." She raises an eyebrow at me, questioningly.

"I'll have a beer, too," I say.

Stu frowns.

"But you don't drink," Rachel laughs.

I glance quickly at Libby and Will who are still lingering intimately by the door.

"Well, I think it's about time I started again," I say.

It's actually a relief to chat with Rachel. She knows what's been going on with me – nothing's a secret in this place for long – but she's either too diplomatic or too disinterested to want a conversation about it. Instead, we talk about a bloke she recently dated who turned out to have a fetish for toes, her inability to get used to the British weather, and her lesbian boss who keeps making suggestive remarks towards her. She's funny, lively, beautiful and, most importantly, superficial and self-centred. That suits me fine; I've had enough of the serious stuff in life.

As time slips by and we have another drink, she touches my arm and suggests going back to hers. I smile at her, but I don't say yes.

"I'm gonna give up on you one of these days," she teases, pressing her leg against mine.

I take a swig of beer. This is only my second bottle, but after so many years of sobriety I can already feel my muscles warming and loosening, my inhibitions relaxing. "Are you saying this is my last chance?"

"I'm saying you're making a big mistake," she says, cocking her head to the side and smiling at me, all eyelashes and glossy lips.

Just at that moment my phone goes. It's Laura.

"Sorry, one minute, I have to take this," I tell Rachel, thinking it could be about my dad or Josh. Unable to hear clearly, I slip out the back door and onto the terrace. I'm surprised to find that darkness has fallen. Two of the outside tables are taken by couples having a drink.

It turns out Laura's just checking in on me. I tell her I'm fine but right in the middle of something. I'll call her back tomorrow.

When I hang up, I look over at the wall. Even with the outside lights on it's hard to make out the painting, and I make my way closer. I study the sky that Josh and I helped paint, the blue-green water of the canal, some brightly coloured riverboats painted in Libby's signature cartoonish style, the winding canal path, the bridge... And when I look closer, I realise one of the boats is *Isabelle Blue*. I recognise the design, the swirl of the red letters on the side. I spent hours on that boat with Libby, and yet I'd almost forgotten what she looked like. Seeing that boat now though brings it all back – poring over textbooks together, our first – or rather second – kiss, lying on her narrow bed, or in the bow under a blanket...

I rub my forehead.

What's the matter with me? I'm such an idiot.

"What do you think?"

I jump slightly to find Libby standing next to me.

I hook my hands in my back pockets and avoid eye contact.

"Looks like you're almost finished," I tell her.

"Hopefully this week, if the weather holds."

"And then I guess you'll be done here."

"Yeah, and Irena's doing much better now so... yeah, I'll be done here."

I feel a wave of relief wash over me. A week from now she'll be gone and I'll have one less thing to deal with.

"Look, I know you have far bigger things on your mind," says Libby, sheepishly, "but when we were in the van the other night looking for Josh... I just... I shouldn't have said what I did. About how you could have given us a shot. I don't know why I said it. It was stupid. I'm sorry. It's been kind of confusing coming back here, there are so many memories and... I think I just... it might not have been the right thing to come back here and—"

"So why did you?" I interrupt, my tone blunter than intended.

"Because you wanted to meet with me," she frowns.

"We could have met anywhere. You're the one who said you'd come here."

"Well, I suppose I thought coming back to Timpton might be good for me. But maybe I was wrong."

"Well, another week and you're done, aren't you?"

I can hear how abrupt I sound, but I can't stop myself. I stare out at the dark water of the canal.

"You're the one who came looking for me, remember?" she says, clearly offended.

"But I never asked you to stay."

I can feel her staring at me.

"Perhaps you would have preferred it if I hadn't?"

I don't answer, but I guess my silence speaks volumes.

"You know, I'm sorry you're going through a hard time, but you're not the only one with past hurts you want to heal," she says bitterly, before turning and walking away.

I close my eyes and clench my jaw, wanting to be somewhere – someone – else.

I lose myself in Rachel. I don't even care about the sound of her housemates drinking and playing music downstairs, I'm just here in this moment. I can smell the alcohol on our breaths, feel my heart racing with anticipation as we pull off each other's T-shirts. It's warm in her room and her hands are hot against my back as she pulls me towards her, starts to unbutton my jeans. She pushes her hips against me and I clutch at her bare waist.

And just then I think of what I said to Libby. The tone I used with her.

I concentrate on the feel of Rachel's smooth, tanned skin beneath my palms. She kisses me with a sense of urgency, running her hands over my chest, through my hair...

Why the hell did I talk to her like that? She's done nothing to deserve my anger.

Rachel kisses my neck, starts to tug down my jeans.

My feelings towards her are my problems, not hers.

"I can't do this," I hear myself murmur.

"What?" whispers Rachel, reaching to unhook her bra.

"I can't… I'm sorry," I say, pulling away and buttoning my jeans.

"You what?"

"I need to go. I'm so sorry, it's not you, I swear. It's me, I'm… I've got stuff going on, I'm sorry."

She looks understandably affronted.

"God, d'you know what, Jay? I'm done with you!" she says, throwing my T-shirt at me.

"Hey, you're the one who kept coming on to me, remember?!"

"And you weren't playing games?!"

I don't even bother answering her. I'm already halfway out the door.

I've never been back to the canal path at night, but tonight I want to torture myself, remember the mistakes I made. As if I ever let myself forget.

I stride through the darkness and the pounding of my trainers against the path reminds me of that night; running fast and yet moving too slow.

Which way? Left or right?

My breath, which that night rasped with the effort of my race, becomes laboured again now, my chest tightening, fighting for air.

Sixty seconds too late.

I quicken my pace, welcoming the surge of pain in my lungs, willing an attack to come on. The lights along the canal path seem to sway and blur, and I remember the sound of shattered glass, a cry of pain, and then blood. Blood on Libby's face. Blood from a knife sliced across my palm. Blood on the pub carpet from my wound.

Out of the darkness, I see a group of men approaching: three of them, one taller than the others. They're talking and laughing, a bit worse for wear. They have accents of some kind and I instinctively know it's the one in the middle who's their leader.

My heart thumps, desperate to break free from the squeeze of my tightening ribcage. There's no escape. I put my head down and plough forwards, my breath coming in wheezy, short bursts.

"You all right, fella?" asks the leader when I reach them.

I don't talk, just stride forwards, but they're taking up the entire path and my shoulder knocks against one of theirs as I try to pass.

"Hey, watch out!" he says, and I think I see him make a grab for me. Without a thought, I lash out, shoving him away from me and into his two friends, who stumble backwards.

"Hey, what the hell?!" shouts the guy I shoved.

"Leave him, Joe," says the third man, nervously.

I stride on, hearing them mutter behind me.

"…just asking if the nutter was okay…"

"…off his head on something…"

None of them has an accent, and none of them is the Leader.

As soon as they're far enough behind me, I stop and lean over, my hands resting on my knees, trying to drag in air.

I climb the steps that lead from the towpath up to the back of the Canal House. Stu spies me crossing the terrace just as he's closing the back doors for the night.

"You all right, mate?" he calls.

"Is Libby around?"

He takes a step to the side and I see Libby and Irena perched at the bar eating a very late dinner of whatever leftovers have come from the kitchen. They both peer at me, forks in the air.

"Can I talk to you?" I call to Libby.

"What about?" she asks, clearly still annoyed.

"I just want a quick word."

She looks to Irena, who gives her a little nod. I have a feeling they've been discussing me.

Libby slides off her stool with a sigh, making it clear that this is an inconvenience at the end of a long evening.

I wander to the side of the terrace, out of view of Stu and Irena, and she follows me. The outside lights have been switched off and I can only just see her in the darkness. I feel agitated and tense, my heartbeat still accelerated.

"Look, I'm sorry about how I spoke to you earlier. I was out of order."

"Yes, you were," she says, arms crossed defensively.

"It's been a horrendous week, and I know that's no excuse—"

"You want me gone, don't you?"

I stare at her. Her eyes shine in the darkness, wide with hurt and confusion.

"Yes."

She shrugs, forlornly. "Why?"

I shake my head and sigh. I don't want her to leave here feeling hurt and rejected. I'd rather tell her the truth than allow that to happen. Besides, I'm too exhausted to lie to her anymore, and she'll be gone soon anyway.

"You and I have a history…"

I stop, unsure whether to proceed. But I've already lost my son, my father, my identity… What else do I have to lose?

"…We have a history, and it's like you said earlier, memories can get stirred up…"

I stare down at my feet, although I can barely see them in the darkness.

"…Feelings," I fumble, trying to explain, "feelings can get stirred up. I thought I could leave the past behind, but seeing you again, all these feelings have resurfaced and—"

"Oh," says Libby quietly, as if she suddenly understands, "oh, I see."

I hold my breath, unable to meet her eye.

"It didn't occur to me that you might feel—"

"No, it's me, my problem," I interrupt, "I know you and I could never—"

"Of course seeing me would bring it all back. I mean, everything you went through around that time, what happened that night…"

It takes me a moment to realise that she's misunderstood me entirely.

I open my mouth to set her straight, but then I stop. This is better, I think.

I nod. "Yeah, I guess I just associate you a bit with—"

"I get it," she says, "I can see why you wouldn't want me around."

"That sounds so—"

"It's fine," she says, holding up her hand to stop me, "I understand."

We stand awkwardly and I don't know what else to say.

"I should go," she says, quietly.

She walks past me, her head down, but stops at the doors.

"I don't know if I'll see you before I leave," she says.

I stare at her face, illuminated by the light from the bar, and realise that this could well be the last I see of her. I drink in her brown eyes, the curve of her lips, the freckles on the bridge of her nose. I feel a mixture of sadness and relief.

"I hope everything works out for you," she says, sounding a little emotional. She turns quickly and heads inside, sliding the glass door shut behind her.

I lean against the cool brick of the wall, taking deep breaths of the night air, feeling like I have nothing left to give.

Just then my phone buzzes. I'm so drained that for the first time ever I consider leaving it, but I can't.

It's Josh.

"You all right?" I answer, worried that he's calling at this hour.

"Dad, I need your help," he says, his voice panicked.

Immediately I go from dead on my feet to high alert.

"What's the matter?"

I can hear shouting around him, swearing, a girl shrieking.

Images flash through my mind of all the threatening situations he could be in, all the people who could be closing in on him, trapping him, wanting to harm him.

"Where are you?" I demand.

"I'm at home. Can you just come? I really need—"

I'm running before he's even finished his sentence.

Chapter 21

Decisions

As soon as I get near our block of flats, I know Josh wasn't exaggerating when he said things had gotten out of hand.

There are teenagers milling about on the pavement, shouting and laughing, bottles in their hands. I can hear the boom of the music from outside on the street, blaring loudly and then fading as if people are fighting over the volume control.

Helen, from the floor below, is standing in the lobby in her dressing gown, having a row with a group of kids I don't recognise. Helen's a good neighbour as long as you don't piss her off, then she comes at you all guns blazing. And tonight she's clearly had enough.

"Get this under control, Jay, or I'm calling the police!" she yells at me as I bound up the stairs.

Chloe, Amelia and the other one – Jasinda? – are huddled anxiously outside my open front door.

"The boys are inside," says Chloe when she sees me. "They're trying to get people out. They told us to stay out here."

I head inside, pushing past teenagers laughing, drinking, swearing and making out in my hallway. My home smells of body odour, cheap fragrances, beer and weed.

As I pass the kitchen, I see Alex and Sam arguing with some other boys and pointing them towards the door.

I shove my way through to the darkened lounge and flick the light switch on. There's a cacophony of groans and swearing as I kill the music.

"OUT! EVERYONE GET OUT!"

For a second I wonder if they're going to obey, or whether I've bitten off more than I can chew. A couple of them look closer to twenty than fifteen, and I wonder whether calling the police would have been a better option. But then a voice booms from behind me—

"COME ON, YOU HEARD HIM! GET OUT! MOVE IT!"

Michael normally avoids confrontation like the plague, but he's in his comfort zone here, using the two skills that earn his livelihood: working with difficult teenagers and using that powerful voice.

Slowly the kids start to move out, blurry-eyed and ratty, mumbling in disgust.

"… thought he said his dad was looking after his old man for the night…"

"… fuck's sake, this sucks…"

"… I was so nearly in there with her…"

"Thanks for the back up," I say, patting Michael on the shoulder as I walk past him.

"I'm sorry, he told us he was—"

"It's not your fault. You can't keep an eye on him twenty-four/seven," I say.

Finding both bedrooms locked, I hammer on the doors until a couple emerges from each, looking both sheepish and disgruntled at the interruption. They slink off, unapologetic.

"Dad?"

I turn to see Josh looking flushed and stressed out.

"I'm *so* sorry."

Another time I might have blown my top, but I'm so pleased to see him, and so relieved he's safe, that I just want to grab him and hold him tight. I'm not stupid enough to do that in front of his peers though. Instead I just shrug.

"Don't worry. It happens."

My miserable-looking son and his equally miserable-looking friends work in silence under Michael's supervision, throwing bottles into bin bags, uprighting furniture, wiping up spillages. The coffee table is singed and scratched, the curtain rail's hanging down, the money from the cash jar is gone, there are burn marks all over the sofa and stains on the carpet I can't imagine will ever come out. The stains on my sheets don't even bear contemplating and I can't tear them off my mattress fast enough.

"Jesus Christ, what a mess," I sigh, throwing the bedding into a pile on the floor and sitting down on my bed next to Chloe. She has a headache and feels queasy.

"It was all my fault," she says, teary. "I was the one who talked Josh into having a party. It was just meant to be, like, ten people from our year and I told them not to put anything on social media. I'm so, so sorry. I just wanted to cheer Josh up. He's been so down and I hate seeing him unhappy like that."

She puts her head in her hands and cries, her long, blonde hair falling around her face.

"It's not your fault," I say, "we all mess up. I know I have lately."

She wraps her arms around herself and shivers. She's wearing a pink, strappy top and her bare arms are covered in goosebumps. I go to my wardrobe and pull out a black hoodie.

"Here, put this on," I tell her.

She pulls it on. It's huge on her.

"So, how do you think Josh is doing?" I ask, sitting down beside her again.

She wipes at her eyes with the sleeves of my top.

"I think he's stressed out and confused," she says. "And I think he's scared."

"Scared?"

"I think he's scared of meeting his mum. And also scared of not meeting her, like, if she just drops contact again. And I think he's scared of upsetting you."

"Me?"

"I think he feels like it would be, like, sort of disloyal to meet up with her? Like, he'd be betraying you or something?"

I close my eyes and shake my head. It had never crossed my mind he might feel that way. But I suddenly realise that's exactly how I've been feeling: that even acknowledging that Jack's my biological father would be somehow betraying my dad, let alone meeting with him.

"I've been trying to talk things through with him and be supportive," sniffs Chloe. "He's always there for me when I'm down, you know? He's always, just, like, really sweet and kind."

"He is?"

"Yeah. I just wanted to try to make him feel better, like he does with me."

I try to imagine my son in this role, providing a comforting shoulder to cry on, knowing just what to say to make an unhappy girl feel better. I've always known he has that empathy in him, but most of the time it's hidden under the swagger and backchat, the cockiness and jokes. I feel proud that he's able to show such sensitivity.

"You're a good friend to him," I tell Chloe, gratefully.

She smiles at me, her make-up smudged around her eyes.

"He's a good friend to me."

I know it's not my place, but I would hate to see these two lose their chance. One of them needs to make the first move.

"Are you sure friends is all you want to be?"

She looks at me, confused.

"Me and Josh?"

"Yeah. I thought maybe…"

"No," she laughs, "I don't feel that way about him. And he's not interested in me like that, either."

You're wrong, I want to tell her, Josh's words coming back to me clearly.

We're already friends and I don't want to put my feelings out there and risk ruining our friendship.

His secret's safe with me, but whatever he feels for Chloe it clearly isn't reciprocated, and my heart aches for him.

"Come on," I sigh, wearily, "let's get you home."

As we stand up, Chloe sways on her feet and leans into me. I put my arm around her narrow shoulders to steady her, and feel a warmth spreading down my side. At first I think it's the heat of her body, but then I realise what's just happened.

"Oh, come on, give me a break," I groan, looking up to the merciless heavens.

She's just thrown up all over me.

"We're majorly pissed off with you," Michael tells Josh, sternly. "You told us you were going out to the cinema with some friends and you came here, threw a party, didn't return my calls… I was just about to call your dad—"

"I know, I know," says Josh, miserably, looking at his socks.

"We trusted you. That was part of the deal about you staying with us, to tell us where you are at all times. We can't have responsibility for you if you're going to lie to us. What if something had happened to you? How the heck would I ever square that with your dad?"

"I'm sorry."

"You damn well should be."

It's two in the morning and the three of us are standing in the hallway under the too-bright lights, surrounded by black bin bags. Josh's friends have been picked up by weary, disgruntled parents.

"So, you coming with me, staying here or what?" Michael asks more gently.

I wait for Josh's answer with trepidation. He looks at me from under his fringe.

"Maybe... I'll just stay here?" he says almost shyly.

I shrug, making it clear it's entirely his choice, but my heart soars.

The next day, Josh walks to Michael's to pick up his belongings, and then spends the afternoon in his bedroom either napping or glued to his phone. Normally I'd be telling him to do something more productive, but today I'm too exhausted to worry about it. I lie on the sofa, my laptop on my stomach, watching YouTube clips on how to remove carpet stains.

And then, mid-afternoon, Josh enters the lounge.

"Can I talk to you?" he asks, quietly.

"Sure," I say, not looking up from my screen. I've learned through experience that he'll talk more openly if I don't look straight at him.

He sits down on the edge of the ruined coffee table and I wait for him to start, but when he doesn't say anything, I look over at him.

He's sitting with his head in his hands, tears streaming down his face.

I sit up slowly, place my laptop on the floor, walk over to him and crouch down.

"What's going on?" I ask, placing my hand on his shoulder.

"I can't..." he sobs, "...I just can't..."

"You can't what?"

He rocks back and forth, gripping strands of hair between his fingers.

"I can't deal with all this, Dad. All this stuff that's coming at me. I don't want to do it."

Tears drip onto the knees of his jeans.

"You don't want to do what?" I ask, anxiously.

"Any of it! I don't want to see my mum for a start!"

I shake my head, confused.

"You *don't* want to see her?"

"No! It's just too much! It all just keeps going round in my head. I can't sleep, I can't think straight. I just want things to go back to how they were." He looks up at me with tear-filled, desperate eyes. "I just can't handle seeing her right now! I just can't!"

"It's okay, you don't have to see her," I say, firmly. "Understand? You don't have to. It's entirely your choice. But if and when you do want to, you know I'm one hundred per cent behind you, don't you? And that I'm completely fine with it."

"I just don't want to! Not right now!"

"That's fine," I tell him, calmly, "then you don't have to, that's fine."

A part of me wants to revel in his rejection of Hellie, wants to throw it in her face. *See what you did? You've lost him! You're too late!*

But, actually, I just feel sad. I'd been starting to entertain the idea that they could have a relationship, that he could finally have his mother in his life. I feel sorry for him, and, surprisingly, I feel sorry for her. They've both missed out on so much.

"Do you want to talk to her on the phone? Email her?" I ask a bit hopefully.

"No!"

"Okay, all right, that's fine," I soothe.

"Maybe. One day. But not now."

He wipes the back of his hand across his nose and sniffs loudly.

"What else?" I ask.

"All this stuff about my GCSEs. I just feel like you're always on my back about my future and—"

"Okay, okay, I'm sorry," I tell him, and in that moment I truly am. Desperately sorry. "I didn't know you were really feeling that pressured—"

"I tried to tell you!"

"I know, and I should have listened. I'll lay off. I promise."

My heart aches seeing him like this, knowing I've

contributed to it, that I've made him feel exactly the way my mum used to make me feel; as though I had to measure up to some higher standard. How is it that the traits you despise in your parents get so easily repeated?

"I just feel like you want me to go to uni and have this great career and everything because you couldn't, and I feel this weight, like this responsibility—"

"It's not that," I tell him, "it's never been about that."

"Then what?"

I give a heavy sigh. "I guess I've always felt like I had something to prove when it came to you. No one thought I could bring up a child. I was young, I was single. I felt like everyone just expected me to fail. And when you went to that primary school... all those cosy little middle-class families... everyone just seemed to look at me like I couldn't do it. And I just... I guess I wanted to prove them wrong. I couldn't give you much, but I thought if you could at least have a good education... but it's my stuff, not yours. That's about *my* insecurities. And I'm sorry. I should never have pushed that on to you. I'll stop. I promise."

"I just feel suffocated sometimes," Josh continues, tearfully, "you're so... I dunno... like, protective. It's too much. I feel like you're just so stressy all the time over me – my schoolwork, my future, where I am, who I'm with, what I'm doing... like, what do you think's going to happen? It's like you don't trust me."

"I do trust you. It's—"

I'm about to say it's other people I don't trust, but I stop myself. Clearly I've been pushing all my fears onto him and I feel terrible about it. I didn't even realise. I thought I was keeping him safe from the big bad world. But look what I've done.

For a moment I wonder if I should tell him; tell him about me and Michael and Max and Tom. About what happened. About how it changed me and how I viewed life. But that's just more of my shit.

"Okay, you're right," I agree ,"maybe I've been a bit much at times. And I'm sorry. I'll try to loosen up a bit, okay? I don't want to make you feel like I'm always on your back about things, I really don't."

"It's just all too much stress, Dad," he mumbles through his tears.

He slumps forward, resting his forehead on my shoulder and I rub his back.

"I know, son," I whisper, "I know it is."

He's still just a boy, underneath it all.

The next day, I make a phone call to Hellie. It's strange hearing her voice again after all this time. I notice the trace of Scandinavian accent is almost entirely gone, overridden by the American after all her years in the States. We exchange very brief *how are yous*, but other than that I keep the phone call purely perfunctory. It's amazing how little two people with a child can have to say to each other.

"He doesn't want any contact with you right now," I tell her.

"You mean, *you* don't want him to have contact with me right now."

"No," I say through clenched teeth, "I mean that after twelve years of not having you in his life he's struggling to contemplate the adjustment. I've told him that he can call you or email you whenever he wants, and that if he wants to see you I'll make that happen. But he's made his choice. For now."

She sighs heavily. "Okay, well, I'm guessing he has social media accounts, so maybe I can just message him or… I don't know… Is there an email address—"

"Hellie," I say, trying to stay calm, "please. *Please* think of him, for once in your life. He doesn't want to make contact with you, and he doesn't want you making contact with him. Not right now. Maybe in a year, two years, he'll feel differently. But *please*, for God's sake, *please* do what any decent mother would do and put what he needs before what you want."

There's a long pause.

"Okay," she says, sounding defeated, "okay, well, will you just let him know that I'm here when he wants to make contact and that I'm thinking of him?"

"Yes," I tell her, relieved that, for now at least, this episode seems to be drawing to a close. "I'll do that."

I'm sitting at the kitchen table typing up invoices on my laptop when I hear the front door open and shut.

I close my eyes and take a deep breath, wondering whether it's all about to kick off again. I should have told Josh earlier about my dad – his beloved grandad – not being related to us in the way we always thought, but I just couldn't bring myself to do it, not when he's been so stressed out. But the longer I left it, the more fearful I became that when he found out he'd feel betrayed again and accuse me of keeping things from him.

In the end, Laura offered to tell him, and I was too tired to argue.

I can't imagine how the conversation went, and I don't even dare to turn around when I hear them enter the kitchen behind me.

Josh comes over and silently places a Starbucks coffee and a paper bag on the table in front of me, and then disappears from my view again.

I hear him shuffling behind me, then feel his arms wrapping around my shoulders.

"I didn't know you were having to deal with all that," he says, sorrowfully, laying his chin on my shoulder. "It sucks."

Laura sits down at the kitchen table.

"Like Josh and I were saying in the café," she tells me, firmly, "we're family, we stick together, and that's all that matters."

I offer her a grateful smile.

"That better not be lemon and poppy seed," I say, nodding to the paper bag.

"Told you!" chimes Josh.

"Oh my God!" cries Laura, slapping her hands over her eyes. "Who in their right mind doesn't like lemon and poppy seed?"

"Chocolate!" Josh and I both shout at the same time. "Always get chocolate!"

I sit at a table outside, the last of the summer sunshine warming my neck, sipping an Americano and gazing at the mural that surrounds the terrace.

It's brilliant, a gentle kaleidoscope of colours that reflects everything that's good about the canal: the reflection of the sky on the water's glassy surface, the vibrant colours of the houseboats, the wildlife, the old bridges... On the towpath, she's painted joggers, cyclists, families taking a stroll, dogs on leads. From left to right, the seasons change in sequence, taking the viewer from a crisp winter's day, through to the bright greens of spring, the warm, yellow days of summer, then, finally, the reds and browns of autumn. The perspective is subtly and skilfully wrong. The houseboats slope cartoonishly, the canal meanders exaggeratedly, the ducks are oversized and the characters look soft and childish, as if they're made of play dough.

It's better than anyone imagined it might be.

Libby's gone. I don't know how I feel about that, just like I don't know how I feel about anything anymore, but I think it's probably for the best. Was it a mistake to go looking for her? I don't think so. I got to make my peace, find out she was okay. And hopefully my apology meant something. At least whatever I'm left dealing with now is all mine.

I close my eyes against the light. My head hurts and my stomach is fluttering nervously.

"Hello stranger," a voice says behind me.

I stand up, slowly, full of trepidation.

"Tom," I say, holding out my hand, unable to believe this is really him, "it's good to see you."

He places his tea on the table and takes my hand in both of his.

We look at each other with some disbelief.

"Christ, when did you get so bloody good-looking?" he asks.

I glance at his soft belly. "When did you get so bloody fat?"

He tips his head back and laughs loudly before slapping me on the shoulder.

"Yeah, that's what the contentment of married life and a sedentary job do to you, I'm afraid," he grins, sitting himself down. "Although you lonely, single labourers wouldn't know about that."

I smile, amazed at how we can fall back into this pattern so easily after more than fifteen years apart.

"I can't believe you're married," I say, "to someone who's actually met you."

"Ouch!"

Out of the four of us, Tom was the only one who was adamant he'd never settle down. He used to tell us it would be a travesty to womanhood if he tied himself down to one person. Now, he brings up a photo on his phone.

"Her name's Kim. Well, that's her English name. Her Chinese name's too hard for us moronic Westerners to pronounce, so she doesn't make us try. She's training to be a cardiologist," he says proudly.

"Wow," I say, looking at the picture. "Good on you. Congratulations."

"Yeah, we started training together before I decided my true calling was fixing people's minds and not their bodies."

I shake my head in awe.

"Doctor Thomas Pickering."

"Who would have thought it, eh?" he quips.

"I would have," I tell him, earnestly. "I always knew you'd achieve great things. The smartest boy in school."

"Ah, yes!" he shouts, punching the air. "Finally he admits it! I win! I win!"

"Apart from me, of course," I add.

"Aghh, whatever," he groans, taking a sip of his tea.

"So, what made you swap from hearts to heads, anyway?" I ask. "Were you drawn to psychiatry by your incredible capacity for empathy? Your naturally sensitive and diplomatic nature?"

He laughs, almost spitting out his mouthful of tea.

"You still know me so well," he grins.

"Clearly not."

"Well," he shrugs, "when you grow up in a nuthouse…"

"Are you allowed to talk about mental illness like that?"

"Only outside of the hospital."

We look at each other, both taking in the changed features of the person opposite. We're both so much taller, broader, with stubbled faces, man-sized hands, the early appearance of faint lines at the corners of our eyes. Where did the time go?

"It's been too long," he says, and I nod, wondering how we ever lost touch.

But then I remember how raw it all was, how messed up and miserable we were. Tom and I were always two of a kind, each of us serving as a mirror to the other one's anger and bitterness.

"So you said on the phone you'd been in contact with Libby?"

"Yeah. Well, I basically hunted her down in the same way I hunted you down."

He raises an eyebrow at me like I might have lost my mind.

I stare into my coffee, suddenly embarrassed.

"You think I need a shrink, Doctor Pickering?" I joke.

He leans forwards, folding his arms on the table.

"I'm not sure yet. Why don't you tell me what all this is about and I'll let you know."

I lean back in my chair, wishing I'd brought sunglasses, less to protect my eyes than to hide the windows to my soul.

"I guess I feel the need to revisit the past and gain closure. Say sorry to certain people, make amends with others."

Tom looks worried.

"Are you sick?"

I chuckle quietly.

"That's what Libby thought too. Although, I dunno, maybe I am, in a way. I feel a weight, I suppose you could say. Like I'm carrying a burden I want to be rid of. I know certain friends and family think I'm closed off, that the way I go about things can be a bit... unhealthy. I don't know. I just got to the point where I had to take action."

"And how did you know you were at that point?" asks Tom.

I shrug. "I guess I just felt like things had reached tipping point."

"What constitutes tipping point?"

"I suppose I felt like I wasn't coping that brilliantly with things. And that the ways I was behaving weren't making me happy in the long run."

Tom nods, thoughtfully.

"So, in what ways has this burden, this weight or whatever, been affecting your life?" he asks.

I smile at him. "Blimey, you really are a psychiatrist, aren't you? I thought maybe you'd just made yourself a certificate in Word and printed it off."

"You're avoiding the question," he smiles, wagging a finger at me.

I tip my head back and laugh, but I feel a surge of anxiety. He knows what he's doing and he's not letting me off the hook easily.

"I think I close myself off to relationships," I admit, thinking about all the accusations Michael and Laura have thrown at me over the years, all the things I've denied but I now know to be true. "I think I sabotage my chances of happiness, I think I spend far too long agonising about the past, I think I won't allow myself to move on from mistakes I made a long time ago—"

"You won't *allow* yourself? Like you're punishing yourself?"

I shift uncomfortably in my seat, the sun suddenly feeling too hot against my neck. I don't like this. I want fun Tom back.

"Why would you need to punish yourself?" he asks.

I shake my head. "I didn't say that, you did."

"Because that's what it sounds like to me."

I stare at the table.

"What did you do that was so wrong?" he asks.

"Look, I didn't invite you here for a therapy session," I tell him bluntly, feeling my heart rate accelerate. "I asked you here—"

"Did you ever talk to anybody about what happened that night?"

"Did you?"

"No. I threw myself into my studies so fucking hard and for so fucking long that when I finally came up for air it felt like something that happened to somebody else. But that's me. And we're not talking about me."

I have no idea why my hands suddenly feel shaky. I clench them tightly in my lap.

"I felt at the time," says Tom, leaning in, "that you somehow felt responsible for what happened that evening."

I fold my arms across my chest and look away from him, but all I see surrounding me is Libby's mural: the canal and all its seasonal charms. Where's the darkness, the people telling me to run like I was their only hope, the point on the towpath where I made the wrong choice? Where's the boy with the blood on his hands, the smashed light, the girl with a bleeding face?

I close my eyes for the briefest moment, my head starting to swim.

"Look, I don't know what other stresses and strains you might have had in your life since I last saw you," says Tom, "but you do at least know that nothing that evening was your fault, don't you?"

I clench my jaw, pain shooting through my back teeth. I have an overwhelming urge to flee, but my bones feel locked in place.

"I thought…" I say falteringly, "…I mean, I had a feeling you blamed me—"

"Me?" he asks, incredulous. "Why would you think that?"

"Because you were so angry afterwards, and because you kept your distance—"

"We were both angry. And I kept my distance because…" he shakes his head, sadly, "because I just wanted to forget it ever happened."

"I had a baby, for God's sake."

"I know," he says, squeezing his eyes shut, the regret evident on his face, "and I never even came to see you, and I'm sorry. I've felt so bad about that, about the way I withdrew. But I never blamed you for anything, you have to know that."

"I was the one who made us late that night," I hear myself say. "I was the one who suggested taking the shortcut—"

"What are you talking about? *I* was the one who made us late, and *Max* was the one who suggested taking the shortcut."

"No," I shake my head adamantly. "I was trying to win Libby a soft toy by shooting one of those stupid air rifle things. I couldn't let it go. I just kept trying until I finally won that polar bear."

"Oh no," he laughs, "you don't get to take the credit for that!"

I frown at him.

"You and I were in competition mode all evening, both trying to be the first one to hit that damn target. We kept going back until you finally hit the edge and won a can of lemonade. I remember because you celebrated by shaking it up and spraying it over me, and then I got stung on my neck by a bloody wasp. Anyway, after that I *had* to hit the target, too.

I was like a dog with a bone. There was no way I was letting you win. I would have stayed there all night if I'd had to."

"But that polar bear… it was mine. I won it for Libby."

"It was *mine* and *I* suggested you give it to Libby."

I gaze at the clouds, tying to recall.

Give the polar bear to your girlfriend. Tell her I won it for her because her boyfriend's a crap shot.

Only after twenty goes!

Doesn't matter. I still hit the bull's-eye. Mind you, Libby probably already knows that you fire too soon and shoot all over the place.

Oh, ha ha, you're so funny…

"*I* was the one who held us up," says Tom. "You three wanted to leave."

"But I was the one who said we should cut through the fields—"

"*Max* said we should cut through the fields and across the allotments. He said he knew a route. Some family member used to grow vegetables there, or something."

I rack my brain, something coming back to me, a conversation I had with Max that night.

My gramps used to have an allotment here. The council have let it go to waste now, but it used to be really nice. He used to grow carrots and lettuces and potatoes…

Hadn't he heard of Tesco?

Nah, it's good, growing your own stuff. More fun than you'd think.

That's 'cause I'd think it would be no fun whatsoever…

"I was the one who said we should run," I say, already seeking the next reason why it must have been my fault, "it was my idea to run—"

"Because we were being threatened!" exclaims Tom in exasperation. "The guy had a knife! Look, you can lay the blame at your own doorstep all you like, but the fact is Michael was the reason we needed to get home quickly, Max was the one who came up with the shortcut, I was the one who thought it was a great idea to go investigate a fire that was none of our business… It was just a series of events. It was no one's fault."

"But I was the one who was meant to get help! I was the one who didn't get there on time. I was a fucking sprinter and I didn't get there because I…"

I trail off, shaking my head.

"Because you what?"

I rub my eyes with trembling hands.

"Because you what?" repeats Tom.

"I stopped!"

Tom frowns. "Stopped? What for?"

"Because I couldn't decide which way to go, all right?!" I snap, hearing an accusation in his tone. "I just froze! I couldn't figure out which was nearer, the Kingfisher or—"

"Hey! Stop," hisses Tom, reaching out and gripping my forearm. "Stop."

I realise I've shouted, that a couple of blokes sipping pints at a nearby table are staring. I feel my chest constricting, sweat beading on my brow.

"I wasted time," I say, staring deep into Tom's eyes, needing him to acknowledge my mistake, needing him to blame me.

"You tried your best," says Tom firmly, "and that was all you could do. Listen, what happened was shit. But it wasn't any of our faults. I've never blamed myself, and I've certainly never blamed you."

His words penetrate me, like narrow beams of light piercing through the calloused outer layer of my heart. I want the layer to crack open and shift apart like the earth's crust, allowing something warm and healing to seep through. But it won't. I just can't accept it wasn't me who made this terrible thing happen.

"So if I was no more at fault than you, then why don't you blame yourself like I do?" I ask. On some level, this makes sense to me; that my guilt is evidence I was to blame, and Tom's clear conscious is a sign of his innocence.

"Because I'm me, and you're you," says Tom. "We're different people, and we process things differently."

He stares into his tea and sighs.

"I think one thing I learned as a child was to draw a line between myself and other people's pain," he says. "I had to. Watching my dad rocking back and forth in his chair crying… I couldn't have coped if I hadn't built a force field around myself. I know you were shocked when you found out I'd gone into psychiatry, but it's not about tea and sympathy. I deal with some fucking horror stories, stuff that would make you lose your faith in humanity. I need that ability to fence myself off, otherwise I'd lose my mind. Whereas you, you were always a bit more sensitive. Plus, you were always a bit more… I don't know… self-doubting. And harsher on yourself."

I think about what he's said. I'd always thought Tom and I were similar, but it's probably true that he had a tougher edge to him. He was certainly more self-confident, more sure of himself. I think maybe that's what I liked about Michael when he came along; that I could see his vulnerability. He was a respite from all bravado and toughness.

"Tell me," says Tom, leaning in, "what it would take for you to let go of this?"

I gaze up at the sky, chew my lower lip and shake my head.

"I don't know."

"Yes, you do," says Tom. "Come on. Libby, me… Who do you need to see next?"

I scratch at my neck.

"Max," I tell him. "I want to talk to Max."

Tom nods as if this was the exact answer he was expecting.

"So let's do it then," he says decisively, "let's go talk to Max."

Chapter 22

Revelations

In the light of the fire, I could see the Leader's face; gaunt, hollow-eyed, grey stubble flecking his angular jaws. His long, skinny arm was draped over Tom's shoulder, the knife dangling.

"What's going to happen now?" he asked in his thick accent, looking directly at me, the firelight reflected in his eyes. "It's all up to you."

I shook my head, not knowing what to say, not understanding what he wanted from me.

He started to count slowly backwards from sixty. I watched him, confused.

"...fifty-one, fifty, forty-nine..."

"I don't know what I'm meant to do," I said, my voice cracking under the pressure.

"...thirty-three, thirty-two, thirty-one..."

"What... what do you want me to say?" I asked in a panic.

"...twenty-four, twenty-three, twenty-two..."

I glanced around, but everyone else – Tom, Michael, Max, the other members of the Leader's gang – was just watching me, waiting for me to act.

"...thirteen, twelve, eleven..."

"What?!" I yelled. "I don't know! I don't know what I'm meant to do!"

"…five, four, three…"

"Stop! I don't know what you want from me! I can't decide—"

"Too late," said the Leader, coolly, slicing the blade across Tom's throat.

Blood gushed from the wound.

And as I glanced down, I saw with horror that my own hands were bleeding profusely, blood dripping onto the hard, dried earth, seeping between the cracks.

"Dad?"

I sit bolt upright, my heart pounding, my chest tight. In the darkness, I can just make out Josh's silhouette in my bedroom doorway.

"Are you okay?" he asks quietly. "You were making weird noises."

I rub my face.

"I'm fine," I tell him. "Bad dream, that's all. Go back to bed."

"*That's* the seventy-millimetre bolt, right? So that should go—"

"It's an error in the instructions, Stu," I tell him again, holding a part of the cot in each hand. I feel exhausted and I'm running out of patience. I wish he'd just leave me to get on with putting the damn thing together.

"Jay knows what he's talking about, Stu," says Irena, grumpily, snatching the instructions from his hand. "Just listen to him."

"I don't think the instructions would be wrong."

"Then why does it say one thing in English and a different thing in Polish?!"

"Calm down, babe," says Stu slowly, "you said you weren't feeling that great, you should be resting—"

"Don't you babe me! Why you ask Jay to have a look if you know what you doing, huh, clever boy? This baby will be sleeping on floor before you are sure! Go to cash and carry and let *him* do it!" she shouts, thrusting the instruction sheet at me.

Stu offers me a look of resignation before sloping out the door, turning at the last minute and making as if to strangle Irena from behind.

"What you doing?" she snaps, turning quickly.

"Nothing, honey," he mutters, disappearing down the hallway.

"Silly man," she tuts, rubbing her back and letting out a little groan. She lowers herself into the new rocking chair and strokes her round belly, grimacing with discomfort. God, I'd forgotten how rough pregnancy looks.

I discard the instructions, pick up a screwdriver and crouch down to get to work.

"Nice cot," I comment, knowing it must have cost a packet. "You know, you can get really good second-hand kids' stuff on eBay—"

"Why I want to get second-hand things for my baby?" Irena interrupts. "I work long hours. What I come to this country for if I can't afford my own things?"

Firmly put in my place, I get to work in silence. I know Irena's spending is a source of stress for Stu. It was initially her idea to get the mural painted, her idea to rebrand the Canal House last year with a new sign, menus, website... But, as Stu admits, the investment pays off in the long run. She's a shrewd businesswoman.

"So, I got text message from Libby last night," says Irena.

My heart sinks. I really don't want to talk about Libby. She's gone. I just want to put her out of my head.

"You're not going to ask how is she?"

"She only left last week, Irena," I tell her, lining up a screw.

"Well, she is split from her boyfriend."

I pause for a second, the screwdriver in mid-air, before composing myself and continuing.

"Split?"

"Yes, split. Finished. Over."

I knew she wasn't happy! I knew it all along. No matter what she said to the contrary, I knew something wasn't right.

"You are not going to ask why?" says Irena.

I shrug, trying to look as disinterested as possible.

"It's not really any of my business, is it?"

"You know he cheat on her?"

The screwdriver clatters onto the wooden floor and I scramble to pick it up. That fucker. That fucking arsing shitty bastard fucker.

"No. I didn't know."

"With his personal assistant." She tuts and mumbles something about all men being pig dicks.

My grip tightens on the screwdriver and I clench my back teeth. I try to imagine what it would be like to bang his head against a brick wall and drive my fist into his face, but having never done such a thing, I have no idea how it would feel. I'm guessing incredible.

"I thought maybe she tell you he did this," says Irena. "It was months ago. Before she even came here."

I pause what I'm doing.

"Before she came here?"

"Yes. So this explains why she is happy to move out of his flat. She wants space from him."

I look over my shoulder and frown at Irena. "But she seemed… I mean, when she was talking about the wedding and their plans…"

"Maybe she want you to think that she is happy."

I think of her playing with her engagement ring when we first met for coffee, flashing it so clearly for my attention. The ring I never saw her wearing again.

"And maybe she try to tell herself she is happy, too," continues Irena. "But very quickly the truth come out with me. He made her very sad. And she was not sure what to do."

I shake my head despairingly and go back to working the

screwdriver, trying to make sense of things. She'd never given any indication that her wedding plans weren't going ahead. If I'd ever doubted the strength of their relationship, it was only through a vague sense that things weren't quite right.

"And so… what? She decided she couldn't forgive him?" I ask.

"At first she try. But once she came here, she decided that whether he cheats on her or not is not the main problem. The main problem is that she realise she doesn't feel for him what she should."

The screw tightly in, I stare at it long and hard.

"What do you think made her realise that?" asks Irena.

I shake my head slowly. "I don't know."

Behind me, I hear a loud sigh of exasperation.

"For clever man, how you be so stupid?" she asks, bluntly.

I look over my shoulder at her.

"Excuse me?"

"She is in love with you, you stupid man! Like you are with her!"

I stare at her, shocked, feeling colour rise in my face.

"You think I don't know? You think we don't *all* know? For weeks and weeks, it is painful watching you two!"

I shake my head and frown.

"I don't think…"

"She tell me this! She tell me how she feels for you! And I promise to say nothing, but how can I? That you are not together is silly! You are silly man!"

"Whoa, whoa, whoa," I say standing up, knowing how Irena is prone to misinterpretation. "What exactly did she say to you?"

Irena rubs her hand over her tummy and shifts in her chair, trying to get comfortable. "I can't tell you that. Exactly what she has said is between us girls."

"Irena," I say firmly, pointing the screwdriver at her, "you can't just make assumptions—"

"She tell me she always struggle to get over you! That

she thought if she come back here she can get over you for good, but instead she fall in love with you all over again! And then she knows for sure she cannot spend her life with Will because she does not have those same feelings for him. She has been trying to make it work because she wants marriage and a family, but now she knows what she has with him is not good enough, is… what do you call… compromise! And she prefer be alone than compromise like that. I say I want her to stay, to carry on working in the bar, but she say she can't, is too hard to keep seeing you—"

"Stop!" I snap. "Just stop!"

She puts her hand over her mouth and gazes up at me with wide eyes. If it wasn't for her pregnant belly, she'd look like a naughty girl snuggled in her oversized chair.

"Okay, I say too much," she concedes meekly, "I won't say another word."

I can feel my heart pounding in my chest, my mind racing to keep up. I can't believe this. Can it even be true? But then I think of the moments when something seemed to pass between us, when the air felt thick with tension like an electric storm was brewing. And the things she said that made me wonder what was happening between us.

You could have given us a chance…

Is she really in love with me?

"Why are you telling me this?" I ask, feeling shaken.

"Because you make me mad! Because I can see you feel same way and is silly that you two—"

"We want different things! She wants a family and stability—"

"And why you not? You have already raised lovely boy! Why no more—?"

"Because I don't want more! I've done it! And because my life is chaos!"

"But you love her, yes?"

I stare at her, my lips tightly pursed.

"Yes?!" she snaps.

I shake my head slowly and look at the ceiling.

"Irena, it's not that simple—"

"Okay, fine, is not that simple. You be sad and lonely and she be sad and lonely. That much more simple. Except she not be sad and lonely for long, you watch! She is lovely, pretty, kind girl who will find nice man—"

"Exactly! She will find a nice man, who can give her everything she wants. Someone way better for her than me—"

"Oh, so you are not good enough, is that it? No. You know what you are? You are scared. Scared to take a chance—"

"No, that's not—"

"Yes, is it!"

I throw the screwdriver into the pile of discarded, cardboard packaging.

"I'm done here," I tell her, heading for the door.

She lets out a groan, as if I'm exasperating her, and suddenly shuffles forward in her chair. For a second I think she's about to stand up and batter me in frustration, but she just sits there, bent over, staring at the floor.

"Are you okay?" I ask, pausing in the doorway.

"Yes!" she snaps, waving me away. "Go. Go enjoy whatever you lonely English men…" She stops short with a sharp intake of breath.

"Irena?" I ask, walking over and crouching down in front of her. "Are you sure you're all right?"

She shakes her head dismissively, but the fact she doesn't shout at me or hit me when I'm so close sends alarm bells ringing.

"I need to lie down," she says quietly.

I support her weight as she stands up, but even on her feet she remains doubled over.

"Aghhh," she groans, gripping my arm.

With horror, I spy blood seeping through the inside thigh of her white jeans. I try to sit her back down, unsure whether she's noticed, but she has.

"Oh no, God, no!" she cries.

"Okay, just sit down," I say, lowering her gently.

"Get help," she whimpers, clutching my arm tightly.

I freeze, unable to draw my eyes away from the blood creeping along the inside of her jeans. And then I hear a voice shouting *get help!* but it's not Irena's, it's Tom's.

My vision blurs, the brightness of the yellow-painted nursery plummeting into darkness. I'm sucked into a sickening swirl of sounds and images: the black canal water flying past me, the glow of the moon, my heart thumping, the thud of my trainers, the smell of bonfire smoke… I feel like I'm being dragged down into a whirlpool, the present moment getting further and further out of reach. But I know I need to claw my way back.

Get help!

Tom's voice echoes inside my head. I see blood dripping from my hands, from Libby's face… I'm running, but I *must* turn around, I *must* get back to the present…

Irena's nails dig hard into my skin, and I feel myself rushing back into my body. I look at my hands as if I'd forgotten they belonged to me, the reddish indentations where Irena's fingers have been.

I stand up quickly, the room spinning slowly around me, a high-pitched ringing in my ears. I feel faint, but I have to act. I force my hands to move, to take my phone from the back pocket of my jeans. My hands are shaking and I'm terrified I'm not going to press the right buttons. I fumble with the digits, unsure if I'm hitting the correct numbers.

Irena cries something in Polish and clutches at her stomach. I crouch down again, taking her hand.

I think I hear Tom's voice in my head once more, but it's quieter this time, like it's coming from far, far away.

And then I realise the voice is coming from my phone.

"Hello? Which service do you require?"

"Ambulance, please," I say, astonished that I managed to dial the right numbers and pronounce the right words.

Irena clutches my hand and I squeeze back, relief flooding through me as I'm connected to the ambulance service.

Chapter 23

Panic

I toss and turn, trying to sleep, but when I do it's fitful and plagued by nightmares. I wake fretful and disoriented, my heart racing.

In one dream, I trudge the length of the canal path for what feels like hour upon hour. As the seasons change, I sweat beneath the baking sun, plod through piles of autumn leaves, then lean into a winter snowstorm that freezes my hands. Suddenly I realise that this whole time I've been dragging a wagon behind me, and in it sit a couple of paramedics – a man and a woman – sharing jam sandwiches. I haul the wagon up the grassy bank, through a copse and over the allotments until, with relief, I spy the bonfire burning.

But I'm too late.

Everyone's dead.

There's no one here, just rivulets of their blood running between the dry, cracked earth.

The paramedics eye me scornfully. I've wasted their time and they have no more sandwiches left.

But then I hear a baby crying.

I rush over to the bonfire, following the high-pitched wail. Irena's there, huddled in the darkness, blood dripping down her naked legs, weeping.

And on the bonfire there's a baby. He's screaming and screaming.

I want to lift him out, but my hands are still frozen from the snowstorm. I can't move.

All I can do is stand, paralysed, and stare at the screaming baby as his skin blisters and burns.

And then, as I look closer, I realise with increasing horror that the baby's not even Irena's.

He's mine.

I'm at home when my phone buzzes. Unusually, it's Chloe.

Before I've even answered, I'm envisaging Josh in a terrible accident, a car coming too fast round a corner, a silly stunt gone wrong…

"Hi. I'm sorry to call you, I just, I wanted to tell you something about Josh," she says, sounding stressed out.

"Right…" I say, cautiously.

"Do you know where he is right now?"

"Yeah, he's gone shopping with Sam."

"No, he hasn't. He's on his way to King's Cross. And not with Sam. He's gone to meet a total stranger."

"What?"

"Did you know there's this girl he likes?"

"Yeeesss…"

"Well, he's gone to meet her."

"Meet her? I thought… I thought the girl he liked was you."

"What? No," she says as if I'm a complete idiot. "I told you we don't see each other like that."

Yes, I think, cursing my own stupidity, *and I didn't believe you.*

"So who is she?"

"I have no idea! I'm sure she's not real though. I mean, I don't think she is." Her voice rises with a sense of urgency.

"Sorry, back up a bit—"

"They've been chatting online for months. They met on

some, like, music forum or whatever. But every time he's suggested, like, calling or FaceTiming or Skype or something, she makes some excuse, which is more than just a bit dodgy, don't you think?"

"Hang on, I'm really confused—"

"I just don't think he should be meeting up with this person on his own. I'm not sure she's who she says she is."

"So, he's been messaging this girl, but he's never talked with her in person?"

"No."

"Or seen her?"

"Only in photos. And she's, like, super pretty, and that makes me suspicious – not that Josh couldn't get with a super pretty girl – but I've been watching this programme on MTV where, like, social outcasts go online and do *exactly* this kind of thing—"

"And he's gone to meet her?"

"Yes!"

"And you knew he was going to do this? Why are you only telling me now?!"

"I didn't know! I'd been telling him not to go, because I told him this 'girl' could be, like, some weird paedo or an axe murderer or something, and he said he wouldn't go, but then I heard that he's going anyway. He's arranged to meet her at King's Cross station at eleven and... hello? Are you still there?"

I hang up and immediately call Josh, my mind racing. What made me so convinced the girl he liked was Chloe? She even told me they were just good friends and I still didn't question whether there might be someone else! Feeling foolish, I realise that I saw Libby and myself in those two and imagined – hoped – that they might have what we once had. Blindsided by my own hankering after the past, I saw something that wasn't there and missed the cues. And now God knows who he's meeting.

"Josh, call me immediately please," I tell his voicemail service.

I then send him a text, repeating the same order, grab my

keys and drive straight to the station. I have fifty minutes to get to him.

I'm already too late when I arrive at King's Cross fretful and anxious, my mind playing out every nightmare scenario. I try to reassure myself that nobody gets abducted in broad daylight at King's Cross station. But what if he's persuaded to go somewhere else? I would have never thought Josh was that stupid. But then I never would have had him down for doing any of this. We've talked about internet safety at home, they've covered it at school. What would possess him to be so stupid?

He's refused to answer his phone, but has at least responded to a couple of text messages, so I know that as of twenty minutes ago he was still alive, something I imagine myself telling the police in a few hours' time. Apparently I wouldn't have let him go to London to meet up with this person if he'd told me about it, seeing as I never give him any freedom and treat him like a child. I reply calmly, ignoring his complaints and simply telling him not to leave the station or follow this person – whoever the hell they turn out to be – anywhere secluded, highlighting cars, vans, empty train carriages and public toilets as areas of particular threat.

When he stops texting, I become so fearful that the woman sitting opposite me on the train asks if I'm okay, as my leg is jiggling up and down at a hundred miles an hour and I'm chewing my thumbnail mercilessly.

I fly off the train, running past the other passengers, swearing loudly when the gate spits my ticket back at me and refuses to let me through. After realising I've tried to stuff my car parking ticket in the slot, I correct the error and finally emerge on the other side, pushing my way through the crowds, searching frantically for my kid.

I turn in circles, frustrated at all the people getting in my way. I see police officers loitering and immediately assume they're here to deal with a reported incident involving my son. I hear an announcement start up over the loudspeaker and expect them to announce a missing child. And for one bizarre moment I think I see him – the Leader – a tall, lanky man disappearing through the barriers on the other side of the concourse.

He came back, this time for my boy.

"You don't have to worry," I hear a voice say behind me, "she didn't turn up anyway."

I turn with a start to see Josh standing behind me. I want to grab him by the shoulder and yell at him, not to ever, EVER do that again! But he looks so dejected, and I'm so relieved to see him, that instead I take a shaky breath, place a hand on his shoulder and steer him back towards the platform for home.

I glance back for a moment, catching a final glimpse of the tall, lanky man. He looks nothing like the Leader. I rub my face, wondering if I'm going crazy.

I grip Josh's shoulder. "You and I," I say through gritted teeth, "need to have a long chat—"

"You wouldn't have let me—"

"Do you have any way of knowing who this person really is?" I interrupt, my anger already rising.

"Yes. I know her. She wouldn't lie—"

"Well, she clearly would, seeing as she's not here!"

"She'll have her reasons. And you didn't need to rush to my rescue!" he snaps, stopping dead in his tracks. "Why do you always think something bad's gonna happen? Why can't you just let me have a bit of freedom? We talked about this—"

"And you didn't even give me a chance! You just went behind my back!"

"What would you have said if I'd told you?"

"I don't know! But it would have been nice to have the chance—"

"Oh, come off it, Dad! You're not gonna just change—"

"You didn't even try me!"

"Josh?"

We both stop and turn towards the owner of the soft voice, a teenage girl who's looking nervously at my son.

"Becky?" he asks, looking stupefied.

"Yes," she nods, smiling awkwardly. "I'm sorry I'm late. My phone lost signal. I was really worried I'd missed you."

She looks down at the ground uncomfortably, holding her head at an angle just like Josh does so that her long dark hair obscures part of her face.

Josh just stares at her.

"You look just like in your pictures," she smiles, sheepishly. "I... um... I know I don't. Look like in my pictures, I mean. But... yeah... this is me."

She laughs nervously and makes a vague, apologetic gesture to herself.

"So now you know why I didn't want to video chat," she says, as is she's admitting a deep, dark secret, "'cause I don't look quite like you thought. All those pictures were, like, airbrushed and stuff..."

Josh shrugs.

"You look... fine," he says, sounding confused. "I mean, you look... nice. You look pretty much like in the photos."

She shakes her head dismissively, but it's clear Josh is genuinely baffled, and so am I. She probably isn't "super pretty" as Chloe described, but she's got pretty eyes, a nice – if slightly gawky – smile. She's very slim, all limbs and angles, and about an inch taller than Josh.

Both of them shift awkwardly from one foot to another.

"I'm probably not as funny as I come across online," offers Josh, trying to even the playing field. "Being online gives me longer to think of witty things to say."

She laughs, suddenly more at ease. "Okay, so you're not as funny and I'm not as pretty... that makes us more even."

"No, you are... you're... I mean, you're really pretty," Josh mumbles, unsure whether to look at her face or his shoes.

Becky looks like she could burst with happiness. I feel a flood or pride and think that I could probably learn a few things from my son. Where did he get the confidence to put himself out there like that? Where did he learn to swallow his pride and say what he feels? I'm not happy about the stunt he's pulled today, but he's clearly able to take a risk where matters of the heart are concerned and that's a good thing. And I feel a little calmer in the face of his competence.

Becky looks over her shoulder and beckons over a woman standing a few feet away.

"This is my mum," she smiles.

Becky's mum is also tall, very slim and looks about fifty. She greets Josh with a smile, her eyes creasing at the edges.

"This is my dad," mumbles Josh, less enthusiastically, gesturing vaguely towards me.

Becky's mum eyes me with surprise and then holds her hand out to me.

"Becky thought I was being too overprotective," she smiles with a roll of her eyes, as if we're in this together, "but I said there was no way I was letting her travel from Reading to London on her own, not at this age, and meeting someone online... well... you can't be too careful, can you?"

I shake her hand.

"No," I say, catching Josh's eye, "you really can't."

We all stand in silence for a moment.

"So," says Becky, smiling a bit more confidently at Josh, "I thought maybe we could go get some lunch?"

Josh looks quizzically at Becky's mum and then at me, as if he's not sure how all this is going to work.

"Oh, I thought I'd just... you know... potter around here for a bit," says Becky's mum quickly, looking around as if wondering how to occupy herself for an hour in Accessorize and Boots.

"And didn't you have somewhere important to be at three o'clock, Dad?" asks Josh.

I check my watch, thinking I've got plenty of time. I can hang around here, stay close. It's not the greatest part of London: too many strangers, drug pushers, groups huddling suspiciously in corners. I can get a coffee, accompany him home...

But he's staring pointedly at me, and I know these fears that seem to be escalating out of control are mine to deal with, not his.

"Yeah, I guess I should get back really," I say. "You're sure you're okay making your way—"

He glares at me.

"Right. Keep your money safe and text me," I say, fighting the urge to drag him home.

But the tiny smile he gives me as I tear myself away makes it clear my pissing off and giving him his own space is very much appreciated.

Later that day, I wait on grass so bright green and springy it barely seems real. I stand beneath a large oak tree, watching people arriving at the crematorium, stepping out of their cars in dark suits and dresses. My stomach turns.

You have to do this, I tell myself, *you just have to.*

But I don't move. I don't want to face what lies ahead. I want to walk back to my van and drive home.

"You okay?" a voice asks.

I turn to see Michael approaching.

I shake my head slowly. I've worked my way through an entire packet of paracetamol this week and I still can't shift the pulsating pain in my temples.

"I don't know how to do this," I tell him.

He sighs, watching the mourners. "There's no right way."

"I don't know what to say, what to do."

"It doesn't matter," says Michael. "What's important is that you're here, that you say something."

I nod thoughtfully.

"Come on," he says, putting a hand on my shoulder and taking a deep breath. "Let's go."

There's a figure crouched in front of the gravestone, a grown man with a broad back and hairy arms. I still can't understand how he got that way, how he grew upwards and outwards without my even knowing.

Michael clears his throat. "Tom?"

Tom stands up, his eyes darting between Michael and I as if he's having exactly the same thoughts as me: who are these *men*?

"Fuck me," says Tom, eyeing Michael up and down. "What happened to that prissy little choir boy I once knew?"

Michael smiles. "Some cocky kid introduced him to metal music and Jack Daniel's. It was a slippery slope from there."

Tom laughs, pulling Michael in for a hug.

They swap life stories – over a decade of love, loss, achievements and disappointments summarised in a few minutes – but it's just background noise to me. There's a slight chill in the air, and the day seems to have a strange dreamlike quality. We're boys, but we're pretending to be grown men. We're standing at a graveside, but we're laughing. Nothing feels right or real.

As they talk, I crouch down in front of the headstone, just as I have done in the past. My eyes linger on the chiselled lettering.

Barclay James Macintyre...

I close my eyes, take a breath and open them again. "Hey, Max," I whisper.

I've tried and tried to prepare for what I wanted to say today. But what's fitting for a friend you lost too soon? For a friend you haven't spoken to in sixteen years? For a friend you let down? I haven't been able to come up with anything.

"We're all here," I tell him, feeling like I'm stating the obvious. "We all came to see you."

I can see him in my mind's eye, watching me, waiting, finding humour in my discomfort, an amused smile on his face. Always, *always* a smile on his face.

I want to tell him I miss him. That I miss his deep, dirty laugh, his jokes and his self-deprecating wit. I miss his ability to cheer everyone up. I want to tell him that I may not have spoken to him in well over a decade, but that I've thought about him every day, that I wish he was still here, that he *deserves* to still be here. Instead, I say what feels easier.

"Tom's a bit of a fat bastard now," I tell him.

Behind me, I hear Tom chuckle quietly, his conversation with Michael over. Now they're both hovering behind me, listening.

"And Blondie's covered in tattoos."

And you, Jay Boy? I hear Max ask. *What about you?*

"And I'm…"

Losing my mind? Not who I thought I was?

"I'm sorry," I say, feeling a lump rise in my throat. "I'm sorry that I let you down. That I didn't manage to get help fast enough. That I made bad choices—"

"Hey," warns Michael firmly, crouching down beside me and gripping my shoulder, "that's not what today's about. It's not about who did what or—"

"This is about saying goodbye," interrupts Tom, crouching down on my other side. "It's about closure, not digging up old ground."

"But I don't know how to do that," I tell them, my throat tightening. I can feel my heart rate starting to accelerate, my palms starting to sweat. I suddenly feel scrutinised and judged, like I'm sitting a test I'm going to fail.

I await instructions from my friends. For a second it seems like they're both about to speak at once, but then neither of them says anything. Because the truth is they don't know how to do this either.

"Is there nothing you've ever wanted to say to him?" I ask somewhat desperately, turning to Michael, searching for reassurance that I'm not alone in this struggle.

Michael looks thoughtful for a moment, but then he shrugs. "I guess I feel like I've said it all. In my music, my songs. I've written it all out."

I remember some of Michael's early songs, those from his darkest days, ones I haven't heard in years, that I would happily never hear again. The slow, miserable ones I always knew were connected to Max's death.

If I could take your hand and lead you to the light,
Then we could start again and it would be all right.
But when I reach for you, you fade again
Into the dust, into the pain...

"There are songs you don't even know are about him," continues Michael, "some of the ones I've written recently. 'Soar'? That's about him."

I wrack my brain. When the tune comes to me – upbeat tempo, all slamming guitars and rapid drum fire – then so do the lyrics.

Fly, just let your spirit rise,
you're beautiful inside, now I can see you in the light.
Fly, inside me, I believe
that you can soar beyond the stars and let yourself
be free.

"I don't ever stop writing it out," says Michael, "because it's always there, it'll always be inside me. But every time I write it out, I work through it. And I'm in a different place with it now. All the guilt and sadness... it's been replaced by something much more peaceful. I like to remember him now for who he was, for his spirit and humour, and if I can write about that, then that's my way of talking to him, I guess. Of remembering him."

I study Michael's face like he's someone I barely recognise, wondering how we've never had this conversation before.

"Plus," he adds, "I've spent a lot of time talking about Max with Catherine. That's also been a way of saying goodbye; talking about him. I've described Max to her, laughed about him with her, remembered him with her."

Tom looks past me to Michael.

"Girlfriend?" he asks.

"Therapist," Michael corrects him.

Tom cocks an eyebrow and nods approvingly.

"And what about you?" I ask, turning to Tom. "Don't you

have anything you want to say to him? Don't you feel the need to say goodbye?"

Tom shakes his head, thoughtfully. "In all honestly, no. Because I don't think he's gone. Not in the traditional sense. I practice Buddhism now, so I look at death with a lot more acceptance than I did at the time. I don't mean that what happened was okay, because it wasn't. It was fucking horrible. And the way I coped at the time wasn't healthy. But now, I don't know… like Michael said, I've already found a way to make my peace with it. Now you just have to find yours."

I close my eyes and shake my head.

Come on, Jay Boy, I can see Max saying, *better out than in.*

But all I want to say is sorry, over and over and over again.

I don't want to say goodbye. I just want to turn back time and make it right.

Just say something! I tell myself, angrily.

Come on, Jay Boy, coaxes Max.

"I can't do this," I say standing suddenly. "This is stupid. I don't know what to say—"

"Jay!" calls Michael as I stride away.

"Just leave me!" I call, my chest suddenly tight, the air suddenly feeling too thick to pass through the tiny passages to my lungs.

"Why haven't you been to the doctor?" asks Tom, once I've managed to regulate my breathing. We're standing under the oak tree, the leaves rustling gently in the breeze.

I shake my head dismissively, my legs still wobbly, my hands still trembling.

"Because it comes and goes. It sometimes takes hold when I'm really stressed out and rundown, but generally I've been okay for a long time. It's just these last few months it's got really bad."

"So, again, why haven't you been to the doctor?"

"I honestly don't know," I sigh.

Tom stands square on and takes me by the shoulders.

"Yes, you do," he says.

"Will you stop telling me I know stuff!" I snap, shrugging him off. "You're the damn shrink. If you think *you* know why I'm doing something, then just say it!"

"Do you *want* to let go of any of this?" asks Tom, making a vague gesture towards Max's grave. "I mean, do you *really* want to let go of it?"

I look at him as if he's mad.

"Why haven't you been to the doctor?" he asks again.

"I told you, I don't know!"

But even as I'm shouting at him, I realise I'm lying. I suddenly recall Laura saying to me – years ago now – that I took a perverse pleasure in my own suffering.

"Maybe because… I don't know… because why *should* I? Why should I get to breathe when he can't? When he *couldn't*? When he was gasping for air because I'd told him to run!"

"You didn't kill him, Jay, the asthma killed him."

I shake my head like he's lost his mind.

"He hadn't had an asthma attack in years. And then he gets scared and he runs and—"

"People get scared. And people run. He was on the football team, for Christ's sake. He played every week and nothing happened. We went paintballing and nothing happened. We trekked for bloody miles in the pissing rain on that stupid school trip to the Lake District and nothing happened. But that night – *maybe* because of the stress, *maybe* because he was running – he had an asthma attack and *unusually* he died. It was a freak event. God, Jay, I remember reading about a case where a teenage girl with mild asthma just died mid-conversation with a friend. She was on the phone, suddenly stopped talking and fucking died. Sometimes these things happen and no one knows—"

"*I* know! *I* know that's why it happened!"

"Who do you think you are? God?! You think you're really that damn powerful that *you* are responsible for this happening?"

I walk slowly in a circle, running my hands over my eyes,

through my hair. I don't know what I think anymore. I see Michael lingering patiently nearby. I know he has nothing to add to this. I know he feels like he's banging his head against a brick wall with me. Let someone else have a try.

"You don't have to keep making yourself suffer," says Tom. "I know you think you do, and I know I can't change your mind about that – only *you* can change your mind about that – but I'm telling you, not as a friend, but as a medical professional, you need to go to your GP. These panic attacks that you're having, along with the dreams, the intrusive memories, the self-blame… it could be that you've got PTSD."

I look at him like he's crazy.

"PTSD?"

"Post-traumatic stress disorder."

"I know what PTSD is. It's what fricking war veterans get."

"It's what people can get after a traumatic event, especially if they've felt extremely threatened, or witnessed a death. And it can start years after the event—"

"I don't have bloody PTSD! It's just been really stressful lately. I found out my dad's not my biological father, my friend nearly miscarried right in front of me—"

"Okay, whatever, I mean, I'm just the psychiatrist. But, either way, you know that what you're having are panic attacks, yes?"

"Yes, of course," I sigh.

"And you know you can get help with those?"

I nod, thinking this is what Josh must feel like when I'm nagging him and he just wants me to shut up.

"But, of course, you need to want help," says Tom. "You need to think you *deserve* help. And if you really believe that what happened was your fault, then there's something else you're going to need."

"And what's that?" I ask him with a weary sigh.

He holds his palms out, as if it should be obvious.

"Forgiveness," he says.

Chapter 24

Intervention

"Where are we even going?" I ask.

Tom, sitting next to me in the driver's seat, looks in his rear-view mirror at Michael, but neither of them says anything.

"This is kidnapping, you know that?" I grumble.

Tom smiles. "Think of it as an intervention."

Wherever we're going, they've obviously agreed it's a good idea, but I have the impression that – as always – Tom is far more confident than Michael.

"Just don't freak out," says Michael behind me, sounding somewhat anxious.

"You trust us, don't you, Jay Boy?" asks Tom, brightly, one hand casually on the steering wheel.

I stare out the window at the motorway traffic passing by.

"Like hell I do."

I'm becoming a mess, there's no other way of putting it. I've been sleeping so little that I'm starting to know what it feels like to be Michael, up all night in the dark and silence. His insomnia is helpful to me right now. We text into the early hours – meaningful stuff, pointless stuff, funny stuff – until he cuts me off and tells me to lie down and rest, even if that's all I do. Michael's work shifts mean he can sometimes nap during the day, whereas I have to be up at six thirty, and nobody should be rewiring some poor sod's house after three hours' sleep.

When I do dose off, I'm plagued by nightmares. I run too slowly. I shout but no sound comes out. I stand – fretful and indecisive – at a crossroads. I see fire and blood, hear cries of pain, and feel the weight of responsibility crushing me, squeezing the air out of me, until I wake, struggling for breath. I see threat everywhere, and at a time when I've promised to give Josh more freedom, I feel constantly torn and anxious.

I also feel angry. All of the time. Knowing how stressed I am, Rob invites me to spend some extra time with him in the gym, bashing it out. There's a certain satisfaction in hearing the thud of my boxing gloves against his pads.

"Harder!" he barks at me. "Work it out of you!"

For a short while, when I'm coated in sweat and practically on my knees, there's no room for thought or feeling. But the relief is temporary, and by the time I'm back home, the pressure's already starting to rise again.

I don't know what kind of intervention this is or what can possibly help me, but right now I feel open to just about anything.

We find a parking space some distance from the seafront, in front of a neatly kept bungalow with a birdbath in the front garden.

I step onto the pavement and shove the car door shut. Seagulls circle and screech overhead, struggling to keep a straight path against the wind.

"Where the hell are we?" I ask.

Tom leans backwards, stretching out his spine, breathing in the salty air.

"Essex."

"Yeah, I know we're in Essex. I mean, where *exactly* are we? And why are we here?"

Tom and Michael exchange a meaningful look.

"Come on, guys," I sigh, "what the hell's going on?"

"We think there's something you need to do," says Tom, decisively.

Michael approaches me apprehensively. "Just stay calm, okay? And remember we're trying to help you."

"Help me what? What are we doing?"

"Come on," says Tom, placing his hand on my back and steering me down the driveway of the bungalow, in between the potted plants and the Nissan Micra.

"What?" I ask, shrugging him off. "Whose house is this?"

Just then the front door opens and a lady steps out. She's in her early sixties, I'd guess, portly, neatly bobbed fair hair, beige trousers and a navy-blue cardigan.

I think I recognise her, but in my confused state I'm not completely sure. And then a man steps out beside her. A tubby, silver-haired gentleman with glasses and a soft, friendly face.

And now I know exactly who they are.

My stomach lurches and my limbs freeze.

We stand still, staring at each other for a moment, before I feel Tom pushing me gently forwards.

"Hello, Jamie," says Max's mum, Carole, smiling warmly at me. "Goodness, look at you!"

Before I know what's happening, she reaches up and kisses me on the cheek.

"Lovely to see you again, son," beams Max's dad, Peter, taking my hand in both of his and pumping it up and down.

His eyes look small and blurred behind the thick lens of his glasses, and I watch his chin wobble as he shakes my hand.

I'm mute and rigid. I can feel my heart pounding. I want to turn and run from these wonderful people who have never known what I did.

I hear Carole behind me now.

"Hello again, Tom," she laughs, and it's clear from the way she says it that they've only met recently, that he's been here already, setting this up.

"And Michael!" Carole exclaims brightly.

I stand there, dazed and lost, as everyone greets each other, shakes hands, plants kisses, as if this is a pleasant reunion of long-lost friends instead the moment of reckoning. I know why I've been brought here and it's not to make chit-chat. It's to own up to what happened, to confess. To seek forgiveness. Tom might have already spoken to Max's parents, but there's clearly no damn way he's told them what happened that night.

"Come inside," says Peter, guiding me indoors, "let's get everyone a drink."

I step out of the wind into the narrow hallway, where I remove my shoes in a trance. From there I'm led into a large, immaculately tidy lounge.

The first thing I see is a photo of Max on the wall, beaming at me. I haven't been able to bring myself to look at a photo of Max in sixteen years. I'd forgotten about that little gap between his two front teeth, the rosy hue of his cheeks. I feel my breath catch in my throat. But when I turn away there's another one on the mantelpiece – Max in his primary school uniform – and another one on the windowsill – Max eating an ice cream on holiday. Around me people talk, but I hear nothing of what they're saying. I feel dizzy and disorientated and I just want to get out of here.

Suddenly a hand touches my shoulder. I turn with a start.

"You okay?" Michael asks.

I look around, but it's just me, Michael and Tom in the room.

"What the *hell* are we doing here?!" I whisper fiercely.

"Think of it as exposure therapy," says Tom, calmly and quietly.

"I don't want any fucking exposure therapy!" I hiss through gritted teeth. "This is insane! What are you trying to do?!"

"Calm down," says Michael, placing a hand on my arm.

I knock him away angrily and he retreats.

"Maybe this wasn't such a good idea," I hear him mutter to Tom.

"Here we go," says Carole brightly, entering the room with a tray of polka-dot mugs.

"We bought chocolate Hobnobs for the occasion," says Peter with a smile, placing a huge plate of biscuits down on the coffee table, "we remembered you boys always loved Hobnobs."

"Barclay certainly loved a Hobnob," mutters Carole, sitting herself down on the sofa.

"Good old Barclay loved anything edible, didn't he?" pipes up Tom, and the rest of them politely chuckle in agreement.

This is too much. It's all too weird – this niceness, this pretending. Plus, when did any of us ever refer to him as Barclay? Not since we were ten and Tom decided Barclay was a naff name that would surely see him bullied at secondary school. We tried out Macintyre for a couple of weeks, but it was just too much effort. Max. That was so much cooler. Jay, Tom, Max. We butchered the names we were christened with – the ones our parents had so carefully chosen – until we were no more than a syllable each.

We sit down, and Carole hands out the mugs. Michael seems to have ordered me a black tea. Or did I do that myself?

Peter holds out the plate of biscuits.

Tom touches the soft swell of his belly and looks like he's going to resist, but swiftly changes his mind. "Oh, go on then," he says, taking a Hobnob, "I think it's what Max would have wanted."

They laugh. All of them laugh. I can't stand this anymore. It's sick.

"Ah, shit!" I breathe, spilling hot tea all over my shaking hands and my thigh. I stand up quickly. "Sorry," I say, realising I've just committed the deadly sin of swearing in front of a friend's parents. And the churchgoing ones at that.

"Let me get you a cloth," says Carole, shuffling forward in her chair.

"No! It's fine," I say, heading out of the room, flustered. "I just need to go to the bathroom."

"On the right!" calls Peter.

I lock the door behind me and immediately run the cold tap, splashing water over my hands and face.

I can feel my chest starting to tighten, my breathing coming in short, sharp bursts.

I lean on the sink and try to count backwards from a hundred, but I can't concentrate. I need to get out of here, but how can I leave? I remember – even though I've spent years trying to forget – the day of Max's funeral. Carole – white as a sheet with dark circles under her eyes – asking us boys to stay in touch. I never did. I never even once called round to the house or picked up the phone or wrote a letter. I couldn't. The one thing his parents asked of me and I just couldn't bring myself to do it. And neither did Michael. And neither did...

But then I wonder how Tom found them so quickly. How did he know where they'd moved to? And the familiar way in which Carole and Peter greeted him. Has he kept in contact all this time?

I lean on the sink, staring at myself in the mirror. I look pale, my eyes tinged pink with tiredness. I haven't shaved in over a week.

I can't do this anymore. Things aren't getting better; they're getting worse. I don't know what will help me, but I need to do something. For me. For Josh. I want to be a better version of myself. A better father. A better brother. A better son. A better friend. But instead I'm sinking. I don't want to reach the bottom. I want to swim.

I dry my face, my breathing slowed, my shaking calmed.

If it will do any good at all, then I need to tell them. I need to just get it out.

We sit silently, the only sound the ticking of the clock on the mantelpiece. No one's laughing anymore. They're just waiting.

"We left the fairground," I start, quietly, "we were later than we should have been. I'd been... Tom... one of us had been trying to win a prize on this stall and we'd lost track of time. So we decided to take a shortcut."

I tell them about the allotments, the darkness, the stinging nettles, the jokes.

The noise. A fox shagging? I think I say this. To Max's parents. I think I actually say the word shagging.

A fire burning, a flickering light against the dark sky. We went to look. I don't know why, but we went to look.

I hear myself talking, but my voice sounds far away...

... lying on the ground... a boot to the stomach...

... tried to run...

... hand on my shoulder...

... be our friends, they said...

... you are leader, like me...

And I remember other things. Things I've tried so hard to forget that I've almost blocked them out.

We were sitting by the fireside on upturned crates. Max and I were huddled on one, overseen by Muscles, who stood intimidatingly close behind us. Through the flickering flames, I could see Michael, sitting miserably on another crate next to Snake Eyes. And nearby stood Tom, overseen by the Leader, who was swigging from a bottle and raving in broken English about his country and leadership, his arm still draped round Tom's shoulder, the knife dangling against Tom's chest.

Max and I were whispering, barely moving our lips.

... don't know what the hell to do...

... need to get out of here...

... make a run for it?...

... don't know, don't know...

When I next looked over at Michael, I could see he wasn't there. I strained to see through the flames. My heart raced harder as I searched desperately. And then I saw him in the shadows, not far from the crate where he'd been sitting, being led slowly into the darkness by Snake Eyes, who had a hand on the back of his neck.

"Where's he taking Michael?" I asked Max, forgetting to whisper, panic taking over me.

My question got the attention of the Leader, who swiftly turned and searched the darkness for Snake Eyes. The Leader called something, a question, in his native language.

"Just a little walk," Snake Eyes called back over his shoulder, lazily. He sounded drunk. And there was something else in his voice, something smug and beyond ugly.

I suddenly felt sick to my core, my heart pounding so hard in my chest that I immediately felt dizzy.

"No!" I heard myself shout out. I jumped up from the crate but was immediately pushed down from behind by Muscles.

I don't know what I thought was going to happen to Michael. I suppose I thought… I don't know…

I just know that those are the worst nightmares of all.

I put my head in my hands and press my fingertips against my eyelids until I see tiny flashes of light bursting out of the darkness. I feel two hands gripping at my wrists.

Michael's there, crouched in front of me.

"It's okay," I hear him whisper. "I was scared, too. But nothing happened."

I feel a warm hand on my back. Tom, sitting next to me.

"Look at where you are," he says.

I open my eyes, take in the bright lounge, the floral sofas, the polka-dot mugs, the flowers on the mantelpiece, the crucifix on the wall.

I see Max's parents sitting opposite me, holding hands on the two-seater sofa. They look so many things – sad, encouraging, shocked, weary – that I don't know what they're making of any of this.

Michael tilts his head towards me and I refocus on his face. He offers me a sad, gentle smile.

"Go on," urges Tom.

The Leader yelled, barking something in his native language. He wasn't happy. He wanted Snake Eyes to bring Michael back. And Muscles wasn't happy about Snake Eyes' behaviour either.

That's how the shouting started. That's why the fight broke out. Before we knew it, Michael was being dragged back to the fireside while the three men argued, shouting things in a language we didn't understand.

… Rocket mouthed at me to run…

… blood was dripping from my hand…

… I stopped and looked back, but I couldn't help him…

… we just ran…

All I could hear was our breathing, fast and heavy, as we bolted over the uneven ground in the darkness. Michael stumbled and fell beside me, and I turned to haul him up, panicking that he might have twisted his ankle on the clods of dried earth. But we kept heading forwards, barely able to see where we were going.

At first, Max kept up with us out of sheer fear and determination. But he couldn't sustain it. He started flagging, slowing us down.

"Come on!" we shouted.

"I can't," he insisted, but he kept going all the same.

After what felt like an eternity but can't have been more than four or five minutes, as if from nowhere, the canal appeared before us. There are no moorings along that stretch of the canal and no lights along the path, but the moon was reflecting off the water's black surface and I could see enough to figure out where we were.

"Left!" I yelled as our trainers hit the path.

"We can stop now," Max called breathlessly, desperation in his voice.

"No!" I told him. "Just keep going!"

"I can't," he insisted.

"You can!" I shouted. "Just a bit further!"

And so we carried on running. Not for long – maybe thirty seconds – before Max finally gave out.

"Stop!" yelled Michael, and Tom and I ground to a halt.

Max was bent over, trying to catch his breath. I ran back to him, took him by the arm and dragged him forwards, determined that we should keep going. He was wheezing heavily, but propelled by fear and adrenaline all I could think was that we had to keep running.

We staggered into the darkness underneath a tall, concrete bridge, but just as we were coming out the other side, Max was done. He yanked at my arm, forcing me to stop and look at him, and for the first time I noticed just how wrong his breathing sounded. And then he slid to his knees.

"Max, come on, we can walk now," urged Michael.

"No, something's wrong," I said, crouching down beside Max.

"Christ, he's having an asthma attack," said Tom, crouching down as well.

I shook my head, confused. It had been so long since I'd seen Max have an asthma attack that I'd forgotten he even had asthma. In fact, if anyone had asked, I'd have probably told them he'd grown out of it long ago.

"Okay, Max, just breathe slowly," Michael said, his own breath laboured. "Just… um… just breathe deeply—"

"He can't breathe deeply, you moron!" panted Tom. "That's the whole point about asthma."

"What do we do?" I asked Tom.

"I don't know!"

"Well, does he have an inhaler?"

"How would I know?"

"You're at school with him every day! I didn't even know he still had asthma!"

"Max, do you have an inhaler?" asked Tom.

Max shook his head slowly. His breathing sounded painful and abnormally noisy, like air trying to force its way through a pinprick-sized hole.

"Let's just stop for a minute so he can catch his breath," said Michael, looking around anxiously. "I don't think they've followed us."

"He can't just catch his breath!" snapped Tom. "This is serious!"

"He'll be okay," I said, my own breathing starting to regulate. "He just needs to stop for a minute."

Suddenly I was jerked into a standing position by Tom yanking me up by the arm.

"This isn't good!" he whispered harshly. "We need to get help!"

"But he'll be okay," I said, confused. "It's not like you can die of it. He just needs—"

"Of course he can fucking die of it! What do you think happens if you can't breathe?!"

I suddenly remembered that day in the school playground when Max had his first asthma attack, and how Tom and I had run to get Mrs Dray. At home time she told my mum there had been an "incident", and that I might be unsettled by it. But I wasn't. Because my mum had given me Nesquik and told me asthma was nothing to worry about.

"Guys, I think we need to get help," Michael said, his voice full of concern.

We looked down at him crouching by Max's side; Max who had sat down on the path and slumped to one side, propping himself up weakly on one shaky arm, his head barely off the ground. The noise of his laboured breathing filled the night air.

"Okay," said Tom, gesturing into the darkness, "that's the entrance to the nature reserve up there, right? So there's a footbridge just past the weir. Look, I'm gonna go get help—"

"I'll go," I said, quickly. "I can run faster than you."

Tom and I were both on our respective school's athletics teams, and we stared at each other now as if this was our final competitive stand-off.

"Okay," nodded Tom, conceding. "You know where you're going, yeah?"

But I was already running, my trainers pounding the towpath, the warm night air whistling in my ears.

"I always thought you were the ones who ordered me to get help," I say, perched on the edge of the sofa, my forehead resting in my hands. "But it wasn't you, was it? It was me. I thought I was the fastest runner—"

"And you were," says Tom beside me.

"Fractionally. Whenever we compared times—"

"I lied. Whenever we compared times, I lied. Of course I wasn't as fast as you. I couldn't run as fast and I couldn't cover the distances you covered, and I hated the fact that you were so much better at it than me. In primary school we were on a level, I might have even been marginally ahead of you, but once you went to St John's you outstripped me by a long way. But there was no way I was going to let you know that."

"You were the right person to go, Jay," says Michael. "It had to be you."

I glance up briefly. He's kneeling in front of me, his face a picture of concern. Beyond him, Max's parents haven't moved. They're like statues, squeezed together on the sofa, listening with a look of silent distress on their faces. They're clutching each other's hand – perfectly together in their suffering. This loving, close-knit family which was torn apart.

"But I stopped," I say. "I couldn't choose which way to go. I remember now you even asked me if I knew where I was going, but I didn't listen. You would have known which way to go, Tom, or you would have chosen quicker. You were always saying I was indecisive, and I was. I still am—"

"What difference would that have possibly made?" asks Tom. "We must be talking a matter of seconds."

"Fifteen seconds. But then I chose the wrong way. And all

together it cost me a minute and I know that because when I ran it again and timed myself I worked out—"

"It's just one minute, Jay," pleads Tom, looking at me as if I've lost my mind.

"Exactly!" I exclaim, holding my hands out as if this is the whole point. "The minute that made all the difference!"

What happened in between my puking up candyfloss on the carpet of the Kingfisher and arriving back at Max's side has always been a blur. There were lights and sirens, but, of course, the ambulance couldn't get anywhere near the spot where the boys were waiting. I had to lead everyone – the paramedics, John Porter and Stan Finch who'd recognised me when I'd burst through the doors of the Kingfisher – to the place where Max had collapsed. I remember darkness, rushing, urgent questions I couldn't answer.

And then we were there, under the bridge, torches flashing, radio controls crackling. Two paramedics – a man with a ginger beard and a pretty woman with blonde hair tied back in a ponytail – were leaning over Max, who was lying on the ground. When the ginger man looked up, I could see something sticky-looking in his beard, glistening in the torchlight. In my fretful state, I had the ridiculous thought that it must be jam, and that he'd been interrupted in the middle of his tea break.

I remember Tom and Michael crouched by Max, being ordered to move out of the way. Tom standing and staggering backwards, unable to tear his eyes away, and Michael frozen, his fingers being prised from Max's arm by Stan Finch before John Porter took Michael around the waist and hauled him aside.

I don't remember any of us talking, or even looking at each other. I think we just stood there, staring in shock. I don't know why, but at that point I still believed everything was going to be okay. I suppose because anything else was inconceivable. A world without Max in it had never, and could never, exist in my lifetime.

And as my mum once told me, asthma is nothing to worry about.

There were mumblings and radioed messages I didn't understand, attempts at resuscitation, codes, numbers and acronyms that made no sense. No one used the word dead, I'm sure of it. But all of a sudden, I knew. It was clear. The bearded paramedic muttered sadly, something about "one minute earlier". And I knew that I'd been sixty seconds too late.

"No, no, no!" I heard Tom screaming, his cries echoing against the vast night sky, and I turned to see John and Stan restraining him, trying to hold him back. "Keep trying!" he was ordering the paramedics. "Fucking keep trying!"

Michael was frozen in the pale light, unable to take his wide eyes off Max's body.

I stepped forwards to look at Max's face, half expecting to see his eyes were open and this was all a misunderstanding. He looked white in the moonlight, his lips parted slightly. His eyes were closed and his glasses had been removed. I wanted to ask where his glasses were. He couldn't see without his glasses.

I didn't cry or shout. I didn't utter a sound or dare to breathe.

This couldn't be happening.

"Come away, son," a voice said behind me, taking me by the shoulders and turning me from the scene. "Don't look."

I'm brought back to the room by the ticking of the clock. I watch the second hand edging round, measuring the passage of time. Another second, minute, hour without him here, where he should be, with his friends and family. I don't remember standing up, but here I am, over by the mantelpiece, my back to everyone. Maybe that's the only way I could tell my story.

Everyone is still. Everyone is silent. I feel raw and exposed, and more vulnerable than I've ever been in my life. It's like I've been turned inside out and every failure, insecurity and ugliness is there for all to see. I press my left thumb hard into the scar on my right palm, watching it blanch.

We made a decision at the time – me, Tom and Michael – not to tell anyone what had happened at the allotments and why we were running so fast. Our story was simply that we were late leaving the fairground, that Michael was worried about missing his curfew, and that's why we were running. We lied, and, like most lies, once we'd said it, it felt impossible to retract.

I remember the day after Max's death, watching from my bedroom window as Rocket emerged from the house opposite. He was battered and bruised, hunched over, a purple eye, a split lip, a limp, one arm in a sling… So, I thought, they didn't kill him after all. His uncle was throwing his bags into the car. I guess he'd finally had enough.

Just as Rocket was about to climb into the passenger seat of his uncle's old Mondeo, he stopped and looked up and across the street, as if he knew I'd be there. Our eyes met and we held each other's gaze for a moment. I guessed he wouldn't know about Max, but the shared knowledge of what happened at the allotments seemed to pass between us like a guilty secret. As the car pulled away, I saw Laura run out into the street. She stood in the road, watching the car drive away. We never saw Rocket again, and I never told Laura exactly what happened that night, or his role in it. I never told anyone.

Peter and Carole have never known the true circumstances of their only son's death until now.

"I'm so sorry for my part in what happened that night," I say, looking up at the ceiling, unable to face Max's parents. "I'm so sorry that the choices I made…"

"There's nothing for you to be sorry about," I hear Carole say, her voice croaky. I can hear she's been crying. "What happened that night… it was just a terrible tragedy. But none of you were to blame."

I can hear her words, but, just like Tom's words, I can't take them in. I don't believe them. I *won't* believe them. Because I don't want to be free of this. Because I don't know what it would feel like to be free of it. And I don't think I deserve it.

"Mate, I don't know what you heard the paramedics say

about one minute," I hear Tom say, gently, "it could have been anything. But the fact is, by the time help arrived, he'd been gone a while. I know I was yelling at them to resuscitate him, so you might have thought he'd just gone, but we... well, we..."

"We already knew," Michael finishes. "One minute, five minutes... none of it would have made any difference."

I can hear what they're saying, but I can't accept it. How can something you've believed for sixteen years be so suddenly overturned?

I hear shuffling behind me, feel a warm hand gently touching my arm.

"You were such a good friend to him," Carole tells me. "I remember him running out of school on his very first day, telling me he'd made two new friends."

"Fwends," corrects Peter quietly.

"That's right," laughs Carole, "fwends, he called you. And then later, of course, he met Michael and the four of you... you were always together. Always laughing. That's what I remember. The *laughter* that used to come through the ceiling from his bedroom. I used to think *what on earth can they be doing that's so funny?*"

I want her to stop. I want her to be angry, to hate me. It would feel easier that way.

"We didn't tell you what happened that night," I tell her, "we lied to you, to everyone—"

"I told them," pipes up Tom from behind me. "I told them a long time ago."

So I was right; Tom was the only one to stay in contact.

"I don't know why I said we should keep quiet about the details of that evening," continues Tom. "That was my idea and it was a stupid one. I think I was scared, that we were all scared. The idea of the police getting involved, having to talk about it and maybe having to face those men again... it just all seemed too much. But lying about it was just another burden to carry."

"We've known about what happened for years," says

Carole, "and we've felt anger and hatred and all kinds of emotions towards those faceless men. We've blamed them. We've wished revenge on them. But, ultimately, they didn't kill Barclay. No one did. We've had to learn to let go—"

"*How*?" I ask, desperately, pushing my hands through my hair, unable to fathom how they, his parents, have been able to move beyond this in a way I haven't.

"It's been a struggle," says Carole, calmly. "We couldn't stay in Timpton. We tried, but everywhere we looked we were reminded of him. We visit him often, and my sister tends the grave, but we couldn't stay there. And I know what we said to you boys the day of the funeral, about keeping in regular contact, but it wasn't fair to ask that of you, and in the end we couldn't have handled it. It would have been too hard, seeing you all grow up without him. It's been nice to have the odd bit of news from Tom over the years, but I don't think we could have coped with much more than that. Not until now."

"But the main thing that's kept us going," says Peter, "is our faith. That's what's got us through. God forgives. And we try – challenging as it might be – to live by God's word."

"But if we'd – if *I'd* – just done things differently—"

"Listen to me, son," Peter say firmly, suddenly appearing by his wife's side.

He puts his two large hands on my shoulders and turns me towards him.

"Look at me," he says.

I struggle to raise my head and meet his eye.

"Look at me," he orders again, inclining his head towards mine.

I take a deep breath and gaze through his glasses, past the tiny smear on his thick lenses, into his green eyes.

"This wasn't your fault," he says, firmly. "This *wasn't* your fault. We have never blamed you. And there is nothing – hear me? – nothing for you to be sorry about."

I shake my head, looking away, a lump rising and lodging itself in my throat. I feel Peter's warm hand wrap itself around my jaw, turning my face back towards his. I try to pull away, but he steadies me with a heavy hand on the shoulder.

"You did nothing wrong," he insists. "*Nothing.*"

I tip my head towards the ceiling, hot tears springing to my eyes, but he places his hands on either side of my head, makes me face him again.

"God loves you, but he doesn't forgive you for this, because you don't need his forgiveness. And you certainly don't need ours. It was just something that happened. And you didn't – you hear me? – you *didn't* make it happen."

I exhale heavily, all the air rushing out of me, a sharp pain stabbing me in the gut as the tears escape.

"It was *not* your fault he died."

I bring my hands up to cover my eyes, tears leaking through my fingers, my shoulders shuddering beneath Peter's grasp.

I feel someone else's hand grip the back of my neck and I'm twisted round forcefully, pulled in and held tightly.

"It's okay," Michael says quietly, squeezing me tight, "it's okay."

I pinch the bridge of my nose in a vain attempt to stem the tears that pour silently from my eyes.

I feel more arms wrapping around me from behind, enveloping me.

"It's all right, mate," says Tom.

I take a deep, shuddering breath, air flooding my lungs.

I let my forehead fall against Michael's shoulder, his grip on the back of my neck pinning me in place, my tears soaking the neck of his T-shirt. I feel the softness of Tom's belly against my side, Carole's gentle hands rubbing my forearm, Peter's warm, heavy hand squeezing my shoulder.

And contained firmly inside this bundle of human warmth and acceptance, I let go, feeling the pain seep out with my tears, feeling the weight finally start to slide from my shoulders.

Chapter 25

Possibilities

Following my meeting with Max's parents, for the first time ever, I take two whole weeks off work. Scheduled jobs have to be cancelled. I have to let clients down. It's alien to me, this lack of responsibility and loss of income. But I know this is what I need.

I take Josh out of school a couple of days before half-term starts and we drive up to the Peak District. We mountain bike, hike, take the cable car up to the Heights of Abraham, which we haven't done since he was about nine. We eat lunch up there, looking out across the wide valley, the subtle spread of autumnal colours just starting to set in, the gentle sun on our faces, not talking much.

I've brought things in the van to start work on the millions of jobs I have to do on the cottage. Normally when I'm up here I'm fixing, mending, painting and making future renovation plans. But this time all the equipment I've bought stays in the van. I can't be bothered. And for the first time ever I wonder if I should sell this place. Laura wouldn't care – she's never been one for the outdoor life – and as she's told me so many times, we could both use the money. I no longer see myself moving up here. I have good friends where I am, people who care

337

about me. Why would I want to isolate myself? It suddenly sounds like a crazily lonely existence. I'm far too young. I have my whole life ahead of me.

At night I drift off in the silence of this tiny, pitch-black hamlet in the middle of nowhere. I slumber in deep, dreamless oblivion and wake up late to the sound of tractors in the country lanes and cattle on the move. While Josh sleeps on until lunchtime, I have coffee, sitting on the brick wall in the small, hopelessly overgrown garden. I breathe in the chill country air, close my eyes and let the dappled morning light filter though my eyelids.

Josh spends a lot of time on his phone and I don't like to pry, but I really, *really* want to know.

"How are things going with you and Becky?" I ask him one evening as we recline on separate sofas, eating giant marshmallows and watching a quiz show neither of us understands.

"Good," he says, not taking his eyes off the slightly fuzzy, ancient TV, "although it sucks that she's so far away."

"She lives in Reading, Josh, not Timbuktu."

"She's actually thinking of coming down again soon."

"Up, you mean. Do you even know where Reading is?"

"Whatever. So would that be okay? If she came for a weekend?"

"To stay?" I consider this. "Sure. I mean, I couldn't let her... you know... I'm sure her parents wouldn't want her staying in your room."

"You mean *you* wouldn't want her staying in my room."

"No, it's not... well..."

"Chill out, Dad. I already said we have a sofa bed in the lounge. For me, I mean."

"The one with burn marks all over it?"

"Yes," he says sheepishly, "although I'm assuming we'll get another one."

I almost laugh and ask him how the hell he thinks I'm

going to afford that right now, but it doesn't really matter. We'll find the money at some point.

"So," I say tentatively, "you really like this girl then?"

He stuffs an entire giant marshmallow into his mouth. I'm about to tell him not to do that while he's lying on his back, that he'll choke, but at fifteen I guess he's probably old enough to know how to eat a bloody marshmallow.

"Umm-hmm," he mumbles, as way of confirmation.

I wait for more, but he just gazes at the screen, where a woman's jumping up and down and screaming because she's won an Audi Q3.

"Am I getting any more than that?" I ask.

Josh chews lazily. "Nope."

We watch the excited woman, who's shocked the host by kissing him enthusiastically on the lips.

"What about you?" mumbles Josh.

"What about me?"

"Don't you ever want to be with someone?"

This is the first time he's ever asked me this.

"I mean, it's probably a bit weird that you're not," continues Josh. "It's not even like you're *that* old really."

"Thanks."

"No, I'm serious though. I mean, you're what? Thirty-four?"

"Thirty-two."

"Same difference. It's not, like, normal to be celibate or whatever at that age."

I smile to myself, amused, wondering if he really believes I've been celibate all these years, or whether it's just too disturbing for him to consider the alternative. When my mum told me she was having an affair, I think part of my horror was facing the fact she had sex at all.

"Talking about what's normal," I say, quickly diverting attention away from myself, "can we have a little chat about some stuff you clearly forgot to delete from the internet history on my laptop some weeks ago?"

Josh's hand pauses halfway to his mouth before he recovers himself and stuffs in another whole marshmallow.

"Stop trying to avoid my question," he mumbles, his mouth full.

"Stop trying to avoid mine," I say, surprised by his perceptiveness.

"It *is* normal to look at that stuff, Dad," he tells me dismissively, not nearly as embarrassed as I might have expected, "everyone does it."

"It's not the fact you're looking at it that bothers me so much as *what* you're looking at."

He rolls onto his side and peers round the arm of the sofa at me, pointing a finger accusingly. He's got my number. "We weren't talking about *me*, we were talking about *you*!" he retorts with a self-conscious smile, his cheeks turning slightly pink.

"I mean, some of that stuff, Josh… you know that's not what girls are really into, don't you?"

"We were talking about *you*!" he reiterates. "Let's talk about *you* and—"

"'Cause if you think that's what sex is really like, you're gonna have one hell of a shock—"

"*You*!" he shouts, throwing a cushion at me. "We were talking about *you* and just 'cause you don't want to answer—"

"I mean the stuff with the cheerleaders?" I say, throwing the cushion back at him playfully. "Seriously?"

"Okay, okay, shut up!" he begs, flipping onto his back. "Although… hang on… that means you watched it!"

"No," I laugh, "it means *you* watched it! I just came across it on my laptop."

Josh clutches his stomach and doubles up with laughter.

"What?"

"Did you *seriously* not hear what you just said?" he laughs loudly.

"What? That I came across— Oh, grow up! You know what I meant."

But it seems like my faux pas is the funniest things ever.

"I'm serious," I say, trying not to laugh. "I'm trying to tell you something here, Josh. You know that's not how you treat girls, right? It's not how you speak to them, it's not what you expect from them—"

"Oh my God, Dad, seriously?! I'm not a complete idiot, you know?"

"Okay, I'm just checking. I just sometimes worry… you know… without a mum around, without any sisters…"

"What? That I'm going to turn into some kind of perv?"

"No! Just… I don't know. I just thought we should have that discussion."

"Well, it was great, Dad. Thank you. I feel like I learned a lot."

I give up and throw a marshmallow at his head. It bounces off the top, onto his stomach and is promptly stuffed into his mouth.

"Anyway," he mumbles, "you're not getting out of it that easily. Back to you."

"What about me?" I ask, feigning memory loss.

"Girlfriends. Why don't you ever have any? I mean, don't you get… um… you know… kind of…"

I can hear he's struggling to spit it out, and I want to help him talk openly.

"Sexually frustrated?"

He makes a noise in the back of his throat that makes me wonder if he's about to choke after all.

"I was gonna say *lonely*, but whatever."

"Oh, right."

Do I get lonely? I honestly never thought I did. I've told myself that I'm too busy with work and parenting and family commitments to have a relationship, that I could never give what would be required of me. But that's all just been an excuse. I suppose you can convince yourself of anything if you really want to believe it.

"Yeah, I guess maybe I do get a bit lonely sometimes," I say, thoughtfully.

"So, like, hasn't there been *anyone* over the years you could see yourself with?"

Since she left I've tried to put Libby out of my head, but even with so many distractions it hasn't quite worked. In fact, it hasn't worked at all. I wonder what she's doing, whether she's okay after her split with Will, whether she's found any work... I think about what Irena told me, and I wonder whether it was all true, whether Irena was exaggerating, or whether something got misinterpreted. But then I always decide the same thing; it really doesn't matter anyway. I made my decision long ago about not wanting any more children, and that's not something I feel I could be flexible about. A relationship, yes. I can maybe see that now. Perhaps I can see myself being with someone. But I can't bring myself to want more kids. I just can't risk that again.

At least, I don't think I can.

"No," I tell Josh, "there's not been anyone I can see myself with."

We fall silent for a while, watching as some generic ITV police drama comes on. It's surprisingly liberating to have a limited number of channels instead of the overwhelming choice we have at home.

"I don't think you should worry, Dad," says Josh suddenly, "about me not having had a mum around."

I stare at the police officer sitting in his patrol car and unexcitedly, but stereotypically, eating a doughnut.

"Of course I worry," I tell him, "it's not ideal, is it?"

"Not ideal," he agrees, "but it's been all right. I feel like I've had lots of people in my life who really care about me – you, Laura, Michael, Brenda, Grandad, even though he's not quite with it anymore. I've always felt, like, loved and cared for or whatever. And I know loads of people with two parents who don't have that. Plus, I think I've turned out okay."

"I think you turned out great," I smile.

"And I think maybe the fact that it's just been you and me, and maybe the fact that you're not, like, nearly as ancient as some of my friends' parents, I think that means maybe we've been, kind of, closer? Like, I can talk to you about more stuff?"

"I hope so," I tell him, touched. "I know I haven't always taken on board what you've been trying to tell me, like about maybe putting too much pressure on you, or not letting you have enough freedom. I know I should have done better there. But I hope you still feel like you can talk to me about your worries, your feelings…"

"I do. Generally."

"I know it's not easy. I know boys especially don't always think they can talk about things like feelings and emotions."

"I talk about that stuff with my friends quite a lot," he corrects me. "Like, if we're feeling depressed or anxious or whatever, or have, like, low self-esteem days or dark thoughts. It's better for your mental health, isn't it? To talk, I mean."

I'm taken aback by his use of language. I think back to Tom's dad, how this puzzling "depression" thing he had was something none of us liked to mention, as if it was some shameful family secret that shouldn't be discussed. If one of us was feeling low, we'd accuse them of being "arsey" and tell them to snap out of it. If one of us showed signs of anxiety, we'd tell them to grow some balls. "Mental" was just a word used to insult one another.

"So, do you talk about your problems with your friends?" I ask him. "Like, I don't know, all this stuff with your mum, or how annoying I am…"

"Yeah, I talk a *lot* about how annoying you are," he says with blunt humour, "and, yeah, about Mum, about the stress of school, about girls and sexuality and all kinds of sh—stuff."

"Sexuality?"

"Yeah," he mumbles, like he's growing bored of this conversation now, "like, I've got friends who identify as bi or asexual or who don't see themselves as cisgender or whatever, so yeah, we talk about it."

I raise an eyebrow, wondering which friends these are, and try to remember what cisgender even is. God, how teenage life has changed in the space of a few short years. I'm pleased – and perhaps a little envious – to hear about their conversations. What would it have changed if my friends and I had been able to talk like that? To say how confused or depressed or anxious we felt? I just don't think we had the words, and if we did we weren't comfortable expressing them. The stiff-upper-lip attitude of St John's had only compounded that. It was only once we'd grown up – only really after Michael had ended up in therapy – that he introduced me to the language of feelings and the two of us had started to establish some kind of genuine emotional dialogue. From that point on, we said, we'd be more open and honest about what was really going on inside us. But it shouldn't have taken one of us being pushed to the brink to reach that point.

"I'm glad you've got friends you can talk to, Josh," I tell him. "Whether it's them, me, whoever… just make sure you don't hold everything in."

"Okay," he says, stuffing the final marshmallow in his mouth. "And don't worry about what I haven't had. You've done okay, Dad."

I smile, feeling a bit emotional.

"Thanks, mate."

That night, when Josh has gone to bed, I head into the cottage garden seeking a decent phone signal and call Michael. I know he'll be awake, even though it's nearly midnight. I've been thinking about that promise we made years ago that we'd be more open and honest with each other. And we have been. Much more so. But we both know it's been a little one-sided, that I've always been holding back, and I realise there are things I haven't told him, things I'd like to say.

"It doesn't matter," he scoffs when I tell him.

"Of course it matters. I was a shit to you."

"I don't remember that."

"How can you not remember?"

"I mean, I remember being vaguely aware of this new boy arriving at school and joining their little gang, and I guess I thought *Oh crap, now there are four of them*, but I don't remember you ever really doing anything to me. I don't even think you spoke to me until that day when you stood up for me."

"We hadn't spoken before that day. But I did join in with them. I remember hiding your bag, taking pieces of your PE kit… I mean, your dad must have given you a bollocking every time you went home with something else missing. And I hate the fact that I was part of that, even for a while."

"Jay, Addison started all his crap when I was, like, eleven. By the time you came along, I'd been putting up with it for three years. Your contribution was pretty insignificant in the grand scheme of things. Plus, you've more than made up for anything you did back then. I'm not even sure if I'd still be standing today if it wasn't for you. You were the one who made me get help, who got me to stop drinking, you're the person I've always been able to turn to if I've needed to talk."

"Yeah, but that's not even true is it."

I've been remembering little things lately, things I'd long ago forgotten or pushed out of my mind.

"When you said that you'd tried to talk to me about what happened that night—"

"You mean the night that Max died," he corrects me.

I swallow hard. Both of us have recently noticed that that's how we've always referred to it – *that night, the night of the fairground, that thing that happened*. We've agreed we need to call it what it is.

"Yes," I concede, "the night Max died. When you said I wouldn't talk about it, you were right. I remember that now. You tried to talk to me about it several times—"

"And you couldn't. And that's fine."

"It's not fine, because you had no one else to turn to—"

"But that's not your fault. You can't fix everything for everyone."

He sighs.

"Look, you haven't got it right all the time, Jay, and God knows I haven't either, but you've been the greatest friend I could ever wish for. When I've been a complete mess, you've picked me up, over and over again. When I've got myself in sticky situations, you've come to my rescue and bailed me out. When I finally found the balls to confess about my sexuality, you said just the rights things... I don't think I would have ever opened up about that without you to talk to. I have never, ever doubted that you have my back."

I feel a slight lump in my throat. After years of feeling like I couldn't quite reach my emotions, lately they've been constantly on the verge of eruption.

"And you've always had mine," I tell him.

He laughs quietly. "Well then, we're all good, aren't we?"

He falls silent, and in the darkness of the overgrown cottage garden, I gaze at the stars and listen to the sound of his breathing in these eerily silent surroundings.

"I fell in love with Libby again," I admit to him.

"I know, mate," he says, sounding sympathetic.

"You didn't say anything."

"I know better than to try and push you to talk. I figured you'd fess up when you wanted to."

I sigh deeply. I don't even know why I bothered saying anything. She's gone now anyway, I don't even know where to, and it's not like I'm going to do anything about it.

"Irena said Libby has feelings for me," I tell him, hunching my shoulders up against the cold evening air.

"You don't say," he replies sarcastically.

I wonder if I really have been blind.

"We want such different things," I say, thinking it through out loud.

"Are you sure about that?"

"She wants kids and I don't..."

"Based on what? A decision you made a long time ago following an incredibly stressful event?"

"My life's just so chaotic, with Josh and my dad and...I dunno, there's hardly any time and she deserves better. She deserves someone who can make her the centre of their world, someone who can give her stability and financial security and..." I trail off, staring up at the night sky. For the first time I'm not even convincing myself.

"And what about what you deserve?" asks Michael.

I look at the stars and wonder, for the first time in years, whether I'm deserving of happiness after all.

On a fresh Sunday morning, following our return from the Peak District, I pull up at the Canal House. I've said I'll take some stuff to the tip for Stu in the van, seeing as I'm going anyway to dispose of a ruined carpet. It's early, quiet, a chill in the bright air.

I go round the back and let myself in through the gate, nearly jumping out of my skin when a cat suddenly races past me. Crumble charges down the side passage and out into the car park like he's running for his life.

And there, on the terrace in front of me, stands Libby, a cat brush in her hand.

We stare at each other, both caught off guard.

"Hi," she says first, looking flustered, "I was just—"

"Hi. I didn't know—"

"...I was trying to brush him—"

"...you're... back. I didn't..."

"Irena's not able to work right now, so Stu asked if I—"

"Oh, right, I see."

"Yeah, sorry. I know you were hoping you'd seen the last of me!" She laughs, but her joke falls flat and we both look away, embarrassed. "I wasn't sure whether to come back, but Stu and Irena were pretty desperate and they've been so good to me..." She waves the cat brush in the air as she talks and

347

sounds genuinely apologetic. "It's just until the baby comes. I'll be gone—"

"No, it's fine. I mean, of course it's fine, it's none of my business, it's nothing to do with me—"

"I'll be working in the kitchen mainly, so we probably won't even—"

"No, seriously, please," I beg her, feeling terrible. This was her hometown too, once. I can't believe I've made her feel so uncomfortable about being here, and not even for a genuine reason. "I've been so busy lately I've barely been around here anyway—"

"Okay, good. I mean, not good, but—"

"Ah, morning!" calls Stu, appearing from the back of the pub carrying a pile of cardboard. He stops abruptly when he reaches us, looking from me to Libby to me again, weighing up what he's just walked into.

"I'm going to find your cat, who I've just scared half to death," Libby tells him, holding up the brush and forcing a smile.

"I told you, you're fighting a losing battle," says Stu. "Oh, can you put these by the bins?"

He piles the cardboard into Libby's arms, and we watch as she disappears down the side passage, struggling to see over the top of the rubbish.

Stu turns his attention to me. "So, Libby's returned," he declares.

"I can see that."

He looks at me long and hard, as if he's waiting for more. "What?" I ask.

He shakes his head, a hint of sympathy in his eyes.

"Come on," he sighs, as if I've somehow disappointed him. "Let's get some coffee."

"I never thanked you properly," says Stu, his hands wrapped around his mug, squinting against the sunshine. We're sitting at the back of the terrace under a clear, blue sky. Light bounces off his shiny bald head.

"What for?"

"For what you did when Irena… you know…"

He stares sadly into his mug.

"I didn't do anything," I tell him.

"Of course you did. You called the ambulance, you stayed with her. She said you were great, that you stayed calm and collected."

Christ, I think, *how could I possibly have given that impression?*

"But you must have been freaking out," continues Stu, not knowing how much of an understatement that is. "It was a really stressful situation, but she was so pleased you were there. And I know you were about to get in the ambulance with her just as I arrived."

"What else would I have done?"

"Nothing, I guess. I just wanted to say how grateful I am."

"Shut the hell up."

"Okay."

We sit in silence for a moment and I study the mural in front of us. It's so busy that I keep finding details that I've never noticed before. The lady in a towel peeping out from behind the net curtain of her houseboat, the dog cocking his leg against a tree, the exhausted-looking jogger who clearly hasn't done exercise in several years. These comical little scenes are so typical of Libby that I can almost imagine her grinning to herself as she painted them. I can't believe that when we first met here all those weeks ago I thought she'd lost her humour, her softness.

"I feel like I'm just counting the days until this baby arrives safely," Stu says.

I nod, knowing so many of us feel the same way. Everyone who frequents the Canal House is rooting for this unborn child.

"You know what the worst thing is?" Stu muses. "I wasn't even sure I wanted this baby. How bad is that? It was all Irena.

She was the one who wanted to get pregnant. I was having fun just the two of us. I thought we had all the time in the world. I had to really force myself into it, you know? Force myself to face the fact that I'm forty-three years old, that I need to grow up. And that we don't have all the time in the world. No one does. When she was rushed into hospital, I really thought…"

He trails off with a deep sigh, and I shudder at the memory of Stu's text coming through from the hospital. For a while there it wasn't just the baby who was at risk. There was a point where it looked like neither of them might make it.

I'm about to tell him that I understand. Not only about the guilt of not wanting your unborn child, but about the fear of losing someone you love more than life itself. I want to tell him that I completely get it if he doesn't want to ever risk a similar experience again, that I'm right there with him. Why would you ever want to make yourself vulnerable to that kind of fear and pain? But it turns out that's not what he's saying.

"It made me realise you have to grab life by both hands. Now, I want everything. I want to marry Irena, have more children, buy this bar in Spain that she's always talking about."

He looks up at the sky.

"I nearly lost her, mate. I nearly lost both of them. All the things we're gonna do, all the experiences that – God willing – we're gonna have. They almost didn't happen. They were almost over before they'd even started."

He shakes his head as if he can't fathom it. His eyes suddenly look watery. He sniffs.

"Anyway," he says, standing up and draining his mug, "I can't sit here and talk shit with you all morning. I'll go get the stuff for the tip."

I make a move to stand, but he waves his hand dismissively.

"You finish your coffee," he says, "I'll bring it downstairs. There's nothing too heavy and her majesty's probably still in her dressing gown. She hates to be seen without her face on. Makes people think she's human."

When he's gone, I think about Stu's words.

All the experiences that we're gonna have. They almost didn't happen...

If Josh had died that night in hospital, what would never have happened? What wonderful experiences would have never been?

The incredible history that Josh and I have shared sometimes feels like a story that belongs to someone else. Occasionally I catch glimpses of the good times – those magical, happy memories – but they're vague and fleeting, like a TV set with terrible reception. I have a sense I could tune that TV – relive the beautiful, meaningful moments – but somehow it's felt easier, safer, not to.

And yet I remember the horror of that night in hospital like it was yesterday. Everything from the smell of the corridors to the squeak of my trainers on the floor and the colour of the plastic seats. I also remember the stress of those early years, constantly struggling, rushing between work and school, always late, always stressed, always broke. I remember being exhausted, frustrated, impatient, feeling like I was never good enough.

But that's not the whole story. And if I can take a moment, just a couple of minutes, to fiddle with the dial on that TV set, I know there's so much more to see.

I close my eyes, feeling the sun's gentle warmth against my skin, and I remember...

I remember arms around my neck at bedtime, excited chatter because the tooth fairy might be coming for the first time. I remember him running down the football pitch to give me a high five when he scored his first club goal. I remember the manic sound of his laughter when I used to tickle him, cuddling up together inside a den made of sheets and pillows, hours spent building Lego together, the first time we went cycling in the Peak District and my amazement that my little boy was now big enough and strong enough to keep up with me.

Despite the tears, the demands, the fear and the exhaustion, it's all been so precious. And I wouldn't give away one single minute of it.

As the memories flood through me, one after another, like a packed closet that's suddenly had its doors flung open, I realise that every day has been worth both the risk of having him and the risk of losing him.

For so long I've dwelled on what I've done wrong, all the mistakes I've made and the ways I haven't been good enough. But look at my son. Look at how he's turned out, how I've helped him grow.

You've done okay, Dad.

And my closest friendship, sustained over so many years despite all the challenges…

You've been the greatest friend I could ever wish for.

When did I stop believing in myself? When did I stop feeling good enough?

Because it's not true.

I might not have it all together. I might flounder sometimes, I might struggle at others, but I can love and I can be loyal. I can have someone's back for as long as it takes. I can be brave and I can step up to the mark.

I remember Libby's words that evening in her attic room. *It's not a house I want, it's a home.*

Maybe, just maybe, I can be everything she needs.

Maybe I already am.

Chapter 26

Running

Ever since meeting with Max's parents I've been feeling things shifting, easing, reframing. It's like a plug's been pulled and the negativity I've been carrying for all these years – all the guilt and fear and self-doubt – is slowly draining away. I sleep better. The headaches are gone. I feel less angry and stressed and overwhelmed. I feel freer.

And clearly I'm not the only one who suddenly feels this way.

"What the hell's that?" I ask, as Michael welcomes me into his flat and closes the front door. I stare at the tattoo on his neck.

"Like it?"

"Sure," I shrug. "Were you going for the *just got out of prison* look, or—"

"Jesus," he moans, rolling his eyes, "give it a rest, Grandad."

"I'm joking."

I examine the ink on his skin. It's very skilfully done. An angel ascending with wings open wide. It seems to counterbalance the weeping, tormented angel on his forearm which I've always found deeply depressing.

"I hate to tell you this," I say, confused, "but a smart shirt isn't going to cover that up when you're summoned to dinner with your dad."

"That's the whole point of it. I met with him yesterday. And I told him… well, everything."

He looks almost smug.

I raise an eyebrow sceptically. "*Everything*?"

"Everything," he confirms. "And let's just say me having a few tattoos, playing in a rock band and earning a pitiful wage actually *weren't* his biggest disappointments."

Right on cue, Rob walks out of the lounge in jogging bottoms and an Aertex T-shirt.

"Now he has a *far* bigger reason to be disappointed in you," he growls in his Dutch accent, wrapping his arms around Michael from behind, squeezing him tight and kissing him hard on the side of the head.

"Ohh, yes," smiles Michael, "well, if you're gonna be a disappointment, why not go all out?"

"Exactly," agrees Rob, releasing Michael and pulling on a pair of trainers that are by the front door.

"Wow," I say, "that's huge. What did he say?"

"Actually, he was surprisingly calm."

"He had to be," Rob adds, "you were in a five-star restaurant."

"True. But that aside, I still think he took it well. He said unfortunately some people just aren't made right, and that it wasn't really surprising given that my mother had weak genes and—"

"Weak genes?!" I exclaim.

"Oh yes, he gave me a long and enlightening lecture about my mother's weak genes," says Michael, adopting a mock-serious tone. "And then he said that as I'm his only son he would *tolerate* my situation – very touching – on the understanding that it remains hidden from all friends and family, and that we never speak about it. Oh, and that he never wants to meet Rob as long as he lives."

"Which hopefully won't be too long," Rob mutters, as he ties his shoelaces.

Michael tuts and shoots him a reprimanding look.

"So what did *you* say?" I ask.

"I told him," says Michael with a smile that suggests he can barely believe his own audacity, "that unfortunately *that* was a situation that *I* could not tolerate, and that if he ever wants to review his terms and conditions, then he knows where to find me."

"Whoa," I say, amazed. "Go you. I mean, I don't know where that suddenly came from, but still—"

"I'm thirty-two," shrugs Michael, as if it suddenly all seems so obvious. "There's only so long you can let fear rule your life, isn't there?"

"Yeah," I nod, although I don't feel particularly convinced. I'm pretty sure I could easily let fear rule my life forever. "Well, good for you. I know that can't have been easy."

I pat him on the shoulder and he smiles appreciatively, but there's a hint of sadness in his eyes. He looks tired, and I'm guessing he hasn't slept since meeting with his father yesterday. He's shown guts, but he's also potentially lost the one person he's spent his whole life trying to please. I can see that he knows this, that he realises the road ahead isn't going to be easy. Still, I'm quietly thrilled he's made a stand for himself after all these years.

"So," says Rob, clapping his hands and turning to me. "Are you ready?"

I look down at my new running shoes.

"As ready as I'll ever be."

"Take it easy on him," Michael warns Rob. "He hasn't run in, like, over fifteen years."

"Don't worry, we're going to build up slowly," he replies, giving me a secret wink that makes me worry about what he has planned. "Go sleep," he tells Michael, kissing him on the cheek.

"If he starts barking orders at you, just shove him in the canal," Michael tells me as we head out the door.

"Gotcha," I call, feeling trepidation creep in.

Interval training is the way it's done now. Not like when I was at school when they just made you run as far and as fast as you could. But perhaps that was just St John's. *Results – no matter the cost.* That would have been a far more fitting motto for the school than the pretentious Latin crap they hid behind.

We run, jog, walk, run, jog, walk, run – and suddenly I just don't want to stop running.

"Okay, so slow it down now," Rob tells me, dropping behind.

But I'm feeling it again, just like I did when I was a boy, before I lost the love of it, before I couldn't bring myself to do it anymore. The repetitive thud of my trainers against the path, the rhythm of my breathing, the cool air filling my lungs, pushing them wide open.

"Slow down!" Rob calls behind me, but I don't want to.

I feel strong and energised in a way I haven't in years. I squint against the light, passing by the narrowboats, the dappled water steadily moving past on one side, thick shrub on the other.

I can hear Rob's breathing just behind me. He's caught up, but he's no longer telling me what to do. He knows I'm working something out and his quiet presence reassures me.

I feel the breeze against my skin, the sweat cooling against my chest and back.

I love this. I could do this forever, making up for all the wasted years.

I run past the lock house, past the weir, past the entrance to the nature reserve. The dogs and their walkers disappear far behind us and the path ahead is open and empty. And just then I see the big concrete bridge approaching, the spot where Max died.

I speed up, the air rushing past me, my feet pounding the ground, faster, faster...

The bridge approaches and I feel a sense of dread set in, but there's no question of me turning back or hiding away from what once happened here. I run full pelt, my legs powerful, my arms pumping, faster, faster, FASTER!

And suddenly I'm bursting through the finish line. The bridge is behind me and I'm out the other side.

I slow down, eventually grinding to a halt, bending over and gulping in air.

"Oh my God," gasps Rob, pulling up beside me, panting. "That's not taking it easy, man."

I use the bottom of my T-shirt to wipe the sweat from my face. I glance back at the bridge, half expecting to see darkness, paramedics, four boys – one of them lying on the ground – Stan Finch and John Porter. But there's nothing but shadow and a bit of weathered, indiscernible graffiti. It's still and quiet, just the sound of Rob and I breathing heavily.

I wander slowly back towards the spot where Max died. I stare at the exact place where his lifeless body lay. There's nothing there. Nothing happens. I don't feel anxious or angry.

I just feel sad.

But it feels right, this aching sadness. I'm reminded of a game little children play, where you have to place the right-shaped block into the right-shaped hole. For too long I've been trying to plug a hole in my heart with notions and feelings that just wouldn't fit, forcing them in until they became distorted and damaged. But this sadness finally feels like it's where it's supposed to be. It's hard and it's painful, but it's home.

If Rob wasn't already aware that this is the spot where Max died, then I'm pretty sure he's aware now. He remains at a respectful distance, looking out at the water until I call over to him.

"Is it okay if we turn back now?"

Our plan was to go about half a mile further than this, but I'm done. He starts to walk towards me.

"You've burned yourself out," he tells me, with the tone of a gentle reprimand.

I shake my head. I don't feel burned out. I feel like I could go for miles.

"I'm fine," I reassure him, turning and starting to jog slowly back along the path. "I just suddenly thought of somewhere I need to go."

"Hi again," I say, "I bet you weren't expecting to see me again so soon."

Max is silent.

"I wanted to tell you something," I say. "In fact, I wanted to tell you lots of things."

I take a deep breath and crouch down in front of his grave. I'm freshly showered following my run, and the scent of my own shower gel and deodorant mingles with the smell of earth and grass.

"I miss you," I say, a lump rising in my throat. "I miss your big belly laugh. I miss your gap-toothed smile. I miss laughing *at* you and the way you always took it in good humour. I miss playing football with you. I miss talking to you. I miss cycling with you, listening to music with you, taking the piss out of Tom with you... I miss... I just miss you."

I gaze at the flowers by his headstone, drooping sadly. For a second I wish I'd brought fresh ones, but that's not really me and he knows that. Plus, it won't be long until they're replaced.

"I've felt so bad for the ways things turned out that night. I've spent so long wishing I'd done things differently, wishing I could have made things turn out okay. I wanted to save you. I *wish* I could have saved you. But I couldn't."

For a long time I stare at his name on the headstone, my mind quiet and empty.

"Would it be okay if I let go of this now?" I whisper, without much awareness of what I'm even saying.

In the stillness, I hear the gentle breeze quietly rustling the leaves of the trees. I feel the early-autumn sunshine warming my back. A single white petal, curled and brown, drops to the ground. I stare at it lying there, wanting it to mean something, wanting it to be a sign.

But there's no one who can answer my question.

No one but me.

Chapter 27

Forwards

For the last four years, at the start of November, Stu and Irena have held a charity fundraiser at the Canal House. It's a ticket-only event, and the place is always packed. There's live music from a variety of local bands, a barbecue, a raffle and, later on, fireworks. Unlike last year when the event had to be moved inside to shelter from the rain, this year the bands will play on a raised stage at the side of the terrace underneath a clear night sky.

Some of the regulars pitch in, selling raffle tickets, promoting the event and helping to get the party started. Michael and I fire up the barbecue, although he's so high on excitement about playing with his band later that he almost sets fire to his own jeans. Then I take over door duty for a bit, checking tickets and turning away anybody without one, taking a bit of aggro from a group of lads who have clearly already been on the beers and didn't read the *Private Event* signs at the car park entrance. Then, like each year, there's a mini-crisis when the banner over the stage falls down, taking a string of lights with it and landing on top of a young female singer and her guitar. Fortunately, she's not hurt, but it takes the shine off her debut at the Canal House, and she has to stop singing while Stu and I climb on stage to a cacophony of good-natured caterwauls and heckling to untangle the mess.

I keep seeing Libby weaving her way through the crowd, collecting glasses, tipping rubbish into black sacks, delivering boxes of hotdog buns to Leo, who's doing a stint on the barbecue, comically squeezed into a striped apron which just about covers his huge chest. In the glow of the patio lamps and multicoloured lanterns she looks rosy-cheeked and slightly flustered, as if she's struggling to keep up. We smile awkwardly at each other as we pass by, and each time I almost stop her.

Can I talk to you?
There's something I need to say.
I need to tell you something.

But there's no time. And on some level, I'm relieved, because I have no idea how to go about this.

I busy myself with anything Stu wants help with – lugging crates of beer, clearing up a broken glass, fetching more ice – until he stops me.

"Right, we're all in order. You're a star, mate. Now go chill out and enjoy yourself."

"Are you sure? If you need me—"

"Go enjoy the party," he orders.

I find things easier when I'm busy, I know that about myself now. When I'm stretched to the limit, being pulled in three directions at once, I might feel put upon and stressed out, but the truth is the busyness – all those commitments – gives me an excuse. An excuse not to get involved in a relationship, not to think about the things that aren't working in my life. An excuse not to live fully.

But I don't want to make excuses anymore.

My work setting up this event is done. I'm free. And, terrifyingly, just for a moment, so is Libby. Besides, how long does it really take to tell someone how you feel about them? There's another thing you could probably do in sixty seconds, if you knew how.

I find her standing at the side of the packed terrace, watching the band from afar. Purple Sway are a local folk band; not my kind of thing, but they've made quite a name for themselves in this town of eclectic music lovers over the last couple of years. The crowd are jigging and foot-tapping in time to the music, drinks in hand. The night air smells of barbecue smoke, hotdogs and booze. The evening has all the right ingredients for a relaxed party, but I'm anything other than relaxed. I don't know if this is the best time, or the best place, but I have to be honest with her. Because even if Irena was wrong, even if Libby doesn't feel the same about me, I need to get it out there. I need to know if there's a chance for us.

But just as I'm about to weave my way through the crowd, a warm hand touches me on the shoulder.

"Hello, stranger."

I turn to see Rachel, her hair hanging in loose waves over her shoulders, an impossibly tiny denim skirt and high-heeled boots showing off her long legs.

"Hi," I say, holding my breath, waiting for her to lay into me. We haven't spoken since the night I went back to her flat and then walked out on her. I dropped her a brief text the following morning – a bumbling apology – but I never heard back.

She leans in close, her mouth next to my ear.

"I'm going home tomorrow," she tells me above the blare of the music, "to Melbourne."

I pull back and look at her in surprise.

"My friend's offered me a job," she explains dismissively, "she wants me to start straight away."

"I'm sorry," I tell her, leaning in to be heard above the noise, "about the last time—"

"Forget it," she says, with a wave of her hand. "You had a ton of stuff going on. I shouldn't have been such a diva. I guess I was just disappointed."

She gives me one of her coquettish smiles.

"I think you and I could have had a lot of fun," she says,

"but I don't think a bit of fun's really what you're looking for."

I glance briefly over to where Libby was standing a moment ago, but she's already gone. I quickly scan the crowd, but I can't see her anywhere.

Rachel reaches out and squeezes my wrist. "Find whatever makes you happy, Jay," she says into my ear, "you're a good guy. You deserve it."

She places a warm hand on the back of my neck, pulls me in and plants a kiss on my lips. And the first thing I see when she releases me is Libby passing behind her, squeezing her way through the crowd, meeting my eye for the briefest second and then quickly looking away.

I want to stop her, but in a flash she's gone.

Rachel sees something in my eye and glances over her shoulder, just catching a glimpse of Libby's back as she's swallowed up in the crowd.

She smiles knowingly at me.

"Go," she tells me, pushing me away from her, and not for the first time I realise how transparent I must be. Does *everyone* know how I feel? Does Libby?

I guess if she does, then what have I got to lose by saying it out loud?

Do you have feelings for me?
    I think there's something between us...
    Is there a chance...?
    "Can we maybe... um... just talk for a minute?"

Later in the evening, when I finally come across her again, Libby doesn't look busy. She's leaning against the wall in the side alley, illuminated by the light from the kitchen window, sipping a glass of water and taking a break from the noise and the chaos. But at my approach she suddenly seems to remember she's rushed off her feet.

"I was just… I really have to get back," she fumbles, making as if to head straight past me.

"Please. Can we just—"

"I can't, sorry, I have to—"

"Are you avoiding me?" I ask, stepping in front of her, thinking it takes one to know one.

"No, I'm not avoiding you, I'm working," she says, sounding affronted.

Just then, the gate that leads from the car park opens and Irena walks into the alley.

"Why you two hiding down here for?" she asks brusquely, shutting the gate behind her.

"I was just getting back to work," Libby says quickly, as if she's been caught skiving.

Irena stops. She looks from me, to Libby and back again.

"Is fine. Take rest of the night off," she orders with a wave of her hand.

"There's too much to do," Libby protests.

Irena checks her watch. "Is all fine. Plus, is already nine o'clock. I tell you only work till nine and then enjoy yourself. Why else I get in extra staff?"

"I don't mind—"

"Don't make me fire you," says Irena, sharply, squeezing past us with her round belly. "No more work tonight."

As she passes me, she jabs me hard in the back of my ribs, making me jolt. I assume this counts as encouragement in Irena's world.

We watch her waddle down the alley to re-join the party. The music has temporarily stopped – a changeover of bands – and despite the hordes of people talking and laughing just around the corner, the air suddenly seems strangely quiet without the thudding of drums and the clanging of guitars.

"So…?" Libby asks, as if she's still needed somewhere else.

"Look," I say, taking a deep breath, my heart starting to race, "I wanted to tell you why I said what I said before…

about not wanting you around, I mean. Because when I tried to explain before—"

"It's fine. I understand."

"No, you don't."

"I do. I know me being here must bring stuff up for you—"

"Yes, but not the stuff you think. I mean, maybe, a bit, but that's not—"

"It's brought stuff up for me, too. Memories and... well, I haven't found it easy either. But I'm just here until the baby comes, and then I'm out of Timpton. I'm sure that for a few weeks, for Irena and Stu's sake, we can—"

"No, I know all that, but that's not—"

"I'm pleased we met up again despite everything, and maybe you don't feel that way, but I really am pleased, even if it has been... unsettling. I always thought about you and wondered if you were okay and I didn't just stop caring—"

"Neither did I."

"—but you and me, trying to be friends... it was probably a bit ambitious. I mean, it took me a long time to get over you and perhaps some things are better left alone. And obviously it's brought stuff up for you—"

"No, but that's what I want to tell you—"

"—I think bringing the past up again, it can get complicated and confusing, and I totally understand—"

"Libby, will you just stop talking for a minute!" I interrupt, a little more harshly than I intend, nerves making me agitated.

She stares at me, wide-eyed, clutching her glass of water in front of her.

"Look," I say, deciding to take a different route in. "I... Do you... do you have feelings for me?"

The second it's out I feel foolish; vulnerable and exposed. She stares at me, the whites of her eyes shining like a rabbit caught in the headlights.

She shakes her head slightly, and with a sinking heart I'm immediately convinced that Irena was wrong, that I was wrong...

"What do you mean?" she asks.

"I just... A few times I've had a feeling that maybe... between us, there was... something. And Irena told me..."

Even in the dim light I can see the flush rise up Libby's neck, colouring her cheeks. She quickly tucks a strand of hair behind her ear.

"I don't know what Irena said, but she shouldn't... she really... I mean, of course I have feelings for you... or about you... It's confusing, seeing you again, that's what I just said, I think maybe coming back here—"

"So then you *do* have feelings for me?" I ask, desperate for some clarity.

"What... I mean, why? Why does it even matter?" she asks, looking flustered. "I know it's not like you and I... I mean, you have this thing with Rachel and—"

"There's nothing between me and Rachel."

"Really?" she scoffs, clearly thinking she knows better. "That's not what it looked like when you were kissing her earlier—"

"She kissed *me*! It was a kiss goodbye. She's leaving."

"Or when you walked out of here wrapped round each other a few weeks ago—"

"When? The night Will was here? No, that... Nothing happened. It wasn't—"

"Whatever, anyway, I don't care," she insists, shaking her head dismissively.

"Well, it kind of... seems like you do care."

"No, I absolutely don't," she says firmly, "that's your business—"

"So why are you even bringing Rachel into it?"

She looks stumped.

"I don't know. I wasn't. I mean, I'm not."

I stare at her, confused. I don't know how I thought this was going to go, but it definitely wasn't like this.

"Look," I say, running my hand over my head, realising

I am making a terrible job of this. "I just wanted to know if you felt anything. For me. Because it seemed like maybe—"

"Okay, I'm not going to lie," she interrupts, "I've had a lot of complicated feelings going on, and seeing you again—" Her voice cracks and she stops abruptly. She stares at the ground silently, recovering her composure.

And in that moment I know.

I know that I'm not wrong.

"What does it even matter to you how I feel?" she asks, her voice having lost its strength.

"Because it does," I tell her, suddenly desperate for her to understand. "Because *I* have feelings. For you. And if you feel anything like the same…"

I watch her carefully, waiting for confirmation of what I'm suddenly sure I know, but she seems to have frozen, her wide eyes staring at me. It's hard to tell in the poor light, but if I had to guess at her expression, I'd say shocked confusion mixed with a hint of fear.

"Okay, listen," I say, wishing I could start this afresh, "the thing is—"

"Why are you doing this?" she asks abruptly, her voice quivering with emotion.

"Why? Because you and I—"

"There *is* no you and I!" she snaps, raising her voice. "How could there ever be a you and I? We want *totally* different things. We want different futures and… and asking me to suddenly *declare* how I feel about you—"

"I wasn't—"

"Although it seems like Irena's already repeated *everything* I told her in confidence anyway! And telling me you have feelings… What does that even mean, that you have feelings? And where has this suddenly come from, because until now you have given me absolutely *no* indication. I mean, one minute I think we're friends and then a couple of weeks ago it became perfectly clear that you couldn't even *stand* to have me around—"

"That wasn't—"

"I mean, your behaviour towards me has been *totally* confusing, I have wasted literally *hours* of my life agonising over it, and now you're telling me what? That you have feelings? I mean, do you think this is okay? To mess with me like this? Because I am *sick and tired* of men messing with me—"

"I'm not messing with you! How am I messing…?"

"—telling me that you have feelings for me and asking if I have feelings for you when you know perfectly well that we want *completely* different things."

"No, but just listen—"

"—And unless that ever changed there could never be any future for us. But if you think I could just give up on everything I've ever wanted – my own family, my own children – that I could just cast that aside just because *you* suddenly decide—"

"I haven't suddenly decided anything! I've been thinking about nothing else for weeks, and if I wasn't sure that I could be on board with what you want for your future, I would never be saying this to you!"

"But what *are* you even saying to me? I don't understand! Do you think this has been *easy* for me? Coming back here? Seeing you again? Do you know how long it took me to move on? Do you know how hard it's been realising that I never actually moved on at all?! I thought – I *really* thought – that if I could be around you…I… Do you… And now you're telling me… What do you even *want* from me?!"

"Libby," I say, holding my hands up in defence, stunned by her reaction, "I don't know what the hell's going on here. I didn't mean to upset you, I just wanted to tell you…" I trail off, searching desperately for the words that might somehow set this right.

"Just leave me alone! Please!" she snaps, shoving past me so forcefully that her water splashes all over my T-shirt.

"Wait!" I call, grabbing for her, but she slips from my hand and bolts down the alley.

I'm left wet, shocked and utterly bewildered.

I re-join the party just as a massive cheer – the biggest of the night – fills the air. Everyone's on their feet so that I'm barely able to squeeze through all the bodies crammed onto the terrace. People are chanting, hollering, whistling…

I hear Michael's voice on the microphone, offering a brief greeting to the crowd, who almost drown him out with their whoops of appreciation. I try to find a path through, searching desperately for any sign of Libby. I don't know where I'm going or why, all I know is I can't leave things as they are. As I search, I see Laura with her arms around Mark, the mechanic she once thought was a dick but now seems to have won her over. I see Amber, the girl with the dragon tattoo, putting her fingers in her mouth and emitting a shrill whistle, supporting her ex-boyfriend on stage while happily entwined with her new one. I see Tom and his wife, Kim, holding hands. I see Tyler and Theo with their respective partners. And I see Rob gazing proudly and adoringly towards the stage. It feels like everybody has someone tonight.

The music starts up to another loud cheer, and Michael's strong, familiar voice fills the sky with an upbeat number that has the crowd jumping and pumping their hands in the air. All around me, people are singing along to his words, rocking their heads in time to his music.

"Dad!" I hear a call. "Dad!"

I spy Josh at the side of the terrace, desperately waving me over, looking stressed. I've been so distracted, I'd almost forgotten he was here.

I force my way through the crowd, wondering what the hell's happened now.

When I reach him, he shouts something at me, but I can't make it out.

"What?" I shout back, putting my arm around his neck and pulling him in close.

"I can't do this!" he yells in my ear.

I look quizzically at his face, and then I curse myself and my own self-centredness. In my fluster over Libby, I'd momentarily forgotten: tonight's his first time performing on stage. He looks anxious, his eyes searching mine, looking for me to rescue him.

My first instinct is to wring his neck. He can't *do* this? After all the hassle he gave me about being allowed to perform?!

"What do you mean you can't do it?" I shout in his ear. "Of course you can do it!"

He shakes his head, grimacing like the very idea is causing him pain.

I clutch the back of his neck and steer him towards the far end of the terrace where there's a small patch of space.

"Listen," I shout, taking his face in my hands and forcing him to look at me, "you are incredible!"

"I'm totally crapping myself! I feel sick!"

"That's fine. It's okay to be scared. Do you remember what Michael said? That he feels like that every time he gets up there?"

"Yeah, but people love him—"

"They'll love you."

"What if they don't?"

"Then fuck them!"

He stares at me as if he can't believe I just said that, and for a second it seems to shock him out of his state of fear. But it doesn't take long for his anxiety to set back in.

"I can't do it, Dad," he says, looking distressed, "I'm sorry. I don't want to let anyone down, but I can't get up there!"

"You can!"

"I *can't*!

"Josh, listen to me!" I shout in his ear. "Sometimes you just have to face your fears. Otherwise you'll never know what could have been."

The music crashes to an end and the crowd cheers and hollers.

"*Ladies and gentlemen*," I hear Michael say over the microphone, sounding slightly breathless, "*tonight I want to welcome on stage with me a very special guest—*"

"Shit! I can't do it!" shouts Josh, grabbing at his hair.

"*—he's a young, talented singer and musician—*"

"Listen!" I shout, grabbing Josh by the shoulders, deciding to go out on a limb. "I'm in love with Libby. I have been for ages, and I think perhaps you already know that. It seems like everyone knows that. But I've been standing in the shadows, too scared to do anything about it. I'm still scared. I'm terrified. But I'm gonna tell her everything. Tonight. And you're gonna get up on that stage, okay? Because if we don't do these things, neither of us will ever know how good it might have been."

He stares at me, stunned. And then a smile creeps across his lips.

"I knew it!" he shouts.

I thrust my hand out.

"Do we have a deal?"

For a moment he hesitates.

"*—please welcome on stage—*"

"Deal!" he shouts, grabbing my hand.

I pull him in for a squeeze.

"*—Josh Lewis! Where are you, Josh? Get yourself up here!*"

"Go!" I yell, shoving him in the general direction of the stage.

There are moments in life when you can barely breathe, and it's not because you're scared or stressed or believe you don't even deserve the air in your lungs. It's because the moment is so special you don't want to disturb it with even the slightest movement.

I gaze at my best friend and my son on the stage, framed

by strings of white lights, playing guitar and singing together, and I'm blown away. They sound so good. They look so good; smiling at each other as they belt out the lyrics, nerves overcome, lost in the beat of the music, spurred on by the love of the crowd.

For a moment I can't believe how far we've come, any of us. All the doubts and fears about whether I've been a good enough dad, they all disintegrate in that moment. Because he's amazing. He's flawed and imperfect and bloody annoying just like we all are, but he's also incredible. Bright, kind, funny, talented... I couldn't want for anything more. And it's not all down to me, of course. It's down to a whole mixture of things. But I'm in there, a huge part of it, and whatever I did, there's no way it could have been wrong. Because just look at him now.

As their second song ends, Michael grabs Josh's arm, holds it high in the air and commands the crowd to give it up. As his new fans whistle and applaud, Josh glows with happiness, and I know that if this is the route he wants to take in life, then I'll support him all the way. For too long I've stifled him in my bid to protect him. But the fact is you can't stop them falling. All you can do is offer a soft place to land if they do.

As soon as he jumps off stage, I make a move towards him, but his friends get in there first, enveloping him in a giant hug. I see Sam and Alex ruffling his hair and patting him on the back, Chloe squeezing him tight and kissing him on the cheek. He grins shyly, modestly enjoying their praise, that cocky charade melted away. But it's also clear he's got somewhere else to be. He extricates himself from the group, stepping towards Becky, who's waiting patiently, the outsider. She wraps her arms around his neck and he kisses her for what seems like an unfeasibly long time while his friends return to their banter and chat.

I decide to leave Josh to his friends and his new girlfriend. As the music starts up again, I begin weaving my way back through the crowd, when suddenly I'm grabbed from behind, arms wrapping themselves around my shoulders with such strength I can't believe this is my child. I turn and pull him in for a hug.

"You were amazing!" I shout in his ear. "I am *so* proud of you!"

"You were right!" he yells above the music, putting his arm around my neck and pulling me down slightly – but only slightly – to his height. "It was *so* worth taking the risk! Now it's your turn!"

He slaps me on the arm and winks at me – actually *winks* at me, the cheeky git! – before rushing away, and for a second I catch a glimpse of the relationship we'll have in the not-so-distant future, when my son is more of a man than a boy.

I search the crowd, knowing what I have to do next. Butterflies rise in my stomach, but I feel stronger, more resolute than ever before. Because they were wrong – my mum, Harmonie, the teachers – all the people that said I wasn't good enough to be with her, raise a child, pass my exams – all the people who doubted me. Because I am good enough, and I always was.

Just then I feel a warm hand grasp my wrist and just as quickly let go. I turn and see Libby stepping away, beckoning me out of the crowd. I follow her through the rocking, jigging bodies, towards the steps that lead down to the canal.

Once on the towpath, she strides quickly, in silence. I keep up with her, waiting for her to stop and turn around. The thud of the music recedes, the bright chaos of the Canal House left behind. Away from the heat of the crowd, the night air feels chill against my bare arms. We pass narrowboats, one after the other, the windows dark, most of the residents out enjoying the party. The moon reflects off the water's surface, and the lamps dotted along our way shed their eerie white light.

"Stop," I tell her eventually, grabbing her by the arm.

"What you were saying earlier," she blurts out, spinning around and shaking me off, "you caught me off guard. You surprised me."

"I know."

We stare at each other, searching each other's faces in the dim light. I can hear her breathing, short and rapid.

"But it shouldn't have surprised you," I tell her, "because it turns out everybody knows how I feel about you. How I've felt about you since…" *Since I saw you again in Camden? Since you came back to Timpton?* "…since forever."

I swallow, willing my beating heart to quiet down.

"I haven't been honest with you," I continue, "but I want to be honest with you now. I didn't just come to find you again so that I could say sorry for how I behaved in the past. I also came to find you so that I could move on from you. Because I hadn't moved on. You and I, that was the closest, most meaningful relationship I ever had, and since then nothing's been able to touch it. Nothing's even come close. And I'd given up. I'd stopped trying. I thought that maybe if I saw you again, saw that you'd changed, that you'd grown up and moved on and weren't the same person anymore, then I could move on, too. But instead I just fell in love with you all over again. That's the real reason I didn't want you around. Not because you brought up bad memories, but because you brought up so many good ones. Because it was just too bloody hard, seeing you all the time, knowing you were with someone else."

She wraps her arms around herself and stares at the ground, silent.

"And even if things had been different," I plough on, "even if you hadn't been with somebody else, I would never have told you how I felt, not all the time I was convinced I didn't want the same things as you, that I couldn't give you what you wanted."

"But how has that suddenly changed?" she asks, risking a glance at my face, shaking her head like she doesn't believe me.

"Because *I've* changed," I tell her. "Things that I believed or told myself for a long time… I see it differently now. I *feel* differently now. I've never been able to see myself having all that with someone – a home, a life, a family – but with you…"

I let this hang in the air, wondering if it's too much. But I'm already halfway there.

"...I can see all that with you. And it doesn't feel scary. It feels right."

She puts her hand to her mouth, covers her lips, but doesn't speak.

"I don't know how you feel," I say, "but I think you feel something. And even if it's only a fraction of what I feel then—"

"How can you not know how I feel?" she asks. "I mean, I was trying so hard to hide it, but I felt like I must be transparent."

"I didn't know," I tell her. "I *still* don't know."

She looks at me, and in the weak light, I can see her eyes are watery.

"Since you barged your way back into my life," she says, her voice shaky with nerves and a hint of anger, "I have tried so hard – I mean, *so* hard – not to think about you, not to feel anything about you. I kept telling myself that it was fine, I was happy, I was going to get married, and maybe I didn't feel like I thought I should feel, but nothing's perfect, right? And then you came along and ruined *everything*. You made me feel the way I used to feel when I was with you, feelings that I'd almost forgotten existed, you made me question what I wanted, what I was doing... but I thought that if I could just ignore all that, if I could just be your friend, then that would make everything okay..."

She takes a deep, shuddering breath.

"I left here because of you," she says. "I lied. Harmonie never had a business opportunity that we moved away for. She moved us on because she knew I couldn't bear to stay here, wondering when I might bump into you. I left because of you and I came back because of you."

I watch her struggling and it takes all I have not to reach out and put my arms around her.

"You know, you actually made it easier when you said you

didn't want me around. Because just for a while I could feel hurt and angry at you…"

She shakes her head forlornly.

"But even then, it didn't stop me feeling all the other things I was trying not to feel."

I watch her closely, waiting, as she wipes at the outside edge of her eye with shaky fingers. She takes a deep breath as if she's about to add something more, but I can't stand it any longer. I step towards her, taking her by the shoulders. She shivers.

"Please don't do this unless you really mean it," she says quietly,

"I mean all of it," I tell her, firmly, "I would never be saying any of this if I didn't."

I lay my forehead against hers.

"I want everything with you," I whisper. "I always have."

We stand silently for a moment, the sound of our shallow breathing mingling with the distant beat of the music. I squeeze her shoulders and she lifts her hands to grip my forearms, her chilled fingers clutching me tight. I close my eyes, breathing in the scent of her. I can barely dare to believe she's here beneath my touch, that she's saying these things to me.

"I kissed you first the last two times," she mutters, and I can hear the smile in her voice.

I laugh quietly, pulling back and searching her face, seeing tears in her eyes.

"Then I guess that makes it my turn," I tell her.

I reach out and gently tuck a stray piece of hair behind her ear. I hold her face between my palms, her scar against mine.

And for the third time in our lives we share our first kiss.

Chapter 28

Goodnight

From the top of the hill, you could see out over the park, above the kids' playground and right across town. We sat on the grass gazing out at the lights of Timpton's houses, pubs and restaurants shining brightly in the darkness.

"I think that's Orion," I said, pointing up at the sky. "Or maybe not. I dunno. Apparently, it's easier to see in winter. Or where there's less light pollution."

The others looked up.

"Where d'you learn that?" asked Max.

I shrugged and smiled to myself. "Libby taught me."

"Libby seems to be teaching you a lot of things," piped up Tom, "apart from what to do with your—"

"Shut up, Tom," I interrupted bluntly.

"Yeah, shut up, Tom," agreed Michael.

"What?" asked Tom, in mock innocence. "I'm just saying—"

"Well, don't," Max told him abruptly.

Tom sighed. "Anyway, talking of girls—"

"Which we weren't," said Max.

"—talking of girls, we need to decide who to invite to Max's party next month."

"I'm not having a party."

"'Course you are," Tom corrected him, "it's your sixteenth. You've gotta have a party. Parties are a great opportunity for getting it on with birds."

Max clucked like a chicken. Tom ignored him.

"Seriously, there are some fit birds at school who are just waiting for an opportunity to get me alone and—"

"Turn you down?" teased Max.

"Punch you in the face?" suggested Michael.

"Kick you in the balls?" I offered.

"Anyway, who exactly are all these girls who are queuing up for a piece of you?" Max enquired. "Jessica Miller, who called you a knobhead in science last week? Lucy Walker, who told you she wouldn't go out with you if you were the last male on earth?"

Michael and I sniggered.

"No," tutted Tom, "just… other girls. Anyway," he said, looking towards Michael and myself, "you two divs must have some fit girls at your school you could invite. Rich girls really know how to look after themselves. And they act all innocent, but I'll tell you what they really want—"

"For you to stay as far away from them as possible?" I suggested.

"Exactly the opposite, my friend. Posh girls like a bit of rough," said Tom.

"Not *that* rough," I told him.

"Yeah, not Allenbrook rough," added Max.

"Plus, you do remember we're at an all boys' school, don't you?" asked Michael. "Funnily enough that means there aren't that many girls."

"But you said there are girls in the sixth form. So invite some of them."

"Why would sixth-form girls from a private school want to come to the sixteenth birthday party of some comp boy they've never met?" scoffed Max.

"Because *I'll* be there!" Tom replied.

"That's definitely not a bonus feature," I told him.

"What about that girl you mentioned the other day?" Tom asked me. "Helen someone."

"Who? Oh, Hellie… God, no. We've only spoken to her, like, two or three times—"

"I don't think Hellie Larsen's going to come to a party with us," Michael smiled at me. "I think girls like her have much better things to do."

I nodded.

"Is she fit?" asked Tom. "That's all that really matters here."

"I'm not even sure why she talks to us," said Michael. "She probably wouldn't give either of us the time of day outside of school."

"God, you two are useless," Tom moaned, "what's the point of you being at a posh school if you can't provide the posh totty."

"Right, I can't wait any longer, I need a piss," said Max standing up. "Anyone coming?"

"Coming for a piss with you?" asked Michael, sounding disgusted.

"Why would we want to do that?" I frowned.

Max pushed his glasses up the bridge of his nose and peered into the darkness.

"Are you scared of going for a piss on your own?" laughed Tom.

"Oh, come on, it's pitch black," Max complained.

"You're joking," I groaned.

"What do you think is possibly going to happen to you in the park?" asked Tom. "This is Timpton, not some gangland in South London. I don't think people are just lurking in the darkness waiting to jump you."

"My eyesight's bad in the dark, I can't see a friggin' thing!"

"Oh, come on, you big wuss," groaned Tom, standing up, "although if you're gonna whip your dick out, I pray *I* can't see a friggin' thing."

Once they'd disappeared into the darkness, Michael sighed.

"God, Tom can be irritating at times."

"Yep," I agreed. "It's all just talk though. Especially all the chat about girls. It's a load of crap. And that stuff about losing his virginity on a camping holiday in Cornwall is bollocks."

"And he needs to lay off with his comments about you and Libby. It's none of his business."

"I'd never tell him anyway. I mean, when me and her do… you know… I'm not gonna just spout off about it. I mean, I'd tell you, but that's it."

"Me?"

"Yeah. 'Cause I think I'd wanna tell someone, and you… well, you're different. I can trust you. I know you won't be a dick about it."

We fell silent for a moment, gazing out at the lit-up town.

"So what about you?" I asked. "Are there any girls you fancy? I mean, I know we're not exactly spoiled for choice at St John's, but what kind of girl would you go for?"

Michael looked up at the sky, chewing his lower lip.

"Can I…?" he started and then hesitated. "If I told you something, would you promise to keep it quiet?"

I shrugged. "Yeah, 'course."

He took a deep breath. "It's just… I think maybe… that maybe I'm…"

"He pissed on my shoes! He actually pissed on my fucking shoes!"

Tom emerged, fuming, from the darkness. Max, doubled-up with laughter, was following behind him.

"I wasn't even that near him and he just swung round and aimed the bloody thing right at me! My new trainers! I'm never wearing these again!"

Max clutched his belly and staggered towards us, laughing uproariously. He flopped down next to Michael.

"I didn't… I didn't mean to!" he gasped, almost crying with laughter. "You spoke to me so I turned around—"

"You just have to open your mouth to reply! You don't

have to swing round and aim your sergeant major in my direction! That's the last time I'm being your piss buddy!"

Max flopped backwards against the grass, his deep belly laugh aiming up at the night sky. It was so contagious that Michael and I started laughing with him.

"Disgusting," muttered Tom, sitting down next to Max, who started protesting that if things were the other way round and Tom had pissed on *his* feet he wouldn't have made half as much fuss.

I turned to Michael. "What were you going to say before?"

"Nothing, it doesn't matter," he said quickly, shaking his head dismissively.

"So come on then, Galileo," piped up Max, pointing up at the night sky, "what's that massive shiny one just there?"

I followed the line of his finger.

"The flashing one? That's what's known as an aeroplane, Max."

Max sat up and peered harder, before removing his glasses and wiping them with the hem of his jumper.

"I wonder what else is up there," mused Michael, "beyond the stars and planets and all the bits scientists have discovered. I mean, how can it just go on forever? I can't get my head round that."

"Heaven?" offered Max, popping his glasses back on. "That's got to be up there somewhere."

"You don't seriously believe that though, do you?" asked Michael.

Max shrugged. "Well, I dunno. Where else would it be?"

"But do you believe in, like, an actual heaven?" I asked him.

"Yeah. Why not? It's where I'm going when I die anyway. I don't know where you lot are off to."

"What, 'cause we're not believers?" scoffed Tom.

"No, 'cause you're gits," said Max.

"Yeah, whatever," groaned Tom. "Well, I'm not going to heaven."

"I don't think any of us doubt that," I told him.

"I should get home," said Michael flatly, checking his watch and standing up.

"Ah, Blondie!" cried Max. "You've gotta get your curfew extended!"

Michael sighed and started to tell Max how he'd already approached his dad about a curfew extension and the angry rant he'd received in response.

"Hey," Tom whispered, nudging me in the ribs, "we've gotta sort this party out for Max, okay?"

"What, so you can try it on with every girl we know?"

"No, you dope, because it's his sixteenth. And because it's Max. We've known him all our lives and he deserves a really good party. He's a legend, and we're his best friends, so we need to make it a special night for him, all right?"

I searched Tom's face in the darkness, trying to figure out what went on behind those eyes. There were times when it was easy to forget that deep down he was a kind soul and an incredibly loyal friend. A lot of the time he did my head in, but despite all the bravado and mockery and insults, I had faith that he'd always come through for me in the end.

"You're right," I said, slapping him on the shoulder, "Max does deserve it. We'll sort something out." I stood up, ready to head back into town with Michael. "You two coming, or what?"

Max and Tom looked at each other.

"Nah, I think we'll hang out a little longer," said Tom.

"Oh, by the way," said Max, "there's a fairground in town next weekend. I saw a poster for it in the window of that place they've just finished renovating in town. The new pub, the Canal something—"

"The Canal House," said Tom.

"Yeah, that one. Shall we go? Might be a laugh."

Michael and I looked at each other unenthusiastically.

"I'm not sure," I said, turning my nose up, "I thought we talked about going to see *X-Men*."

"But you already saw it with Libby."

"Yeah, but I missed half of it. We got there fifteen minutes late and then she kept nattering the whole way through and asking loads of questions."

"We can see the film Sunday," said Tom.

"Let's vote," said Max, "all those in favour of the fairground…"

Max and Tom both raised their hands, and then, tentatively, so did Michael.

"Might be fun," he shrugged at me.

"That's a majority vote then," declared Max.

"Fine," I yawned, "whatever. We'll see you next weekend then."

"Have a safe walk home, boys," called Tom, lying back on the grass, "don't go talking to any strangers!"

"They don't come much stranger than you, Tom," called Michael as we headed down the hill.

"Ha ha! Later, Blondie! Later, dickhead!"

"Later, shitface!" I called back.

"Goodnight, gentlemen!" called Max.

"See you, Max!" replied Michael.

"'Night, Max!" I called, glancing back over my shoulder, but he'd already faded away into the darkness of the star-studded night.

Acknowledgements

I would like to thank the team at Legend Press for their continued belief in my work, and for enabling me to share these people, places and events which insisted on invading my imagination whether I wanted them to or not. I would also like to thank my children for putting up with the numerous canal-side walks I dragged them on during the summer of 2019.

Lightning Source UK Ltd.
Milton Keynes UK
UKHW012057140221
378768UK00002B/62